TITAN'S FOLLY

STEVE HIGGS, BRYON ARNESON, JOSEPH DANIEL

For Mary,

whose encouragement has been my light in dark places,

when all other lights go out.

Also, for Paul H.

The first to read most my books

CONTENTS

1. Chapter 1   1

2. Chapter 2   13

3. Chapter 3   27

4. Chapter 4   33

5. Chapter 5   43

6. Chapter 6   50

7. Chapter 7   60

8. Chapter 8   71

9. Chapter 9   87

10. Chapter 10   100

11. Chapter 11   120

12. Chapter 12   131

13. Chapter 13   140

14.	Chapter 14	152
15.	Chapter 15	157
16.	Chapter 16	167
17.	Chapter 17	175
18.	Chapter 18	184
19.	Chapter 19	199
20.	Chapter 20	208
21.	Chapter 21	224
22.	Chapter 22	240
23.	Chapter 23	263
24.	Chapter 24	275
25.	Chapter 25	287
26.	Chapter 26	293
27.	Chapter 27	314
28.	Chapter 28	318
29.	Chapter 29	331
30.	Chapter 30	338
31.	Chapter 31	353
32.	Chapter 32	361
33.	Chapter 33	373
34.	Chapter 34	395
35.	Chapter 35	400
36.	Epilogue	415

37. Ready for the next adventure?   417

39. The Stolen King   419

38. Want to know more?   420

CHAPTER 1

THREE WEARY DAYS OF travel had passed since Sir Matimeo Navara killed his first man, and he was at a crisis of conscience. Sir Navara traced the stubble along his sculpted jaw, peering at the red satin curtains inside the carriage. He'd always been called a handsome man, a claim he struggled to believe of himself. His brow furrowed beneath dark hair, bunching up his neatly trimmed eyebrows as he continued to stare into the curtains. Red was a familiar color to Matimeo.

He hadn't wanted to kill the man, but he had warned the meddler not to impede the promotion. Threats of blackmail demanded a swift response, especially threats concerning momentary indiscretions from Navara's past. The prospects of a minor noble in the Gilded Islands were grim. Most ended up as knights, others made it among the merchant vessels or took double pay positions on imperial ships. A close friend of Navara's by the name of Agreo, the younger brother of a baron, had made it as a crewmaster the last he'd heard. A secure position. Safe. Unassuming. Expected. Rarely did a minor noble reach the ranks of *true* power.

Sir Navara smiled softly, tapping the fingers of his right hand against the window of the carriage. The many rings he wore clacked against the glass as he exuded a soft sigh, recalling all the adventures he and Agreo had gotten into as youths. Agreo's brother had paid shush money to more than one young woman's family after the pair's night time indiscretions. But Agreo, for all his camaraderie, had always been the better of the two. He, at least, had half a conscience. Matimeo had even spotted his childhood friend praying to the gods on occasion. Navara gave fealty only to Nameless Death. He found the devotion fitting.

Navara listened to the clopping hooves of the carriage horses and peered out the window at the passing inland countryside. In the distance, he spotted the Monta Gabri, each mountain in the range reaching towards the sky in devotion to the sun. Even a man from the coast could appreciate the beauty of Southern Godshaven.

Besides, this was his chance after all. It had taken convincing and a good sum from his merchant father to lacquer the palm of the young Commodore—whose own father had passed the year before—but Matimeo Navara was now the newly appointed reeve of Titan's Folly.

"Reeve Matimeo Navara," he murmured softly to himself, tasting the delectable words as they snuck past his lips. The first step on a noble's path to power. He could be patient. He could be charming. Within ten years, perhaps, he could insinuate himself with the barons—maybe even a Lord Captain.

The three day's journey from his father's coastal manor had gone quickly enough. Three days of distance from his past. Three days of distance from his most recent kill.

This kill had been Matimeo's first *man*. He'd killed a good number of women already in his twenty six years. They were much more his type. Murdering the man had been an unpleasant necessity and had evoked no pleasure within him. Navara frowned at the thought, rubbing his manicured hands against his slacks as if wiping off a layer of soot. His handsome face grimaced, recalling the way the man's head had caved in from the blow. He hadn't even been looking when Matimeo had crept up on him. Matimeo felt tarnished, in a way; sullied even. His hands weren't meant for taking a man's life any more than a sailor's hands were meant for sheering wool.

But the women? His past indiscretions? The prizes he'd claimed, wedding himself in soul and mind, as the blood drained from them? He knew the number off the top of his head; no need to count. If ever his collection attempted to slip his mind, he would remind himself.

He smiled again, softly, glancing at the seven rings on his right hand. There had once been eight. He preferred them married and young. He avoided noble wives, though that one time, three years ago in Dumas... He'd nearly made the mistake of courting a Lord Captain's bride.

Navara shuddered at the recollection. It had been a close thing. Rumors had followed him home. The same rumors that had nearly cost him his promotion. But his stepbrother should have known better than to threaten Navara.

You're not fit for the promotion! He'd said. *I know you had a hand in Sophie's death. I might not be able to prove it, but I'll be damned before anyone gives you an ounce of power!*

Navara had tried to reason with his stepbrother. He had known, at the time, the previous year, that taking Sophie—his sister-in-law—would come with consequences. But he hadn't imagined his stepbrother clever enough to put it together. A simple oversight.

I'll tell the baroness. I'll tell the Genevese! I'll tell the pyrite miners. I'll tell every godsdamned one of them. I don't care if your father is trying to ship you off! Two miles or two hundred miles, he can't cover for you. He can't save you, Matimeo! I know what you are.

Sir Navara hadn't wanted to, but he'd been forced to strike his stepbrother as he'd turned to leave. He'd used a marble bust on his father's mantelpiece, and snuck out the body in the usual way. A quick trip to the cellar, a couple of sharp cleavers and three wax-sealed satchels. Normally, it only took two satchels—but his stepbrother was a large man.

He'd buried the body next to where he'd buried Sophie's. It had been the right thing to do. But it had felt dirty, somehow. As if he were giving Sophie *back*. Sir Navara eyed his fingers. Only seven rings now. He'd returned the eighth—even placing it in his stepbrother's grave, before piling on the dirt. He couldn't have kept the ring even if he had wanted to. It felt foreign to him the moment he'd struck his brother, as if by killing him, in the same way he'd killed his wife, he was sharing an intimate, vulnerable part of himself.

He grimaced again, wiping a bead of sweat from his brow.

For the last three days they'd traveled, stopping only to rest the horses. He hadn't had a chance to *replace* Sophie. And he desperately felt the urge coming on. He needed a new bride. He licked his lips, which felt suddenly dry as the thoughts curdled through his mind. He needed a new wedding. As reeve, with more power, he hoped that it would give him every opportunity to fulfill his urges—to honor Nameless Death as best he knew how, with an offering of flesh.

Three days was a long time to wait, though, when the urge came on this strong. It wouldn't leave him until it was satiated. He didn't want it to leave.

Sir Navara smiled and pushed his head out the window, allowing the wind to buffet his face and paw at his hair. He inhaled the scent of wheat grass and earth. Perhaps living inland wouldn't be so bad either. He had grown up on the coast, but with the rolling hills and thick forests, he could grow accustomed to the heart of Godshaven as well.

Just then, there was a soft whistle, followed by a clicking noise.

"Whoa, steady, uh?" said a voice, emanating from the coachman's seat.

Navara frowned, his head still jutting out the window, he turned to try and spot the coachman, but only glimpsed the side of his sleeve.

"Excuse me, sir," he called, ever the polite eldest son. "But what are we stopping for?"

"In the road, uh? See?" the man replied.

Another voice from out of sight in the ridealong seat grunted as well.

Normally, one driver and one guard would have been a small escort for a reeve. But Navara had never been escorted before, save when he accompanied his father on his travels. A rare occurrence due to Navara's nasty bouts of seasickness and hatred for the smell of the boats. Besides, the coachman and the guard had come highly recommended by the owner of *Wickwood's Transportation and Steeds,* a discount business Navara's father had hired—always in search of the deal, his father was.

"What's in the road?" Navara said, pushing his head further out the window, he twisted his neck, frowning.

Then he spotted her and his mouth came unhinged, his chin tapping against the bottom of the window.

He gaped at the single most beautiful woman he had ever laid his eyes on. Her pale skin glistened like silver. Her raven hair framed razor-sharp cheeks and a celestial nose, upturned like drawn porcelain. Her clothing fit loosely in parts, but snugly in all the appropriately provocative places.

Navara swallowed softly, at a loss for words. He squeezed his right hand, feeling the rings tighten in his grip.

"Should we pull over, uh?" said the carriage driver. "She's waving for help."

Vaguely, past the churning sea of his thoughts, Navara thought the request odd. At least, it was highly unprofessional for a hired coachman and his fellow guardsman to suggest their client stop for a commoner on the road, even a beautiful one.

But then again, nothing about this woman was ordinary. She was the perfect bride. And, even from this distance, as the carriage rattled along at a snail's pace, coming to a full stop, he could almost feel her gaze boring into his.

"Yes. We stop," he managed to croak out as he met her eyes across the long distance. As he did though, staring at her, she stared back. Normally, young women would glance down given such attention, or look away. Some of them might blush due to Navara's good looks. Others might think him presumptuous and glare in return, though, secretly he knew they enjoyed the attention.

This woman, though, didn't smile, nor did she frown. She didn't blush or glare. Instead, she just watched, observing him with no small amount of interest. There was something in her gaze that set him at unease. Something unnerving in the way the beauty beheld him. He felt, for the faintest moment, like he was peering into the eye of a storm.

"Perhaps... Perhaps we should keep going," he said, astonished to find the words spilling from his lips. He shook his head, trying to clear his thoughts.

It was just a woman. There was nothing to be afraid of. There were three of them, besides. Perhaps the coachman and his guard would like a taste too, as Agreo often had. Navara felt the urge rising in him again. He'd long since buried any sense of shame at the desires. Now, he acknowledged them as old friends. And like any good host, it was up to him to accommodate his friends.

The carriage had finally reached a full halt and Navara pushed open the door. Had he been thinking clearly, it perhaps would have occurred to him that despite his change of mind and new command, the coachman had made no attempt to continue traveling.

Navara pushed open the carriage door and stepped out of the back quarter. His feet felt unsteady beneath him from so much time sitting, but he managed to take a couple of stumbling steps towards the woman.

"Hello, lass!" He called, his voice clear and genial. She couldn't have been any older than he was, perhaps even younger. Though... as he met her eyes, the uneasy feeling crept up in him that she wore her age like a garment, and that she might toss it aside at any moment for one that better suited her mood. Not that it mattered. Maiden or matron, she was beautiful and that beauty called to him.

As he approached, the woman just stood in the middle of the road, watching him. There were no signs of horses and no signs of traveling companions. It was a strange thing to find such a beautiful woman alone on a road which was still distant from Titan's Folly by a good thirty miles. As far as the eye could see, he spotted hills and trees and more trees.

He inhaled through his nose, his nostrils flaring. He could feel a warmth creeping over him as the distance between him and the woman closed. He pressed his teeth together slightly, like a wolf testing its jaws before the feast.

"Don't be afraid," he said quietly. "I'm here to help. Do you need a ride?"

The stunningly gorgeous woman with the near silver skin just continued to watch as he approached.

Navara glanced back, but the carriage driver and guard were sitting in their seats, watching him with disinterest.

He would, perhaps, not share this particular prize. The forests nearby, th ough... Those offered quiet. He would court her there, and then, perhaps, ask her for her hand... Though, as he glanced at her fingers, he spotted no ring.

He frowned.

"No suitors?" he said. "No engagement? A fine woman like you—I'd imagine you're beating them off with a club."

The woman eyed him up and down as he approached. "What is it you want?" she said.

"Your name," he replied, with a would-be roguish wink. "That is a fine start."

"Mirastious," she said, softly.

Navara frowned in surprise. "After the goddess? A bold choice by your parents."

"I have no parents."

"I—I..." He frowned again, then noticed her lips turning at the corners. The urge often came with bouts of fury, and one was rising in him now. "Oh—I see. You're mocking me? Is that it?" He reached out and grabbed her by the wrist, yanking, hard.

She stumbled towards him.

"Come with me," he snapped. "I have something to show you." He began dragging her towards the forest. One step. Two.

The woman said, "You shouldn't have. I told him he couldn't. Not unless you hurt me. And you have. You shouldn't have." She sighed softly. "The secrets lurking in your brain... I could have spent a year sifting and searching through every nook and cranny. But—alas—another time... I suppose."

He wasn't sure what she was going on about. Her voice came strangely calm as he continued to yank at her, pulling her still.

"Sir Navara?" a voice called behind him.

"What?" Matimeo demanded, whirling around with a snarl.

The short coachman dismounted and leaned against the carriage with a bored look towards the newly appointed reeve. Every so often, oddly enough, the coachman would glance to his shoulder and speak to the breeze, muttering beneath his breath as if to a ghost. The coachman removed his hat and displayed a strangely shaved head—one side completely bald, the other braided into dreadlocks and adorned with pieces of colored glass, beads, and baubles.

The guard also dismounted and now stalked towards Matimeo with quick, agile movements that reminded him of the Signerde who sometimes frequented the harbor outside his father's mansion. They too moved with a strange, dancing rhythm as if in motion to some unheard music, their feet always finding firm footing, even aboard a ship in a gale. The man's eyes were dark and laden with a strange sadness. The same sort of sadness Navara's stepbrother had exhibited ever since the loss of his wife.

But the man's face... This *most* unnerved Navara.

For it was Navara's own countenance that peered back at him. The same handsome features, straight nose and neatly trimmed eyebrows beneath thick dark hair. The same firm jaw and dusting of stubble across his chin. He was a couple of inches shorter, but not by much.

Navara gaped. He frowned, shaking his head, certain he was staring into a mirror. But his doppelganger just kept coming. In his left hand he clutch ed...

A pistol.

"Who are you?" Navara said, his voice straining. "What do you want?"

The guard had been wearing a helmet obscuring his face last time they'd stopped to water and rest the horses. But now, the helmet was nowhere to be seen.

"I know men like you," said Navara's sad-eyed doppelganger. He shook his head slightly. Matimeo noticed, with a start, the double was holding the pistol in his *left* hand. He shuddered, he knew the foul luck that followed those who led-with-their-left. "I know you *much* better than you might think. I once had a wife, you know..." A small, black bottle dangled from the man's neck, swishing back and forth across his chest.

Navara's eyes widened. He couldn't account for the eerie similarity of their features, but the way the man was speaking... Double hell—his past had finally caught up with him! One of the husbands of his brides had found him. He'd never thought it would happen! Despite Agreo's warnings, despite his father's veiled efforts to correct his eldest son's behavior, he'd been smart. He'd been careful!

"No," said the man simply, studying Navara's expression. "It's not what you think. My wife was taken by another. And most my ire is reserved for that man."

Relief flooded Navara, and he found himself gasping. He was still gripping the arm of the woman who'd called herself Mirastious.

"Though," the man said. "There is some hatred to spare." He didn't smile, he didn't blink. Instead, with a swift motion, he raised his pistol and—

"No don't!" Navara screamed, throwing up his hands.

—fired.

CHAPTER 2

Augustin bit his lip against a sharp jab of pain.

Damnation! Any more of these godsdamned brackelthorns and I'll be shredded before I even get there. He lifted his bleeding hand to his lips and sucked the pin-prick of blood welling up from his palm. Covered from the waist up by only a hardened leather vest, Augustin's arms and neck already sported a series of small nicks and scratches from the hard, thorny branches. He rested a moment to readjust the rapier and dagger hanging from his hip. From his place on the ground, the light of the half-moon came through a small copse of dead trees in ribbons, and only a bare fraction of it crossed the scrubby brush around him to grab hold of his dark hair and glimmer in the deep brown of his hawkish eyes.

Pausing a moment, Augustin peered through the remaining brush to the warm, orange glow of a campfire ahead. Twelve men with half as many horses slouched around the meager fire in the bank of a trickling creek that cut through the hard and dusty land. The horses milled about, chewing

13

the tough grass protruding from the weakly running creek bed. Among the mottled bays and grays stood one black horse a full four hands higher than any other in the group. To Augustin's eye it was a magnificent creature, and he couldn't help but wonder how the brigands had come by it. The firelight caught the steel guards of daggers and short swords at their hips and the scraped leather of their travel-stained boots and leggings. A thin-limbed man in a billowing linen shirt held a leather haversack between his knees and sorted its glittering contents in his hands before putting them back into the bag.

"Fifty six, d'oro," he said to his companions, placing the last of the red-gold coins into its pile. "Plus the twenty from the wagon last week means—"

Another man interrupted the counter. "Means it's time to leave." He spoke with a gruff, round tone of authority, and Augustin watched the other eleven look his way. "The valley door's been good to us. Best not tempt Dulomora by sticking around." A few of the other men nodded with muttered assent, and Augustin saw more than a couple wave their hands in a warding gesture. Brigands or not, they were still common folk, and that meant they had a healthy respect for the god of mischief and misfortune.

The man with the commanding voice ran a rag over the gleaming brass of a blunderbuss. The stubby rifle's flared barrel made it look like a trumpet, and Augustin grimaced at the sight of it. When they could get their hands on them, highwaymen and brigands loved the blunderbuss. It didn't require expensive cartridges to fire, and Augustin had seen them loaded with everything from lead shot to broken glass. At Trelliman's Folly, he had even seen a desperate rebel load one with a fistful of silverware. Well, there would be nothing for it now. He hoped the brigand at least had the sense not to clean a loaded weapon.

As Augustin peered around the campsite, he wondered if the others were in position yet.

Crawling forward on his forearms, Augustin tried not to crack the dry brackelthorn bushes around him as he reached the very edge of the brush and the outer limit of the brigand's campfire. Four days of wilderness tracking all came down to this. They would wait silently until the brigands fell asleep. They were outnumbered, so the element of surprise would be key.

A brigand tripped over one of his companions as he stumbled away from the fire, and he flailed his arms for one tentative moment before regaining his footing. "Oye, move yer arse," he said. The kicked man grunted in response and threw up an obscene gesture at his passing comrade, but did not stir from his spot. The man took five weaving steps towards Augustin's hiding place, spitting into the dirt as he unlaced his trousers. Augustin's heart began to beat faster. It was too soon. With all the brigands awake they would be outnumbered, and that was a risk they could ill-afford to take. Augustin bit down on his tongue in an effort to hold himself perfectly still. With the fire behind him, the staggering man formed a distinctive silhouette over Augustin's prone body as he began to piss into the brackelthorns. Augustin heard the stream of urine feeding the dry earth to his left, and held his breath.

Mercusi, be just. How much can a man piss? Augustin clenched his hands, resisting the urge to grab the dagger from his hip. The man above hummed to himself, and Augustin heard the trail of piss rolling in a looping circle.

One loop. Two. Three. He felt a string of gentle taps as the line of urine trailed across his back, letting out a heavy spluttering as it hit the hardened leather of his vest.

"What in the hells?" The moonlight highlighted the confused brigand's eyes as he looked down at Augustin's prone body, and a brief moment passed where they locked eyes. A look of realization spread across the brigand's face as resolve settled in Augustin's. The once lord-captain leapt forward, his powerful forearms propelling him up out of the clinging brush like a pouncing leopard. The brigand floundered backward, wailing in surprise as he held his trousers with one hand and reached for his dagger with the other.

"Ambush!" the man shouted, and behind him, the other brigands flew to their feet with shocked alacrity.

Grabbing hold of the man's wrist, Augustin gave a sharp twist and sent the man's dagger to the ground. With a cry of pain, the man released his grip on his trousers to try and throw a punch at Augustin, but as his pants fell around his ankles, Augustin gave a quick shove that sent him sprawling, and the man's punch flew wide.

"Get him!" shouted the leader with the blunderbuss. A chorus of scraping steel rang out as the brigands drew cutlasses and daggers. Augustin reached to his side and pulled free his own dagger and rapier as he fell into a defensive posture. Surging forward, the first two brigands to reach Augustin drew up short, eyeing the long blade of his rapier. He had the reach on them, and he could see that they knew it. They looked at each other, and Augustin glimpsed the pair muttering to each other. With a nod, the sword-wielding brigand to Augustin's left jumped forward. Augustin paid no mind to the obvious distraction. The man had not even bothered to swing his sword, instead keeping the blade up defensively. Half-a-second later, the brigand to the right lunged in, swinging the heavy cutlass in a wide slash. Calculating for such a strategy, Augustin pivoted to meet the slash, guiding it away with his rapier as he brought the point of his own blade into line with his opponent's body. Swift and efficient, Augustin's thrust slipped in and out of the brigand's exposed chest as if he were made of smoke, and the man fell to the ground with a scream of pain.

The remaining brigand's eyes went wide, and he looked over his shoulder to the rest of the group. "What are you all standin' about for? Get him!" This time the remaining ten brigands rushed forward in a mob.

A seven foot shadow loped out from the copse of dead trees to Augustin's right. Holding a heavy, wooden maul in both hands, the giant of a man planted his feet and swung the cudgel at the charging brigands. Augustin saw the attack crash into the foremost brigand's side, and hurl the man back, knocking his allies behind him to the ground as he careened through the air. The giant stepped beside Augustin. The moonlight highlighted a row of scars across his bald head, culminating in a criss-cross patchwork of flesh where an ear should have been. In a heavy Dumasian accent, the giant rumbled, "This is what happens when you mention Dulomora. Speak his name and mischief appears."

Augustin shook his head at his friend. Two of the brigands would not be getting up, but in spite of the ten still standing, Cristobal still found a moment to ponder the divine portents of the encounter. Augustin turned aside one of the brigands' attacks, landing a smart cut across the man's arm.

Despite Cristobal's sudden appearance, the brigands pressed on, and soon all of them whirled in a bladed melee.

Augustin twisted his dagger, turning aside another sloppy attack from the brigand's cutlass, but in the opening another of the group managed to catch the edge of Augustin's shoulder before his rapier could fully parry the slash. Even for a swordsman of Augustin's caliber, a group of brigands attacking together put his skills sorely to the test.

"Where the hell are the others?" he grunted to Cristobal as another brigand fell, clutching a fresh stab wound in his gut. He didn't hear the big Dumasian's reply. Steel sang out by his ears as Augustin swept his rapier and dagger to catch two of the brigand's blades, his strong arms straining to parry the cuts that flew within a hand's breadth of his head. With his arms upraised, his eye caught the moonlight glinting off a third brigand's short sword as it thrust for his exposed ribs. His muscles tensed as he jerked his dagger down in a desperate attempt to parry the thrust he had spotted too late.

A flash of light announced a thunderous snap as a flintlock roared. In the sudden gout of sulfurous smoke, the brigand's short sword fell as the man slumped to the ground. In his place stood a ragged figure in a muddy red frock coat. Shaking a mane of black dreadlocks, the figure dropped his smoking pistol and daintily turned a basket-hilted rapier to engage the brigands.

"What's this, Gus?" A rough and rasping voice called out playfully. "Thought you could have all the fun, eh? Leave ol' Vicente to pick up the scraps? No, no, no, I says!" With a mad cackle, Vicente threw himself at the brigands, unleashing a wild flurry of thrusts and slashes that drew the three remaining opponents off of Augustin as they raised their weapons in panicked defense. Cristobal laid out three more of the brigands with his maul while Augustin harried them with his blade.

Taking a quick count, Augustin saw two of the remaining brigands retreating from Cristobal. Two more writhed on the ground behind Vicente as he pursued the skinny brigand in the billowy linen shirt. Six more littered the ground around him, wounded or dead. That left- Augustin whipped his head around as he wildly searched the campsite. He found what he was looking for, and a spike of fear leapt in his chest. The brigand leader, six paces away from Vicente, threw a tamping rod to the ground with a wicked grin as he raised the blunderbuss.

"Vicente, look out!" Augustin shouted. With a curt slash of his rapier, Vicente jumped back from his current target and spun around to follow Augustin's gaze.

"Oh, shark-shite," Vicente groaned. A metallic click sounded as the blunderbuss' flintlock hammered down. In the same moment, the metal of the gun's flared barrel rang as a long spear dropped from the shadows and slammed down across it, driving the weapon down towards the ground. Fire belched from the blunderbuss, and skirted across the dry earth like dragon's breath as a concussive blast shocked the air. The horses screamed and bolted, all except the big black. Vicente let out a harsh cry of pain, and the black linen of his left trouser snapped back like a flag caught in a stiff breeze. He shook where he stood a moment, then his legs went out from under him, and Vicente collapsed onto the ground. The owner of the spear, a handsome man in a chain-hauberk, stepped into the campfire's light and spun the haft of the weapon around, cracking the strong wood against the brigand leader's face. The man sprawled back as the gun flew from his fingers.

Leaving Vicente behind, the brigand in the billowy linen ran for his leader. With the haversack of coin jangling on his back, he pulled the bigger man to his feet. "Come on, we gotta run, boss!"

The man with the spear lowered the point. "Surrender," he said. His strong, clean shaven jaw carried the words melodically, and his blue eyes were open and reassuring. "In the name of Pardi, I swear no harm will be done to you until you are tried before the reeve."

The brigand leader spat, leaning on his smaller companion. "That's some deal. Surrender and we'll make sure someone else kills you later. I'm gonna pass." With a sudden shove, he tore the haversack from his ally's back, and pushed the smaller man forward. The spearman darted to get around the sprawling figure, and the leader of the brigands mounted the black horse, spurring it away from the camp.

Augustin ran after him, squinting into the darkness, but the shadowy stallion quickly outpaced him. As he stared after it, a small silhouette leapt up from the brush at the escaping brigand. The man let out a yell of surprise, but with a swift kick, he knocked the smaller figure away as quickly as they had appeared. Sheathing his rapier and dagger, Augustin sprinted towards them.

Sprawled in the dusty earth lay a young woman in brown linen shirt and pants. She rubbed her shaved head and heaved with heavy coughs. Augustin lent her a hand and together they rolled her onto her side. Still gasping, her breath came a little easier, the young woman shook her head. "You—al—you al—let him—get away."

Augustin grimaced. She was right, of course. Their ambush had turned into a fiasco; even now the leader of the brigands escaped deeper and deeper into the wild with their plunder. "Are you alright, Catali?" Augustin asked, helping her to her feet.

Catali waved away his concern. "I'm fine. Just got the wind knocked out of my sails is all." Putting an arm over Augustin's shoulder, Catali let him help her back towards the campsite. "You're just lucky I was here."

Augustin cocked one of his dark eyebrows. Scratching at the flecks of grey in his close cropped beard, he chuckled. "And why is that?"

"You almost let him get away."

"Almost?"

Catali gave a mischievous grin. From her side she held up a long surgeon's knife. The thin edge caught the starlight and trapped it in the ruby glow of a smeared blood stain. "Think this is enough for Vicente to work with?" Augustin nodded grimly, and Catali's smile faded. "What's wrong?"

"Vicente's been shot."

"Blue fire and black fish," Catali swore, shoving herself free of Augustin's support. "Why didn't you say so? Walking me back like we're on a goddamn picnic." Catali continued to mutter, but Augustin lost the thread of it as she hurried ahead of him.

Back at the camp, Cristobal helped hold down Vicente's leg while Catali poured the contents of a clear bottle from her surgeon's bag over the wound. Judging by the string of oaths from the ragged knight's mouth, Augustin assumed it hurt like hell, and as the liquid washed the initial flow of blood back, the wound pulsed with a fresh flow of red.

The handsome spearman stepped beside Augustin. His chain hauberk jingling as he rolled his shoulders, his expression heavy with concern as they both stared down at their friend. Then as Vicente let out another groan of pain, the golden haired spearman lay down his weapon and rushed to kneel by the wounded man's shoulders.

"Vicente, hey hey, look at me, my friend," he said, his voice rising with an encouraging lilt.

"Tristan? What in blue hell—Oh, shark-shite, I'm dyin' aren't I?" Vicente moaned.

"What?" Tristan replied, letting out a small laugh, "Of course not. Why would you say that?" Tristan looked over his shoulder to Catali, but the young surgeon did not meet his gaze.

"You're kneeling by my head, Pardi's sun in your hand. Blue fire and black fish, Tristan yer a good boy, but holy hell are you a terrible liar." Vicente barked out a harsh laugh that turned into a cough, and Tristan let go of the amulet he had been clutching, letting the little iron sunburst dangle around his neck.

"You caught me," Tristan replied, his eyes wrinkling with a worried smile. "But you're not dying." He took Vicente's hand and the two of them held each other's wrists. "Catali's got this," Tristan added reassuringly, "But is it alright if I ask Pardi's help too?"

From his position on the floor, Vicente nodded his head, and in a soft, nearly whispered voice Tristan began to pray.

At their side, Augustin felt a dull thwack at his shin and looked down to see Catali extending a metal probe, thin and long as a knitting needle, towards him.

"If you'd like to do something *actually* helpful, go heat this in the fire. It's treated for the purpose so it shouldn't take more than half a minute."

Augustin took the probe, and without waiting for his reply, Catali turned back to Vicente's leg.

True to her word, the metal instrument had barely been in the fire when it began to give off the soft glow of scorching heat. Augustin returned it to Catali, who glanced at the heated end with a satisfied nod before saying, "Cristobal, hold him tight. Tristan, pray harder, I guess. This is going to hurt like hell."

Without waiting any longer, Catali inserted the thin rod into the pulsing wound. Vicente let out an agonized scream, his body trembling and twitching as Cristobal held the wounded leg immobile. Tristan continued with his quiet prayers, but took hold of Vicente's shoulders to try and hold his friend still. The charred smell of cauterized flesh rose up, as a pink stream of steaming blood rose, the departing ghost of the sealed injury. After another moment, Vicente relaxed, and Catali let out a relieved sigh. She turned to face Vicente as she packed away her tools and retrieved a meager coil of linen bandage. "You're going to be fine. It wasn't as bad as it looked. You got lucky."

"You know, I feel lucky," Vicente said with a weak smile. Catali smirked back at him, and for a while Tristan's prayers, rolling like a singer's melody over the rhythmic sound of Catali bandaging the wound were the only sounds in the campsite.

With the moon glowing down on him, Vicente's mismatched eyes seemed to almost glow. The left a deep, oaky brown, while the right held a bright yellow band. Licking his lips, he tilted his head toward Tristan and said, "I'm no mystic, but shouldn't Pardi be asleep right now? Being a sun god and everything?"

Cristobal looked up at Tristan and nodded solemnly, as if this made perfect sense.

Tristan shook his head. "No, Pardi is always present. Even when he's not obvious." Tristan pointed to the half-moon in the sky. "It's funny though, when I crossed the Reach last year, I heard a scholar who said that the moon doesn't actually glow with its own inner light like the cult of Mirastious always said. He claimed that the moon catches the sun's light and shines it back to us like a mirror." A look of gentle awe hung on Tristan's face as he stared up into the sky.

Cristobal and Vicente looked from one to the other, then with a sound like an avalanche Cristobal began to laugh. Vicente quickly joined in with his own cackling rasp, and after another moment Tristan shook his head with a resigned laugh of his own.

"That's ok. I know how it sounds."

Catali shook her head at the lot of them. "Mirastious, save us from ignorance."

Vicente winced as the young surgeon cinched a bandage around his leg. Satisfied, Catali fished out a bottle with a thick, honey-like syrup. She looked at the near empty bottle in frustration and seemed for a moment as if she might put it back into her bag. With a sigh she said, "I'm giving you a little senza, because we might need that sight of yours."

Taking Vicente's dreadlocks in one hand she poured a bit of the pain-killer into his mouth. The relief on Vicente's face swiftly made itself apparent, and disappointment followed as soon as Catali withdrew the bottle. Catali pursed her lips then put the bloody surgeon's knife on Vicente's chest. She tapped it with a thin finger. "That's the last brigand. Whenever you're ready." With that, she stood and walked away from the campfire. Augustin followed.

Falling into stride beside her, they walked past the firelight's edge, until the sound of the crackling wood fell away behind the chirping of crickets and the soft burring of wind-pulled grass.

Augustin said, "We can track the brigand after a bit of rest. You know how Vicente's eye taxes him. If he's wounded, he'll need to take it slow."

Catali rubbed her shaved scalp with one, thin hand. She looked over her shoulder, then in a hushed voice said, "That's the last of the senza, I just used my last bit of bandage cloth binding up his leg too, and I'm nearly out of gut thread, if I have to sew one of you up." She locked her eyes on

Augustin's. They carried no accusation, just a declaration of fact propped up by a knowing worry. "I'd love to take it slow, but the fact is we need to get paid. If we don't get paid, I don't have what I need to keep you all alive." The weight of her statements hung like a cold stone around Augustin's neck. He nodded, looking back towards the group. He knew Catali had done everything in her power to stretch her supplies, but—

"Listen," she said, drawing Augustin's gaze down again. She seemed to be weighing her words carefully. "I know you haven't given up on your crusade to find that bastard. Trust me, I want to see you catch the tomb raider."

The Viper. Augustin's mind flared with the thought of the man. The tomb raider who had eluded him these last ten months. Chasing the Viper had cost him everything. His title and position. His ship. In the span of a week his rising star had fallen under the weight of the man: from being in a place to make things right with Isobella de Morecraft, to essentially an outlaw. At times, it felt as though the man might claim his sanity as well.

"Hey." Catali's voice snapped Augustin to the moment. He blinked to focus his attention back on her. "We can't keep going like this. You have to let us take more jobs that pay. Jobs like this." She pointed back toward Vicente. Even with the pain of his leg, he turned the bloody knife in his hand, focusing on it, letting his eye find the blood's owner. "If you don't," Catali sucked in a breath and released it slowly, "there isn't going to be enough of us left to help anyone."

CHAPTER 3

EDMOND MONDEGO STARED AT the corpse of Sir Matimeo Navara. The sound of wheels against dirt startled him from his reverie, and he glanced sharply back up the road, relaxing only when he recognized the approaching cart. Their backup had been hiding behind a copse of trees, along a dirt road beyond a switchback over the dells. Edmond was pleased to see how quickly they responded to the pistol shot. He'd never worked with bravos before, but over the previous year, he'd discovered they were the best hires he'd ever made. There had been the nasty little re-negotiation an hour after their first contract was up, but once the gunsmoke settled and the sabres were sheathed—and the eight bodies were disposed of—Edmond had managed to hire the remaining crew for another seven months.

Two months remained on that contract. If nothing else, he could count on that. Bravos *never* broke a contract. They honored d'oro too much for that. But once the contract completed... well, like last time, they might come calling late at night in Edmond's room with serrated knives. At least now, he'd be expecting them, rather than lulled into a false sense of security by their compliance, utility, and loyalty during the contract period.

Kurga's two sons sat in the elevated carter seat, while other bravos had piled in the back. Kurga's sons were, almost comically, much larger than their father. They had boyish faces of lads shedding their late teens, and their braids on the side of their heads were shorter, woven with fewer baubles and trinkets. They had the same pale skin as Kurga and would often mutter to each other in Chellek. Unlike their father, their hair was pure white, and the few strands of fuzz protruding from their upper lips and chins were similarly discolored. Beside the short cutlasses at their sides, both the boys carried rifles—or, more accurately, *half* a rifle. It was unlike any musket or firearm Edmond had ever laid his eyes on. The gun, when assembled, was massive; nearly twice Kurga's height. It gleamed with polished steel and varnished wood, boasting a strange array of mirrors and telescoping lenses on top of the barrel. Sunlight glinted off of a hammer, but the strange weapon held no pan or flint cap or frizzen. Pearl inlay etched up and down the side of the enormous weapon. Despite the boys lugging the rifle everywhere they went, Edmond had yet to see it put to use. The previous year, barring the renegotiation, had been a bloodless one. Plans and research and preparations had been set into motion.

Edmond's past attempts at conversation with Dorgo and Calub—Kurga's boys—had convinced him that Kurga's ability to speak Emperor's Common was a rarity.

The cart full of bravos pulled to a dusty halt, spitting dirt and scraping mud. The horses whinnied at a tug of their reins, clopping to a firm-hooved stop. A second later, like piranha's swarming a goat in a river, the bravos spilled out of the cart and rushed to Sir Matimeo's side. They brushed past Edmond in a whirlwind, quickly pulling and pocketing every item of jewelry on the corpse's body. Rings vanished from fingers, a locket disappeared from his throat, and even his buttons and shoe buckles were pried off by the edge of daggers.

Then, shovels appeared from the back of the cart, and the ten bravos, under the lead of Kurga's sons, darted into the undergrowth, carrying Sir Navarro's corpse and hurrying towards the border of the nearest line of looming, dark-needled fir trees.

"Take him a quarter mile in!" Edmond called after them. "Make sure to mark your way out!"

Kurga grunted from the direction of the wagon, tisking his tongue. "They know, uh?" He said, inclining a dark eyebrow over pale skin. "They know what they do."

Edmond raised a hand in deference. He could feel Mirastious' eyes boring a hole into the side of his skull, and with a reluctant sigh, he finally turned to face her. "What?" he said. "I stuck to our agreement. I didn't hurt him, until he hurt you."

Mira pursed her lips, but simply shrugged. "I didn't say anything."

"No—but you're thinking it. *Loudly.* Isn't that right, Kurga?" Edmond glanced at the bravo leader.

The short man had opened his coat, revealing a criss-crossing bandolier adorned with pistols of many sizes and sheen. Each looked more well-kept and ornate than the last. Kurga had a small rag out and was busy rubbing the grip of a silver flintlock. At Edmond's words he grunted and waved a hand dismissively towards Mira.

"Cannot hear her thoughts," he said, shaking his head. "The Scry is silent with her."

Kurga reached up, brushing aside his dreadlocks, revealing a silver ear. The same ear he inclined towards the air. His hand stopped dabbing at the pistols and instead, he pointed towards Edmond. Eyes closed, Kurga whispered a couple of times, his ear still inclined towards the sky.

"No... I not say this, uh?" Kurga whispered. "He not like." The pirate hesitated, still seemingly listening to the breeze. "Okay. I say this."

Edmond waited patiently, watching the pirate. Over the last year, he'd grown accustomed to both the sellsword's sense—or lack—of hygiene, and the invisible 'ghost' he called *Scry* who he listened to on occasion.

Edmond didn't believe in ghosts—neither did Mira. And half the time he suspected the pirate was simply sunstroked, or insane. Not that he minded. He liked his employees a bit unhinged.

Kurga tapped his chin, still pointing at Edmond with his other hand. "Aye," he said. "Scry says you is find enemies in Titan's Folly. Scry says blood will spill."

Edmond shook his head. "Does Scry say anything nice?"

Kurga hesitated, his silver ear glinting beneath his dreads. Then, he shrugged. "Scry says perhaps you find friends too. Perhaps not, uh? You a deadly bastard. Friends with the Man of Faces is a danger thing, uh? When the tide is low, every shrimp has its own puddle. "

"Scry said all that?"

Kurga flashed a grin, revealing surprisingly well kept teeth above rotting gums. "Kurga say that." He nodded towards the forest where his boys had vanished with the body.

Edmond withheld a smile of his own, and gave a respectful bow of gratitude towards the bravo leader, keeping quiet the skeptical thoughts churning through his mind. Kurga was far too good a shot with those pistols of his to risk offending. But silver ear or not, invisible ghosts or not, Edmond would author his own fate. Be he godsdamned or otherwise, he had once resurrected a goddess. His very breath was defiance to damnation itself.

Edmond swallowed, then turned to the carriage, gesturing the others should follow. "Titan's Folly is another few hours away. We'd best hurry before nightfall. I'd like to familiarize myself with the town."

"Yes, Reeve Navara," Mira said, coolly, brushing past Edmond and politely accepting Kurga's offered elbow to lift herself into the back quarter of the carriage.

"Reeve Navara," Kurga cackled. He winked at Edmond, then took a couple of hopping steps for momentum to launch his diminutive self into the metal stirrup leading to the coachman's seat.

Reeve Navara. Edmond echoed the title and name, allowing a small smile to curl his lips. He stowed the now-cooled pistol at his belt and joined Mira in the back of the carriage, leaning against crimson cushion and peering out the windows at the imposing outline of Monta Gabri towering ahead of them. Titan's Folly was situated in a valley beyond the mountain pass.

Gold was in those mountains, but Edmond was in search of a different sort of treasure entirely.

With a soft sigh, he leaned back, closing his eyes, allowing his mind to rehearse the plan they had constructed over the previous year again... again... and again...

CHAPTER 4

FROM THE BACK OF the big, black stallion, Vicente's ribald singing announced the Order of the Honorable Lily's arrival in Wickwood. When the senza had worn off, Cristobal had volunteered a brown bottle of whiskey that had done much to take Vicente's mind off of his leg wound, though Augustin pondered the wisdom of this compassionate gesture as the villagers of Wickwood, framed in the early morning light, shot silent scowls to the group.

The brigand leader, bruised, limping, and bound at the wrists, marched ahead of them. Behind him, four of the brigand's horses walked with the bodies of the remaining criminals bundled across their backs. Augustin rubbed his tired eyes. It had taken the whole of the night for Vicente's demon-eye to track down the brigand leader, but none of the party had any desire to camp in the wild with their new captives. Beside him, Tristan's soft eyes tracked the pink glow of the rising sun as he murmured a prayer to his sun god. It only made the rings under Augustin's eyes feel all the more heavy.

"So what blessing does Pardi have for us today?" Augustin asked. He had no qualms with the gods. Like many soldiers and knights of the Empire, he had notched Mercusi's scales into the back of every shield he'd ever borne, and he at least thought he understood Cristobal's superstitious gestures and the small totems he gave the gods when luck smiled on them, but for Tristan it was different. For him, Pardi wasn't just sun-baked treats every year on Mittlemass. The sun god pervaded his thoughts each and every day. If Augustin hadn't known the fellow knight for years, if he had not traveled with him in the Order, he might have thought so much devotion indecent. Augustin waited patiently while Tristan silently finished his prayer. His eyes seemed to be searching the horizon, and though Augustin could see nothing by the climbing pink and blue of the imminent sunrise, it seemed to him that Tristan did.

"We are going to help someone today. Someone who really needs it." The comment came with a satisfied nod and the same assurance of a fisherman declaring the coming of a storm. Augustin turned as Cristobal grunted in acceptance; the big Dumasian also squinted into the morning light.

Augustin closed his eyes and let out an exhausted sigh. He didn't know what else he had expected, but something in the hopeful pronouncement turned his stomach. He shivered and felt a sudden chill. When he opened them again, they stood in the shadow of a tall manor house. He remembered it from when they had accepted the job—the Navara family manor.

The bruise-faced brigand inhaled sharply. Augustin spun around, in case the man had decided to make a break for it, but the brigand leader had not moved. Augustin's hand froze on the hilt of his rapier as he eyed the man.

"This is where you're takin' me? Not the village reeve?" the brigand said as he eyed the stone and wood of the manor.

"The reeve didn't hire us," said Catali.

The brigand pulled his eyes from the dark windows of the manor and turned his head to face her. "Filthy bounty hunters," the brigand said with a note of disdain. "Just slit my throat here then and be done with it."

Augustin looked to his friends, but all of them appeared just as puzzled as him. Even Vicente had ceased his singing and now leaned precipitously off his saddle to peer at the highwayman. Having their attention, the brigand leader spoke again, "That's Matimeo Navara's house. If he's the one what hired you, I'm as good as dead anyway."

Vicente blew out of his lips in a derisive burst. "You said las' night that the reeve would hang ye anyway. I remember. I was paying very close attention because you'd just shot me leg. So die here or die there. What's the difference?"

The brigand glared at Vicente, but the ragged knight had already turned his attention back to the bottle of whiskey. "The difference," the brigand spat, "is that the reeve will see us hanged. Now I'm not looking forward to dancin' the hempen jig, but I'm a man. I knew that would be my lot one day." With his back straight and his bloodied chin up, the morning light gave the brigand an almost noble bearing. Almost. Rubbing at his nose with his bound hands, the brigand pointed to the cold manor. "But I've heard stories about Matimeo Navara that would curdle your blood. Screams at midnight. People go missing from Wickwood, and later all they finds is bones. I spoke with a latchboy once, broke into the Navara house.

35

Said he found a whole collection of bloody knives, all kinds of wicked shapes, and he runs out of the manor because Matimeo Navara came in with some kind of heavy bag, all bloody, and it was *moving*. So no, handed over to Matimeo Navara is not any kind of way for a man to die."

A long pause hung in the air. Augustin had heard all manner of stories from desperate men. In the years he and the Order first traveled, he had seen bandits who claimed to have been framed by their wicked twins, to be the bastards of royalty, and even one who claimed an alchemist changed his face to frame him. That last one had begun to haunt him on quiet nights, but for the most part, Augustin believed in Mercusi's justice. Right and wrong. Good and evil. Brigands should be caught and turned over for their bounties, but if what this brigand said had truth in it—

Tristan met Augustin's eyes, he had a hesitant look to him. Flicking his eyes towards the rising sun, he gave Augustin a meaningful look. *We're going to help someone today. Someone who really needs it.*

On his other side, Cristobal ran his meaty fingers over his scarred chin. "A torturer is a hateful thing. Mercusi's law is not a law of vengeance. If the reeve will take him—"

"Oh, tell me you're not buying this shark shite." Catali turned and looked around at the four knights with an incredulous expression. "Depths below, they're stories. Even if there was a latchboy, which I doubt, scary looking knives don't prove a thing. Hells, *I* have scary looking knives." Rummaging through her surgeon's kit, Catali pulled free a curved surgeon's knife, and a squat, toothed bone-saw. Looking to Augustin, she pursed her lips. "Imperial bounties haven't even posted for them. If the reeve decides to give us anything, which is no guarantee, there is no reason for him to match even half of what the Navara offered." After her statement, Catali held Augustin's eyes.

He thought about the empty bottle of senza in her pack and the stained bandages on Vicente's injured leg. *A torturer is a hateful thing.* He couldn't remember if the expression came from Mercusi or from life-giving Ververiona—*Maybe it's a Dumasian thing.* Tired, Augustin gripped the swept hilt of his rapier, and the tendons of his calloused hands creaked with the momentary strain. *I have to keep us going. I have to keep us together.* He clenched his jaw.

"We can't afford to go back on our deal now. We made this bargain with Rollo Navara, not Matimeo. We can't chance a deal with the reeve, and we're not oath-breakers." He folded his arms behind his back as he spoke. His tone brooked no further question, and he forced himself to look his companions in the eyes. Cristobal nodded quickly, and Catali's face seemed to practically melt with relief. Tristan held his gaze the longest, then he walked back to help Vicente down off the big black. As an afterthought, Augustin turned to the brigand leader. He felt his tongue on the precipice of apologizing, but caught himself, and pushed down the niggling remorse in his heart. Instead, giving the man a short, hard look before turning to mount the manor steps.

When they had first arrived in Wickwood, the Navara manor had been, while not exactly cheery, at least lively. They had seen servants in the livery of their merchant lord, moving through the yard, running out horses, and attending to the lord and lady within the manor's main hall. Now, as Cristobal pulled the bell chain at the manor's door, no sound of scuttling feet came from within to greet them. Vicente pulled Tristan after him as he limped to the windows of the manor, trampling a cluster of blue flowers as he did. He glanced down at a frayed piece of parchment—folded like a pamphlet, trampled in the dirt.

Vicente stooped down, eyes narrowed examining the bold lettering across the muddied pamphlet. "W—wi..." he tried to sound out, but then waved Tristan over. "Oi, Beautiful. Ol' Vicente's eyes are failing him. Mind givin' that a read?"

"Your eyes aren't the problem," Catali snorted.

Vicente pointedly ignored the comment while Tristan stooped in the dirt, picked up the pamphlet, and showed the colorful, red and green inked parchment towards the others. "*Wickwood's Transportation and Steeds,*" he said. "Looks like a new business in town."

Vicente shrugged while Tristan stowed the pamphlet, and the ragged knight turned back to the manor's windows. "The curtains are shut, but," Vicente shook his head then turned back to Augustin. "I don't see any light behind them."

Tristan half-dragged Vicente back to the door as Vicente kept craning his neck to peer at each of the windows. Back at the front door, Tristan said, "It could just be early. Perhaps the servant did not hear. Ring it again." At a nod from Augustin, Cristobal pulled the bell chain again. Another moment passed, but no answer came.

A nervous look passed among them, and Augustin narrowed his eyes as he raised a fist to pound on the heavy door. At the first blow, the door swung open. It drifted, silent as a shadow, on well-oiled hinges. Within, the manor's entry hall lay dark and cold. A wide stairway covered in a thick red carpet led to the manor house's second story and at its peak hung a six foot portrait. The oil painting showed an older man with a severe look, glowering from behind a bushy set of mutton chops. At his back stood a dignified woman in a long green dress with her hands on the man's shoulder as though he were an unruly dog that would bolt after the portraitist if she let go. From his first visit, Augustin knew that these were the merchant lord and lady Navara. To either side, so that their lord father would sit the middle of the portrait, stood two men in their mid-twenties. The one to the right turned his handsome jaw in a charming smile, and rings of gold and silver adorned his exposed hand. The other's rounded features held a simple geniality as he stared out from the portrait. Augustin could not help but wonder now which one was Matimeo. No servant had come through the entry hall to draw the curtains for the morning light, and the dim glow that flowed in from the door cast an eerie shadow that seemed to highlight the portrait's eyes, as though they were alive and staring down at him.

"Hello," Augustin called into the darkness as he stepped into the manor house. He waved a hand backward as Cristobal made to follow him in. He had no desire to scare anyone if a servant were to come in suddenly. Still, no answer came.

A soft clatter sounded as Tristan leaned his long spear against the side of the manor. Augustin heard Tristan tell Cristobal to keep an eye on their captive, then the sound of soft footfalls as he came up beside him. "This isn't right. Where is everyone?" Tristan asked.

Augustin had been thinking the same. The manor lay as silent as a grave-yard. Early though it was, there should at least have been servants awake to work the kitchen and stoke up the fires. Instead, the air hung still and cold. "Keep everyone outside for now. I'll do a quick search of the manor. If something foul is afoot, I'll call for aid."

"Like hells you will," Tristan muttered. "The others can watch the bandits. Blue fire, I'm not about to let you wander off alone into some *murder* house." Tristan often did his best to avoid cussing or taking oaths, but when his friend's lives were in question, he seemed to care less about his code than his convictions.

"Tristan, you're being ridiculous."

"Why are you so insistent on doing this alone? If you think two will make too much noise, I'll go ahead and—"

Stepping between them, Catali stuck first Tristan then Augustin with a frustrated stare, "Oh, blue fire and black fish. Neither one of you soft-h

eaded *knights* is going alone. Now let's start with the upper floor. If the lord and lady are here, that's where they'll likely be."

His shock passed quickly, and Tristan held up a gauntleted hand. "You're right, it's probably nothing, but on the off chance it is something dangerous, well, you really should let us handle it."

Jabbing a finger into the ring-mail of Tristan's hauberk, Catali said, "That's why I'm coming, you pious-stick-swinging-dunderhead." From the doorway, Vicente let out a hearty guffaw, and Catali shot him a quick smile before her face fell back into a mask of impatient irritation. "Someone could be hurt. I'm coming. Now, stairs." Tristan sucked his breath between his teeth, but gave an apologetic nod as he turned to lead the way.

Within two steps, he and Augustin fell into sync. They took the stairs by slow steps, examining the hallway cautiously. Between steps, Augustin held his breath, listening for any sound from the blackness of the manor halls. At intervals, Tristan called out in his clear, strong voice, but once they reached the second story hallway he stopped. If someone did hide in these dark halls, they likely didn't want to be found.

Together, they checked the manor's rooms. The first few seemed to be guest quarters, pleasant, but with none of the personal effects one would expect from someone's private quarters. The bedsheets held no dust, and the wardrobes stood empty. As they ventured further down the halls, the manor seemed cared for, but for the absence of any of its inhabitants. Here and there they opened windows to allow in light where they could, though the morning sun did little to illuminate the manor's inner halls.

Feeling a tap at his shoulder, Augustin followed Tristan's hand as he pointed to the frame of a nearby door. A deep gash revealed bright wood under the painted finish. *That's fresh,* Augustin thought, nodding to Tristan. The lightness in the cut told him that the air and moisture had not had a chance to darken it. Augustin drew his dagger, and motioned to Catali to step back. She slipped near the wall, behind Augustin as Tristan took hold of the door handle.

As he opened the door, light spilled into the hall. Augustin stepped into the doorway, and noticed the window stood open. A chill morning breeze followed in the bright light of the rising sun, and a shiver ran across Augustin's bare arms. A long shadow stretched from an object on the floor. Kneeling, Augustin found it was a marble bust. The same severe expression and curling mutton chops from the entryway portrait adorned the figure, but as Augustin turned it in his hands he saw the white marble stained with the rusting red of dried blood.

"Don't touch it!"

Augustin whirled as the gaunt form of a wraith-like woman rushed towards him. Her eyes were wide with menace and bulged from black rings that stood against her pale flesh like bruises. Her hair, matted and stringy, blew behind her, and she raised her sharp fingernails like claws. "Don't you touch that!" she shrieked.

Augustin dropped his dagger as the woman lay hold of his neck, her nails biting into his skin and drawing thin lines of blood. Augustin grabbed the woman's wrists. He tried to pry back her hands, but she held on by some preternatural strength. Tristan rushed into the room, his chain hauberk jangling as he whirled around Augustin.

"It's not right. It's not right," the woman said. Her dark eyes seemed on the verge of tears, but quickly filled with rage as Tristan grabbed her around the back and pulled her off of Augustin. She shrieked as Tristan threw her to the ground, and with a sudden jerk, he drew his own dagger from his belt.

"Stop!" Augustin shouted. Tristan froze. He did not look back to Augustin, nor did he lower his dagger. The woman lay on the ground, her screams of fury turned to sobs as her dark hair shrouded her shaking body. Between deep breaths, Augustin rose to his feet, and pointed to the woman. "That's Lady Navara."

CHAPTER 5

THE ORDER OF THE Honorable Lily sat in the parlor of the Navara Manor. Cristobal stood pouring cups from a silver teapot, Tristan coaxed a fire out of the cold hearth, and lady Navara sunk into the plush fabric of an armchair with a heavy blanket around her frail shoulders. She had spoken little since attacking Augustin in the upstairs study, but allowed herself to be led, docile as a lamb, downstairs. She accepted the hot cup that Cristobal offered, holding the steaming tea under her chin and laying her palms around the cup to absorb its warmth.

Catali had warned them not to ask her questions yet, but to wait patiently. So Augustin held his peace and folded his hands against a tremor of unease. While they waited, once he'd finished stoking the fire, Tristan had taken Vicente's place watching their captive brigands. On the table between them all, sat the marble bust, it's bloody side turned up for all to see. At length, Lady Navara sipped her tea, and said, "My son has been murdered."

Augustin sat up. Looking to Catali; he waited for the surgeon to give him a gentle nod, then turned to face Lady Navara. The lady took another slow sip from her tea cup. Augustin took a breath to steady himself, "What happened? We were here only a week ago."

Lady Navara closed her eyes. She shuddered and for a moment, it seemed she might burst into tears, but instead she opened her dark eyes and looked to the bloody bust. "I found the bust hidden in the hearth... But that's only the start of it. Five nights ago, my husband received a letter. A ransom request. My step-son, Matimeo, has been gone nearly a month. He was commissioned to be reeve, a heady promotion for one so young as him." Augustin looked to Catali, but she raised a finger. The woman's voice drifted with an indifferent grey melody, as if she were reading a diary entry. "His road would take him near the coast, and the letter said he has been captured by pirates. The pirates now demand a ransom, which my loving husband has left to fulfill." A sarcastic thread began to weave between her words, and its bitter sound made Augustin feel as though he were listening to some spiteful joke. "He said, 'do not worry, your son, Sebastion, he will be home in a few days once he concludes his business in Gavelwood. He will keep the house while I am away to ransom Matimeo.' So I waited. I waited, but Sebastion did not return." Augustin thought of the portrait in the entry hall, and pictured the handsome face of one young man across from the genial face of the other. Which was Sebastian, and which was Matimeo? Only time would tell. Here Lady Navara's eyes welled up with tears and two wet lines traced across her cheeks, joining familiar runs already stained with her sorrow. "I sent a messenger to Gavelwood to inquire on my son's delay. He returned the next day, and he tells me, 'Sebastion never arrived in Gavelwood.' He has not been seen there in months. How can this be? I thought. He left the same day that my step-son, Matimeo, left to take up his commission." Her lips trembled, and her nostrils narrowed as she took a sharp breath. With a crooked, accusing finger she pointed to the bloody bust on the parlor table. "That was when I found this." Now she looked up, her eyes were mad with rage as she cast a dark look to each of them seated around her, and Augustin felt a chill settle in his heart.

"I know what they say in the village about my step-son, but I have lived in this house for years now. I have closed my eyes to more than those gossips and tale-spinners can dream in their twisted little hearts. Matimeo is a monster. He flatters and smiles. His father's indulgence covers any slip up that might stain the family name." Lady Navara twisted her head, her fingers shaking around the tea cup. "Rollo has been good to me and my son. I'm his second wife, but he has treated me kindly, so I said nothing. I said nothing about the midnight sounds and the blood stains, or the servant's whispered fears." With a sudden twist she threw her cup. The porcelain shattered in the fireplace with a hiss as the tea splashed across the burning logs. "I will be silent no more."

Lady Navara stood, and Augustin rose to meet her. Stepping to the knight she said, "My lord husband promised you a tenth of what you recovered from those brigands, yes?" Augustin paused for a moment, taken off guard by the sudden change in topic.

He folded his arms behind his back and nodded, adding, "Plus twenty d'oro for their capture." Lady Navara nodded bruskly and walked to a cabinet set opposite the fireplace. With a slender brass key she opened first the wood cabinet, then a metal safe within. She withdrew a purse of coin, and held it up.

"This is fifty d'oro. Take it. Consider your contract with my husband fulfilled."

Augustin eyed the purse. Trepidation played at his heart, as he began to see where Lady Navara's intentions lay. "What of the brigands, my lady?"

"Turn them over to the reeve. Release them. Kill them. I don't care. I need you for something more important." She pressed the purse of coin into Augustin's hands, but as he attempted to take it, she took hold of his hands. "If you take my coin you are in my employ until I am satisfied." She looked hard into Augustin's eyes. A sort of mad zealotry spoke out from her gaze.

"My lady, what do you want us to do, precisely?" Augustin asked cautiously.

"Find my son's killer. Bring me justice for my child." Her voice rasped as her throat could no longer bear the emotion welling up from her heart. "My prayers to Mirastious remain unanswered, but my soul says that it is Matimeo. Whoever the monster is, I want you to find out, and I want you to see them punished in kind."

Here she released the coin purse and stepped away. From the fireplace hearth, Cristobal spoke up. "Lady Navara," his thick accent dripped out heavy and slow as he tried to be sure he would be understood. "To be sure. Your son, Sebastion, is missing, and the blood is damning, but how are you sure he is dead?" Lady Navara slumped back into the overstuffed chair by the fire.

"A mother knows."

A tense moment passed, while Augustin thought of how he might reply, but before he could, Vicente gave a groan and limped towards the bloody marble bust. He waved away Cristobal's offered hand, and took hold of the sculpture.

"Well, we can know for sure."

Lady Navara raised a quizzical eyebrow as Vicente's calloused fingers began to probe the dried blood that painted the statue. The fireplace light glinted off of the ring of yellow within Vicente's eye as it began to spin. The yellow pupil vibrated and started to wander within its socket. A pained expression crossed Vicente's face, and he nearly dropped the bust as a shock ran up his body, tensing the muscles of his arms and legs. Augustin and Catali jumped together to steady him as the moment passed. When Vicente next blinked, his yellow eye had drawn itself to the edge of his periphery. He turned his head to follow it, as his expression fell. "Oh," he said, "Oh, Nameless Death be kind." Then, licking his lips, he looked to Augustin. "We're going to need a shovel."

***

The noon-day sun fought to pierce the heavy clouds when Cristobal pulled the last parcel from the dark earth. Vicente had told them where to dig. He had even told them to go slowly to avoid missing the disparate pieces of Lady Navara's son, but even he had not expected there would be so many of the wax-paper wrapped packages. As Augustin looked at the pile, it took no guessing to know it held too many pieces for one body. Too many by far. Lady Navara watched the grim affair from the manor's back stoop with

Catali standing respectfully near her. As Cristobal pulled himself out from the hole, the pair began to walk towards them.

Vicente shuffled the parcels, picking out one in particular. With his dagger, he slit the paper open. The stench of decay flowed out like water from a spring. Not minding the gore within, Vicente fished through the decomposing contents of the bag, with the grim determination of a fisherman pulling in a catch. Augustin held his breath to drive back the nausea that rose in his stomach at the sight.

"That's it, come to Vicente," Vicente muttered. Then, with a sigh of relief, he pulled his clenched hand out from the parcel. Vicente wiped his hands on the grass as Augustin and Cristobal stepped closer. It was a ring, pale gold and set with a sapphire.

"That's Sophie's ring," Lady Navara intoned. The group looked to her, and her gaze hardened. "Sebastion's wife. She disappeared more than a year ago." She took several deep breaths, covering her nose with the back of her hand. "Of the many rings that choke his filthy hands, that's the only one he ever saw before it was owned—Matimeo, I mean. He helped Sebastion pick out the ring. That monster. I'm sure it was him now," she said. Once more she turned to face Augustin. "I'll give you one thousand d'oro if you bring him to justice. A princely sum, surely enough for you all."

The knights looked at each other in stunned silence. With a thousand d'oro, a person could buy their own ship outright. It was an extravagant amount, so much so that Augustin didn't quite believe his ears. With that kind of money they could live for quite some time. He thought again about Catali's supplies. With this money they could easily replace her stocks. They could even replace the tools she had lost over their year of travel. They wouldn't be out of meals. They could stay at village inns instead of camping on the edge of town. This was a chance. *Today we're going to help someone. Someone who really needs it.* Augustin didn't know if Pardi had guided them to this place, but if this wasn't the person they were meant to help, who else would it be? "My lady," Augustin said, "We would be honored to take up your cause."

CHAPTER 6

The Choking Pass curved into a steep, winding road, which carried the carriage through and across the numerous engineering projects poured into the road over the centuries. The tangle of stone bridges and switchbacks made a maze of the three mile pass through the jagged and craggy peaks of the Monta Gabri.

Edmond had been expecting this, however. He'd studied more than one map—geographic, climatic, political, topographic. The year leading up to this had been one filled with information. He knew about the rumors concerning the late Matimeo Navara's bloody pastimes. He also knew Titan's Folly had hired him as reeve. But Titan's Folly offered *other* prospects as well.

It all hinged on the Tenth Annual Commemoration Tournament.

Edmond knew the region well—as well as he could having never set foot within it.

He barely even glanced up as they passed the ruins of Fort Dentimosi. Flanking the narrowest portion of the pass, its wood and iron gates removed years ago, the remaining stone of the keep reclaimed by mountain scrub and the desperate, climbing roots of pine trees.

The carriage came to a momentary halt outside the fort. Men moved to and from the cart. The majority of the bravos moved—as Edmond had outlined earlier that day—into the fort, preparing to take up temporary outpost for the time being.

Kurga's sons, toting their half-rifles and white hair joined the carriage, climbing up onto the coachman's seat with their father, the beads in their dreadlocks tinkling against each other. Now, they were wearing hats to disguise their hair and proper crimson livery with the golden badger crest of house Navara. Edmond had instructed them to do so, knowing that bravos this far inland would raise uncomfortable questions he'd rather leave unasked. Kurga also had donned the disguise. Bravos took great pride in their hair, the length of their braids and the number of beads and baubles woven throughout. Edmond still wasn't certain of the significance, but it had taken a herculean effort to convince Kurga to wear a hat. Finally, he'd agreed to do so for a bonus fee of ten gold d'oro. The one loyalty higher to a bravo than their hair was their purse.

The two sons and their father muttered quiet, ominous sayings in Chellek, their voices resounding through the thin wood of the carriage's top quarter.

Mirastious snickered, raising a hand to cover her lips, her eyes twinkling.

Edmond frowned, shooting her a sidelong glance.

"What?" he demanded.

"Oh," she said, still chuckling. "Nothing—only, well... They're right. You *do* look a bit constipated, sitting there all grit and furrow."

Edmond started. "I beg your pardon?"

Mira held up her hands in mock surrender. "I didn't say it! They did." She pointed towards the front of the carriage and snickered again as another bout of Chellek conversation drifted through.

"You speak Chellek?" Edmond asked, stunned.

At this, Mira's expression soured somewhat and she picked distractedly at a splinter beneath the window. "I know nearly fifty languages, not to mention various regional dialects," she said.

"Impressive."

"Don't. I'm serious. Don't. No, don't act all innocent. You know what I mean. I can tell, just by looking that you're trying to figure out the best way to exploit this. I'm only surprised you didn't know."

"I'm not trying to exploit anything. Though your ability with languages might come in useful after all. I'm surprised you didn't tell me. All those times Kurga would rattle off commands to the men—you knew exactly what he was saying?"

"It was mostly just a translation of the instructions you gave him. Except that one time he told Abedgo not to stab you during negotiations."

"Abedgo?"

"The one with the longest braids and ebony crystals dangling from his locks."

"Oh. Well. I'm glad he didn't stab me."

"He wasn't glad."

Before Edmond could retort, the carriage pulled along a bluff, spitting stones and dust over the edge of a precipice and sending them skittering down the mountainside into the holler. As the carriage turned, winding down the dipping path, Edmond fell quiet, peering over Mira's shoulder and staring to the valley floor. He swallowed slightly, and for a moment he forgot to inhale.

"What?" Mira frowned. "What is—" She followed his gaze through the window, then fell silent herself. "Oh..." she said simply. "There it is." Her tone carried with it an undercurrent of delight—the crystal cool splash of melted water sloshing onto a river bank and teasing life from once-dry earth.

"There it is," Edmond repeated, his voice barely more than a murmur.

Even the yammering of the bravos had ceased for the moment as the pass spilled into a broad and empty basin, dry as salt, still as death. The distant silhouette of a plateau, no more than a shadowy smudge across miles of cracked flat earth, stood as the sole resident of the Folding Valley. Edmond could only imagine that was what caught the bravos' eye as well. They were there. Titan's Folly.

The last half-dozen miles brought them across the valley floor to the base of the plateau. Edmond only spared a cursory glance for the log platforms and wooden supports built into the side of the cliff both north and south. He cared little for the carts and carriages hefting supplies back and forth along a massive boulevard twisting its way like a snake through arid and depleted terrain. The riphouses where they would separate metals from minerals and stone were of passing curiosity, spewing multi-colored smoke into the air—likely sourced from alchemical fires. The many pockmarked holes scattering the face of the mountain, again both north and south, rising from the valley floor and dotting their way to the peak like snake dens large enough for humans, also received only a passing glance.

Edmond only had eyes for the namesake of Titan's Folly. The wrecks.

An enormous ship had been ripped in two on top of a mile-long plateau.

The ship's prow—an angled behemoth of a wooden and metal structure, boasted a figurehead as large as most towers. The figurehead was of an indeterminable form claimed by decades of rust and salt-tinged wind—perhaps a god, or perhaps an ancient king, a sword clutched in one hand and a golden net tangled in a bunched fist at its side. Six imperial frigates could have easily fit inside the prow alone.

The stern was equally large, but the severed portion was facing the carriage across the valley floor like some severed corpse revealing its innards. And, while the titan still had multiple decks—Edmond counted seven—it wasn't spacious, nor was it filled with cargo or armaments and crews quarters. He'd never been on a titan, so he didn't know what they did with all that space normally. This particular, severed ship, however, was a small city.

Wooden platforms extending from the guts of the ship protruded out, crisscrossing with walkways and ladders and curling stairs. Full-sized buildings and shops of wood and steel siding were built into the side of the titan, disappearing up alleys which ventured further into the back half of the ship.

Edmond supposed, though he couldn't see the heart of the prow, that the front half of the ship was also similarly engineered. On the top deck of both ships were two enormous houses.

A giant, palatial estate surrounded by a wooden palisade was built on the top of the stern. The white-painted mansion of stone and wood was surrounded, astonishingly by a green garden filled with mountain shrubs and resplendent flowers. Tangled vines poking up the top of the palisade further served to disguise the contents of the ship-topping estate from view.

The stern also boasted an enormous structure on the other end of the plateau, separated by nearly a mile—in Edmond's estimation—from the prow. This second structure, though, was more castle than mansion. Edmond suspected he knew where the gates to Fort Dentimosi had disappeared to. Thick stone blocks and towers faced the mountain-pass, orange lights glinting dully even at this distance.

"You're now the reeve of this place," Mira said, a cattish playfulness to her tone. "Do you think you can handle it?"

"We're going to find out, won't we? I need to speak with the baroness, though."

"Won't that offend the baron?"

"It may. But I'll speak to him too, eventually. The baroness, however, is still sponsoring applicants to the tournament. So she's our best bet."

"You're sure the information was reliable?"

Edmond gave her a significant look. "It was good enough for us to ambush Navara wasn't it?"

Mira made a face like sucking lemons, glancing back towards the valley once more. Her upturned, celestial nose placed in immaculate features cut a statuesque silhouette against the horizon. Strands of midnight-black hair curled past her silver-pale cheeks, resting on the soft curve of her shoulder.

Edmond looked away, frowning in thought.

In his readings of the area, and the few conversations he'd managed to have with people—tradesmen and travelers mostly—who had visited Titan's Folly, he'd ascertained that no one quite knew *how* the titan had found itself miles inland. The red-grey outline of the Monta Gabri ringed the basin of the Folding Valley, an elemental fortress separating the region from the cool breezes of the Western Sea and the green hills of southern Godshaven—isolated from sea and river like a well-sealed cask under its pale, cloudless skies.

Some suggested that the gods had placed the titan there. Still others supposed that it had been carted in, exchanged for gold, pyrite sulfur, and gunpowder, one large piece at a time over the span of decades. Still others suggested that there had once been an enormous river running through the heart of the valley, but it had been dammed off long ago, stranding the massive ship.

Edmond, of course, knew *exactly* how the ship had arrived. It was all part of the plan.

Whatever the case, Edmond was now responsible for keeping the peace in the divided lands.

"How long have the baroness and baron been feuding?" Edmond said, glancing towards Mira.

"Since they were born," Mira replied without blinking, peering with her inky gaze in Edmond's direction. "They both inherited the feud from their families."

"It was a murder, correct?"

"Tito Genevese," Mira said, again without hesitation, as if she were commenting on events from earlier that morning. "Ninety-seven years ago. He was murdered in a land dispute. They suspected Deneme Alverdo, but no charges were brought. The Genevese took matters into their own hands..."

"Feuding for near a hundred years now." Edmond whistled softly.

"A dangerous land for dangerous folk. Neither the Genevese nor the Alverdo family will take kindly to strangers."

"I'm the reeve," Edmond said, pointedly. "That should count for something."

"Hired by the young Commodore. Don't forget it. The baron and baroness had no say in the matter. And the new Commodore who commands this region is not like his father. He isn't strong or feared by either the baron or baroness. The tournament was put in place to give the feuding families an outlet for their aggression and a path to knighthood for the populace. It was, and remains, a distraction."

"A distraction that we will benefit from."

"Be that as it may. With the death of Commodore Radichelle last winter... Now more than ever, the chance of the blood feud escalating is a tinderbox simply waiting for a spark. Neither the Genevese nor the Alverdo much appreciated the Commodore's hand in their business, but they at the very least feared the man. With his son... It may not be the case."

Edmond tapped the front of the carriage lightly. "That's why I brought them. And that's why we're going to stick to the plan. I have no interest in eliciting too much attention from either family. If they want their feud, they can have it."

"You say that now. But you have a thrice-cursed way of sticking your nose where it doesn't belong."

"Last time I did, I resurrected you," he said, sweetly.

"And you'll never cease to remind me, will you?"

Edmond's silence accompanied by a self-satisfied smirk was all the answer Mirastious needed, prompting her to fall into a dark mood and glare out the window at the village below as the carriage trundled along, carrying its cargo down in the valley and on towards an uncertain destiny.

Edmond couldn't shake Kurga's words from earlier. *Scry says you is find enemies in Titan's Folly. Scry says blood will spill.*

For a moment, prickles crept across Edmond's skin. He glanced down at his hands in his lap and noted a slight tremor to them.

His eyes narrowed, though. Edmond could live with the consequences. He dealt with Navara and he would reserve a similar fate for anyone who came to him looking for trouble. Blood would spill, perhaps. But as long as it wasn't Edmond's, he didn't care if the streets ran red with it.

He glanced at his hands again.

They were as steady as stone.

CHAPTER 7

IN THE MIDST OF the Folding Valley, there lay a five mile ring of cracked and barren flat land, a landscape of dust where only the faintest of breezes arose like the final death rattle from the dry throat of a sun-blistered corpse. The ground glinted a bone yellow, whitened only by the thin layer of salt that robbed the air of the meager moisture that managed to cross the mountains into the skeleton valley.

Rising from the ground like a mirage stood the craggy cliff-face of a plateau, nearly a mile wide at its top. Its eastern shadow protected a criss-cross of irrigated channels supporting rows of ruddy red beanstalks and tough, spiky vegetables. Situated on top of the plateau, rested Titan's Folly. Rings of stone houses lay in the shadows of the two massive wrecks. And as the carriage trundled past the first row of the houses, Edmond could feel the eyes fixated on them, burning like rays of sunlight into his skin.

He glanced out one window, then the other, confronted by weary, grim-faced men and women without a second of leisure among them, either hefting mining equipment, or covered in dust from the day's work, some lugging children in their wake, wash baskets under one arm, or groceries wheeled along by trolley. The quiet popping sounds of distant explosions—likely mining efforts—only further added to the ominous atmosphere which fell on Edmond and his companions.

Another thing Edmond noticed: everyone was armed.

But unlike most of the Gilded Islands, sword and dirk weren't on display. Rather, nearly everyone carried pistols at their hips or muskets strapped to their backs.

Gunpowder... Edmond remembered. Alchemically derived from the sulfur in the valley's pyrite mines. Titan's Folly's biggest export. Another bout of unease shot through him, but he pushed the thought away with a sniff. There was no turning back now. Too much was at stake.

Edmond tapped the window and pulled the sliding glass so he could call out. "Kurga—the reeve's manor is supposed to be smack-dab in the center of town. Look for a—" he glanced back down at the series of opened letters scattered across the seat between him and Mira. He scanned the letters for a moment—settling on the one he needed, and, after another moment of re-reading the contents, he called out, "Look for the emperor's symbol—the heron. It should be painted blue and gold on the door!"

Kurga clicked his tongue in response. The bravo leaned so far over the side of the driver's platform, Edmond worried he'd tumble, but then he remembered the man was used to climbing monkey-rigging in a gale on a ship during high storms, and his worries faded. At least Kurga was wearing his hat and the red livery, disguising—at least on cursory glance—his identity as a bravo. "No need to whisper to a chicken, uh? It has no ears."

"I still don't know what the bloody hell your sayings mean, my friend!" Edmond shouted out. "Just get us to the manor. We'll venture forth from there."

The shouting back and forth between the newcomer in his fancy carriage and the coachmen in the driver's seat only further elicited sideways glances and flat out stares. Edmond had been counting on this. Word would spread that the new reeve had arrived, which, in turn, he hoped would act as a deterrent to any bad blood between the Genevese and the Alverdos.

Kurga navigated their carriage through the streets of Titan's Folly, moving closer and closer to the giant wrecks, pulling past halted carts loading heavy boxes outside armories, and maneuvering around horse riders clopping through the mud or racking up their steeds to the hitching rails.

It was as they rounded a sharp turn past a large storehouse with greasy windows, that a commotion broke out ahead. Three large men, built like brick houses and sporting dusty braided beards and long, tangled hair were dragging a scrawny lad through the mud.

The boy—who couldn't have been more than twelve—was hooting and hollering something fierce, kicking out with his feet and trying to shake them free from where they gripped him by the wrists. He was also uttering the most colorful string of obscenities Edmond had ever heard from the mouth of a child. "You shite-covered, godsdamned, blue fire, cocksucking pieces of fuckstained ass juice!"

The three large men paused momentarily, in the middle of the road, readjusting their grips on the lad and forcing the carriage to come to a momentary stop.

One of the men held up an apologetic hand towards the carriage. "Pardon us!" he called, in a deep, rich voice. The man had a broken nose above a prickling mustache and his face was streaked with dirt trails and sweat stains. He wore a leather frock and thick heat gloves.

"Miners," Edmond murmured.

The adolescent kicked and fought and continued to shout various observations about the reproductive endeavors of the miners' mothers, daughters, and sisters, but the only reaction he received was a couple of clouts to the back of the head and another heave across the street.

When that didn't seem to work, the boy shook his head wildly, his shaggy red-hair shifting with the motion above his childish face. "I didn't mean it!" he shouted, shaking his head vigorously. "I'm apologizing—see, this is me apologizing! I never meant a word of it..." Again, the men didn't react except to continue dragging him. The boy's pale face flushed red. "You ballsack-licking, gold-sucking little bitches! I'll kick your dusty old asses! Let me go!"

Edmond watched in mild interest as the boy with the colorful language and his accompanying captors moved to the other side of the street.

Mira glanced across at Edmond, almost expectantly.

"We're not here to make any friends," he said in a quiet voice. "We're going to lay low and keep our noses out of it."

She looked back out the window at the struggling figures. Despite being outnumbered, and the sheer size difference, the lad was putting up one hell of a fight. He had managed to bite one of the men on the arm and was chomping down like a wolf with lockjaw, refusing to relinquish his grip.

The man being bitten howled and whacked at the boy with his free hand, pummeling the side of his face until he let go. "None of that now!" the miner roared, stepping forward so he was staring down at the boy draped in his companions' arms. "I don't care whose son you are! We caught you red-handed. Now behave properly or—"

The boy had been nodding along, hanging his head and glancing demurely down, but the moment the large miner stepped too close, he headbutted the man. As the boy was still draped over, practically on his knees, his head collided with a particularly delicate portion of the enraged miner's body—given the choice of words the boy had used earlier, Edmond figured he'd given fair warning as to the nature of his attentions. The miner gasped, as if he were choking on a cough and buckled over, heaving.

The boy cackled delightedly. "See if the missus prefers a rope toy to a bullet, ey?" he chortled. He received another couple of slaps and one rabbit punch to the nose which sent him into another series of painful expletives. The man who'd been headbutted managed to regain his posture, gasping and glaring daggers at the red-headed boy. The bulky miners managed to drag the boy completely out of the road, to the side of the street with the warehouse.

Edmond looked away and tapped the roof. "Keep going, Kurga—can't be far now."

Reins snapped and the temporary coachman whistled, but over the renewed sound of clopping, Edmond heard one of the miners shout. "He likes rope toys? I'll give you rope. Get me some of the braided stuff from indoors. We'll string the ashen bastard up right here!"

Mira glanced at Edmond again, tilting one eyebrow. The make-believe reeve stared resolutely ahead.

"Help!" a voice screeched suddenly, in a bloodcurdling screech. The inhuman sound was offset only by a series of gulping sobs. "Help! Fucking help me, please. I'm fucking begging—"

The sound became muffled again. And an unfamiliar voice shouted, "Keep his mouth covered, you fools! You looking to get roasted? Here, gag him with this!"

"Ack! It's an ass rag! The ol' perv is trying to shove his ass rag in me mouth! Help! Fire! Rape! Murder! Tits! Fu—" But the boy's protests were cut off as a dirty cloth, the sort used to clean machines, was shoved in his mouth.

Edmond heaved a defeated sigh. He threw up his hands as if in surrender and tapped the carriage roof again. "Wait!" He called. Then, eyes narrowed, he fixed Mira with a look. "We *should* be laying low. Mixing it up with the locals will only get us in trouble."

"I didn't say an—"

"Don't start with that shite." Edmond kicked open the carriage door with disgust and hopped into the street. He stretched for a moment, pushing his shoulders forward and leaning back at the neck.

There was more muffled shouting, followed by a few soft thuds. Edmond sighed and turned, striding towards the three miners and their captive. The door to the warehouse was ajar, and the large, bearded men were trying to drag the lad in. The man with the broken nose and heat gloves was prying at the young lad's fingertips which he had managed to somehow latch onto the edge of the large sliding door.

Edmond wasn't the most intimidating presence, and wearing this particular face—handsome and clean cut as it was—he knew it would only further alienate men like these. But there was nothing for it. Putting on his best, no-nonsense voice, Edmond called out. "I don't mean to intrude—honestly, looks like you have things managed. Was wondering if I might be able to lend a hand though?"

He approached the warehouse, keeping his expression casual while his gaze darted rapidly from man to man, trying to gather as much information as he could.

The man with the broken nose grunted, and waved Edmond away.

"We have it handled," he said with a grunt. His 'v' sounding like an 'f'. "Thankee for the offer." The man had a sing-song way of speaking that wasn't entirely unpleasant to Edmond's ears. The warehouse door had widened a bit more, giving Edmond a glimpse inside. One of the other miners had a grip of the captive lad's legs and tugged him, trying to drag him in. Meanwhile, the third miner had a length of rope, which he'd tied off as a noose and ventured to toss over a metal beam stretching the base of a walkway above.

Edmond continued to approach. For a moment, his gaze fell on the hapless lad. He was, perhaps, thirteen or fourteen years of age and boasted bright, red hair above a pale, freckled face. Where the miners' skin was rough and stained, the boy's was smooth and untouched. His lips were so red, Edmond half expected rouge.

Also, strangely, the boy's veins across his cheeks and especially down his neck, seemed to glow with a strange, orange light. Similarly, where Edmond could see the boy's arms, which were still being yanked away from the door by the broken-nosed miner, he had a trail of glowing, spiderweb patterns across his pale flesh, as if emitting from beneath the surface.

"Alchemist?" Edmond said sharply.

The broken-nosed miner hesitated, glancing back at Edmond. The miner did a double take, then he loosed his grip on the boy, momentarily. "Keep his gag on," he directed over his shoulder, but continued to face Edmond. "Aye, it is alchemy. One of Baroness Alverdo's bastards. Burned down a stable, he did. Alchemical prick." The sing-song accent made the 'S's sound like 'Z's.

"He's an Alverdo?" Edmond pointed at the man. "I guess that makes you Genevese, then."

The man nodded firmly, tapping his chest with a closed fist in a gesture of pride.

"Well, I suppose that makes me the spoil sport."

"Don't rightly know what you mean," said the bearded man, coolly.

Edmond noted a dirk tucked in a sheath at the man's hip, accompanied by two flintlock pistols sheathed in a chest bandolier.

"You're not from around these parts, are you?" said the miner. "It isn't that I don't recognize you. Though, I don't. But damn near impossible keeping track of the thousands of souls on this plateau, not to mention the tradesmen coming in and out. More so, the look about you." The miner lifted his head and sniffed at the air, then exhaled softly. "You a sailor?"

Edmond hesitated, then, remembering the situation, he said. "No, but I have spent my life in my father's house on the coast. My name is Sir Matimeo Navara. Or, I suppose, *Reeve* Navara."

The bearded miner stiffened. One of his hands slipped, surreptitiously towards a pistol. "Reeve is it?" he said. "Can't help but notice where you keep your pistol, reeve. You lead with your left?"

Edmond glanced down at the pistol on his left hip, then gave a half-shrug. "Suppose I do."

By now, the red-haired youth had been dragged into the warehouse and the two other miners had him gripped firmly by the shoulders. "Agh—he's pissing on me!" snapped one of the men, yanking a hand back in disgust.

The other man punched the boy in the stomach, doubling him over—still gagged. A couple moments later, the noose was now around the boy's neck and the men were busy trying to keep the lad still while simultaneously tugging at the other side of the rope, to yank him bodily off the floor.

Edmond tilted his head slightly to the side as if to say *just-so*. "Afraid I can't let you lynch the child," he said, nodding past the miner.

The man spread his legs slightly, taking a firm stance in the doorway, angling his shoulders directly at Edmond. "You know what happened to the last reeve who came meddling in affairs not his own?"

"Can't say I do."

"He was shot."

"No," called one of the other miners over his shoulder, who'd overheard the conversation. "That was *two* reeves ago. The last one was cut up and pushed off the Prow."

"No!" the third miner grunted, in between tugs on the rope. "That was *three* reeves ago. The last one was either drowned or poisoned."

"Well," said Edmond, raising an eyebrow, which one was it?"

"Drowned," said the broken-nosed miner.

At the same time, the miner tugging on the rope said, "Poisoned."

The third miner nodded significantly, peering through the dingy store-house, out into the street. "Poisoned *and* drowned."

Edmond knew an intimidation play when he saw it. He'd faced worse.

"Be that as it may, I still can't let you hang the boy."

"You heard me, right?" said the broken-nosed miner. "The boy burned down a stable. He's an alchemist. Not to mention, he's an Alverdo. Never met an Alverdo I didn't like to hear scream."

"If you like hearing them scream, how come you have this one gagged?"

69

"Told you. Alchemist. He swallowed fire."

Edmond hesitated, frowning. Reeve Navara wasn't known to be an alchemist, and Edmond didn't intend to let that tidbit slip any time soon. Inwardly, though, he was mulling over the potions he knew, and the ones he'd heard of... *Fire swallowing? A specialist?* There were some alchemists who specialized in certain ingredients or outcomes in alchemy. The glowing patchwork of veins up and down the boy's body *did* have the look of alchemy about it. But what did—

Just then, the boy—seeing Edmond's efforts on his behalf—redoubled his thrashing and kicking. The noose tightened around his neck as the miners pulled it taught. But in their efforts to hang the poor fellow, they neglected further attention to his gag. Finally, the boy managed to tear down one corner of the gag with his teeth. Gasping, and inhaling with a rattling breath accompanied by a gulping swallow, the boy, gasping, managed to say, "Now you've fucking done it." Then, he began to exhale.

It sounded like the stoking swoosh of a newly heated furnace. The veins across the boy's skin began to glow bright, bright orange, as if he were illuminated from the inside. As if his blood itself, coursing through his veins, were trying to escape his skin.

At the same time, fire began to pour from the boy's mouth, spilling across the storehouse ground, and sweeping towards the miners, threatening to consume them.

CHAPTER 8

ALCHEMIST. BLOODY HELLS. EDMOND lurched back, dancing scatterfoot away from the swirling vortex of flame spewing from the boy's mouth.

The two miners inside the warehouse cursed, letting go of the rope and racing towards the door, but their path was cut off by a wall of flames, trapping them inside the storehouse. They scrambled back from spreading flames, shouting and hollering at the tops of their lungs. Red-faced, stained with sweat and a smattering of ash, they shouted past the alchemist child, glaring wide-eyed and gesturing chaotically at Edmond.

"Don't leave us!" one cried as Edmond continued to distance himself from the flames with hurried backwards steps.

"Do something!" another shouted. "You're the reeve aren't you," he screamed. "Stop this maniac."

Edmond took a tentative step forward, but the boy continued spewing fire almost as if he couldn't control it, like someone who drank more than their fill bent over a gutter late at night. The boy's eyes flared with red, the veins standing out against his pale skin like blood marks through a snow bank.

Edmond continued his backpedaling retreat, holding up one finger towards the clamoring miners trapped in the warehouse as if to say, *just one second.*

The broken-nosed, bearded miner was beating at the flames with his apron, but to no avail.

The miners inside the warehouse shouted after Edmond, screaming in indignation and terror as he fled. Still holding up a finger, Edmond beat a hasty retreat across the road back to where the carriage awaited him.

He took the last couple of steps with leaping strides and jumped, latching onto the side of the carriage and poking his head through the open window. "Mira," he said, trying to keep his tone conversational. "Quick question—"

Mira though, was looking out the other window, seemingly disinterested now with the events across the street. From his time with her, Edmond knew that the goddess wasn't particularly fond of overt displays—the sorts of public spectacles available for everyone to purloin with their gaze and discuss for years to come. The more ears inclined towards an event, the less interest Mira had in it. And currently, half the street was staring in the direction of the storehouse. Edmond, as a person, was quite a secretive fellow, switching faces and hatching plots; it was one of the reasons Edmond figured she kept him around. A scream pierced the sky, and he cleared his throat again, "You wouldn't happen to know anything about glowing veins and fire pouring from someone's mouth would you?"

She sniffed, and in a bored tone, she said, "Oh, is someone interested in my opinion after—"

"Not to interrupt," Edmond winced apologetically. "I'm sure whatever sarcastic exchange you had lined up would have been witty and scathing. But I'm in a bit of a hurry, if you don't mind. What might cause one's veins to glow as if smoldering?" Edmond glanced frantically back over his shoulder towards where the boy was still standing in the doorway spewing flames. The doorframe caught ablaze, smoldering, flames licking higher, threatening to consume more of the building. Luckily, about the frame there was a buttress made of stone.

Still, those miners inside would roast like chicken in a brick oven if Edmond didn't hurry.

"Well," Mira said, shaking her head and causing her silken locks to shift across her shoulders. "There are all sorts of things that might do something like that."

"What sorts of things."

"You have to describe it to me, you've barely given me so much as—"

Edmond scooted back, giving a clear view of the front of the storehouse, jabbing a finger towards the boy who was now clutching his head and falling to his knees, gasping in pain amidst billowing clouds of ash and dust.

Mira peered across Edmond's chest, focusing on the boy, and her eyebrows flicked up ever so slightly. "Curious," she said. "That," she said, "is an amateur."

"Amateur?"

"An alchemist who specializes in only one sort of alchemy."

"Wouldn't that just be a specialist?"

"Same thing as an amateur. You wouldn't call someone who knows all the synonyms for the word, "timidity" a linguist would you?"

"No, but I don't think—"

"It's the same thing. Just because someone memorized a vast swathe of knowledge about a single component of alchemy, doesn't mean they're an alchemist. Though..." She paused, her face forming a slight frown. "If not an amateur... he *could be a*... Well, no, it isn't likely. Not in Titan's Folly. Not in *that* appearance. I doubt he is one of them."

"You're not making any sense."

Mira waved his question away though and sniffed, nodding once as if making up her mind. "He can't be. He's not *that*—he's an amateur. That is all."

Edmond normally would've pressed the issue, but as time was of the essence, he shook his head demurely and waited for Mira to continue."

"Likely, there is a gelatin cap in one of his teeth—the sorts you stopper your depths droughts with. He broke it and swallowed it the moment he got scared. It's the way that a lot of these sorts of alchemists like to distribute their pre-brewed ingredients around their bodies. Feathers from a hawk's tail, sunflower seeds, and the blessings of Pardi himself, or someone he has blessed as devout."

"The sun god?"

"Exactly. I spend most my time courting the night, and have interacted very little with Pardi."

The sounds behind them were growing louder and more intense. Edmond clenched his muscles to stave off the need to act. He needed more information.

"Well, how do I stop it?"

"Just wait for him to vomit it up," she said in answer. "Oh, and keep your distance, fire from a *scorchmouth,* which is what they're called, burns three times as hot as normal. Of course if he turns out to be that *other* thing, well, then you should kill him where he stands. But I'm sure he's an amateur—I can't imagine he'd be anything else."

"How so very intentionally vague."

"Secrets aren't free."

"Fine, so as long as the boy isn't this other mysterious 'thing' is there nothing I can do to diminish the effects?"

"Nothing without ingredients or time, and, oh look, your scorchmouth is spewing up something."

Edmond turned and almost immediately wrinkled his nose as the boy was now hunched over, coughing and spewing flecks of what looked like ash and black shards of egg. Every couple of hacking coughs, new spurts of flame erupted from the boy's mouth, but beyond that, even his veins were returning to a less illuminative hue. The flames were also diminishing, as the fire guttered like a candle caught in a breeze.

"That's not right," Mira said slowly, her eyes narrowed on the black shells on the ground.

The miners tentatively stepped back towards the still-smoldering doorway, their eyes wide. Once they realized the boy seemed incapacitated, and the flames faded, they threateningly approached again.

The red-haired alchemist groaned once, and held his hands up to protect his head. He burped, and a jet of flame spat out singeing one of the miner's shoes, sending the large man into a fit of horrified shouts, and a flurry of retreating steps as he tried to stamp his own foot with his other to put out the blaze, which only ended up sending the men tumbling to the ground in a heap.

The lad burped again, still shaking and dazed, but he managed to cough out a single word between painful chuckling, "Bitch."

"If he swallows those flakes though," Mira said through the window, "He will burn the lining of his stomach, and you will see his intestines fall out of his gut, leaking like lava dripping through heated stone." A bit of the interest had returned to her voice. Now that the flames had receded, a good number of townsfolk were continuing on their way, distancing themselves from the spectacle.

Edmond took this, and the distinct lack of flames, as his cue to scurry back across the street towards the now extinguished boy. The child hacked and coughed, gasping at the ground, spitting more black eggshell pieces.

The miners hesitantly eyed the display, which allowed Edmond to sweep past them and drop to the lad's side. He avoided the more singed sections of the ground, careful not to brush up against the smoldering doorway. These black shells certainly didn't *look* like gelatin caps—when Mira had seen them, she'd seemed troubled. But if the boy *wasn't* an amateur—or a specialist—then what was he? Edmond tentatively touched the lad as if testing a cook pan that had been left to cool. When he found the boy's skin warm, but comfortable enough to touch he'd gripped the lad by his shoulders and righted him, pulling him to the side so that his head was aligned with the rest of his body. Then, he slapped the boy on the back a couple of times for good measure, saying, "Spit it up, there you go. You'll be fine. What's your name boy?" he added quickly.

The child eyed his rescuer through a tear-stained, ash-streaked face. His voice weak, he said, "You a perv too?"

Edmond raised an eyebrow. "No. I'm just asking your name?"

The miners were muttering now, but Edmond ignored them, keeping his attention fixed on the fiery boy.

"You look like a perv," said the lad, nodding once, looking Edmond up and down from where he hung in the tomb raider's arms. "Creepy perv at that."

Edmond hesitated, then shrugged. He couldn't take offense. Matimeo Navara was, perhaps, the sole definition of "creepy perv."

"I do a bit," Edmond said. "You're not wrong."

This answer seemed to stump the boy. He allowed himself a small, painful smile, veins still glowing slightly in the side of his neck. Then, he said, "Dante Alverdo. I'm the baroness' youngest son. Know what that means?"

Edmond began to shake his head, but Dante interjected, raising his voice and directing his comments towards the miners. "Means I'm a big fucking deal! And these naked, butt-scratching apes were trying to rape me! Jealous of me good looks an' charm! The ass-gutted snipes."

Edmond, refusing to rise to the intended shock-factor of the boy's words, kept his voice bland and disinterested. "I'm pretty sure they were trying to *lynch* you."

"Yeah? Trust a skeevy perv to know the difference, ey? The lot of ya—you ash-toasted bastards!"

"Who you calling bastard?" snorted the broken-nosed, bearded man with the apron and gloves. He still spoke in the sing-song, lilting way of his, but his words were clipped and careful, accompanied by an undercurrent of venom. "This here," he snapped, addressing Edmond, "Is the baroness' adopted son—bastard brew."

The miners growled, shaking their heads, slowly circling in, but not lunging yet, as if waiting to make sure all forms of fire had vacated the foul-mouthed child.

Dante gasped and gagged a couple more times, tears streaming freely down his young face, trickling past pale cheeks and freckles. Edmond felt a flicker of sympathy for the boy; as much as he couldn't spare empathy in a place like this, he couldn't help but feel this child had somehow scored the sour end of a salt stick.

The whole town was split in two, the Genevese and the Alverdos had been fighting each other for nearly one hundred years now, and Edmond was quickly surmising this was his first introduction to the feud. But this boy was just a child. One of the adopted children of baroness Alverdo if the miner's comments and his own research was anything to go by. The bastard alchemists were feared, and judging by what had just happened, it wasn't without good reason. Though, Edmond supposed the boy hadn't shown much control over his alchemy.

Swallowing ability, inducing draughts, was one of the more finicky alchemical endeavors. It required a certain precision to create a brew that would work well after you had finished preparing it; a certain stability to keep the alchemy from breaking down. Unstable draughts were never good. At best, it meant a fizzling mess that did nothing but upset the stomach. At worst—Edmond briefly thought of the black amorphous flesh of the djinn he had conjured in Sile. It was part of the reason why Edmond restricted himself to two draughts and knew them so well that he could prepare them in his sleep: The Depths Draught so he could breathe underwater, and the Faciem to change his appearance.

He heard the sound of shuffling feet and low grumbling and glanced up to see the three miners slowly shambling forward, taking tentative steps towards the boy who had spewed fire. They were all glaring at Dante now, their eyes white in grimy, soot-stained faces. The large man with the beard and the apron scowled in full force, his brow little more than a rutted field in the hot sun. "You one of them?" he said, his voice rough, losing some of its lilting quality. "Don't be gentle with that bastard. He nearly cooked us. It's proof, he burned down our stables."

Edmond waved a hand in their direction. "That's not proof. He's just a child." Then, directing his attention back towards Dante, he said, "There you go, cough it up now, yep, one more good one."

The three miners though didn't seem satisfied with this response and their looks of fury only doubled. "Well, I'm not going to tell you this twice, stranger," said the bearded man. "But back away from the boy. He's ours. Around these parts, justice is everyone's responsibility. And I plan to fulfill my end of it."

"It doesn't have to be at the end of a rope though," said Edmond. "Besides, I'm the new reeve. I say the boy comes with me."

Edmond knew he couldn't allow anything to happen to Dante. Not only did he feel a bit of sympathy for the child, but on a purely selfish front, he needed an audience with the baroness. He required her sponsorship to join the tournament. The entire plan hinged on his ability to make his way into the tournament ranks. That was the first step. After that, of course, he would have to find someone to fight in the tournament for him. He sized up the three miners, but then just as quickly discarded the thought. They were already angry with him, and they didn't seem particularly gifted with any sort of weapon. They just seemed mean, angry, and intent on causing Dante harm.

"You're not some bleedin' heart are you?" snapped the bearded miner. "Willing to let children run roughshod simply on account of their youth?"

Edmond gave a shake of his head, grateful they were still talking. As long as they were talking it meant fists weren't flying and fire wasn't spewing from Dante. "Hang children, hang women, hang 'em all," said Edmond with a noncommittal wave. "I don't care. Just don't hang *this* one. I need him for something."

"Knew you was a perv," Dante muttered.

Edmond kept his expression impassive, but stepped on Dante's foot, murmuring beneath his breath so only the boy could hear, "I'm trying to help you, you lummox." Edmond stepped quickly back as the boy tried to spit on him, and just as promptly changed his tone, once more addressing the miners. "How about you all just go home now and let me handle the bastard."

The miners didn't look convinced. "What do you mean handle it?" their leader asked. "You can hang him yourself. Rope right here."

One of the miners pointed towards the noose dangling from the rafters.

Edmond give a quick, curt shake of his head. "What I do is gonna be my business. This town needs some law and order, and I intend to see that it—"

Edmond cut off mid-sentence and ducked out of the way. It had been a bluff, and the miners either took it as such, or didn't care. One of them had launched a metal bucket, aiming for Edmond's head.

The bucket zipped over his ducking head, clattering into the streets. A couple of passing horsemen yelled in surprise and anger, but they didn't slow their march as they hurried up, away, heading, likely, towards more welcoming parts of town.

Edmond cursed, holding his hand in front of his face lest another projectile work its way towards them.

"Don't do it," he spat. You better be careful about—"

He trailed off as one of the miners pulled a short pick-like item from the back of his pocket. It was sharp, with a long piercing end from a black hilt. Edmond licked his lips nervously, trying not to contemplate the thing puncturing his chest again and again. "Careful," he said, "don't do anything rash."

The man seethed, spit dripping from his tongue glancing from the bearded leader to Dante. "My brother were in the fire," he spat. "Barely got out with his life, could've burned him. Coulda deformed him forever."

"Yer brother was an ugly nub to begin with!" Dante called out, but this time received an elbow to the stomach for his efforts and started coughing again.

"Whoops," said Edmond blandly, withdrawing his arm. "Sorry about that. As for you, I'm sorry about your brother. Truly. By the sound of things he made it. Don't go costing yourself by doing something rash now."

The man stepped forward, pointing his pick at Edmond's face; it wasn't exactly a rock pick—it had too many teeth on one side, and looked instead, like the sort of tool that might have been used for gouging chunks of material from the ground, and then sifting that material later. Edmond didn't know what the tool was called, but he did know from a debacle with some of his Signerde friends panning the mouth of The Dandelion River in Northern Godshaven that this was the sort of tool used for mining small amounts of gold.

The man with the pick flashed a grimace in Edmond's direction, revealing at least four different golden teeth. Edmond stared. Then, as if sensing Edmond's distraction, the man darted forward, pick raised.

Edmond cursed and tried to reel back, but the man tripped him, hooking a booted foot behind his. This was no stranger to violence. In a town like this, everyone had to know how to carry their own weight.

Edmond's weight was currently careening towards the ground. He struck the dirt with a painful thud, inhaling dust as he tried to push back to his feet. A heavy foot pressed against his chest slamming him back into the dirt.

"Gregor," said the bearded man with the gloves, glancing nervously back and forth. "Maybe you shouldn't. Careful now, doing in the boy is one thing. But the new reeve? We don't have the baron's permission."

The man named Gregor's eyes were wide and bloodshot, his teeth set, and he was shaking his head quickly from side to side. Edmond had seen the look before; it was common to have those sorts of eyes and disposition from someone who partook in black gum, chewing on the hallucinogenic far too often.

The man growled, showing more teeth, the four missing teeth capped with gold likely had been replaced from gum damage—black gum was notorious for causing oral decay. Edmond knew that Sophia Diladrian, the leader of the Roosters up in Carabas had even outlawed the substance among her own gang—too expensive replacing her men.

Edmond grunted and tried shoving the foot off his chest. But his ribs ached as the man pressed down with near superhuman strength, lost in a delirious state, intending to stab him with the pick.

Edmond tried to shout out in protest, but he couldn't get the words to leave his throat, they were jammed as if from the dust. He choked, spitting and swallowing, trying to reach for the pistol at his back, but from where he lay, weirdly angled, the pistol was trapped between his body and the dirt. He had a knife on his hip as well, but as his fingers scrambled for it, he knew he was going to be too late. His eyes widened as the pick came arcing down towards his left pupil, but just then, before it struck, there was a loud blast.

A grunt.

A clatter, as the pick hit the ground, a few inches from Edmond's face.

Then, with a slight gurgle, streaming blood from directly in the middle of his eyes, Gregor toppled over backwards, collapsing to the ground and kicking up more dust.

Edmond surged to his feet and spotted Kurga in the carriage. The short man was standing in the driver's platform, pointing one of his fancy silver pistols in their direction, a thin trail of smoke curling up from the muzzle end. Kurga's pale-faced boys were clapping politely and nodding their approval. Edmond swallowed, relief flooding him. He glanced at Gergor and felt another spat of sympathy. This wasn't like Matimeo; the miner wasn't some serial murderer. He had just been in a bad situation, and a bad town at a bad time. Edmond gave an apologetic wince in the direction of the two other miners, tried to say something, but couldn't think of anything worthwhile, so he closed his mouth again.

One of the remaining miners stepped forward, shock on his face and violence in his eyes, but Edmond snapped up a halting hand. "See that short man back there? He's dressed up all fancy like right now, but he's a cutthroat through and through. Don't let his look fool you. If you try anything now, he'll not just hit you like he did that one, he'll do it before you even blink. The best shot I've ever seen. I've been sailing with him for near a year now, and I haven't seen him miss with those pistols of his. He buys himself one for every ten kills he gets, as a sort of treat. There's," Edmond made a big, finger-waving show of counting, "seven hooked into his belts now. He's killed more men in battle than you can remember names."

The miner glanced shiftily from Edmond to the body at his feet, then, reluctantly, raised his hands in capitulation and stepped back next to the bearded leader. The bearded man was grumbling, and coughing, shaking his head in disgust and sadness, staring at the lifeless eyes of his friend's corpse. "The baron will hear about this," he said, growling.

"I suspect he will. You can relay the whole truth. The part where your man came at me with his picker, and I was just doing my job. Or, will you leave that part out, I wonder."

The bearded miner shook his head in disgust, but then sighed softly. "Not looking for a world where one can't tell the truth. No plans to be dishonest. I'll tell them what I saw." He pointed a finger straight at Edmond. "I'll tell the baron that the new reeve and his bodyguards killed one of his employees. The Bull is a dangerous man if you're not careful—be up to him to see what happens."

The second miner shook his head, gritting his teeth as he tugged at the first miner's shoulder. "Can't just let them get away with that," he was murmuring. "They murdered him-cold blood!"

"And what would you do about it," the bearded man growled back, turning slightly as if to shield their whispered conversation with his body. Out of the corner of his eye, Edmond noticed Mira perking up and leaning out the window for a better look.

"Want to be picked off by that shooter of his? Another bullet between your eyes too? You know Gregor, he wasn't worth nothing to nobody anyhow. Wife left him near seven years ago, children beaten black and blue every night. Some might even say they done a mercy to us."

"Ain't right killin a man. He wasn't perfect—not claiming it. But ain't right."

Edmond fidgeted nervously, but couldn't help but agree with the man. This Gregor wasn't fit to be around others it seemed, but killing him was a step he wished hadn't been necessary. When it came down to it, though, if he had to choose between his life and Gregor's... That was a choice that all the gold in Titan's Folly couldn't sway.

Chapter 9

THEY TRUDGED UP THE disjointed staircase, ascending from one platform to the next—it would have been a relatively uniform process if Dante didn't spend every few seconds darting one way, then the other, peering over the edge of the platform to the ground far below and chucking coppers he pulled one at a time from his pocket.

With every launched coin, Dante would cackle and duck under Edmond's grasping hand to move to another angle and launch another coin.

"Godsdamned fire-headed wastrel!" Edmond bellowed the fourth time this happened, his hand swiping through mid-air, whisking over the head of the boy. "What are you—six? Stop pelting the town!"

Dante glanced over his shoulder, smirking. He waved a hand dismissively to the North, "Thereaways is Genevese territory," he said, deftly flicking a coin from one thumb to another. He skipped a step back as Mirastious joined them on this platform. Kurga and his boys had been sent ahead to the reeve's mansion to secure the place and prepare it for arrival. Also, though they were now wearing the crimson livery of the Navara household and hats to disguise their hair, Edmond didn't want to afford the baroness the opportunity to examine them too closely. The presence of bravos in Titan's Folly would only raise uncomfortable questions.

Mira examined the boy, a curious expression on her face.

Dante looked back.

She said nothing.

Neither did he.

Mira smiled softly.

Dante glanced at Edmond, then thumbed in Mira's direction. "Fine set'a tits on her, ey?" He nodded appreciatively. "I mean, real? Ever just buried your face in them and—" He wiggled his head back and forth causing his cheeks to wobble.

Edmond stared, stunned. Then, fast as lightning he reached out and swatted the boy across the back of his head, sending him reeling.

"Owowow!" The boy howled, stumbling forward. "Wha' was that for you giant fucking cow! Not my fault she aint lettin' yer put the bat in the belfry, is it! You cock!"

Edmond scowled and took another step towards the boy, ready to swat him once more, but Dante quickly cowered, ducking behind his upraised arms. "I didn' mean it!" He said. "Don't do me like Ma done that Genevese pup last week."

"Edmond, please stop hitting the child," Mira said.

Edmond raised a hand again and Dante flinched—hand still raised, Edmond glanced over at the goddess. "Isn't that what your kind is on about? Smiting and blighting and whatnot? Well—here I am." He wiggled his upraised hand. "Smiting."

"Don't lettem!" Dante exclaimed, his voice high-pitched. "Will pop me eye straight out. Take an hour to replace—it will. Once knew a bloke—popped an eye. Bloody mess it was!"

This, more than the look of good humor on Mira's face, stayed Edmond's hand. He pointed to Dante's mouth with a knowing smirk and said, "Not to mention that cap of yours, hmm? In your teeth, then? That's where you store your alchemy, right?"

Dante winked and gave a small grin. "I don't do alchemy," he said. Then, he darted towards the next platform. "Better hurry!" He called over his shoulder. "If I reach ma first, I'll tell her you done struck me! Cross the mouth an' everything. All because you're tryin' ter impress the goldstrike o'er there!"

Edmond ripped off a cufflink and launched it after the boy, watching as the metal clasp ricocheted off a staircase.

Dante stuck his head between the stairs, making rude gestures in Edmond's direction. "That's a *nice* thing you outsider prick! Goldstrike means pretty."

Edmond glared straight ahead, ignoring Mira's snickering. "I wish I'd let them hang him," he muttered, stomping up the next flight of stairs.

As Edmond joined the colorful youth, the boy said, "So," Dante glanced surreptitiously out of the corner of his eye at Edmond. "Why do you want to speak to mother?"

Edmond glared at the boy, his teeth gritted, "Maybe I'll start with telling her how you've been talking to women in her absence. Or, maybe I should mention how you burned down some stables."

Dante pulled a face, as if he were sucking on lemons. "I did *not* burn down the stable. They made it up. One of those idiots was smoking black gum—the tar shite. Chinning it down with one of those glass curling pipes. Saw him do it. Set the fire, roasted a horse before they even had the wherewithal to know the place was burning. The guy with the black gum was so fried he almost choked on the smoke. If I hadn't been there, he would've died."

"You helped him get out?"

"I put out a couple of fucking fires in the cocksucker's jacket."

"Oh, how exactly?"

"Smotherered them. Handfuls of horse shite." Dante grinned. "I'm a fucking great shot."

"You strike me as the sort that might enjoy playing with horse shite. But that doesn't say what you were doing near a Genevese stable? As far as I'm aware the Alverdo don't venture near that part of town. There's bad blood between your families."

"It isn't what you think," said Dante, flushing suddenly. For a moment, his rough, calloused way faded to something more timid and uncertain. The boy swallowed, his cheeks turning red. "I wasn't there to burn nothin'. Just because I sometimes belch a flame or two, don't mean I go around pissing it everywhere... I'm not burning *you* am I?"

"Damn near did back there."

"But I didn't. And I wouldn't."

"So if you weren't there to burn the place, why were you there?"

Dante shifted uncomfortably, scratching at the side of his chin. His cheeks took on a deeper hue of red, and he muttered into his hands, staring at his feet as he traveled along the top flat platform towards a brace of metal gates at the far end. The wooden ground beneath their feet didn't even creak or give at all as they walked. The boards and beams were so large and thick that it didn't even feel like they were walking on wood. Edmond's stared at the side of Dante's face, trying to read the boy.

But, at that moment Mira stepped forward, her eyes blazing with a new-found interest. "Tell me," she said, her voice unyielding. "Who is it? What's her name? Is she *that* pretty? Prettier than me?"

Dante had turned to Mira and was staring at her chest again, but it was more of an interested glance, like the way someone might examine the fur color of a dog—a passing interest in the unusual more than a lecherous ogling. Also, Edmond was pretty sure Dante was trying to unnerve the goddess. But Mira didn't shift, nor sway. The first time Edmond had en-countered her, she'd been completely starkers, without an ounce of embarrassment. Over the past year, it had taken him a good number of pleadings to stop her from walking around naked on deck for all to see. Eventually, following a duel to the death between two bravos over who could 'lookout' the next morning, she'd finally agreed to resume wearing clothes.

Needless to say, the young boy's improper attentions received him another swat from Edmond, but no sort of reaction from Mira.

She studied the boy—who rubbed ruefully at the back of his head—then her raven-colored eyebrows flicked up. "Ah," she said. "I see. Not a girl is it?"

Dante's own gaze snapped to Mira's now and he flinched as if Edmond were about to strike him again.

Mira smirked, nodding to herself. "I see. A boy?

Dante shifted again uncomfortably, his cheeks now practically matching the color of his hair.

"What are you on about, Mira?" Edmond said.

Mira rolled her eyes. "You can be so dense sometimes. Our young adventurer here, our specialist, was visiting a lover."

Dante made a face at this declaration, sticking his tongue out slightly and opening his mouth in a gagging sort of way. "I'm not a specialist—like I said, I don't do alchemy. And also, we're *not* lovers," he snapped. "We're just friends is all." His cheeks were still flushed red.

"You wouldn't be turning the color of a beet if friends were all you were, at least, if that were all you wished to be," said Mira, purring like a cat.

Though, now that Edmond watched her, she more had the look of a spider, her black hair like the furry back of an arachnid settled in the center of its web, pulling its prey one thread at a time closer into its silky embrace. Dante didn't know it yet, but his private thoughts, his uttered secrets, were like the smell of a sumptuous banquet to Mira. Though perhaps, the shudder of flies caught in a spider's web would be more accurate.

"He is a person I can't tell you about. I can't tell anyone," said Dante, his words surprisingly devoid of expletives. "Please, don't tell mother. Don't tell her anything about, just, if you have to, tell her I was there to burn down the stable. She'll take it better than if you told her that I had feelings for a Genevese. I know—I know it's wrong, but…"

He trailed off as Mira was eyeing Edmond now.

"What?" said the tomb raider.

She continued to stare at him, inflecting her gaze with a slight, prompting tilt of her head.

Edmond huffed, but then sighed and muttered, like a child caught with his hand in his mother's purse, "I won't use the boy's romantic attractions as ammunition against his mother. Fine—is that all?"

Mira continued to stare at Edmond then inclined her gaze towards Dante, who was now quiet all of a sudden, staring embarrassed at his feet.

Edmond rolled his eyes and mouthed, over Dante's head, out of sight, *No. I won't. No. You do it. No.*

Mira kept insistently nodding towards the fire-headed youth until Edmond threw out his hands. "Fine!" he declared.

Dante shifted slightly, glancing up.

Edmond cleared his throat quickly and said, "I mean—you're doing just, er, just fine. Don't beat yourself up. I mean, I'm sure illicit relationships with the family member of someone who wants to kill you can't be anything but good..."

Mira was now scowling at him.

Edmond sighed; he watched Dante for a moment, then, in a softer, gentler tone, said, "I know what it is to love someone I can't have. I'd burn down heavens to get her back..."

Dante glanced out of the corner of his eye, head still hanging. Edmond reached over and patted the boy on the head.

"Perv," Dante muttered, jerking his head away and doubling his pace.

Edmond scowled and called after him. "Did you really piss yourself back there!"

"Fucking weirdo," Dante called back, but his mood seemed much improved.

Edmond gave Mira a significant glance, and she flashed him a winning smile. Edmond rolled his eyes and shouldered past Mira, who was savoring the newly harvested secrets with a delighted expression.

Edmond caught up with Dante, grabbing the boy by the wrist. "Look; call me a perv if you want. I have the face of one. If you don't want me to tell your mother about you and some Genevese boy, I won't tell her a thing, but you need to tell me how I can get what I want."

"I can't make her fuck you," Dante jerked a head towards Mira.

"That's not what I want!" Edmond snapped. "I'm looking for entrance to the tournament. Your mother is still sponsoring challengers."

Dante waved a hand. "Just show her that you're a wizard with a blade or something, then I'm sure she'll be happy to sponsor you."

Edmond let out an explosive sigh. He knew full well he wasn't particularly good with a sword. He had some training, but it wasn't much. More likely than not, in a straight up duel he would have his serial murderer ass handed to him up and down the dueling grounds.

"Well, what if," Edmond paused, rephrasing in his mind. "What *other* thing might convince your mother to sponsor me?"

Dante eyed Edmond. "You're the reeve," he said, "aren't you? It's a little strange for you to be asking me this stuff."

"And it's a little strange for you to be lurking around the stable right before it catches fire and blame a man smoking black gum, isn't it? It's a little strange for you to fall in love with a boy from the family yours is feuding with. In fact, it's practically theatrical."

"I'm not in love," Dante snapped, clenching his teeth and his fists at his side. "We just like spending time together is all. You said you wouldn't tell mother."

"I said I wouldn't tell her if you help me out. You're being nothing but a legendary blister on my ass at this point."

"Fine," Dante rolled his eyes again. "Just tell mother how much you hate the baron Genevese. Mention what you did to those miners. Mention that you had one of your men shoot one. She'll like you for that, more than anything."

Edmond cast a sidelong glance at Dante as they finally all came to a halt now, outside the giant metal gates built into the shrubs. Edmond studied Dante, trying to determine if the boy was joking. But it didn't seem like he was.

"Your mother hates the baron that bad then, does she?"

Dante snorted. "What a stupid question. The reason she has to have all of us adopted and didn't carry us herself is because they took her ability to have children. Poison. Tried to kill her. Ruined her insides—she spends half the night in pain before being able to drift off to sleep. Yes, I'd say she hates them. Don't get me wrong, she loves us. All of her children, bastards or not. But she hates the Genevese for taking her ability to have children from her own womb. I don't blame her, and I've never felt less love from her for it. But if you tell her that you hate the Genevese, and that you did in one of their loyal miners, she'll like you more for it. I'll throw in a good word too. As long as—"

96

"Yes, yes, I'll not to say anything about your romantic romps in the hay. Thanks."

"There was no romping! And, it wasn't in the hay."

"Oh, indeed? Where was it?"

"Why? Creepy old man need something to spank his plank to later tonight?"

"Does your mother just let you speak any old way you like?"

Dante shrugged, and Mira give a half smile. Any further conversation was interrupted by a sudden creaking noise. The double gates began to move.

Edmond peered through the bars and spotted a few men wearing green uniforms, pushing the gates from the inside. The men were shorter than Edmond, though not by much, and they had a wild, unkempt look about their features despite their neatly pressed uniforms and trimmed facial hair. Their eyes were just a little bit too wide, their mouths held in just a little too loose of an expression. Their hair, unlike their beards stuck out at odd and strange angles from beneath red pointed hats. At their sides, they all carried weapons of some variety, and the green uniforms they wore nearly blended in with the shrubbery around them. Also, much like Dante, their hair was quite red or dark brown. One of the men with a small moustache and mutton chops, a fellow even shorter than the others—perhaps even Kurga's height—was hefting a small golden pocket watch. He gestured elaborately, scanning from Edmond to Mira to Dante. He did a double take, emitting a theatrical sigh and holding up the pocket watch, allowing it to dangle in front of his mutton chops.

"You're late Dante," said the man, swinging the stopwatch around like a cudgel. Edmond noted that the man's fingertips were stained and his knuckles bruised. As he spun the golden watch, it seemed, almost, to spin towards the man's face, as if drawn to a magnet. Edmond noted the guard was wearing earrings made of gold which were dangling at odd angles, as if attracted to some unseen force in the man's jaw. Another of the bastard alchemists? "And I see you've brought friends," said the guard. He eyed Mira and Edmond with a suspicious expression.

Before the short man could say anything, Edmond stepped forward, waving. "Reeve Matimeo Navara," he said, nodding once. "Here to see Baroness Alverdo."

A couple of the men in green shifted slightly, and Edmond couldn't help but notice their hands moved closer to their weapons.

"Ah, don't be a bitch about it, Fero," Dante said, "They're friends—er, well, they're not enemies. Let them in."

"What did you call me?" the man with the pocket watch asked, glaring. The watch was spinning faster and faster now, moving with such speed that it was little more than a blur at this point.

"A crippled, drooling, no good, incontinent little *bitch*," said Dante cheerfully, pronouncing each word with much gusto. Then, he darted through the opening in the gates and dodged the swiping pocket-watch.

As the man named Fero glared after Dante, he snorted in disgust. "Don't let my little brother's manners trick you," he said.

"Oh, it's quite alright," Edmond began, but Fero cut him off, continuing as if he hadn't been interrupted.

"Because you're not welcome. Strangers never are, reeve or not."

Then, Fero let go of the spinning watch, but it continued to spin, rotating rapidly through the air as if on its own accord.

"You're an alchemist too?" Edmond said shrewdly.

"Not an alchemist. Neither is Dante." Fero smirked, but instead of explaining further, he gestured for Edmond to follow and led them away from the hovering, spinning watch, guiding Mira and Edmond towards the mansion built into the surface of the dismantled titan.

Chapter 10

Strange pools, glinting with streaks of silver and gold swirled like vortexes as they moved up the garden path towards the looming mansion. Even stranger hedges, chopped and trimmed into dark creatures, lined the pathway. Edmond shivered as he passed under the hulking form of a hedge trimmed in the shape of a familiar creature boasting tentacles and enormous eyes peering out of a flat squid-like face. He clicked his tongue, seething as he muttered beneath his breath, "Why would anyone memorialize a marid."

One of these fourth-tier demons had nearly killed him the previous year and had killed two of his accomplices at the time, twin pearl divers from Sile. Edmond glanced to the left into a swirling pool stained with strands of ink. Inside, as he peered into it, he could have sworn he glimpsed faces leering back at him. Inhuman faces that belonged only in nightmares and storybooks. Edmond looked away sharply, determining to keep his gaze focused straight ahead; he could hear Mira next to him, shaking her head and muttering beneath her breath a series of oaths, mainly to herself. This whole garden was strange and unusual; exactly the sort of thing Mira normally enjoyed, but now, none of the usual curious delight radiated across her face, and instead she looked simply disgusted.

As they approached the mansion, the shrubs grew larger, and more dangerous creatures leered out at them. Some of the shrubs were nearly as tall as the mansion itself with fangs, muscular arms, and glinting eyes. Edmond determined some of the features were alchemically induced; the eyes alone were light stones, resplendent with prearranged colors glinting through transparent crystal.

"Someone likes their alchemy," he said in a low voice.

Dante had scampered up ahead with two of the guards, but seemed to hear this, and he turned on his heel, walking backwards with a slight skip to his step. The boy chuckled. "Mother used to be one of the most powerful alchemists in Godshaven," he said. "Ask Fero!"

The short man with the mutton chops nodded once, still watching Edmond and Mira with a suspicious glare.

Dante, unperturbed by his disgruntled older brother, continued. "She knew sixth level potions; the sorts of concoctions that could change the course of history itself. The Emperor often employed her, calling her to the great city to perform her alchemy for him. She even trained under some of the court alchemists."

"Is that true?" said Mira, a note of unease in her voice. "And what is with her affinity for the tainted ones?" She waved a delicate finger towards the hedges trimmed in the shapes of demons. "And what are these pools? I've never seen the like before."

It sounded innocuous enough, but this last sentence more than anything set Edmond on edge. For a goddess like Mirastious to have never encountered something before, in her thousands of years of existence, was, well, unusual would be putting it mildly. Unique felt more appropriate. He started to wonder what other secrets lurked in Titan's Folly, and if perhaps, he had put himself in a game without knowing all the rules.

Dante shrugged, stooped to pick up a pinecone, and launched it through an archfiend's face. Edmond only knew what the creature looked like from drawings and sketches he'd found in an old copy of the *Nominii Daemonia* he'd read as a child. The hellcatcher's manual had been cryptic, but it had at least been clear that an archfiend was the second most powerful demon that could be summoned by failed alchemy. It towered as high as the trees and had three curving horns protruding from its eyes in the top of its head, pointing downwards like grasping fingers. Even though the demon had only been carved into leaves and twigs, aided by alchemical stones, the archfiend sent chills shivering up Edmond's body. The thing carried a tail that split into spikes on the very end, and its claws were most unusual of all. Each of the jagged points protruding from the enormous hands of the archfiend had strange faces etched into them. As if they carried a tormented person trapped in each leafy claw. Agonizing expressions and grimacing countenances peered out from the tips of the claws like finger puppets.

Dante noticed Edmond's attention, and shook his head grimly. "I don't like that one," he said.

"Stop talking to them," Fero snapped.

"They're guests," Dante retorted.

"They're only allowed in because mother wanted to speak with the new reeve," Fero replied, scowling at his little brother.

"How does your mother know what these things look like?" Edmond interjected, shaking his head. "They're so deeply detailed, it's not just imagination."

At this, though, both Dante and Fero sealed their lips and gave a similar sort of half shrug.

One of the guards behind Edmond clicked his tongue and pushed him with his hand, sending the grave robber stumbling forward. "Keep your eyes ahead," snapped the man in the green uniform. "You're not welcome yet; Dante's invitation and your status as reeve doesn't mean the mistress won't kill you where you stand for trespassing."

Edmond looked over his shoulder, frowning at the guard's scowling face beneath his red cap. "Do you make a habit of murdering reeves?"

The guard replied, "Reeves in Titan's Folly don't last long. We've learned not to grow too attached. Whether you die here, now, or a year from now, the end will be the same. Whatever you do, keep your questions to yourself."

Edmond decided that he wasn't going to get anywhere with the surly guard, so he looked back ahead keeping his mouth sealed.

Fero waved a hand, and, without being touched, a second metal gate opened up, ushering them into the mansion's courtyard. The enormous structure was reminiscent of a palatial estate unlike any mansion Edmond had seen before. The architecture reminded him of the coastal homes he'd seen back in Wickwood—the ones Kurga and the boys had desperately wanted to rob. The mansion was white with pillars and marble siding. Tangled ivy curled up the side of the mansion, tastefully probing the roof. But, also, the mansion seemed to be an alchemical experiment all unto itself.

The windows alone glinted with a strange shimmering sheen. It was as if alchemy had been baked into the bricks. Edmond could practically feel a buzz emanating from them as he eyed jets of electricity zipping from stone to stone, tracing the ivy and then darting back towards the ground again. Peculiar lights glowed from the windows, and a couple of the windows upstairs flashed with explosions preceding a distant commotion of shouting voices.

Dante clicked his tongue. "Sounds like the young ones are practicing," he said with a shrug. "Mother won't be happy they are doing it indoors again."

Fero snorted and shared a significant glance with his younger brother; the meaning of the look was lost on Edmond. The guard noticed the grave robber's confusion, and chuckled again.

"Wouldn't be wise to try to break into this place without an army. And even then, that army would be toasted. There's more defenses and protections around this place than most of Godshaven put together."

"She's not worried of things escaping?" Edmond said, softly, still watching the mansion and trying to track the two adopted brothers out of the corner of his eye.

"What sorts of things?" the guard snapped.

Edmond hesitated; it was considered the blackest luck among alchemists to discuss alchemy with non-brewers. Even the Signerde didn't approve of sharing secrets among their kind, and their community treated each other as family.

Still, Edmond's curiosity and mounting worry got the better of him. "Demons," he said. "Isn't she worried with children around and an entire town pissing distance that way," he gestured from where they had come, "that one of the creatures might get out. If even one of the alchemical spells breaks, it would be disastrous."

"We've killed demons before," the guard said with a self-satisfied grunt. "Nothing to be feared about *reeve*. Alchemy is not so tough—not that you would know. Don't trouble your pretty head."

Edmond didn't move to correct the man. While it was true he hadn't dabbled in any sixth tier potions, nor had he even touched a fifth tier, Edmond was a relatively accomplished alchemist. He trained with the Brewers themselves, among the Signerde, though that had mostly been due to his wife's connections. He fidgeted, reaching out to touch the simple black vial beneath his shirt. Then, he sighed softly. "What sort of demons have you killed? Describe them; were they large? Did they change forms and shapes. Did they try to bite you, or were they more the sort that spewed gas and odors?"

If the man had fought an imp it was one thing. Imps commonly escaped beginner alchemists, but they were little more than embodiment of the bedtime stories of mischievous fairies, who would curdle milk, or try to trip someone down some stairs. They had their harms, and could lead to real damage if one didn't contain them quickly, but normally they only served as a hard lesson for the burgeoning alchemist. But beyond them... Djinn. Marid. That's when things got dangerous. Edmond had once heard a story where a marid had eaten an entire town before the hellcatchers arrived. At the time, he'd laughed at the notion that a demon could eat a whole town. The Brewers hadn't laughed, and Edmond took the implication to heart as well as a newfound respect for hellcatchers. The order of hellcatchers specialized in hunting down loose demons. They were above the law on most islands, except for the Crook—where everyone *else* seemed to be above the law.

If the guard wasn't talking about imps, then second-tier incubi were a bit more dangerous and would often lurk in the dark and hunt weary travelers. Edmond shivered at the memory of the hellcatchers he'd encountered, and doubly shivered at the memory of the form-shifting third-tier djinn that had almost killed him and Mira back in Sile the previous year. It had trapped them in a houseboat while they had been trying to escape retribution for the death of those pearl divers.

"Mother doesn't do alchemy anymore," said Dante with a slight scowl on his face, regaining Edmond's attention. "Uncle Rodergo says it's too fucking dangerous. He says for the good of everyone in Titan's Folly its best she doesn't." Dante frowned as if in consideration, chewing on the side of his lip. "I've honestly never seen mother listen to uncle Rodergo like that before. He's one of the few people she listens to at all, but she doesn't take orders from anyone. It must be something serious for her to agree with him and give up alchemy completely."

Edmond scanned the doorway traced with glowing veins and the windows above glinting in the sunlight from arcane sources. His eyes flicked to crystals infused with alchemy buried in the stonework all up and down the mansion, painted white but still conspicuous. He shook his head. "I don't think that she's completely abstained."

Dante followed Edmond's gaze again and then gave a small snort of laughter. "You're stupid for a smart man aren't you? She did all that *before*."

Fero nodded in corroboration of his younger brother's words.

This only doubly served to bother Edmond. This whole mansion filled with alchemical stones and glyphs and wards and protections had been built more than a decade ago. The chance the creations had become unstable over time was much higher. Prickles crept up Edmond's spine, nipping at the base of his neck, and he set his teeth together. He didn't like the idea of entering a place like this, unprotected and unprepared. The single shot pistol in his belt wouldn't do anything if a horde of demons came bursting out of the walls. He wished he'd brought Kurga and his boys. He glanced over at Mira, who was eyeing Dante with a renewed look of interest.

"Your mother teaches because she has the memory, but she no longer has her power," said Mira with more than a note of sympathy.

Dante shook his head. "It's a rumor, you know. We're not alchemists—I know they call us that. But mother doesn't teach us. And no, she *can* still do it, she's just not supposed to. I don't know exactly why. I think it hurt her a few years ago." He gave another shrug. Edmond couldn't help but notice the boy didn't call *Mira* stupid, or a perv. In fact, since they'd entered the compound, he'd been treating her much more respectfully. Edmond scowled.

"Anyway enough jawing," Dante said cheerfully. "If you want to meet her, follow me."

"Still not sure we should allow strangers into the house," said one of the guards behind Edmond.

Fero waved a hand dismissively. "She wanted to meet the reeve."

"How do we know he is that?" said a guard, flicking his eyebrows up.

"He's my guest—he might be stupid and ugly and fat, but he's still my guest," said Dante.

A second guard tried to protest further, but both the Alverdos shook their heads and waved any further comments away with dismissive gestures. Edmond heard the men behind him mutter darkly. "Uppity little unwanted bastards."

Fero didn't seem to hear, but Dante flinched. His cheeks flushed, and he had clearly heard the jibe, but didn't reply to it.

Eyeing the mansion once more, his mind filled with images of demons charging across a room, swallowing him whole, Edmond followed Dante through the front doors into the mansion.

More guards awaited them inside. And, if it was possible, the interior of the place was even more reminiscent of an alchemist studio than the outside had been. Imbued crystals jutted from desks covered in onion bottles and percolating pots. Ingredients dangled from small terrariums around the room, set on shelves and shoved under desks with sunlamps and alchemically infused light fixtures. The stone floor itself seemed to glow with a strange energy. Edmond tentatively stepped onto the floor, sidling past a couple of the red-haired guards blocking the entrance.

They scowled at him at first, but when they spotted Dante they looked uneasily past Edmond at the guards beyond.

"They're here to see the baroness," said Fero in a clipped tone. "Is mother here? Or at the hellcatcher's?"

"Upstairs," said one of the guards.

The older brother frowned. "What are you waiting for then, go!"

The man turned, and hurried away, his green uniform shifting with each rapid step up the staircase, and his booted feet clomping against the stairs.

Edmond normally would have examined the room, looking for escape routes or potential weapons to be used in case of catastrophe. But he was disjarred; something intimidating about the whole atmosphere left him unnerved. He was an alchemist; it was one of the few advantages he held in most of his encounters with others. But, surrounded by a place filled with the very advantage that protected him—It was almost as if he lost what made him special. Granted, face-changing among alchemists was incredibly rare and difficult. He was one of the few he knew who had perfected the potion, and who could do it without much trouble. But beyond that, it felt as if most of his skills had been compromised simply by nature of their ubiquity. He hated the idea, as he glanced from terrarium to crystal to pot to potion, that he wasn't the most powerful alchemist in the room. Dante's fire—whatever fake toothed caps he crushed were more powerful than most of what Edmond was capable of. But Dante was a specialist—even though he denied being an alchemist, it was obvious. By the sounds of things though, his *mother* was a full-blown alchemist who had trained with the Emperor's brewers. And judging by the items around him, she knew her craft.

Edmond shifted nervously and, despite himself, found that he took a hesitant step in Mira's direction, almost like a child approaching their mother. For her part, Mira didn't comment on this in her usual way. But instead she stepped slightly in front of him, in a protective gesture, placing a hand out and patting him on the wrist.

Edmond swallowed softly, and Mira flashed him the slightest smile, accompanied by a half-nod of either mockery or assurance—it was hard to tell with Mirastious sometimes.

He didn't know when it had happened, but he was starting to consider Mira one of his friends. Who would've thought it. A godless man befriending a god. It wasn't like he could trust the friendship of course; goddesses were notoriously tricky beings, who enjoyed bamboozling humankind. But still, even though she was powerless, and he normally protected her, he felt a strange sense of comfort standing next to her in the atrium filled with mysterious secrets and arcane sources.

"Well," said an abrupt voice at the top of the stairs, "what?"

Edmond's gaze snapped to the stairwell, fixing on the guard who'd been sent to fetch the baroness. The guard stood off to the side, pressing against the wall so hard that it almost seemed like he was trying to be swallowed by it, putting himself as far out of the way as possible to avoid inconveniencing, in any way, his companion.

The woman descending the stairs didn't wear the sort of finery one might expect of a baroness. A tunic and leggings took the place of a more conventional dress or robe. Large earrings dangled from her ears, flickering like diamonds. In addition, she wore clothing traced with silver.

Edmond frowned at the clothing. It must have cost her a fortune. In a town filled with gold, it was a strange thing to see silver spun tunics. He knew the sorts of seamstresses in Godshaven who could do such a thing, but creating thread from silver was a nearly impossible task without alchemical help, and it required enormous amounts of time: this outfit would be worth its weight in gold.

But the outrageous cost of the ensemble wasn't Edmond's primary concern. Silver garments were a time-honored tradition among the most powerful alchemists in the isles. Demons found silver offensive and painful to the touch. To clad oneself in silver was a necessary, if expensive, precaution for those who entered the higher tiers of alchemy. But if Dante was telling the truth, and she didn't practice alchemy anymore, why was she wearing silver? Granted, in the mansion, it still made good sense to be protected against all the alchemical efforts that could go awry, but there was still something about her silver tunic and pants that left Edmond uneasy. As she took hold of the banister between them, Edmond saw that the baroness also wore a black glove, but only on her left hand. It was a thick glove, almost too thick. Larger than a normal hand ought to need. Her other hand lay bare, and tanned, like many of the people he'd seen in the town heading to the wrecked stern of the titan. She had similar red hair as her guards and Dante, though her face was noticeably devoid of freckles. This, Edmond supposed was due to the efforts of her past self. Young girls with potions altered their appearances rather quickly rather than relying on nature. He knew there were all sorts of beauty potions and alchemical oils that young alchemists misused or overused before they knew better. Her face was stunning, if not particularly beautiful. She had the stern, sharp features of a marble statue carved by artisan's knives—the features approximating power. Perhaps it was her position, high above and looking down on him, but unlike her guards, she seemed quite tall, standing at least to Edmond's own height.

Edmond didn't care if she'd altered her appearance, of course; he himself had changed his face more times than he could count. And the face he now wore was quite a bit more attractive than his normal fare. Not that it mattered. He was not interested in the allure of physical attraction. Not anymore. The striking baroness with her dangling, large diamond ears, and her silver clothing, waved her gloved hand in their direction. "Well," she snapped. "What?"

Edmond hesitated, and Mira, taking this as a cue, sidled smoothly another step in front of him, almost blocking him from view like a mother guarding her young.

She met the baroness' gaze and held it. Something in the baroness' eyes flickered, and she glared back; this was a woman used to having her way. But she was faced off with Mira, another woman, if that's what she could be called, who was also used to having the same.

For the first time in a while, Edmond was happy to keep silent.

"We're here to speak with you about a knighthood sponsorship for the tournament," Mira said without missing a beat. "Also, we're here to return your child, Dante. He had some trouble in town."

The baroness' gaze snapped to her eldest son, and Fero nodded. She switched her gaze to Dante. "Trouble," she asked?

Dante nodded, a disgusted look on his face. "A gaggle of Genevese miners," he said with a snort. "Double fucked pricks."

The baroness gave the slightest tilt of one of her eyebrows in his direction, and Dante quailed immediately, coughing into his hands and holding up both of them apologetically in a gesture of concession that Edmond with all his threats and slaps hadn't been able to evoke in the entirety of the walk here.

Something about the baroness' aura contained more threat in her lifted eyebrows than Edmond had managed in all of his bluster. He watched her for a moment, cataloging the gesture, wondering if perhaps he could use it in the future.

"Sorry," Dante said quickly. "I mean to say, three Genevese miners, gold miners. They thought I burned down a stable."

"Did you? This isn't like last time is it? Back at the chicken hutch—"

"One of those nasty buggers *pecked me*. But no, it isn't like that," Dante said quickly shaking his head.

"Good," said the baroness.

Edmond found it strange there were no follow-up questions, nor further scrutiny. As if she took the boy's word as simple truth.

"And what happened after that; why are they here?" she asked, still addressing Dante.

"You don't need to speak to the child, when we can speak for ourselves," said Mira.

The baroness' gaze flicked to her and sized her up. "I don't know who you are," she said with a sniff. "My son, on the other hand, won't lie to me. So, I'll ask him again, who are they?"

Dante gave a sort of half shrug. He pointed at Edmond. "That one likes to ask about the sexual escapades of others. Though he's not fond of her tits." He pointed at Mira.

The baroness flicked an eyebrow up again, and Dante quickly amended, "I mean to say, the perv helped me escape." He pointed at Edmond again. "He might be some sort of depraved deviant, but he did rescue me from the miners. One of his men shot Gregor."

"Gregor?"

"He's a no one," said the guard behind Edmond, stepping forward at this point. "Just a miner, doesn't even have a wife. A black gum addict."

"Will we have trouble from it? Should we shore up the line?"

The guard shook his head, but then hesitated. "Gregor won't matter much. I'll send a couple of men later tonight just to be sure, but he's not the sort that will be missed. I don't think the baron will start anything over that.

Though," the captain of the guard hesitated. "Tiny has been looking for trouble, at least that's what I hear. He's searching for any excuse to pick a fight after last year's finals."

"Very well." Baroness Alverdo turned her gaze back to Edmond and Mira, a less severe expression on her face. "You saved my son?" She tapped her gloved hand against her waist, but there was something about the way the hand moved that unnerved Edmond. And then he realized, there were only four fingers. Was she missing a finger? Was the glove specially made? He found himself staring at it, but then quickly looked away as the baroness continued, "You killed one of the Genevese men. One might take that to mean you're not allied with them. Who are you then?"

Edmond quickly said, if only to take his mind off the glove, "I'm the new reeve. Reeve Matimeo Navara. At your service."

Almost like a curtain being pulled back, or a cloud dissipating from an ocean breeze, the baroness' countenance changed dramatically. In a second, she turned from cold, stern, unyielding authority, to a warm, dimpled, smiling host.

She flung out her arms, the black glove jutting towards one of the bay windows. "Welcome, Reeve Navara. You have saved my son, and for that I am in your debt. And who is this lovely woman with you? I see fire in her eyes—she's not the usual sort of sheep, is she?"

Edmond smirked, but Mira answered instead, "I'm no sort of sheep. But I keep my fangs hidden until someone threatens me or mine." She inflected her words with a significant tone.

The baroness' new countenance didn't fade one iota; there wasn't even a hesitation as she gave a crystal clear laugh, which peeled down from the staircase, and she began to walk towards them again, taking the stairs one dainty step at a time. All of a sudden, she had the bearing of a girl, a princess. She was dainty and delicate, and moved her hips in a seductive flow that belied her age. Her striking features almost seemed to soften as if bathed in a different warm light.

Still giggling like an adolescent, and smiling so that her cheeks dimpled, Baroness Alverdo reached the bottom of the stairs and took two quick steps forward, throwing her arms out and embracing Edmond.

Edmond flinched at the familiar gesture, trying to recoil, but then thinking better of it, he reached up to pat the woman on the shoulder. She pressed against him, and he felt the softness of her breasts leaning into him. He swallowed as she leaned over and kissed him on one cheek and then the other. Still laughing musically, she declared, "Welcome indeed; Titan's Folly has been looking forward to your arrival my reeve."

The smell of her perfume wafted in, reminding Edmond of roses, tulips, fresh moss, and nighttime carriage rides through a rain-slicked forest. Everything about it left him disconcerted. They were all smells he quite enjoyed. This, suggested to him that perhaps there was more at work than just natural perfume. She leaned in again, still holding him tight, and whispered in his ear. "And some of us have been looking forward to a reeve of such appealing proportions. It's been a while since we've had a handsome man in charge of keeping the peace. You're left handed, no?"

Edmond squirmed and coughed, keeping both his right and left hands stuck firmly to his sides. He'd been trying to hide favoring his left hand, but it was a difficult task to undo a lifetime of conditioning.

Mira was surprisingly frowning at this point. She glared at the back of the baroness' head, and almost moved as if to pry her away from Edmond, but the baroness extricated herself at last, and turned to Mira. "And you, you beautiful star you, you lovely, remarkable creature. Are you his wife? I noticed there were no rings on your finger—"

"No," Edmond said quickly at the same time as Mira said, "Of course not."

Edmond glanced at her. "Of course not? I wouldn't say it's *of course* not."

"It's of course not. I'm his adviser," she said, glancing back at the baroness who watched them with an amused expression.

"Adviser is it? And what sort of advice do you give?"

"Well to start, I told him to come here. To look for a sponsorship for his knighthood."

"You told him that did you? And is that because you knew the baron has already filled his docks?"

"Yes—" Edmond started to say, but the half-formed word vanished behind Mira's commanding voice as she said, "We wouldn't serve the baron even if we could. We have no interest in helping that lecherous, violent tempered man."

The baroness nodded in agreement, smiling again and causing her cheeks to dimple once more. She was perhaps forty years old, though she both looked younger and older at the same time. Much like Mira, her features were fresh and lissome, but her eyes held a weight and a burden that no child had ever encountered.

"Well, you speak well. But do you fight well?"

"No," Mira said shaking her head. "He's hopeless. But, he can learn."

Here, Edmond interjected, glaring at his 'adviser'. "I've been training. I'm incredible. I'll do just fine—don't listen to her. She's just jealous."

"Jealous?" The baroness said tittering. "Jealous of me? I hope not."

"Mother," said Dante, "Can I go upstairs, please?"

The baroness waved at him, but said nothing and watched as Dante bounded out of the room with a gleeful expression.

"Children," she said with a smile.

"I hear you have a lot of them," Edmond said conversationally.

"Yes, a few. All of them adopted."

"That's very..." Edmond struggled to find the word. "Not everyone would be so selfless."

The baroness didn't seem to take offense at this; if anything, this second part of her personality was quite winsome, but she did clear her throat and replied, "Is it any more selfish to want children of your own? I just happen to be blessed enough to choose my children. I assure you, any parents must make sacrifices, but just because one child is birthed from your body instead of another's, doesn't mean you want to love them less or more. And it doesn't mean it's a charitable gesture one way or the other."

Edmond acquiesced with silence, but Mira said, "You're quite right. There are mothers with many children, who they didn't birth, but who they grow close to over the years of conversation and relationship and prayers."

"Prayers?"

"What she means to say," Edmond interjected hastily, "Is when you pray together, teaching your children right from wrong—that sort of thing."

"Oh? That's what you meant?" The baroness glanced back at Mira.

"No," said the once-goddess, but then offered no further explanation.

Before Edmond could try to readjust the track of the conversation, the doors to the mansion swung open again, and a very peculiar man entered the room.

CHAPTER 11

EDMOND KNEW IMMEDIATELY, THIS was a dangerous man: the same way a person knows a dangerous dog when it crosses their path or the preternatural dread that rises when a snake appears at their feet. Whether by the sheer musculature displayed beneath his formfitting clothing, or the emanating confidence in which he strode past the guardsmen without even a glance in their direction, or the alarming collection of weaponry dangling from his belt, hanging from bandoliers, tucked into sheaths, stowed in his boot, and strapped to his back in quivers protruding over his shoulders. There were knives, dirks, daggers, hooked chains, a morning star, a miniature crossbow, one compound bow, a longbow, three different pistols, and what looked like the round form of a grenade. Each and every weapon fashioned from wood and silver.

The man's skin glinted as he approached, and Edmond saw the glimmer resolve into the swirling patterns of silver tattoos. The tattoos stretched up his face, along his cheeks, meeting in twisting patterns on his forehead, even looping past his ears. He was completely bald as if to make more room for the intricate silver tattoos which patterned the top of his head all the way down his spine and disappeared into the collar of his tunic. Even his bare hands, visible past the hem of his shirt, also boasted the silver markings.

This man, Edmond knew immediately, was a hellcatcher. He even had the official emblem stenciled on the front lapel of his shirt. An image of a horned head with a golden spear protruding through the neck.

The symbol of the hellcatchers was jarring, but it was nothing compared to the nature of the sulfur-sniffer's order itself. Edmond had encountered hellcatchers before. Once, while Edmond had been perusing the tomb of a Gamorian noble. The villagers had thought the tomb haunted. They sent their local hellcatcher to investigate along with a couple of reinforcements. The demon hunter hadn't even tried to enter the mausoleum. Instead, he had flooded the entire place by breaking a damn nearby with explosives, trying to drown out anything and everything lurking inside. Hellcatchers were above the law and shorted no measures in their efforts to kill any demon released through catastrophic alchemy.

Edmond stared at the man, licking his lips nervously. He twisted his hand along his waist, brushing his fingers across his thigh, probing at the phantom pain; he had been impaled on a silver spike while trying to escape the flooding tomb, and while he had managed to flee with his life, remnants of the pain sometimes came calling. Face-to-face with one of the order, he found himself having flashbacks of the horrific day.

"I caught the beastie up in the North Fields," said the man in a rich, musical voice. He beamed across the room at the baroness, still seemingly oblivious to the others in the room. "Took some doing, but Mirabelle here did her job." He tapped one of the pistols on his bandolier, and smiled. "Of course,

Sasha was jealous, he tapped a dirk tucked in his waist, but I'll gladly take her out for another swish later this evening—that should appease her."

The baroness cleared her throat, still smiling, still adopting the more cheerful personality. "Hello Rodergo," she said with a welcoming tilt of her head, then she nodded significantly towards Mira and Edmond. "These are our guests. Perhaps we shouldn't discuss business just now."

Edmond's research informed him Rodergo Alverdo was uncle to Dante and brother to the baroness. He was the only hellcatcher in the Folding Valley worth his salt. And, he had a notorious reputation for using his powers to flaunt the law and go after his sister's enemies in the Genevese clan. There were rumors that he had murdered the baron's sister and father twenty years ago by loosing a demon into their carriage.

Edmond shivered. He didn't like the idea of a hellcatcher who made use of the beasts they were sent to hunt instead of killing them.

Rodergo glanced at Mira and swept into a gracious bow, then he turned to Edmond and adopted a similar posture. "Fancy meeting you two here," he said. "I of course recognize both of you."

Edmond flinched. "You do?"

"News travels fast in Titan's Folly. I heard about the handsome couple in the red carriage. You're the ones who killed the Genevese miner."

Edmond shifted uncomfortably. "It was actually one of my men. The miner was about to stab me with a pick."

Rodergo waved away the explanation with a laugh. "Oh, I'm not accusing you of anything. I don't care. Better let those bastards chase themselves one at a time into a hail of musket fire. Someone should burn the lot of them to the ground."

Edmond flipped an eyebrow, and the baroness quickly stepped in, "But of course," she said, "we will be abiding by the laws of the town. Especially with the reeve present."

Edmond gave a sort of half shrug with one of his shoulders. Rodergo met his gaze, unblinking, and still grinning jovially. "Of course, of course. Laws," said Rodergo in the same way a fish might say 'air', "What lovely inventions. I would like to say that I would follow yours, but, of course as you must know, my order has immunity." He tapped the lapel on his shirt.

"As long as what you do is in service of your official position," said Mira quietly. "I do believe that part is often left out of the immunity clause."

Rodergo turned to her and winked. "Oh I know what the clause says. Don't need to remind me. It also tells me I can detain anyone at any time for any reason as long as I suspect them of meddling in alchemy or releasing demons intentionally."

Again, Edmond shifted uncomfortably, finding there was just something about this part of the floor he didn't particularly like; he moved his weight from one foot to the other. If Rodergo knew anything about Edmond's past year, or past ten, he likely would have captured him right then and there and thrown him in a fort dungeon. This man was not someone to ally with. This man was a threat, and Edmond had hoped to avoid him.

123

"Well," Mira said, noticing Edmond's discomfort. "We actually need to be going soon. But, about the sponsorship..."

The baroness began to open her mouth but at that moment the door slammed open again, and four men carrying a large crate between them struggled into the room. Each of the men wore a full suit of plate steel that covered them completely. The rondels at their shoulders were emblazoned with peering eyes, and intricate embellishments in silver and gold wrapped their cuirasses in fantastic images of feathered wings and birds of prey. Each step they took came accompanied by a singular tapping of metal on the hard floor, and as Edmond looked down he saw each metal sabaton that covered their feet held a tapered metal point, like a stiletto dagger that extended from their toes, a weapon made for kicking hapless infantry from horseback. The suites were completed by polished wooden scabbards on their hips, holding broad swords as wide as a hand is broad. Green plumes protruded from their helmets, and half capes bearing the symbol of the house of Alverdo draped over their shoulders. The crest of Alverdo, now that Edmond had seen the mansion, was quite a bit more ominous than he'd first anticipated. What he'd initially taken for the yellow glare of an owl at night protruding from green fabric now harkened to a far more ominous implication.

The four men in armor were clearly knights, but it was a strange thing to see men of such station performing menial labor. The crate they carried rocked and shook back and forth as they heaved it into the room. Snarling sounds emitted from the box, followed closely by rabid growls that trembled in the air.

"What is—" Edmond began to say, but Rodergo cut him off with a spurt of laughter.

"Don't trouble your pretty little law-keeping head. It's just a cougar we found recently."

"In the North Fields?" said Mira innocently.

Rodergo gave her a shifty glance, his smile diminishing somewhat. As it faded, like ice melting from a stone block, it revealed a far colder and calculating countenance. Much like his sister, Rodergo Alverdo the hellcatcher wasn't all he seemed. "Perhaps in the North Fields," he said. "Perhaps in the graveyard beyond the Stern against the tilt of the plateau. There are a good number buried there, you know—people who asked too many questions." He allowed the words to hang for a moment, then loosed a jovial laugh and chuckled. "I'm only jesting, only jesting. Come!" He beckoned at the knights. "Take it in the back, into the basement. Don't let any of the children near the box—you know the rules!"

All the men grunted or nodded to show they'd heard, and began heaving the box through the partition door Dante had exited through. Once they disappeared from sight, the baroness cleared her throat, and said, "Those knights are the winners of the last four years of tournaments, all of them wearing Alverdo colors." She smiled. "We often manage to pick the winner. So, you must understand if I'm not jumping at the opportunity to sponsor someone I only just met."

"Those knights claimed the last four tournaments?" said Edmond with a frown.

"That's what she said," said Rodergo. "Now they work for our family."

"Is that how it always goes?" said Edmond.

The baroness smirked at the look on Edmond's face. "My sponsorships are often quite generous," she said with a soft chuckle. "The Baron Genevese tries as he can, but unless they're robbing us of our gold mines or encroaching on our territory, they just don't have the funds to recruit as far or wide as we do."

"And it's important to win this tournament then," said Edmond.

"Of course, the prize money alone can set a man—

"Or woman," the hellcatcher reminded, idly.

The baroness made a sour face, and didn't correct herself. "The tournament can set a man up for a long time. It also gives him land."

Edmond shifted, trying not to show his interest. "Land," he said pretending as if he didn't know exactly this. "And what parcel might be given out this time?"

Actually, said the baroness, "this year is the most prized parcel we've offered in decades. Fort Dentemosi."

"The abandoned, broken down fort on the way here?" said Mira.

"It may need some work," said the hellcatcher, "but it's costing too much for Titan's Folly to try to maintain. To be honest, it's not a matter of funds, but of manpower. Most of the town seems to have gotten into their heads that the place is haunted."

The baroness quickly interjected, "but, of course it's not. And we're not trying to get rid of it, we just know it's a wonderful prize. How many knights that you know are gifted a fort?"

"A broken down fort," Mira added.

"Whatever the case, it comes with the same privileges that title and land-holders own. It's no small prize."

"No small prize indeed," said Edmond. "And I know of *no* knights offered such a thing. None in all of Godshaven, or in any of the tournaments in the surrounding islands."

Mira made a face in his direction as if to tell him to pull it back a notch, which Edmond did, wiping the gleeful look from his face—mostly.

"Well," said Rodergo, "my wife is actually waiting for me back home, I should probably get going."

The baroness shook her head quickly though and said, "Actually, Rodergo, I had something I needed to discuss."

Rodergo raised a querying eyebrow. "Is it something that can wait? My wife is *waiting for me*," he said, absolutely no inflection or significance to the words themselves, or the tone. Yet, something in the hellcatcher's eyes flickered, and the baroness' eyebrows twitched, suggesting there was far more behind that statement then Edmond realized. But, he decided he wanted to know nothing about it. The less he involved himself in the politics and intricacies of these two ancient families, the better chance he had of succeeding at his mission. And of course, the prize of Fort Dentemosi was crucial to what came next.

"Well," said Edmond, "What do you say? The sponsorship?"

The baroness sighed through her nose, her nostrils flaring delicately across a severe face still alight with would-be mirth. "I suppose I could sponsor you. We already have a good number of high quality candidates in the tournament. But, you would owe me a favor."

"I'm the reeve," said Edmond, "I can't promise anything that would—"

"You shot one of the Genevese, I don't need you to *tell* me that you will do anything, I just expect that you will when the time comes. Do we have a deal?"

"I'm not going to sign over just any favor," said Edmond. "But if it's within reason I'm happy to do it if I can."

Beneath his breathe, though loud enough so that Edmond could hear, Rodergo murmured, "If you think you'll be able to refuse *anything* we ask, you may be surprised."

The baroness smiled at Edmond and reached out to pat his cheek, "You look so handsome when you're flustered." She winked. "If ever you're lonely, and you want to be rid of this adviser of yours," she glanced at Mira, "please do come calling. The younger children go to bed at midnight."

Edmond felt his face heating up, and he coughed slightly. "Is it normal for children to sleep so late?"

"Nothing normal about her 'children'," Rodergo snickered, but quailed under a sharp look from his sister.

"Is that a yes?" Edmond said, shifting back on track. "You will sponsor us?"

"I will. The favor I have lined up isn't for you to murder a man, or rob a mine. It's really quite pedestrian."

"What is it?"

"I'll tell you when the time comes." She smiled sweetly.

Edmond glanced down at the baroness' gloved hand, which she kept rigidly against her hip. The fingers seem to be moving as if of their own accord; though the baroness' eyes were fixed on him, her fingers almost seemed to be grasping as if to flee Rodergo, moving in the exact opposite direction of where he stood.

Edmond shivered. "Well, I agree then."

"Perfect," said the baroness. "In that case, I will tell you when the time comes and that time is now. I wish for you to keep an eye out for Tiny Genevese. I've heard rumors that he is looking for trouble with my family and has been encroaching in Alverdo territory. Tiny is a dangerous, mule-headed infant of a man. Do you think you can do that?"

"I can always keep an eye out."

The baroness patted him on the cheek again, a bit harder than necessary, but her smile remained affixed to her face. "Fero!" she called towards her son who was lounging against a wall with one of the guards, beneath a crystal. "I need you to get the proper papers, the sigil—the same as we did with the last knight."

The red haired son nodded once and scurried off. As he did, Edmond realized that all of her adopted children resembled her in appearance. He wondered if alchemy was involved in that too.

"I'm looking forward to doing business with you," said the baroness, and she reached out again to touch his chest. "I'm especially looking forward to seeing you fight."

Edmond swallowed for more than one reason. He gave a nervous little chuckle, and said, "Oh, well... I promise I won't disappoint you."

"Better not," said Rodergo, a smile still fixed to his lips. But as for his eyes, they were like chips of ebony, darker and colder than any of the things he hunted.

Edmond could only nod again and inwardly start listing the ways he could find someone to fight in his place. He needed someone who could *win*. Someone he could trust.

CHAPTER 12

FIVE WEEKS LATER

"Pardi above, I repent of my sins. Forgive me, sun-father. Yer ways are the light. My ways are shite-black. Please, don't kill us. I'll ne'er ever drink ag'in. I promise. Ok, maybe one more time, but after that ol' Vicente will ne'er touch the bottle again. Maybe twice." Vicente held his frock coat over his head, shading himself from the blistering heat of the sun. His leg had mostly healed, and he had no difficulty holding himself in the saddle of the dappled grey horse. The scraggly black of his closely cut beard glistened with the sweat that ran freely down his face, and as Augustin looked his way, the heat rising off the dry valley floor warped and wavered making it look as if his friend were underwater.

The windless valley floor kicked up no dust, and no rain or mist fell from the cloudless sky, so there was nothing but the fluttering heat to interrupt their vision. With the craggy reds and greys of the Monta Gabri Mountains ringing them, the flat bottomed valley gave the impression of a rusted iron skillet, an image only embellished by the scorching sun. Augustin knew from examining maps of the region that beyond those western mountains lurked the sea, but the tall peaks formed a wall against the wind and rain as unassailable as the staunchest fortress in Godshaven. So the Folding Valley sat like a stoneware bowl, dry and empty but for the mining towns that speckled its rim. Well, almost empty anyway.

From behind him, Augustin heard Tristan call out to Vicente. "Slow down. You'll tire out your horse, if you keep letting it pull you ahead like that." His voice had a halting quality, as if he couldn't quite catch his breath. Despite packing away his armor, Tristan seemed to be having the most difficulty with the Folding Valley's oppressive heat, and in contrast to Vicente's joking calls to the sky, he clutched a small metal icon of Pardi's sun and moved his lips in quiet prayer for the better part of the day. Tristan didn't pray like most holy men Augustin had known. His words came soft, and unrehearsed. There were pauses and good load of 'umms' and 'errs.' It was almost as if he were having a conversation. Despite struggling in the heat, Tristan had made double rounds with the water sack, checking that his companions' thirst was quenched.

Augustin smiled slightly, watching as the knight offered to lead Vicente's horse so the man could take a bit of a kip in his saddle. He'd forgotten what it was like to have a den mother—for that's what Tristan had always been to the group. A stark contrast to his sister—Serenia. Augustin's smile slipped somewhat.

Cristobal had wound a spare shirt around his head, letting a tail hang back to cover his neck. "This is a bad heat. A dry heat," the big Dumasian said, licking his lips. "We should have plenty of water still. Drink. Refill your flasks." From the saddle, he patted the keg of water Tristan brought past him, moving towards Catali. Tristan paused, allowing the giant access to the water from atop his big black horse. When they had decided to keep the brigand's horses for their journey, they quickly discovered that only the big black would bear Cristobal's prodigious weight comfortably, and after two weeks overland, Augustin could tell how fond of the horse his large friend had become.

"He's big enough to bear the burdens of others. Like me," Cristobal had said one night as he brushed the valley's dust and grime out of the big black's coat. In addition to the feed they had bought, Cristobal slipped the horse dried slices of fruit from his provisions, and Augustin knew enough of the Dumasian tongue to know that Cristobal had named her Bellenio—Pretty—and grown fond of telling the creature what a sweet and gentle beast she was as he cleaned her hooves and removed her saddle each night.

Augustin pulled free a wedge of dried apple from his own satchel and fed it to the bay he rode. As he closed the satchel, he felt the heavy gold band of the ring they had found in that monstrous grave, and the edge of a heavy gold coin that Lady Navara had given him. They had left Wickwood a few days after making their deal with Lady Navara. Catali had wanted Vicente to rest his leg a bit, and guarantee infection did not set in now that she had the proper materials. When they were stocked with provisions and ready to leave, they had been caught in the village square by a crowd. The surviving brigands and their leader filled a hastily erected gallows, and despite the crowd's taunting cries, the men held their backs straight and their heads high up until the moment the reeve had pulled the trap door from under them. Augustin had remembered then the fear in the brigand leader's eyes when he thought they were to be turned over to the Navara. He remembered the foul stench of the dismembered bodies hidden in the garden. It now seemed to him that they had been right to be afraid. What kind of monster must this Matimeo Navara be, that even hardened highwaymen like them feared to be in his power?

The group had plenty of time on their journey to discuss their plan. Despite the urging of the Lady Navara, they still could not know for sure what she had told them was true. Once out of the village, Vicente had been quick to point out, "The rich are the schemer's schemers. They scheme at levels you and me only dream of. There may be some deeper game here yet. By Dulomora's black nose, I would not be surprised to find that Lady Navara had put some of those bodies in the ground herself." Catali had been repulsed at the idea, and for the first few days swore that Lady Navara's grief had been real, but as they reached the Choking Pass, she had admitted that even if the lady's grief was real, it did not mean she was innocent in all this. No, as much as Augustin wanted matters to be simple, they would have to find the truth about this new Reeve Matimeo, evidence or a confession. Once they had the measure of the man and knew him, then, and only then, could they attempt to capture him. Then, it would be a matter of figuring out how to bring the reeve, the arbiter of justice for the town, to justice.

Augustin pulled the heavy coin from his satchel and looked at it again. It was larger than one of the red-gold d'oro and brighter too. Its edges tapered out like a pancake, and a grinning skull surrounded by ivy adorned the front. Turning it in his hand, he felt the rough grooves of old letters, worn with time. *My husband drew from the ancestral vault for the ransom*, Lady Navara had told him as she handed off the coin. *It's old. Not proper d'oro, but pure gold, stamped with the seal of the First Kings. Pirates aren't picky.*

Gold is gold, after all. But, if you find a coin like this in Matimeo's possession, then my suspicions are right and he was never kidnapped. It's just another scheme to get his father's gold.

Augustin pocketed the coin. He groaned inwardly, and shifted in his saddle as he thought about how foolish he had been to think of this as a simple job. He took a pull from his flask then splashed some of the remaining water on his face, rubbing it around his eyes and forehead. As he blinked away the water, his refreshed eyes caught the shadow of a horned plateau rising in the distance.

"Titan's Folly," he murmured.

The shimmering reflection cast by the broken halves of the ancient titan nearly blinded them as they rode up the western ramp to the city's heart.

"What do you think is happening there?" Catali asked, to the shadowy side of the plateau.

Where she pointed, Augustin spied a group of men putting the final touches on long fences and what seemed to be new scaffolding of raised seats. A place on the wasteland's floor seemed to have been cleared, and as the evening passed, he guessed the place would be shaded by the plateau's shadow. It was a sight that he had seen in innumerable variations in a hundred different places when he was younger. "A tournament," he said simply. As Catali looked over to him, he shrugged. "It looks to me like they are arranging a joust or perhaps a melee," Augustin said.

"Mirastious sake, what kind of knights would come to a place like this?" Catali replied, looking up to the beating sun.

Tristan licked his lips. "Could be they are hoping to attract some. Tournaments are good for that. Even godsforsaken places like this will draw hedge-knights looking to come into a lord's service."

Augustin frowned. He pointed towards the field's edge where a line of three bodies hung from a wooden gallows. Across their chests hung painted signs that read, 'cheater'.

"Stay sharp," he called to the group. "You gather enough swords in one place, someone will want to use them."

With their heads low, they tried to follow the piecemeal streets of old and cracked foundation stone. Once or twice, Vicente fell back to urge Tristan forward. The man had a habit of stopping to talk with every beggar who approached him, whether he could spare them a coin or not. By halting stretches, they passed the bustling market with its savory smells of cooking beef rubbed with colorful spices. A sun-browned merchant in a billowing blue robe tried to tempt them with similar garments of bright yellows and pinks, and Augustin started to wave the man away before changing his mind.

"Excuse me, good sir," he said instead. The merchant gave a broad smile in return, his shaved chin wobbling with the motion. Augustin tried to smile back and could feel his sun baked skin crackle under the effort. "We have just come into town and need to find an inn. Do you know where we can find one?"

The merchant's smile fell at this unprofitable question. Folding the robe over one shoulder he crossed his arms and asked, "That would depend. Who are you for?"

"I'm sorry?" Augustin said.

The merchant slapped his forehead with his palm, then tilted his head, speaking more slowly. "The baron or the baroness. Who are you for?"

Augustin looked to his companions, but they appeared just as puzzled as him. The stories about the Folding Valley and Titan's Folly were few and far between in the North. He had only half believed the wild descriptions of a broken titan in the middle of a wasteland plateau until he'd seen the shape of it rising out of the valley floor. Local politics were well beyond his realm of knowledge. "I'm sorry, but whatever marital issue is dividing the baron from his baroness, I'm afraid I don't know anything about it."

Here the merchant's eyes shot wide, and he leaned forward. He spoke in a conspiratorial whisper to the group as they edged their horses closer. "Don't you know anything? The baron and baroness aren't married. They hate each other." Here the merchant shot a finger to the hulking stern of the wrecked titan, looming above them. "South side is the baroness Alverdo's domain. The bastard alchemists." Augustin could see a pair of banners hanging from the wreck's bricked up face, an owl's eye gleaming from a green background. As soon as he had the sight of it, the merchant spun and pointed to the prow of the dead titan on the far side of the plateau's table. "North side is the baron Genevese. Dumasian stock. Deals in pyrite sulfur and recently gold." The sun baked stone that made up the titan's castle-like facade held two banners as well, like a twisted reflection of the first. Only, the device on these banners held a yellow serpent slithering over a black field.

"The city is in two baronies at once?" Catali said. She spoke with an incredulity that begged for clarification, and the merchant swiftly waved his hands to dismiss the thought.

"No. Titan's Folly is divided. Officially, it is the edge of two baronies, North Fold and South Fold, but—" Here the merchant gave the group a hard look. "If you don't want trouble, I recommend deciding which side of town you are staying in, and staying there."

"This is ridiculous," Augustin muttered, drawing a sharp look from the merchant. "They all answer to the Commodore. This is petty and childish. We're still in the Empire."

"Ha," the merchant shook his head. "Try telling that to the Alverdo or the Genevese. See how well that goes for you."

Stepping forward, Tristan looked between the two fortified wrecks. "Is there no neutral ground in the city? We are here on business with the reeve."

At this the merchant gave them another appraising look. "Do not say that you were not warned, but the center of the city, around the reeve's mansion, that's as close to neutral as you will find." The merchant shook his head, and let out a resigned sigh. "Look for the blue heron on the big house. That is the reeve's mansion. The closest inn will be the Pipe and Lady. There will be a sign with a woman playing a flute." At this, the merchant stepped back, his expression saying that the matter was settled. Augustin took the hint and urged his horse onward towards the heart of the city.

A divided city, he mused as they wound their way through the sun baked houses and businesses on the plateau's surface.

Behind him Vicente's rasping voice said, "Feuding lords pay very well. Perhaps, while we are here it might be profitable to take a side." Catali pursed her lips, murmuring in hesitant agreement.

Tristan shook his head, propping his spear into the stirrup. "We have a job to do already, and we shouldn't stir up trouble. It looks like these people have more than enough to deal with on their own."

Augustin nodded. "Focus on the reeve. We want to leave this town better than we found it, not worse."

CHAPTER 13

THE FRONT OF THE Pipe and Lady Inn smiled into the street like a tooth-less old man. Its broad window sloped and cracked at its edges, and worn imprints, like rotted gums, lay in its edge to show where shutters and glass had once been embedded. The round, wooden sign held deep cracks that broke up the flaking paint displaying the inn's namesake, and the whole affair hung on a brittle chain that would have snapped if any wind ever came to the valley. Luckily for the Pipe and Lady, the mountains that encircled the Folding Valley, the Monta Gabri, kept the sea winds back as tightly as a well-sealed cask.

Inside, the Order of the Honorable Lily found an assortment of discarded barrels and planking roughly hewn to approximate tables and chairs. Men and women in the same sort of loose fitting robes and pants that they had seen in the market clung to clay mugs of beer and some strong smelling spirit that Augustin could not quite identify. In the northern corner, a group of men in green livery shared a pitcher while they laughed and talked in loud, harsh voices. Pistols hung from their hips, as well as short-handled arming swords. Unlike the sun-toasted inhabitants of the valley that he had encountered so far, a few of these men had pale skin, pinked by the heat, and fiery red hair that complimented the baked brick of the inn.

"Let's get a few drinks and we'll see about rooms," Augustin said. Taking a table near the center of the room, Augustin raised his hand to a woman passing by with an empty wooden tray. She turned, and for a moment, he lost the thread of what he had meant to ask her. The woman had tied her long, black hair into a tight braid that fell between her shoulders to her hips. Her luminous brown eyes sat in a smooth sea of caramel colored skin, and her hand held a gold ring bound to a thin gold bracelet by a trio of light chains. She waited expectantly for his order, the gold bangle tinkling softly as she pushed back her braid. Feeling the flush of attraction rising in his chest, Augustin ran his fingers through his own dust-coated hair, pushing the tied-back tail over his shoulder.

"Hello. Could we have a round of beers, if you please?" His parched throat struggled slightly with the words, and Augustin turned to cough as he tried to smile to the woman. She nodded with a sympathetic grin.

As she started to turn, Catali held up a finger to stop her. "And a pitcher of water with something to eat as well?" she asked. The woman's dark eyes flicked to Catali's shaved head, and her smile broadened.

"Of course, medici," she said, and the woman retreated with her tray towards the bar at the back of the room.

"Medici?" Tristan asked when the woman had gone.

Catali shrugged. "I haven't heard that since my apprenticeship. It just means doctor, but only the small islands use the word anymore. Didn't think I'd hear it here on Godshaven."

Augustin licked his lips. "Isolated as the Folding Valley is, it's easy to forget we're still on the continent." He looked back towards the men in green livery. They now had their pistols out, and they were passing them around, admiring the weapons. "Seems it might be easy for them to forget as well."

Cristobal gave a grunt of agreement, and for a short while the group sat in uneasy silence. A shadow passed over the Pipe and Lady's door, and the dirt floor scraped with the sound of boots. The chatter and laughter from the other tables ceased, and a spectre of tension, like the sound of a distant wolf's cry, settled over the room. Augustin looked to the door. Four men in loose, black tabards stepped in. Gilded pistols hung from their belts, and hand-axes of fine steel sat in leather loops on their hips. They were large and broad at the shoulder, with the squat heavy features of Dumas. On their tabards sat the symbol of a serpent in embroidered yellow.

The men in green ceased their chatter, and glared at the newcomers, and Augustin thought about what the merchant had said. *Neutral ground, indeed. More like no-man's-land.* Augustin gave his companions a hard look to draw their attention, but they already saw the same brewing storm that he did.

The black tabards—Genevese men, if Augustin remembered correctly— took a table on the southern side of the inn. The apparent leader of the group, a man whose enormous stature and rail thin limbs combined to give the impression of a black-clad scaffolding brought to life, gazed at the green-shirted Alverdo, his dark eyes appraising them coolly. His long fingers

142

caressed a golden amulet at his throat, shaped to form a skull with a crossed pick and shovel beneath. *Corundos,* Augustin thought, recognizing the sigil to the god of mining and precious metals.

"We should go," Catali said, leaning close to Augustin. "We don't want to get caught up in something like this." Around them, the hard shuffling of chairs and the tapping of coins being dropped to tabletops played like a prelude, and the work-stained men and women shuffled out of the bar with their eyes down cast, looking to neither side as they did.

"I wonder," one of the red-haired Alverdo called out in a theatrically loud voice. "With all that gold the snakes put on their pistols, do you think the Bull can even afford shot for them to fire?"

"Nah," said another of the Alverdo men, looking straight at the black tabarded Genevese. "Look at their livery. The old Bull can't barely afford to keep 'em in shirt sleeves. No wonder they haven't won a knight from the tourney in over six years." The Alverdo men laughed at this, pouring more beer from their pitcher as the Genevese glowered.

One of the heavy-set Genevese, patting the grip of his flintlock, said, "If you doubt we can use these, I know a sure way to find out." The scaffolding shot his man a hard look, and he put his hand back on the table, but the words were already out. Now the Alverdo were the ones casting dark looks.

"Well, what's the hold up?" The Alverdo shouted, an edge of anger rose in the question. "Too heavy for you, Tiny?" he directed the insult to the Genevese's tall, gaunt leader. "Or maybe you can't bear the touch of it because that gold's dug from Alverdo lands."

Tristan held his spear in one relaxed hand, his eyes expectantly affixed to Augustin. Catali had her surgeon's bag in her lap, while Cristobal turned his head to look between the two other groups of armed men like a guard dog waiting to be let off its chain. Augustin put his palms on the table. They would find another inn. There was no reason for them to get involved in this. If these two groups of idiots wanted to shoot each other, he would be more than happy to let them.

"Here you are," the dark haired barkeep set down her tray and started to settle the clay mugs of beer around the table, but as she caught Augustin's eye, her expression froze, realization settling into her face.

"Suffer no impurity within thy heart." The scaffolding—Tiny, it would seem—stood, intoning the words like a prayer. The black tabards of the Genevese rustled within a chorus of clattering chairs as the men stood, drawing themselves up around their leader. In answer, the Alverdo stood. Clutching his amulet, Tiny continued, "But by fire, alloy thyself to the glint within."

The pistols of the Alverdo snapped up towards the Genevese, and the gilded pistols of the Genevese to the Alverdo. And between them, Augustin tackled the dark haired barkeep to the floor. A thunder of gunfire tore the Pipe and Lady apart as gouts of dark smoke belched out to fill the room. Cries of pain flared up from both sides of the room, and through the ringing in his ears Augustin heard the woman screaming with fright.

"Stay down," he told her, and through the haze that filled the room, he saw her nodding fervently.

With their pistols spent, Augustin heard the Alverdo draw their swords. He assumed the Genevese would have their axes in hand. They had not hesitated. They had not waited. The thought drove a heated iron of anger through his chest as Augustin stood. By their livery Augustin had judged them to be knights. Fighting each other was one thing, but firing across people who had nothing to do with your feud? Endangering the people their lords were meant to protect? Augustin drew his rapier and dagger.

In the fog of acrid gunsmoke, Augustin's world narrowed to a six foot ring where the shadowed forms of the other men wavered in and out of sight. Here and there his rapier leapt from the mist, and he felt the satisfying punch of the blade as it drew incapacitating ribbons through the shoulders and legs of the pale Alverdo and the broad shouldered Genevese alike. He heard the sweeping crack of Tristan's spear as he slammed the shaft through the melee and the heavy rumble of Cristobal's voice as he charged around the room, overturning tables and throwing chairs as he went.

Augustin did not know how long it took for the gunsmoke to find its way out the broad, smiling window of the inn, but when it did, he found himself surrounded on all sides by the laid out bodies of the green and black uniformed knights. A few lay unconscious, but most were in various states of agony. Tristan held one struggling Alverdo pinned to a wall with the butt of his spear, and Cristobal held Tiny in a headlock that kept the thin man's long body bent double. Lowering his rapier, Augustin's eyes darted to the space on the floor where he had left the barkeep and found it empty. A rush of anxiety rose in him and his dark hair whipped behind him as he searched the room. *Mercusi, be just, but if she's been shot—*

"Where is the barkeep, did anyone see where she went?"

"Oye," Vicente called. Behind the heavy wooden bar, Vicente stood pouring a dark brown draught from a clay jug. At his side leaned Catali, and the dark haired barkeep knelt crouched behind the lip of the bar.

She raised her hand, and with a nervous smile called out to Augustin, "I'm alright. Thank you."

"You're welcome," Vicente said, not looking up from his pilfered drink. Augustin gave a small sigh of relief. He felt the wave of anxiety slip away, and he sheathed his blades. Turning on his heel, he strode over towards Cristobal, and the big man pulled Tiny up to face Augustin, releasing his neck to take hold of his arms. No longer struggling, Tiny cast a baleful glare down into Augustin's eyes that sent a shiver of unease through him.

"Release me," Tiny said. His voice hissed out like the sigh of wind through dead trees. Even with his hands held behind his back, the tall Genevese spoke with a voice that anticipated obedience.

"No," Augustin replied. "Not yet."

Tiny's lips drew into a thin, impatient line. "Who are you to hold the baron's son?"

Drawn up to his full height, Augustin could see that despite his thin, gaunt features, Tiny actually stood taller than Cristobal, and his friend tilted his head to the side, giving Augustin a worried look from behind Tiny's thin shoulders. From the bar, Catali's youthful voice and Vicente's harsh rasp said in unison, "Blue fire and black fish." Augustin, turned and gave them both a hard look, and Vicente held up his hand apologetically.

146

While he had his back to Tiny, Augustin used the moment to think. Attacking the son of a lord could land them all in far more trouble than he had bargained on. He cursed his luck, then took a breath. Trouble or not, they were in it now. If he backed down now, he had no leverage at all. *And, I can't let what he did slide.* Augustin looked at the broken tables and the shattered remains of clay mugs around the room, then to the dark haired barkeep. *No, this cannot stand.*

"Is the baron's son above the law?" Augustin said. In his boiled leather vest and dust worn trousers, he looked the part of a sell-sword, but the old clip of command rose in his voice as naturally as ever. Maybe it was the subtle grinding of the dirt floor, or a particularly harsh blast from the tall Genevese's nostrils, but Augustin could sense the rising agitation in the man.

"The laws of the gods overrule the laws of man," Tiny replied. His thin voice rising like a tea kettle about to boil. Augustin turned around to face the man and saw color rising in his face. The amulet of Corundos bounced as his chest swelled with his quickening breath. "Is gold adorned and chased in iron? Should the glory of the god's own chosen be stifled by the mewling concerns of the unworthy?"

Augustin waved a furious hand around the inn's ruined front-room. "You could have killed someone."

With a haughty sneer, Tiny's voice dropped back to a cool, liturgical cadence. "In fire will you know the proof of the metal."

Augustin looked at the man in disbelief. *He truly sees nothing wrong in what happened here. What sort of town is this?*

At that moment, a gruff voice called out from the inn's open doorway. "What in Pardi's scorched balls is going on here?"

Augustin turned to see a short man with a heavy truncheon in his hands. The leather wrapped steel creaked as he twisted it in his grip. A patchy grey beard hung in a bristling arc below his chin, and his eyes were a muddy brown that stood in the wide whites like flies in an open sack of flour. A handful of other men armed with clubs stood in the street behind him. And on his chest, an iron broach held the symbol of the Imperial heron over a blue strip of cloth. *The reeve?* Augustin thought for a moment. The man looked nothing like the handsome portrait they had seen in Lady Navara's home. *A deputy then.*

"Clasco, you buffoon," Tiny said to the deputy. "Come in and arrest these vagrants." Augustin shot Tiny a dangerous look, but the lanky man paid him no mind. The deputy, Clasco apparently, squinted in as his eyes adjusted to the dim light of the smoky inn. He gasped and stepped inside, coming up short as he nearly stepped over one of the unconscious Alverdo knights.

"You." Clasco pointed the truncheon to Cristobal. "Release him. And you," he turned, whirling like a cornered animal, to face Tristan, "drop the spear and let him go." Tristan looked over the frothing deputy to Augustin, but with one curt nod he reluctantly lowered the spear and let the pinned Alverdo man retreat. Cristobal released Tiny as well and he stepped away, rubbing his wrists with a languid intentionality.

"Corundos smiles on me still," Tiny muttered. "For he sent you, imperfect tool that you are, to be the device of my escape."

Clasco's eyes narrowed as he forced out a smile. "Yer too kind, baronson Timeteo." Then, like a man realizing he's about to burn his dinner, Clasco yipped and spun around to face the green uniformed Alverdo. "And, what of you and yours?"

The Alverdo man waved a hand at Tristan, then jabbed a finger to Augustin. "We were just having a drink when these lunatics attacked us out of nowhere. Look at how cut up we all are. It's a miracle none of us were killed."

Augustin ground his teeth. "Trust me, if we'd just let you two fight it out there'd be a lot more dead men in this inn."

"It's true." From behind the bar, the dark-haired barkeep lifted a hand and pointed around the room. "The Alverdo and the Genevese drew pistols. You can check their guns. I stood right in the middle. If these strangers hadn't intervened I'm sure I'd be dead."

Clasco waggled the truncheon at her. "Ana, stay out of this. I can see for myself what happened here." Folding his arms, the stubby deputy looked first from the Alverdo then to the accusing face of Tiny. He swallowed hard, and wiped at his forehead. "Yes, I see what this is. You strangers come in here. Making a ruckus, riling up the place. With the first bouts of the tournament this afternoon, you thought you could take out some of the competition. You entered in yourselves? Looking to get a knighthood out of such base cheating? Only one rule 'round these parts we take as divine—no *cheating*. Specially not with the tournament comin up."

Augustin glowered down at the deputy. "We had no idea there would even be a tournament until today. As she said," Augustin nodded towards Ana,

"These so-called-knights drew steel on us, and we did what we could to prevent them from killing anyone, including each other."

Vicente slapped down his glass on the bar. "Ah, you see that was our mistake. I'm thinking we probably should have let these clay-brained-whoreson's kill each other."

Clasco slammed his truncheon on the dirt. "That's it. All of you, surrender your weapons. You are coming with me to the reeve."

A tense moment passed and Augustin tightened his grip on the handle of his rapier. He had no doubt that the Order could cut through the deputy and his posse, but what would they do then? They had to investigate the reeve. *Hard to investigate when you're fugitives.* With a swift series of snaps, Augustin popped the leather sheath of his dagger and rapier from his belt. "Fine," he said. "Take care. I'll want these back after we speak with the reeve, and I'll hold you responsible for any damage." Clasco eyed the weapons suspiciously, then with a gruff command, nodded for his men to gather them. Tristan handed over his spear with a cheery smile while Cristobal passed over a whittling knife no larger than his little finger.

"Oh, you drownin' bastard," Vicente muttered, throwing Augustin a sarcastic grin, pulling free his own rapier. "If we get hanged, I'm gonna kill you." The reevesman waited with growing concern as Vicente placed three pistols onto the bar to join his rapier, then his dagger. A belt-knife. A boot-knife. A smaller pistol drawn from within his trousers, and finally a set of brass-knuckles from the inner pocket of his coat. He gave the man a lopsided smile and followed as he walked back towards the front of the inn.

Satisfied, Clasco turned to Tiny and the Alverdo knight. "I think it best if you both left now, don't you?"

Tiny gave a faint smirk. "Don't worry. We'll be on our way." He then spoke to Augustin. "I won't keep you from the reeve. It seems you will have a great deal to discuss."

CHAPTER 14

EDMOND, STILL WEARING THE face of Navara, leaned against the wall, inhaling deeply through his nose, savoring the scents of the dusty streets beyond which wafted through the open window to his new offices. The reeve's manor was the most comfortable place he'd ever stayed for more than a week (with express permission). He smiled softly, swirling the contents of a glass which he plucked off the table. Mira sat across from him, opposite a thick, oak desk inlaid with blue and gold trim, studying a rolled out parchment of blueprints—outlining the construction of a dam.

"So? Is it doable?" Edmond asked in a drawl, sipping from his drink.

Mira held up a shushing finger, still hunched over the unfurled paper.

Edmond rolled his eyes and glanced towards the door where Kurga and his boys stood.

"Did you manage to rid us of the lackey yet?"

Kurga nodded once beneath his large, floppy hat. His head looked quite small with all his braids tucked out of sight. The short bravo teased a finger across the pistols jammed into his belt and said, "Common sense is like perfume, uh? Those who need most, never use, uh?" Kurga itched at his silver ear, but kept his gaze focused on Edmond.

Ever since they'd arrived, nearly a month ago, at the reeve's mansion, they'd been trying to rid themselves of the local deputy, a man despised by both sides of the town for trying to keep the peace by *not* taking sides.

"The nuisance be gone, uh? Be out in streets-lodged in inn. He no come back soon."

"Good," said Edmond. "And as for you and your boys—any luck locating the vault with the titan's guns? We need to be moving on that soon."

This time, Kurga's boys, Dorgo and Calub stepped forward. They muttered something in Chellek and nodded quickly.

Edmond glanced at Mira and, with a weary sigh, she looked up from her structural drawings. "They say that they have the location and now they're starting to plan."

"The gold?" said Edmond. "From the ransom for 'Reeve Navara'," his voice inflected the feigned identity as did the tilt of his eyebrows. "Secured away?"

"Spent," said Kurga.

"Already?" Edmond asked.

The bravo nodded once, again. "Mostly," he said. "The armor—tricky to find. Short time, uh. And ehh... other expense, too, uh." He hesitated

153

as if listening to the breeze, then smiled softly, but added no additional comments.

Edmond knew better than to doubt the word of Kurga—the man had proven loyal to his contract, as did the other bravos. It was their sole moral conviction and, Edmond had seen, once, on a dark night, when a particularly drunk bravo had tried to pinch a silver knife from Edmond's office, the others tie him to an old rusted anchor and drop him off the prow of their ship.

It had given Edmond nightmares for weeks hearing the screams of the man followed by a sudden gurgling silence.

But he was beginning to understand *why* the bravos stuck to the code. To do otherwise meant certain death, especially under an unyielding leader such as Kurga.

"Well, good then," said Edmond, drinking a longer sip this time in an effort to drown the memory of the sinking bravo. "I won't need you around here for the rest of the day. Do try to be back by the evening though—if you don't mind."

Kurga and his boys nodded, tapping two fingers against their thighs in a sign of understanding and then turned, hurrying out the door, leaving Edmond and Mira to their papers and thick silence.

"Anything yet?"

Again, Mira held up a shushing finger, scowling at the parchments, and again Edmond rolled his eyes and took a drink.

A good thing too; had he not, he wouldn't have spotted the two groups intersecting out the window. First, he spotted Kurga and his boys striding away, moving up the street back towards one of the local taverns. Then, coming from the opposite direction, Edmond spotted an entirely different group of people.

Clasco was in the lead—the reeve's deputy scowling and blustering something fierce to the men and woman over his shoulder. Edmond began rolling his eyes at the nuisance deputy, but then he froze as he spotted the rest of the group.

He nearly choked on his drink and, still leaning back, forgot to catch his balance as he kicked his legs to try and get a better view. As a result, Edmond tumbled from his seat and smacked his head against the wall. Dazedly, he hopped back up. Mira ignored him and continued to study with a furrowed frown what lay in front of her.

"Godsdamned luck above," Edmond whispered fiercely to himself. "It can't be." He scurried to the window for a better look, and his heart plummeted.

He recognized the giant Dumasian, the man with the dreadlocks and golden eye and, most of all, the hawk-faced fencer: the Lord Captain from Carabas.

"Mira," Edmond said quickly. "You have to hide!"

"Hold on," the once-goddess snapped. "I'm not about—"

The front door creaked open, and Edmond could hear boots stamping in the room beyond. He cursed again. There was no time, no exit door besides the main one. Edmond vaulted across the room, slamming the door to his office shut. He would have to have a word with Clasco about just leading anyone into the parlor of the manor.

Still cursing, Edmond glanced one way, then another. "Mira, I'm serious," said Edmond. "They'll recognize you as sure as shite. You have to hide!"

"Who?" Mira demanded, looking up for the first time in nearly two hours, her dark, glittering gaze flashing with annoyance.

"Oh, no one much, just an old lord captain we've encountered before and his motley crew of thugs."

Mira hesitated for a moment. "Which lord captain? You've pissed off quite a few in only the year I've known you."

"The one whose *ship* we stole," Edmond said significantly. "You *need* to hide. They won't recognize me, but *you*... You have a face that's hard to forget."

"Oh dear."

Just then, the door shook with a rattling knock.

CHAPTER 15

"ONE MOMENT!" CAME A squeaking, agitated voice. "Just stay right there, your reeve commands it!"

From the mansion's hallway, Augustin stared into the polished grain of a fancifully carved wooden door. Clasco held his elbow in one hand and his truncheon in the other. Behind the sealed doorway, Augustin heard the rapid scraping of wood proclaiming what sounded like a series of cabinets and drawers being hastily shut. Judging by the blast of impatient breath from Clasco's nostrils, the situation of being ignored was all too familiar under the new reeve's supervision.

Augustin held his shoulders back and his chest high. He had not had a good look at Reeve Matimeo Navara, but if the man were as sloppy and disorganized as he sounded that could only bode well for his investigation. *Careless. Such men incriminate themselves. I'll have to be watchful.*

When the door opened again, the reeve motioned both of them in. Augustin kept his eyes lowered as he stepped in. Men with small titles often insisted on the most respect in his experience. The office itself held a wide desk of polished oakwood. Small purses sat open and the light from the glass window at the room's rear caught their contents, casting the red-gold glint of d'oro across the wood-beamed ceiling. Leather portfolios lay across the desk's surface in a haphazard geography of disinterest, and a half-empty bottle of rum sat next to three small glasses. To Augustin's eyes, it was the office of a man who cared not one whit what anyone might think of him. *What on earth was he shutting away then?* Looking to the closed doors of the waist high cabinets that lined the office's left and right walls, Augustin could only imagine.

As the door shut behind him, Augustin heard the reeve say, "Now what, Clasco? I'm very busy with the tournament. It's starting tonight, you know?"

"Yes, m'lord reeve. I'm very sorry, but—"

"But you're going to insist on bothering me anyway," the reeve interrupted, stepping to look out of the room's back window. Was it Augustin's imagination, or were the reeve's hands trembling, if ever so slightly?

"Yes, m'lord. I mean-No, m'lord-wait—" Clasco paused for a moment, letting go of Augustin's arm as if he'd forgotten why he'd brought him here. In the window's light, Augustin saw the reeve's finery hung in a loose-fitting way, and he wore a pair of satin house slippers. For a noble of Godshaven, such a state of undress only further pressed the idea that Reeve Matimeo cared as much for appearances as a fish might care for the price of salt.

The reeve raised a finger and waggled it over his shoulder. "Enough. It's hot enough in here without your blustering. Just come out with it."

Clasco put a hand on Augustin's back and shoved him forward. The unexpected push sent him stumbling for a moment, but Augustin gave the carpet a quick stomp and regained his balance at once. Looking back at Clasco, the man seemed disappointed that he hadn't fallen on his face, but gave his report to the reeve regardless.

"This one and his gang of vagrants was brawling in the Pipe and Lady. They assaulted baronson Timeteo Genevese and his retinue as well as a group of the Alverdo's sworn swords."

The reeve's fingers twitched. His left hand came up towards his throat, and he seemed to be adjusting the buttons of his vest. There was the faintest of bulges beneath the neck of the vest, Augustin thought, but it was hard to determine the source. A pause stretched between them, and Augustin looked down at the desk. At the reeve's back, one of the wide drawers hung slightly ajar. A bit of folded leather peeked out towards him.

The reeve turned. Locking eyes with Augustin, he pushed the drawer shut. His dark eyes were sharp and appraising, and they looked at Augustin as though they held an important question for him. Augustin narrowed his own eyes in response. Whatever the reeve expected him to say, he would let the man speak first.

All at once, the reeve's dark expression dropped and a smile spread across his handsome jawline. "You fought Alverdo knights and Tiny Genevese's retinue in a barroom brawl? You must have had a couple dozen men to pull off such a feat. How many of you are there?"

"Five." Augustin kept his reply clipped and professional. Something in the reeve's expression concerned him.

"Five?" Reeve Matimeo repeated. He tilted his head to look at Clasco. "Five vagrants assaulted the sworn swords of the baron and baroness?" The deputy held up his palm as if he might explain, but after a few stammering syllables the reeve pinched his fingers in a gesture calling for silence. "Are the other four here?" he asked Augustin.

Nodding, Augustin said, "They are being watched in your front parlor by the deputy's men. They will not cause any trouble."

"I'm sure," the reeve said, his smile ticking into a smirk. "Clasco, go and make sure the rest of the group are comfortable. Get them some water if they want it."

There was a slight murmur of protest which quailed under the look of sheer indifference on the reeve's face. More grumbling, then Augustin heard the door shut behind him, followed by the trudging of Clasco's booted feet as he retreated up the hall. After another moment, the reeve stepped around his desk and put a reassuring hand on Augustin's shoulder, giving it a squeeze. "Just a wild guess, but I'm thinking that you all didn't start that scrap?"

The reeve's easy familiarity did nothing to put Augustin at ease. *This man wants something from me,* he thought. Augustin's encounters with the merchant and with the feuding knights in the Pipe and Lady had made it abundantly clear that the baron and baroness were less interested in law and order and more in protecting their own interests. Whether he started the fight or not hardly mattered. He had injured their knights and threatened the baron's son. They would want their own brand of justice. That the reeve would care about his side of the story at all told Augustin the man either had an extraordinary sense of justice and great respect for the law, or that he would want to trade his protection for some favor. Augustin thought about the ring and pure-gold coin in his belt-pouch, and guessed it was the latter.

With a hesitant feeling like stepping into some hidden snare, Augustin said, "No. We had just come into town and were taking a rest at the inn when the Genevese men came in. The Alverdo were already present, and after the two exchanged a few taunts it became clear they would fight." Reeve Matimeo listened eagerly as Augustin laid out the events leading up to Clasco's arrival.

"It sounds like a simple misunderstanding," the reeve said as Augustin finished. "I'm certain I could clear it up for you with the baroness Alverdo and Baron Genevese. The Bull is a stubborn old man, but he's not unreasonable." The reeve stepped behind his desk and grabbed up the half-empty bottle of rum, swirling it casually as he spoke. "Of course, I do have a few questions myself first. What are you all doing in Titan's Folly?"

Augustin licked his lips. *Finding out if you murdered your step-brother,* he thought as he watched the reeve pick up two of the short glasses between his fingers. He had anticipated this question as Clasco marched them towards the reeve's mansion. "We are here for the tournament," he said. The reeve raised an eyebrow, and Augustin clarified, "My companions and I are members of a knightly order, the Order of the Honorable Lily."

The reeve turned his back and poured the rum into the two glasses. Augustin thought he heard the choke of a stifled laugh, but when the reeve turned around he set down the bottle of rum and waved to his face. "Apologies. The dry air makes me sneeze sometimes. So," with a drink in each hand, the reeve waved his arms in exaggerated confusion, "you came all the way out here for our tournament? I wouldn't have figured you for the type to settle down as some inland baron's sworn sword."

Now it was Augustin's turn to raise an eyebrow. "Why do you say that?"

The reeve drank one of the small glasses of rum, then turned to refill it. "Just a feeling," he said, watching the pour.

Augustin wished he could ask what the reeve was thinking at that moment. The man had a peculiar way about him, a sort of nervous energy, like an actor playing the part of a reeve on a fairground stage. Augustin remembered what Lady Navara had told him. Matimeo had only been appointed reeve two months before. Perhaps he was simply new to this sort of authority?

"You know, I envy you actually," the reeve said. "I've never been much of a fighter. Never fought in a battle. Don't really know how to use a sword or gun. Oh, I know the basics. I even received some measure of formal training, but a tournament like this, with experienced fighters looking to prove themselves—" The reeve shook his head. "I would get killed."

Watching the younger man's strange loping gait and animated gestures, Augustin was inclined to agree.

"So, I have a deal for you."

Augustin stiffened. Just as he expected, here came the favor. Would the young reeve want him to kill an enemy? Go off on some mission to steal something for him? Help him to cover up some crime?

"I want you to be my second," said Reeve Matimeo.

Augustin stood silent a moment, unsure he had heard correctly.

"For the tournament," the reeve continued. "I'm terrible with a sword, and you seem to be extraordinarily capable. It makes perfect sense."

Augustin's forehead wrinkled in confusion. "My lord reeve, if I may ask, why do you wish to enter the tournament? These sorts of tournaments offer great opportunities for young men looking to prove themselves, but... for someone with a station already..." Augustin allowed the question to linger.

"It's embarrassing," Reeve Matimeo said at last. "But, I've never been knighted. My father is a merchant noble so my step-brother and I were never squired. As I've said before, I'm terrible with sword and gun so I'd never be able to win it on my own, but—" Here the young noble raised one of the rum glasses, holding it out for Augustin. "If I had a cunning swordsman, like yourself, to fight for me as my second, we could win. I could finally have my knighthood. It would mean respect, and honor, and all that other chivalric stuff."

Augustin looked down at the glass of rum skeptically. His heart chilled with silent unease, and yet, how could he afford to say no? If he didn't help the reeve, then it would be a simple matter for Matimeo to turn him and the Order over for the harsh justice of the baron and baroness. If he accepted, he would be close to the man he needed to investigate. It made perfect sense for him to agree, and yet he hesitated. When Augustin looked back up into the reeve's eyes, the man gave him a smirk that could not have been more clearly read if it had been written in ink. It said, 'We both know you don't really have a choice, so just take the damned drink.'

Augustin reached and took the glass, and the reeve smiled. As he did, Augustin noticed that Matimeo's hands were bare. He thought of the pale gold ring in his belt-pouch and the portrait in lady Navara's manor. *Did the loss of one make him discard the rest of the rings, too?* It seemed strange to Augustin, and as they drank their rum, he watched the excited young reeve with growing curiosity.

"Oh, Augustin, my friend," said the reeve. "We are going to do great things together."

Augustin frowned, a shiver across his spine. Had he told the reeve his name? He hadn't thought so—but he couldn't exactly remember either.

His expression impassive, Augustin glanced at his drink, then threw it back in one burning gulp.

***

Closing the door behind Augustin, Edmond dropped the rum bottle onto his desk with a heavy clunk. He rushed to the cabinet doors and pulled them open. Mira's contorted body tumbled out, her face flushed red with a furious scowl.

"If you *ever* shove me in a cabinet again, I'll bury you beneath the Wise Oak so deeply that not even the Blind Seers of the Starless Library will know where your miserable bones have gone!"

Like most of Mira's threats, Edmond found it as incomprehensible as he did harmless, and he raised a shushing finger as he helped Mira to her feet. "Didn't have a lot of options, now did I?"

The goddess's dark eyebrows beetled momentarily, before she raised her chin in a haughty display of condescension. "How would you know? You never consider your options. Oh, sure, when you're on the road it's all grand plans and schemes, but as soon as the unexpected happens it's whatever hole you find first. I'm surprised you haven't tried to disappear straight up your own ass, yet. Though—" Mira shook her head in a patronizing stare, "Maybe that's exactly what happened here."

Edmond gave Mira a curious look over his shoulder as he sank into the desk chair, kicking off the house slippers. "Not sure I like where this is going," he said, grabbing up a pair of heavy boots.

Mira crossed her arms. "Making him your second? Have you lost your mind? Granted you haven't seen the man in months, but the last time you did, he tried to skewer you on that rapier of his. And that was *before* you stole his ship."

"True," he replied. "But, at least I know he can fight."

Mira pinched the bridge of her nose with a frustrated sigh, "That really wasn't the point I was making. You don't seriously believe he's here for the tournament do you?"

"Nope. Don't believe that for a second," Edmond stood, straightening his shirt as he buttoned his cuffs and collar. "But, as long as I've got him here, better to keep him where I can have an eye on him, right? And if he fights well enough, I might even be able to resell that bleeding armor at a half decent price."

"Oh, yes." Mira closed her eyes, giving her words a sage air. "As long as you're trapped in a room with a tiger, best to stay as close to the tiger as possible so you know where it is."

Edmond paused as he reached for the door. "You know, I think you've finally got this sarcasm thing down."

Mira smirked. "Must be all the time I'm spending around you mortals."

CHAPTER 16

"PERFECT. NOW LET ME see you with the visor down." Reeve Matimeo eyed Augustin from a stool at the far end of the tent. When he had agreed to be the reeve's second for the tournament he had expected to spend some time with him, but he had not expected the man to be so involved in the process.

Matimeo had insisted that Augustin take part in the opening duels, and rushed the lot of them down the main streets of Titan's Folly to the clustered tents and pavilions that surrounded the tournament field. In the reeve's tent, two young men with whitened hair had been helping an older, shorter man into a set of armor, but when the reeve arrived, he ordered them out. The older man had seemed relieved, smirking at some unspoken joke and carelessly dropped the armor into a clanging heap as he left while the young men simply rolled their eyes, shouldering a pair of strange devices that Augustin did not recognize as they made their way out. The exchange was just one more piece in the strange puzzle that was Matimeo Navara.

Augustin lowered the visor on the armor's helmet. It bore down on the padded coif wrapped around his head, but the narrow eye slits allowed him to see clear enough. He had not worn plate armor in years, and Augustin rolled his shoulders and hips as he got used to the extra weight. Even for tournament use, it hung heavier than he would have liked. The overlapping steel plates were thin and strong, but they were overlaid with copper and gold decorations of bird wings and twisting ivy, riveted in place and burnished until they seemed to glow with a pinkish light. As he stretched, Augustin felt the curling ornamentation clip and hook against the armor's joints, limiting his movements. It felt to him like someone had taken good armor and tried to turn it into a ceremonial piece, making it ill-suited for either use.

The reeve gave a satisfied nod, and grinned, "Yes, I believe that will work."

At Augustin's side, Tristan held a two-handed longsword. He examined the blade, pressing his thumbnail to the edge as he tested the bite. "It's sharp," he said, turning to give Augustin a concerned look.

Catali looked to the reeve, folding her arms over her chest, "You're not using blunted weapons?"

The reeve shook his head. "No," he said. "Not for the duels. But, remember, it's not to the death. Just until one of you surrenders or falls unconscious. Killing your opponent would go very badly-for both of us."

"I don't like it," Catali said. "Too many things can go wrong, even in a tournament, when the weapons are lethal."

Augustin continued to stretch and roll his legs, careful to keep the ornamented gold from catching. With the visor down, no one could see the scowl he gave. Catali was right. The longsword wouldn't cut through plate armor, but if the slender tip made its way between the joints, a solid thrust could push the ring-mail apart and drive deep enough to kill. Augustin lifted his elbow and felt a curl of gold ivy hook on an ornamental bronze feather. He pulled it free barely a heartbeat after, but if a blade had been coming for him, that moment could mean his death.

The reeve simply shrugged, "I didn't make the rules, but if you're worried, check over the joints again. I won't object if you want to take every precaution. Remember, if you win, I win." Catali sniffed at this, but took the reeve's offer and tested the plates, pulling on them to be sure they would not shift or expose the more vulnerable mail beneath.

At the tent's flap, Cristobal stooped to peek in. "Bellenio is ready," the big man said. Behind him, Vicente held the reigns of the big black horse. The reeve stood and walked over with a broad smile on his face.

"Good good," he said. "She took to the caparison then?"

"Like she were born to it," Vicente laughed.

Through the flap, Augustin could see Bellenio draped with the elaborate, dyed garment. Her natural black coat and mane seemed to embolden the red stripes and blue herons that the caparison adorned her with, and despite her gentle eyes, she seemed every bit a warhorse. The reeve inspected the lay of the cloth and ran his fingers through her mane. Bellenio whickered and shied back from his touch, and the reeve respectfully stepped back.

STEVE HIGGS, BRYON ARNESON, JOSEPH DANIEL

"You brushed her thoroughly?" he asked.

Vicente snorted, rolling his eyes, "Yes. Seems to me a lot of trouble for just riding out to a duel, though."

Augustin had to admit he agreed. In tournaments, presentation and pride mattered as much as skill in arms, but his first contest would be a duel. Neither he nor his opponent would be mounted. It seemed ostentatious to him that he would ride out onto the field, then dismount to fight.

Cristobal said, "I will hold her if you wish to examine yourself." The shadow of his wariness lay over the words, and he stroked Bellenio's neck as he spoke to the reeve.

"No, no," Reeve Matimeo smirked. "I believe you. Thank you."

At that moment, a trumpet blared, sending its call across the tournament grounds. Matimeo clapped his hands and said, "That will be the duels. We should get you mounted."

Augustin twisted his hips and stretched his shoulder. The metal scraped again as a bit of decorative gold ivy caught the pauldron. He cursed as frustration boiled up in his chest. *This suit is a death-trap,* Augustin thought. *If I can't move, I'm just as likely to lose my life as the match.* "Hold," Augustin said. The others turned to face him as Augustin lifted the helmet's visor. "This armor is going to kill me."

Matimeo rolled his eyes. "A little late for that. We have your match and if you don't show, I forfeit." His gaze turned serious as the reeve stepped closer. "And, that wasn't our deal," he said with a hint of menace.

170

Augustin paid no attention to the threatening look, but turned his head to look around the tent. "Does anyone see a set of tin sheers? A hammer and chisel would do the trick." Everyone except Matimeo turned to peruse the tent, turning over boxes and looking under stools and benches while the reeve crossed his arms.

"We don't have time for this," Matimeo grumbled, looking anxiously towards the tent flap.

"We'll make time," Cristobal rumbled as he triumphantly held up a set of short snips.

Augustin felt a sigh of relief escape his lips as he waved the big man over. "Here, help me get these ridiculous snares off." Augustin indicated to the curling golden ivy and trailing bronze feathers.

"Now hold on—" Matimeo held up a hand in protest, but too late. With a small squeal of peeling metal, Cristobal clipped the first bit of gold ivy. As Cristobal moved over the armor and cleared the joints of all their fanciful decoration, Augustin saw Matimeo watching the fallen trimmings. Beside him, Vicente drank from his flask and stared down at the scattering of gold and bronze. Both men had a look of calculation on their face, but where Vicente's was a hungry look, as if he were eyeing a rabbit he hoped to make his dinner, Matimeo's eyes were a cold calculation, like a surgeon deciding where to saw off an infected limb.

Augustin stared at the reeve. *He lives in a mansion in a city of goldsmiths, but to look at him you'd think he had no way to replace these decorations.*

As Cristobal switched to Augustin's left side, Matimeo's eyes met Augustin's. Abruptly, his expression changed to irritation, and the reeve gave an exaggerated sigh out the side of his mouth, shaking his head as he muttered, "Damaging perfectly good armor. You're lucky I don't charge you to have it replaced."

Interesting, Augustin thought. *Does our reeve perhaps have money problems?* Coin could drive men to do unspeakable things. If his step-mother's guess was correct, and he had also cheated his father out of a ransom, what else might he have done? *How* do *you spend your money, Reeve Matimeo?*

Cristobal clapped Augustin on the back, sending up a metallic ring. "Try it now."

Testing each joint in turn, Augustin felt much more limber. With a grin he reached out and took the longsword from Tristan.

"Not exactly a rapier," Catali said, eyeing the two handed blade. "Looks heavy."

Augustin held the blade up with one hand, feeling the muscles of his forearms turning the steel. He looked along the blade's edge. *Straight and true,* he thought as he said, "Not as heavy as you may think. The rapier's weight is in its grip, so it feels lighter and allows you to move the point more quickly. The longswords' weight is balanced into its blade-you can take a man's arm off with a longsword, but you could never do this with a rapier-but both weigh two, maybe two and a half livre." He turned to Catali with a smile. The young surgeon eyed the blade with a look of concern, and Augustin's grin faded. "I'll be fine," he said more quietly. Catali gave him a hard look, then turned and stepped out of the tent, scraping her palm over her shaved head as if it itched.

As Catali stepped away, Vicente slid in to fill her place. His yellow eye danced from the blade to meet Augustin's gaze. "Fascinating tid-bits aside. It's been more than a few years since Borgo Tortrugha," Vicente flicked the longsword's blade, and it rang as the trumpet outside gave a second blast. "Do you still remember how to use that sword?"

Augustin flinched, and his fingers loosened for a moment before he regained his grip. He stared into the well-oiled blade and caught his own reflection. His eyes were indecisive, and he turned away from his own staring face. "This isn't a battlefield, Vicente. It's a tournament."

Vicente chortled. "Have you not been paying attention to this town, Gus? The whole village is a battlefield. The tournament is just one stage in it."

The thought sent a coil of unease in Augustin's stomach, and he lowered the point of the longsword.

Vicente put a hand on his armored shoulder, "Why don't you let ol' Vicente take this one, eh?"

"There's no time." Reeve Matimeo stepped forward and practically slapped Vicente's hand from Augustin's pauldroned shoulder. "We had a deal, Sir Mora. Now get your whiny-metal-arse out on that field or—"

Augustin did not hear the rest of what Matimeo said. A third blast sounded from the trumpet. He looked down into his reflection in the longsword's blade. Feeling his chest tighten, Augustin pulled down his helmet's visor, his face becoming a mask of militant resolve. "I have this," he said, and he stepped out of the tent.

CHAPTER 17

As Augustin steered Bellenio towards the dusty oval that made up the tournament grounds, he found himself looking over his shoulder. Matimeo had declined to follow them out of the tent, but his parting words had been so earnest that Augustin wondered if perhaps more was at stake for the man than simply the title of tournament champion.

Around him, the gathered crowds roared from the raised wooden benches as others pressed against the guard rails that encircled the field. It seemed as if half the town had turned out, and the long sides of the oval arena were packed ten deep. The gallows that he had seen on the way into town had been cleared of its ropes. Now, men and women in dusty robes crowded it for a better vantage of the field. At the center of the western and eastern sides, mid-field to give the best vantage, were wooden boxes, raised above the roaring commoners. Festooned in the green owl-eyed symbols of the Alverdo, the severe-faced woman seated in the eastern box's shade paid little attention to him as he rode onto the field. She wore a strange glove on one hand and silver jewelry glittered across her hands and shoulders in a dazzling display that nearly washed out her house colors.

Turning to western box, Augustin saw a bald man, broad of shoulder, but so hunched that he seemed to lean on the prodigious grey beard that drooped behind the box's wooden front. A solitary black banner with the yellow serpent of the Genevese dangled from the wall beneath him, and Augustin wondered if the old man was the Bull that he had heard so much about. Around the baron and baroness stood their families. Pale, red-haired, and chattery on the Alverdo side. Tall, heavy lidded, and grim on the Genevese's.

As he rode onto the field, a murmur rose up in the crowd. Augustin peered through his visor as he surveyed the field. Thirty paces ahead of him, a man in much simpler plate armor stood with his longsword over one shoulder. His helmeted head tilted and Augustin heard him shout over the muttering crowd. "It seems you have come to the wrong event, sir. This is a duel, not a joust. Or are you afraid someone will steal that nag of yours if you do not ride her out?"

The crowd laughed at the rib, and Augustin saw the baroness Alverdo scowling down at him. A flush of embarrassment rose in his collar, and Augustin dismounted his horse as Cristobal ran out to grab the reins.

"I had hoped we could count on our host to at least get the matters of custom correct for us," Augustin grumbled.

Cristobal took Bellenio's lead and leaned down to say in a low voice, "Do not fret about it. Fight. Win. Any missteps in tact are his own."

Augustin nodded beneath his helmet, and Cristobal led the horse back at a jog. Once his friend cleared the field, Augustin turned to face the other swordsman and raised his blade in salute. His opponent gave a curt wave of his own blade in response, nothing that could be properly called a salute.

A commotion stirred beneath the Alverdo box, and Augustin saw nearly swallowed by the press of people around them, a smaller box holding a cluster of old men and women in muted robes of black and grey. Their hands and necks sparked with gold adornments, and they were talking to a young man that Augustin could only barely make out. With a shooing motion the young man ran out from the group of grey-beards and mounted a small podium on the edge of the field. As he did, the crowd roared in response. He wore a wrap around his head of purple silk, and the tail draped over the puffed shoulder of his satin doublet. As he raised his arms and his voice in a call for quiet, the crowd fell into a practiced silence.

"Eleven years ago, on this day, peace came to our town. The feuding of the noble houses of Alverdo and Genevese, Genevese and Alverdo, ended. In brotherly love, our two noble overlords commemorate the end of those days of violent strife with a glorious tournament. Pride and honor are shared this day, as each sponsors the inclusion of many brave and noble warriors. As is tradition, the victor of the tournament, proclaimed one week from today, shall be invited into his sponsor's retinue, to the glory of Titan's Folly. Peace and Honor!"

"Peace and Honor!" the crowd roared in response.

Augustin could not believe what he had heard. *Peace? Brotherly love?* He wondered if anyone in the crowd actually believed the rhetoric the herald had announced. He could only guess, but from the rehearsed tone of the words it sounded to him like the speech was the same year to year. *Delusion,* he thought grimly as he looked around at the cheerful faces of the expectant crowd.

The herald's firm voice pulled Augustin from his thoughts. "As is the tradition of our most noble lords, a unique boon is given to the winner of each tournament. By the approval of the esteemed leaders of our bright city, the winner of the tournament shall receive the keep of Dentimosi and by right of that noble and ancient fort be named Lord of the Pass." As the crowd enthusiastically cheered the proclamation, one of the grey-beards stepped forward to join the herald. A short man, particularly beside the handsome, young herald he seemed to stand on his tip-toes as he held a silver broach of office up over his head.

The sun glinting off of the broach as well as what Augustin could only assume was a gold rimmed monocle, gave the man an almost celestial appearance. But, as he lowered the broach and retreated, Augustin could see the box of elders for what it was. A tournament committee. A group of self-important old men that the families had employed to run the tournament so neither side could accuse the other of rigging the field.

A fanfare of trumpets from the Alverdo box gave some time for the herald to graciously applaud the tournament committee, and as the final blast sounded he turned his smile back to the crowd. "Our first event is the duel. Twenty knights have been paired, and the first draw has fallen to Eldin of Carcos, sponsored by Baron Genevese, and our own reeve, Lord Matimeo Navara, sponsored by Baroness Alverdo. Gentlemen, are you ready to begin?"

Eldin raised his longsword in one hand over his head. Augustin hesitated. The herald had made no mention of a second. *Does he think that I'm the reeve?* Augustin thought for a moment of stopping the bout to clarify, but instead clenched his jaw and pushed his own sword up overhead. *I'm going to have to have a word with our reeve when all is said and done,* he thought.

A lilt in his voice, the herald threw his hands into the air with a shout. "Then, lay on!"

Augustin guessed that Eldin sensed his hesitation, because the other swordsman rushed to close the gap between them like a charging warhorse. With a clash of steel, Augustin met the onslaught with a series of close guards. Plate armor was heavy, and if Eldin wanted to tire himself out with an opening assault, Augustin would be happy to let him. The sharp edges of their longswords rang together five times in rapid succession before Eldin drew back. Augustin saw the other swordsman's shoulders rising and falling with his breath.

Hoping to make a quick end of me, eh? Sorry to disappoint. Augustin plunged forward, twisting his longsword in an upward slash. Eldin brought his guard up to catch the slash, but at the last moment Augustin leveled the grip of his sword. The blade looped around his opponent's guard and gave off a terrific clang as it clashed against Eldin's helmet. The crowd cheered and Eldin slipped back, a bright slash smiling from his now dented helmet. Not content to let his opportunity slip away, Augustin scored two more strokes across Eldin's shoulder and thigh before he could get his guard up.

Had he been fighting in another tournament, a judge would have called the bout and announced points to Augustin before resetting them for another round, but Augustin knew there would be no second or third round. As

Matimeo had told him, this fight went until one of them yielded or could no longer fight. Feeling his blood racing in his veins, Augustin let himself be swept up in the fervor of his attacks.

His precise and calculated swordplay moved Augustin like a dancer around his opponent. An efficient music of steel and muscle sang a brutal melody as the crowd joined in like a chorus, to echo each blow that rained down on Eldin, and for a moment Augustin lost himself in the savage simplicity of it. His body knew what to do. He could let go.

Augustin drove another dent down into the top of Eldin's helmet with his longsword. The man swayed on his heels, and Augustin brought his blade in a low slash for Eldin's knee. The force of the swipe drove a weak parry aside, and as the steel blade rang against the metal joint, Eldin spun and fell to his hands and knees. Augustin's body knew what to do. He no longer heard the crowd. The hot, wasteland sun above turned to the oppressive hell of burning buildings in his mind. The pounding in his ears became the roar of cannons as the guns of Borgo Tortrugha blazed around him. His body knew what to do. The back of the neck. Between the helm and the cuirass. The longsword spun in his hands, arcing for the exposed gap.

"Stop!" A woman's voice called out to him, cutting through the din.

Augustin froze, turning his head to look. "Serenia?" he whispered. At the edge of the tournament field he saw the Order staring back at him, and at their center, Catali with her hands lifted to cup the sides of her mouth. His memories fell away, and Augustin's mind returned to the tournament field. He still had a fight to win. He turned back to Eldin.

A spray of hot dirt and sand flew into his visor, and Augustin cried out in pain. The crowd split between triumphant shouts and low, bovine boos. Blinded, Augustin lashed out with his longsword, swinging it one-handed while his other hand reached up to his helmet. He blinked rapidly, trying to clear his eyes, but in the tight confines of the helmet he could see little more than the dimmed impression of sunlight around him. He swung his sword again as he stepped back, desperately trying to buy himself some time while his other hand groped for the latch to his visor. *I have to get my eyes clear,* he thought. His fingers felt the small latch and yanked. The visor did not budge. He pulled again and again, each time more forceful as he tried to gain access to his own eyes. *Corundos, confound this bleeding contraption,* Augustin swore, but the visor would not come loose.

"Something in your eyes there, reeve?" Eldin's voice taunted from beyond Augustin's blinded sight.

Augustin raised his guard. His gauntleted hand let out a snap as Eldin's longsword came down, and Augustin felt the sharp pain as his wrist buckled, then with a violent tug, he felt his longsword plucked from his grip. A soft piff rose from the dirt nearby where the steel blade fell. He thought to dive for the blade, but he knew that would put him in as vulnerable a position as Eldin had been moments before, if he could even find it. Raising his armored hands in a guard, Augustin continued to blink fiercely beneath his shuttered helmet, the tears streaming down his cheeks as he tried to clear the debris from his reddening eyes.

"Figured you for a ponce," Eldin continued. "Think you can just kill our miners, do you? Think the Genevese will just roll over? You and the pint-sized bastard."

A heavy slash rang against his shoulder and forearm, and Augustin immediately shifted for the follow-through, dragging his leg back to deflect the second strike. Eldin let out a frustrated grunt, and Augustin grit his teeth. He needed a strategy. He couldn't continue to guess and dance. The thought to yield crossed his mind—given the circumstances, who could blame him— but as he blinked Augustin began to catch the foggy outline of Eldin's armored form in front of him, and a different plan took its place.

"I want you to remember this," Eldin said as he circled Augustin. "When I'm swornsword to the Genevese, and you're back in that cushy mansion of yours. I want you to remember who thrashed you on the field." Eldin swung in for Augustin's legs.

As the blow rang, Augustin dropped to one knee. Then, he prepared for the follow-through. Still half blinded, Augustin twisted and lowered his head. The slash glanced off the curved top of the helmet, slowing down the strike, and he reached up with his gauntleted hands, grabbing the extended longsword. A moment of stunned silence gave him the chance he needed, and Augustin twisted his body, jerking the sword out of Eldin's grip. Wielding the weapon by the blade, Augustin slammed the heavy steel pommel against Eldin's knee like a club, dropping the other man to the ground with a cry of pain. He struck again and again, blindly cudgeling Eldin with the guard and pommel of the sword.

Pausing, Augustin pushed himself to his feet, righting the sword in his hands. "Do you yield?" he shouted through the snot and tears streaming down his face. His heart pounded and his ears burned with the coursing drumbeat of his heart. He heard no reply, and Augustin brought down the sword in a vicious strike to the prone Eldin's helmet. "Do you yield?"

From behind him, Augustin heard Vicente's let out a low jumble of curses.
"Aye. I think ye got 'em," he said as Augustin felt him take the longsword
from his hand.

CHAPTER 18

THE NIGHT AIR BROUGHT a chill over Titan's Folly so cold and sudden that its promise of relief from the sun seemed to become a hateful pronouncement, as if Nameless Death himself descended on those windless currents. Augustin stood from his seat, his leg creaking from the battering he took only three hours before. He walked to the window and pulled in the wooden shutters. Their suite in Reeve Matimeo's mansion afforded them three bedrooms that opened into a common sitting area. Here, they sat around a circular fireplace, like a campsite, looking to each other over the flames. Augustin looked to the doorway connecting the suite to the rest of the mansion. Matimeo had left a few minutes before with the promise of food, but Augustin didn't feel much like eating. He had questions.

"How can a place so hot, be so bleedin' cold?" Vicente grumbled, tugging his coat close to his chest.

Cristobal held his hands out over the fire, rubbing them together. "There are deserts, worse than this, in Dumas," he said. "When the air is dry, it does not drink the sun's warmth. As soon as the sun leaves, so too does all her warmth."

Tristan shook his head slowly, and in the firelight Augustin thought that his blond hair took on a quality like molten iron. "What is it, Tristan?" Augustin asked as he took his seat once more by the fire.

His eyes, pensively scanning the firelight, Tristan let out a soft breath before he spoke. "I'm thinking about our reeve. I watched him as we walked to the tournament pavilions. I stared at him under the light of Pardi's sun, while I prayed to Pardi to reveal his truth to me."

Catali let out a sarcastic sigh, and Augustin shot her a quick glance. She shrugged apologetically, before motioning to Tristan to continue, but he did not seem to have noticed.

"There is something not right about this man, but—" Tristan pursed his lips, his eyes distant and puzzled. "I don't see him cutting up all those bodies. Burying them in the garden. No, I don't think our murderer is here."

Intuition or divine intervention, Augustin knew that Tristan's instincts about people tended to be correct. Even so, they were hardly evidence.

Cristobal made a rumbling sound from the bottom of his throat, and stretched. "Then where are they?" he asked.

Tristan turned up his palms in resignation. "I don't know, but my heart tells me that they are somewhere Pardi's light does not shine."

"Oh!" Vicente called out. He had slumped down so far in his chair that his shoulders nearly touched the arm-rests, but a lop-sided grin spread across his face. "Maybe, the next place to check is up the reeve's arse. Might be, we can find out what else he's lying about. Come on, Beautiful," Vicente's harsh voice scraped out his sarcasm in flitting bursts, like a bag of dropped coins, "The man's a con-artist. He's been playing us since the moment we walked in. He lied to Gus about needin' to ride onto that field on a horse, and I'm willin' to bet that's not the only lie he's fed us. Trust me, Pardi might know what goes on in the sun, but a liar knows a liar."

As Vicente folded his fingers over his stomach, Tristan's eyes sloped in almost embarrassed concern. "Liar or not. I don't think he's our murderer."

Augustin stood. "My visor was stuck shut." The group looked back to Augustin. "When he threw dust into my eyes, I tried to open the visor to clear my eyes, but it would not unlatch."

"You took a pretty good knock there, Gus," Vicente said. "Sure you didn't just fumble it?"

"No," Augustin replied. "I hadn't been struck in the head, yet. I put the helm on myself. I even felt the latch but it wouldn't come loose."

"You forgot about the safety catch by your ear. You hadn't undone it. I noticed it when we got you back in the tent," Vicente said, squinting his eyes with a look of friendly pity.

Augustin cut his hand through the air. "I'm telling you. I didn't set that. The helm was tampered with."

A brief knock sounded at the door, and Reeve Matimeo stepped in. Back in his house slippers, his cuffs hung loose about his wrists and he pushed the door shut behind him with his foot as he hoisted in a silver platter decked with cheeses and a loaf of nutty smelling flat bread. A stack of clear glass cups teetered precipitously on the tray, but Matimeo seemed unconcerned, his strange, loping gait seeming to rebalance the tipping tower with each step. Despite his claim that he knew nothing about fighting, Augustin saw a strange sort of grace in the helter-skelter movements. He wondered briefly if Matimeo had perhaps studied dance. The group fell silent. They all watched as Matimeo set the tray on a narrow end table, dragging the piece nearer the group.

"Well," the reeve said, picking up a slice of cheese, "Do you want to eat first or just start right in with the accusations?"

Another lengthy pause passed while the Order all looked to each other. Augustin had not known what to expect, but this certainly hadn't been it. Matimeo folded his arms, chewing and swallowing the cheese while he appraised the group. From his seat, Vicente let out a sniggering laugh, but said nothing, contenting himself to give Tristan a look of smug satisfaction instead.

Matimeo looked to Augustin, his gaze inviting him to speak.

Very well, Augustin thought, stepping toward Matimeo.

Augustin asked, "Did you tamper with my helmet?"

"Yes," Matimeo replied cheerily, taking another bite from the tray. Augustin frowned. The reeve had moved to pick up the piece with his left hand, but then, as if remembering himself, switched to his right. *Strange...*

"For what it's worth," the reeve continued, "I didn't figure Eldin to be the type to throw dust in a man's eyes. Knowing the type this tournament attracts, I probably should have, but then again so should you. So, let's call that one a wash, eh?"

Augustin blinked back at the reeve while he absorbed the response. He could feel his neck flushing with indignity at the reeve's cavalier attitude. "Why?" he finally demanded, his voice hot with restrained frustration. "I couldn't clear my eyes. I could have lost or been injured. Why did you do it?"

"Well, what's the point of cheating if you don't take a few precautions to avoid being caught?" Matimeo replied.

A momentary silence hung in the air, then realization fell into Augustin's stomach, cold, hard, and naked. To his side, he vaguely heard Catali mutter: 'You drowning bastard' as Vicente let out one barking 'ha!' Cristobal rushed forward like a tidal wave, and before Augustin realized what was happening, he grabbed Matimeo by the throat.

"You set us up! Used us to cheat?" Cristobal spat. He lifted Matimeo off the ground, slamming him against the mansion's lime-washed wall with an audible crack. The reeve's eyes bulged and his hands grabbed hold of Cristobal's wrist, while his flailing legs kicked over the silver tray, sending the teetering cups spilling across the stone floor in a glittering tide of broken

188

glass. The muscles of Cristobal's arm stood out like a nest of snakes beneath his skin, and Matimeo gave out a choking gasp as he fought for air.

In a moment, Tristan and Augustin were both on their friend. They took hold of his arms and pulled backward, trying to pry him loose from Matimeo, but to Augustin it felt like trying to reign in a charging bull. His heart raced, and Augustin's bruised leg trembled with the effort of pulling on the giant. He saw Cristobal's lips pulled back in a snarl as his clenched teeth ground together. His heavy Dumasian brow beetled down into a gruesome mask of wrath. The urgency of the moment drove Augustin's confused thoughts back, and the only feeling coursing in his veins was the panicked thought that Cristobal might close his hand and snap the reeve's neck.

"Cristobal," Augustin shouted. He tilted his head up and spoke directly into the scarred mass of Cristobal's missing ear. "Let him go."

"Why?" Cristobal rumbled. "This snake has already sentenced us to death? What more would it cost me to crush his lying throat?"

"What are you talking about?" Augustin demanded.

Cristobal looked down at him. "He used us to cheat in the tournament."

At that moment, Augustin remembered the hanged men out front of the tournament grounds; the painted signs on their chests that read 'cheater'. He saw Tristan's eyes go wide.

"Pardi, shield us," he muttered. Apparently, he had the same thought.

"So?" Catali stepped forward. "He cheated, not us."

Around Cristobal's grip, Matimeo choked out the words: 'All—of us.' He tried to speak again, but couldn't muster the breath, and let out a stifled gag as his face began to purple.

Vicente shifted in his seat, "Nah, he's got us. Good and proper he's got us. Gus, you were wondering about the horse earlier? That's part of it. We could try to deny it, but everyone in the tourney stable saw me 'n Cris brushing out that horse. Fittin' her with her caparison. I'd bet my last d'oro that a fair few would remember your pretty little face fetching that blade out from the smithy too, Tristan. And, I'm goin' to go out on the rope here and say that this tournament doesn't allow 'seconds' does it, m'lord reeve?"

Matimeo let out another near silent croak.

"Cristobal, for Mercusi's sake, put him down," said Augustin, "We don't know enough yet."

With a snort like an angry stallion, Cristobal let go of Matimeo's neck. The reeve hit the floor, his heels driving him back against the wall as he drank in desperate gulps of air.

Augustin stood over him, arms folded, his hawk eyes staring daggers into the reeve. "Even with the penalty being death, you cheat. Worse, you bring me and mine into your cheating and risk our lives for a knighthood? Just to add one meager title to your prestige?"

"Not just about the title," Matimeo said. "I'm sorry. I just had to be sure I had your commitment. You can't trust anyone in this town. Could I count on you to do what needs doing for my sake? Pheh—" Matimeo gave a raspy laugh that ended in him spitting onto the stone floor. "But for the sake of each other? That, I could count on. Trust me, we are all in this together. If we get caught the baron and baroness are not going to patiently divide out the blame. They will hang all of us together on that tournament field, even if they have to extend the gallows."

"Why then? If not for the title, why gamble on cheating?" Augustin asked.

Matimeo looked to them all. He drew himself up, straight backed and defiant. His black hair and handsome features seemed to fall away, and Augustin found himself staring into his eyes. A silent sorrow seemed to hover within them, like a gull's keening cry lost in seaward fog. They held a desperate resilience and flinty determination that told Augustin he would do anything to accomplish his purpose. It held a chill and a fire that felt at once alien and strangely familiar to Augustin, as though he were looking into a mirror or into the eyes of an old friend he had not seen in months. Then, Matimeo blinked, and the look vanished, buried beneath an expression of pleading sympathy, like a curtain draped to soften the grief-stained hardness beneath.

"This town has a cancer," Matimeo began. "You've seen it yourself. The division. The fighting. The endless one-ups-manship of the two 'noble' families. Did you know that the wrecked titan, the broken halves that the families now use as their homes, it used to have its guns?" As he spoke, Matimeo stepped lightly to the fallen tray. Picking it up slowly and placing the fallen flat bread back onto its shining surface. "Ornithopters too. Perhaps a half-dozen that were still workable in the wreck. The Commodore was so afraid the Alverdo and Genevese would destroy the town, he had them disarm the guns—seal them away in one of the old mines so that no one could use them again—but neither side can bury their hate. Both families

191

still check on the mine. They have inspections where they oil and maintain the weapons. They both go down there to ensure the weapons still work, and that none are missing. Even this godsdamned farce of a tournament is nothing more than a recruitment drive so they can both keep killing each other. If it doesn't stop—if *we* don't stop it—they are going to destroy this town." Matimeo picked up the last of the fallen food, a squashed bit of cheese. He stared at it a moment then threw it into the fire, eliciting a soft pop.

"I'm sorry that I conned you into this, locked your helmet so they wouldn't see your face and know it wasn't me. It's not your fight, but I wasn't lying when I said I'm terrible with a sword. If you hate me for this, that's fine. I can live with hate. But if only for your own sakes, I need you to stay and fight for me."

"That doesn't answer my question," Augustin replied. "You don't really want this knighthood. Why is it important to win the tournament?"

Matimeo frowned, then gave a small chuckle. "It's a start. Trust me. Once my plan is accomplished, you are free to go. In fact, I'd prefer if you did, but until then I need your help. Now, can we agree to see this through civilly? I'd like to get at least a little sleep without wondering if you're going to stab me." Matimeo extended his hand, offering a handshake to Augustin.

Augustin looked around the room. Everyone stared up at him expectantly. Tristan wore a soft smile that seemed to take Matimeo's speech as hopeful proof that he had been correct about the man, Vicente's one yellow eye stared up with bemused acceptance, Cristobal seemed to be waiting for permission to begin strangling the man again, and Catali's troubled eyes darted from the reeve to Augustin with a subtle shake of her head.

"My lord reeve," Augustin said, turning back to Matimeo. "If what you're saying is true, and I would hope for your sake it is, then, our paths may have crossed for some higher reason." Augustin took hold of Matimeo's hand, gripping it tightly. The reeve winced slightly and tried to shake, but Augustin held his grip firm. "If you betray us, there will be consequences," he said, locking eyes with the reeve. Matimeo gazed steadily back at Augustin, giving a subtle nod, and Augustin released his hand.

"So, what's our next step?" Augustin asked as Matimeo worked the circulation back into his fingers.

"Well, tomorrow's event is the lesser melee. Two teams of six warriors each. Still armored, but with blunted weapons. You can choose your weapon this time too, so expect some hammers, maybe a polearm."

August nodded. "Well, we have four here. Did you have anyone in mind for the other two? Those men who were suiting up in your tent before we got there?"

Drawing in a sharp breath, Matimeo looked as if he'd just swallowed something unpleasant. "Well, that's the thing. Because none of you were entered, the teams have already been drawn. Your companions won't be able to fight with you."

Augustin's mustache curled to ride his frown. He did not care for the idea of fighting alongside men he did not know. He would have to keep a sharp eye to be sure he did not get separated. "No matter," he said, smoothing his hair with one hand. "If the teams are randomly drawn then our opponents will have the same difficulties to deal with."

Again, Matimeo gave the uncomfortable expression of someone biting into a lemon, and Augustin braced himself for what the reeve might say next. "Well," Matimeo began, dragging out the word. "There's random and then there's *random*. You must have made an impression today. I got a look at who you're up against, and if I had to guess, I'd say the Bull might have had his thumb on the scale."

"Great," Augustin muttered. "Let me guess. It's the six strongest fighters the Genevese sponsored."

"No, no, no," Matimeo reassured, waving his hands in front of his chest. "I'm sure it's a spread across their top twenty, unless you meant strongest smelling. Then, you're probably right. They'll have to scrub the Dog's Eye for a week to get their stench out from the walls."

They exchanged a few more words before Matimeo retreated from the room with a parting recommendation to get some rest. Once he had gone, Catali stood and strode over to Augustin. "What are you doing?" she demanded.

"What is necessary," he replied.

"Necessary? We've stepped into the fire with this murderer, and you feel it's necessary to walk in further? We've already gone too far with him."

"We're investigating him," Augustin said, lowering his voice. "We can't exactly ignore him. If he wanted to, he could change his tune and then we'd have the baron and baroness after our skins."

"You think they wouldn't be in a forgiving mood if we told them the charming story of how their reeve is cheating at their tournament? I feel like

194

we've got the upper hand on him, and he's trying to convince you it's the other way around. And, if he's strung up for cheating in the tournament, it doesn't really matter if he killed those people back in Wickwood. It's not like we could dig him up and hang him again." Catali shook her hands, throttling the air between them as her whisper spilled out in harsher tones, like a drunk trying to hold her drink.

Augustin sighed. "It would matter," he said.

Cristobal grunted beside him. "Mercusi the just, would know. If he did not kill those people, we have to know. We are still obligated to find out, for Lady Navara's sake."

Her eyes set, Catali opened her mouth to speak twice, before spitting out: 'Mirastious, save us from ignorance' and storming out the door into the manor hall.

A tense moment hung in the air, then Augustin stepped toward the door to follow her.

"Erp-wait-er-um," Vicente sputtered. He fell out of his chair as he hurried towards Augustin. Reeling momentarily, he blinked before he steadied himself. "Gus, what are you doing, you drownin'-tin-brained-jackass?"

Taken aback, Augustin gestured to the door. "I was going to talk to Catali. She seemed upset."

"Yeah, you really do have the eyes of a hawk to realize that, you great blunt-hearted-scarecrow. You realize you are ah—you're gonna be the last person in the Isles that she wants to see right now, right?" Vicente stepped between Augustin and the door.

"I just thought, if I was perhaps unclear in what I said—"

"Oh-ho-ho, I'm gonna stop you right-there. No, no, no. How did you lead a whole ship without knowing how to talk to people?"

Augustin stared at Vicente with a flinty gaze. "They tried to hang me. You were there."

Lifting a finger, Vicente pointed to the center of Augustin's nose. "Exactly. So you stay here. Let ol' Vicente talk to her, eh? Don't you worry."

Like a rat squirming into a crack in a wall, Vicente wriggled through the door, and disappeared into the hall.

Behind him, Augustin felt Tristan walk up and clap his shoulder. "That's alright," he said. "Vicente may be crazy, but he knows how to cheer people up. Somehow. You should rest, like the reeve said, you've got a day ahead of you tomorrow. I've made the beds the reeve set aside. There's an extra pillow I managed to borrow for your leg—do you need anything else?"

"Thank you," said Augustin, clapping Tristan on the shoulder. "You didn't have to."

"'Have to' isn't the point, Augustin. But, if it makes you feel less guilty, if I don't keep you in one piece, my sister is likely to get all her tough Rooster friends together and beat me down. So, take care of that leg for my sake."

Augustin chuckled, rubbing his nose with the edge of his thumb. "No, she'd come break *my* legs for inconveniencing *you*. Then, she'd try to sail you to Carabas and get you to sign up in the Kindly Roosts." Augustin grinned, but the expression tasted bitter and it swiftly faltered then died.

196

"What is it?" Tristan asked, a shadow of worry flitting across his face.

Augustin briefly considered lying, but only briefly. "I thought about her today," he said softly, as if unsure what to make of his own words. "On the field. I lost myself. With the armor and the longsword. I thought for a moment I was back at Borgo Tortrugha. Not really, but it was like my body believed that I was. I almost cut his head off. I saw a chance. Could have broken him, flesh and bone. I don't know what Catali saw, but she must have seen something. She shouted to me. Told me 'No'. Only, I didn't hear Catali. I heard Serenia. I heard your sister."

Augustin stared into the fire pit. He heard Tristan sigh beside him.

"She always thought the best of you, Gus."

"I'm certain that's no longer the case," Augustin muttered.

The fire popped as Tristan licked his lips. Augustin could see from the corner of his eye that he was debating what to say next. His tired eyes spoke volumes in that moment.

"The mind plays tricks, Augustin," Tristan said carefully. "I know things, well, things ended poorly between you and Serenia, but something like this—Chalk it up to the heat and the fight."

Augustin gave a nearly imperceptible nod, and Tristan clapped him on the shoulder.

"Get some sleep, Augustin." Tristan turned to stoke the fire, allowing Augustin to exit the room with another, longer sigh, limping with each step as his feet tapped against the floor.

Things ended poorly, that's putting it delicately, Augustin thought as he slumped onto his bed. He remembered the way she'd screamed in his face.

"What do you want, Augustin?" she'd yelled, tears running down her cheeks.

Isobella. The answer had always been Isobella, but even now, when she was only a memory, his lips silently mouthed, *'you'.*

CHAPTER 19

AUGUSTIN FELT THE HEAT of the burning city around him. Flickering flame from wood and daub lit the cobblestone street in a sharp contrast while black smoke choked the sky, muddling the distinction between heaven and earth. At the street's end, he saw the outline of the town's belltower in relief against the setting sun. Another mad bellowing of cannons proclaimed the tower's death as he watched the stonework blow outward and scatter into the streets below.

He ran through the streets, fear clutching his heart. Horrific tableaus leapt from the licking flame like the illuminated pages of a hellcatcher's manual. He had seen a copy of the *Nominii Daemonia* only once, as a child, but the colorful renderings of alchemical horrors devouring hapless peasants and nobles alike had been indelibly etched into his mind. He would have preferred those horrors. Instead, he wove through the bloodied and mangled bodies of men and women torn apart by blade and shot, some wearing the emperor's black heron, most not. Blank eyes gazed up at him, stained with their own blood, and broken fingers reached for him. He plunged ahead, wheeling wildly through the hellscape. He had to find his friends. He knew they were here somewhere. Why couldn't he find them? At his heels, the ghoulish corpses rose to follow him. Every way he turned, Augustin saw them hobbling on splintered legs or dragging their spilled intestines as they shambled after him. He ran, but no matter how fast he pushed his legs, their shuffling gait brought them closer and closer. They surrounded him with the slow tightening of a noose, and Augustin felt panic rising like a cold tide, threatening to seize his roiling heart.

"Afraid to stain your blade, lad?" A grey and flinty voice found him over the pressing bodies. Past the mutilated swarm, Augustin saw a figure in a dark cape. He stood on a wooden pier. In one hand, he held a long dagger with a swerving blade. With the other, he held a man by his hair. In one fluid motion, Augustin saw him draw the blade across the man's throat tossing the body off the pier. The caped figure looked over his shoulder. Black, stringy hair hung over pale, moist skin, and he stared with milky grey eyes towards Augustin. "Do you still know how to use that sword?" As he spoke, Muergo's face became Admiral Morecraft's. The buzzing of ornithopters filled the air as they swarmed past, peppering the ground with musket fire.

In his hands, Augustin felt the grip of a longsword. Had he been carrying it this whole time? The thought failed to take root as he spun into the swarming press around him. He hacked and slashed, screaming out as his terror animated his arms into a brutal whirlwind. Blood misted and sprayed until it filled his vision and he swung blindly.

"Stop!" a woman's voice cried.

Augustin froze. He blinked his eyes. His arms extended, the longsword hovered in the air beside a woman's face. A leather strap bundled her dark hair behind her shoulder, and the glint of spectacles on her narrow face caught the fire light as if they were the window of a furnace. She met his eyes only for a moment before she turned to look behind him. Augustin turned to follow them. The longsword fell from his nerveless fingers. Behind him, the waters off the pier ran red, reflecting fire and blood. Dozens. No, hundreds of bodies floated there. As he watched, they pushed at the debris of a city brought to its knees, slipping past splintered wood and algal clouds of ash to float South; drifting like dark leaves on a river across the still water.

A musket shot cracked the air.

Augustin woke screaming. He clutched his ribs as he felt the rapid beating of his heart beginning to slow down. The cotton sheets of his bed in the reeve's mansion were stained with his sweat. He kicked them off. Despite the night air, he felt hot. As his breathing settled, his fingers lingered on his ribs, feeling the raised scar tissue. The old wound gave him no pain, but the flesh seemed to itch with the memory of the decade old musket shot.

Looking around the room, he wondered how long he had slept. Vicente's bed lay undisturbed, and the sounds of night insects still muttered from outside his window. He lay there for several minutes, but even after his heart stilled and his breath returned, his mind refused to quiet. With an aggravated groan, he pushed himself up. If he could not sleep, he would at least have some water to cool himself. Augustin threw on a loose fitting shirt and cinched his trousers. Stepping slowly, he passed through the empty sitting room, and by the light of the still burning fire found his way to the door. They had ready access to the mansion's courtyard, and a red, stone fountain burbled at its dusty heart. Stepping to the fountain, he felt a shiver run up his spine as the cold night slipped its icy hands down his loose collar. He cupped his fingers in the fountain and took a handful of the cool water to drink, rubbing his damp palms across his neck and face afterward.

"Having trouble sleeping?"

Augustin turned. At the courtyard's gate stood Ana. The cloudless sky let the moon and stars illuminate her raven black hair and copper skin as she leaned her arms between the wrought iron gate's bars. Wrapped in a shawl, her breathing gave off small puffs of steam nonetheless. Augustin had not expected to see anyone, let alone the Pipe and Lady's innkeeper, and for a moment he slipped on the mask of a smile while he wiped the rest of the water from his hands. Last he'd seen her, he'd been tackling her out of the way of gunshot.

"Perhaps a bit," Augustin said, stepping towards the gate. "Not that I'm unhappy to see you, but what brings you here so late?"

Ana gave a small shrug, her lips curling into a non-committal smirk. "I just closed up for the night. Clasco told me that your group were now staying as the reeve's guests. That's quite the turnaround. I thought for sure I'd be petitioning the reeve just to try and keep you from being hanged."

"Well," Augustin said. "We managed to come to an agreement."

"I can see," Ana laughed. "Truthfully, I didn't believe Clasco at first, but here you are."

"Here I am," Augustin echoed. The smile on his face warmed as he relaxed.

For a moment, they stood in silence, the metal gate between them rattling with Ana's slight movements as she adjusted her leaning arms. In the stillness, the shadow of his nightmare faded from his mind, and instead, he found his thoughts preoccupied with the shapely curve of Ana's wide eyes and full breasts. She looked away from him, her smile becoming bashful in the growing silence. Augustin looked away too. She had apparently come back concerned about them. After the brawl in the Pipe and Lady, that made sense. He decided then that Ana must have a good heart.

Augustin cleared his throat and asked, "Did they come back? The Alverdo or Genevese?"

Ana seemed distracted for a moment, then her eyes met Augustin's as she caught the thread of his question. "No," she said. "At least, not that I know. Bredo, he minds the bar when I'm not there, he didn't mention it when I came back from the duels. Did you see the reeve's bout? I saw your friend, the one with the black dreadlocks and dirty coat, he helped the reeve off the field at the end. His leg looked pretty bad."

"No," Augustin said hurriedly. Ana turned her head, giving him a strange look at the outburst, and Augustin repeated, more calmly, "No. I wasn't at the duels." He avoided her eyes.

"Funny, I'd have thought with your friends down there I'd have seen you too. Did the reeve not permit you to come? Something to do with your agreement?" she asked.

"No. I mean, yes— in a way. Yes. I offered to stay behind. I was sure the reeve would have more questions, and I needed rest from our journey. We had been on the road many days." Augustin felt a nervous energy run through his body. His guard had been down, and he struggled to compose the lie. Distracted, his injured leg twinged, and he hissed with a momentary pain as he reached out to steady himself on the gate. Rubbing his bruised knee with his free hand, he looked up as he heard a soft gasp from Ana. She looked at his leg through the iron bars, and the expression of startled realization stood stark and clear on her face.

A moment passed where Ana composed herself and Augustin regained his footing. As she continued to stare down at his injured leg, a feeling of weary resignation spread through Augustin's body.

"So, that's your agreement then," Ana said.

Augustin nodded, then said, "I hope you don't think less of me for it. If I had my will, I would not have—"

She held up her hand, and Augustin held his tongue. When she looked back into his eyes, her expression held no condemnation or judgment, but pity. "Trust me," she whispered, "this tells me more about the reeve's character than yours. I have lived in Titan's Folly my whole life, and even as a child I understood the plotting that goes on behind the tournament banners." She leaned in close, lowering her voice further, and Augustin bent forward to hear her.

"I had hoped to repay you for protecting me by protecting you from the reeve's judgment. It seems you'll need another sort of protection."

Ana reached forward, sliding her hand between the bars, and wrapped her fingers around Augustin's hand where it held the gate. He felt a small thrill run through his heart as the chill of the gold ornaments around her wrist and fingers traced his knuckles, a cold counterpoint to the warmth of her hand.

"I'll guard your secret. And, if things get bad, promise me you'll come to the Pipe and Lady. I have a basement room that I can keep you and your friends in for as long as you need."

"Ana," Augustin murmured. "Don't. Please, I know we're in a tight spot, but don't put yourself in danger for our sake."

"Don't you condescend to me," she scoffed. "I'll not have my hospitality turned down for pride. Like you're good enough to help me, but my help isn't good enough."

"No, I didn't mean that." Augustin fumbled his words, taken aback.

With a sardonic grin, Ana shook her head. "You meant what you said, but so did I. So swallow your pride and promise me. Promise if things get bad, you'll come to me."

Augustin looked into her eyes. Wide and luminous, they held a fiery resolve. He did not want to make that promise. It felt too much like bringing her into the conspiracy. She meant well, but if things got that bad, could he bear to have her fate on his conscience?

Augustin sighed. Keeping his voice gentle and low, he said, "Ana, no. I can't have you risking your life on my account, or for my companions. If things get bad. If we're discovered, we'll find our own way. I won't bring this down on your head too."

"You have no right," Ana replied. Her voice was far from gentle now as she narrowed her eyes. "No right to put me in your debt. To put yourself between me and a pistol, and then say that's the end of it." The moonlight caught the edge of a tear breaking free from her eye and glittered across the small path it drove along her cheek, and she took a shuddering breath before continuing. "They can't keep getting away with it. They can't keep playing their spiteful game. Using people up like powder and shot, so they can keep firing at each other. You don't live here. You're not theirs. No matter what they think. Not Alverdo. Not the Genevese. Not the reeve. If things get bad, I don't want you to die because of me. I want you to live because of me. Now," she wiped the tear from her cheek and blinked as she found his eyes, "promise me."

Augustin stood for a moment. Her words resonated in him like a song he had not heard in years. Would he demand any less, if their positions were reversed? He placed his hand over hers. "I promise," he said solemnly.

From between his hands, Augustin felt Ana squeeze his knuckles, and a look like relief and disbelief broke over her face, and he realized that she had half expected him to refuse her again. She opened her mouth to speak, then closed it again, taking a breath before she continued.

"Alright, then," Ana said. "I hope you don't take it amiss if I secretly wish things get worse for you," she pulled her hand free and stepped back with a mirthless chuckle. "I don't much care for being in other people's debt." Starting to turn, Ana paused and said over her shoulder, "And tell the reeve if you get injured, he should at least pretend he's hurting too."

Augustin watched her leave. As the icy, night air began to shiver his bones, he returned to his bed. Staring up into the stone ceiling of the room, he felt his stomach turn with indecision. He shouldn't have accepted her help. People who tried to help him got hurt. Even the Order, professional knights, thick-heeled and hardened, they got hurt. Why did anyone follow him? He wondered. Why did anyone ever feel like they owed him anything? He didn't know, and he was too tired to think on it a moment more.

CHAPTER 20

EDMOND PULLED THE HOOD further over his face, obscuring his features for the first time in a long while with cloth rather than alchemy. For this, he would have to be quiet and careful. Already, standing on the Genevese side of town, he'd learned a thing or two about the family in the northern wreck of Titan's Folly. The Genevese section was more rundown and dilapidated than the Alverdo's. The buildings were grimy, stained, splattered by the exhaust and fumes from the riphouses, where silver minerals and gold were separated from the rocks the miners carted in. Brown sludge that stank like a sewer poured down in rivulets along the sides of the road, and everywhere Edmond looked, he glimpsed shadowy forms standing in alleys, or, through windows, carousing the various pleasure establishments. Despite the late hour, it felt like this section of the city was awake with a lively energy. He could hear the clink of glasses, the raucous laughter, and the sound of at least two fistfights, and that was just this corner.

Still, pulling his hood closer over his face, Edmond sidled up the alley that led to the fighter's barracks. He had discovered the location of the baron's tournament sponsors from the baroness. More than anything, especially following his defeat for the last four years, the baron wanted a victory. Rumors had it that he had even gone into debt to secure the sponsorship for some of these knights. Even a bladesman as powerful, swift and trained as Augustin wouldn't be able to match six of the baron's picked men.

The barracks was in a short squat building against the hull of the stern of the tatterdemalion Titan. The enormous shadow of the gigantic ship swallowed the small building, encapsulating it in a dark embrace. Flickering lights from torches and candles glowed from inside the barracks, illuminating the street and the walls of the soot stained buildings outside.

"Hey!" shouted a voice.

Edmond stiffened, glancing sharply over his shoulder towards the mouth of the alley.

A silhouette cut dark against the night, but his back was to Edmond, and it seemed as if he'd been simply traveling across the alley towards one of the buildings on the other side. He was waving at a man standing by a glass window and two spinning doors. "Wait for me!" the silhouette cried, emitting a burbling laugh. "First round's on me!"

The second man called back something indeterminable and slurred, slumping against a wall and banging his head accidentally. Edmond supposed he had probably already had his first, second and fifth rounds.

But the more chaos in the streets, the louder the town was, the better for his endeavor.

Pulling a key from his pocket, Edmond eyed the barrack door.

Alright, Rodergo. Don't let me down. The key clicked in the lock after a couple of tries, the sound bringing with it a sense of relief washing over Edmond. As he pushed his way through the door into a dark, descending corridor, he made a mental note to thank the hellcatcher the next time he went to visit the baroness. Adjoining the corridor, a staircase leading up was placed in the far side of a vacant hall, but Edmond ignored this. He wasn't interested in the knights themselves, whose quarters were upstairs. Rather, he was interested in the armory and the kitchens. Both of these, he had learned from Rodergo, were downstairs. Though that had been the extent of the baroness' brother's information. If they were guarded, or how many men watched the place, was entirely a matter of chance.

Edmond hoped that behind a locked door and a barracks filled with tournament knights, no one would have seen fit to also include guards. He hoped that after the day's combat, the knights would be carousing and drinking and whoring away.

"Oh, I hope they're whoring," he murmured quietly to himself. It wasn't a sentence he was all too accustomed to saying, but it certainly wasn't the first time it had left his lips. Still slinking along, Edmond patted the two vials he'd prepared in his pockets. Mira had been more than helpful in concocting the creations, and had even added a couple of ingredients to spice them up.

"Their bowels will feel like fire," she had said chuckling delightedly before adding slivers of wormwood. Kurga's boys had picked it up from one of the local apothecaries, and it had cost them a pretty penny. Edmond tried not to think of his still dwindling supply of gold and d'oro.

Glancing down at his left pocket and then his right, Edmond made a mental note of which potion was in which pocket. It was absolutely crucial he didn't mix them up. If he did... Edmond shuddered, separating the thought from his mind with a shake of his head, refusing to contemplate it. It was simply better for all involved that he didn't make that mistake.

Carefully, with one padded foot in front of the other, he made his way down the stone stairs, slipping his sole along the lip of the stair so that he made as little sound as possible. His hand reached out, fingertips brushing the wall, tracing the cracks and crevices in the cobweb covered stone as he moved into the lower part of the building.

"Hello?" he said quietly. "Is anyone there?"

No answers were forthcoming. He reached the bottom of the stairs and found another hall stretching before him, this one separating into two atriums on the left and the right, as hemispheres. From the open hemisphere areas, one slightly staggered in front of the other, Edmond could hear voices through doorways. If one were looking from above, this whole section might have appeared to be an ornate cross—one of the symbols of the Betrayed Mother. Edmond shuffled forward, hesitantly. He glanced left and then right, sliding along the wall, keeping his movements as quiet as possible and trying to control his breathing. He supposed he would find the armory first. By the sounds and smell of things, the voices were coming from the kitchen. He would have to tend to the food later.

He stepped into the first atrium and then moved through the door, but found that it was shut. He tried it, using the key that Rodergo had given him, but to no avail. The door remained resolute. *"Dammit,"* he murmured quietly, glancing back over his shoulder. The hallway remained empty. He glanced back at the sealed, metal door. It took Edmond far longer than he would ever admit, and the fact of it would never reach Mira's ears, but after several seconds of careful prodding, he recognized the push door for what it was: a pull door. In his surprise and embarrassment he nearly missed another key bit of information as the door swung open, brushing against him and bumping gently to a halt against the leather of his boot.

It had already been unlocked.

Edmond glanced at the lock and frowned, noticing scrape marks around the keyhole.

This time, he didn't probe into the darkness of the armory with his voice. Instead, hand to the dagger in his belt, he stepped into the room, facing whatever lay in store.

He spotted no one.

But, perhaps that was due to the shelves of armor, racks of weapons, and cumbersome grinding stones. The expansive room stretched far beyond him into shadowy, gloomy corners, illuminated only by the torchlight through the door and moonlight through a window high in the wall; the narrow window bars rose ankle-height to the street outside.

So far, the hellcatcher's advice had proven correct. This clearly was where the knights kept their armaments. Six of them were staying here, as far as he'd been told, four of them would be in the sortie with Augustin. He didn't know what set of armor belonged to which knight, but all six sets were glinting dully from wood mannequins set around the room. *Just have to treat each of them,* Edmond thought as he stepped further into the room. He pulled up sharp.

One of the suits of armor had been pulled off the mannequin and lay in its various pieces on the floor. The person who had pulled it off, however, was also on the floor, crouched over the armor and muttering quietly to himself as he used one hand to fiddle with the joint of a pauldron, and used the other to take swigs from a green bottle of dark liquid.

Edmond winced as a second later he caught a whiff of the strong stuff from the bottle. It smelled like cleaning fluid.

"Lookin' for trouble they are—those fish-tongued-ass-scratchin'-whoresons," the man muttered to himself. "Don't know whose mead they're pissing in, the pole-headed-nonces. Think they can tip the scales on Gus, eh?" He paused to take a swig, smacking his lips with a sigh of satisfaction. "Have to come through ol' Vicente. They want to tip scales, we'll tips scales. Tip 'em right on their heads. Ol' Vicente will make sure they do."

Edmond stared astonished at the shifting dreadlocks of the man he recognized as Augustin's demon-eyed companion. The old knight hadn't yet noticed Edmond. In his right hand he had a knife, which he delicately slid across leather straps or pried between rivets in the armor. As Edmond stared agog, he watched the man jam pieces of twisting metal into joints so that the plate wouldn't move properly. All the while, as he did so, he suckled from his bottle and chuckled delightedly to himself, almost as if holding a conversation with his own head.

"'Course, of course," he said, "wouldn't dream of. Well—no. Dreams often enough, don't you? Dreams for the two of us. Dreams of the dreadful sort. But Vicente would never" a swallow, "—ah, that's the bleeding stuff." Another chuckle emitted from the gloom, spreading out from the hunched form of the man and claiming the room like frigid air.

Edmond stared at Vicente's back, trying to make sense of it. At last, he cleared his throat.

Vicente whipped around, faster than Edmond would've thought possible, the knife in his hand already leaving before Edmond could cry out a warning. The knife spun through the air, cutting a whistling path to Edmond's chest. It struck the vial hanging at his throat with a sharp sound of ringing metal. Edmond cursed, his hand fluttered up, testing to make sure the bottle hadn't shattered. His fingers felt the smooth surface of the reinforced glass, and he let out a murmur of relief. The contents of this bottle were far more precious to him than his own throat had ever been.

He stared as the knife clattered to the ground, and then whipped his eyes back up to Vicente. "Are you a maniac!" he whispered fiercely.

Vicente eyed Edmond with a similar expression. Then, faster than Edmond had reached the conclusion, the drunken knight chuckled, he gave a little twiddling wave with his right hand. "Blue fire and black fish, but you have Tempa's own luck," he said nodding towards the knife at Edmond's feet. "Mind giving it back to me. More work to do."

"I'm not fucking going to give it back to you. You just tried to kill me!"

214

"Trust me. If ol' Vicente were tryin' to kill yeh. You'd be dead. You just startled me's all. Didn't kill you."

"No, and that's why we'll keep the knife right here where you can't use it."

Vicente frowned, nodded once, then pulled another knife out of his boot and began sawing at the armor between his feet again.

Hesitantly, Edmond approached, testing the darkness with quiet mutterings of his own. "What are you doing," Edmond said at last.

"Thought it would be obvious, my ol, sharp-cheekboned-sharp-assed reeve-of-a-bitch."

"It looks like you're tampering with the armor."

Vicente tapped the knife to his nose and nodded once, "Clever man, my reeve."

"*Clever*, not exactly, that's Mira's job."

"Mira, who is that? Or is it a what? Or a how?"

Edmond coughed into his hands and shook his head. "Just someone I used to know, don't worry about it. You know, it's against the law to tamper with the tournament. Penalty of death."

"Aren't we a little past that, yer reevey-ness? We get found out, you get found out. You get found out, we get found out. I seem to remember you giving a very dramatic speech about the whole affair. I know I was touched. So why are you down here with ol' Vicente?"

Edmond looked around the room, unsure how much to tell the old knight; unsure how much the loon might already know. "I'm spying. Getting the scope of the competition. Sizing them up," he said.

Vicente chuckled and tapped the knife against his forehead with a knowing grin. "No, you're not. You're here for the same reason ol' Vicente is, aren't you? Interested in spreading a little mayhem. Causing a little trouble." He made a kissing sound. "The seasonings of life. I know the way of it."

"I'm here to make sure that an injustice is righted."

"The injustice being they set the man you're cheating with, against other men by cheating?"

Edmond hesitated, trying to track exactly what the old knight had said, but he found himself distracted, eyeing the yellow band in the man's face which began to shift and twirl and swivel. Vicente frowned suddenly. "Old Scratch keeps growlin' whenever you're around," he said. "Won't tell me why. Almost as if it recognizes you."

"Well I have a very recognizable face," said Edmond, shifting nervously.

Vicente stared at him for what felt like an extraordinarily long time. Then, with a shrug, he mumbled, "Or maybe he just doesn't like you."

Edmond managed a small grin. He remembered how the oculomancer had tracked him down in an alley behind a Kindly Roost the previous year. He had gotten word since then that the Signerde fighter who worked there had been murdered, tortured to death. He didn't know if Augustin's order of knights had anything to do with it, but judging by the number of knives this man carried on him, he wouldn't put it past them. The thought drove a surge of anger up through his stomach, but only briefly before he quelled it.

No, he decided, he didn't think these men were the sorts to torture another to death, not even a Signerde. But, these were also not men to be trifled with. And that was exactly what Edmond had been doing up to this point, *trifling*. Everyone from the giant Dumasian to the new lad in the shiny armor and the doctor with the shaved head, not to mention Augustin—Edmond had found it amusing to use them for his own ends. But, watching Vicente now, he realized there was a bit more to this order than he'd initially anticipated. The sort of man that would sneak into a barracks and sabotage the armaments of another party's knights was also the sort of man to be feared. These were dangerous people, and Edmond couldn't forget it again.

He nodded in acquiescence towards Vicente. "You've done a decent job on this one," he nodded towards the armor, "but I have some things that might move this along a bit quicker."

"The same sorts of things that stop throwing knives from cutting you a new smile? Not alchemy is it?" Vicente eyed him shrewdly, his yellow band swirling in his pupil.

Edmond hesitated, and then nodded once. "How did you know?"

"There aren't many things that can beat a sharp blade."

"Well, I had a friend make this for me." He patted his pocket.

"You're no alchemist yourself then?" Vicente asked.

Edmond frowned. "You ask a lot of questions."

Vicente shrugged and slowly got to his feet, kicking a gauntlet into a loose greave with a dull clang. "I didn't know you were an alchemist is all. Usually its common knowledge a reeve can brew."

"I can't brew. And I'm not an alchemist. A friend made the potion for me."

"You said that, but I can't help but notice you didn't mention what friend. Not your father, is it?"

"My father?"

"Yes; lives in a big ol' coastal home. All sorts of interesting things in the backyard..." At this, Vicente fixed Edmond with a piercing gaze.

But Edmond just frowned, shaking his head. He didn't know anything about a backyard. "You heard that did you?"

Vicente stared across the dark room at Edmond, their eyes locking, illuminated only by the torchlight flickering through the cracked doorway, and a moon beam pouring through the slatted window.

"Is there something I can do for you friend?" Edmond said slowly.

"Well, Reeve Navara, I don't think so. Clever that, what you tricked Augustin into. Making him take your place in the tournament and all; a bold move."

Edmond shrugged. "Mistakes happen."

Vicente cackled delightedly, slapping a hand against his leg and moving animatedly in a slight circle almost as if he were dancing a jig. "Mistakes happen," he said with another laugh. "Suppose it's the same mistake that allowed you to creep into a barracks, at night, with a bulge in that pocket of yours too big to be your pasty-half-erect-noble-cock. That's where you're keeping the corrosive stuff, at least, that's what I'm guessing, yes? The first note of a sonnet, two dashes of rock salt... Is that about the sum of it?"

Edmond half moved to correct Vicente. There was no rock salt in the potion, but then, he hesitated. Eyeing the shrewd man. "I don't really know what goes into it. Like I said, I'm no alchemist. But you sound as if you might be."

Vicente tapped his yellow eye, "I knew one once, and dabbled meself years ago. Serenia was..." he grinned wickedly. "Dangerous. You don't get these eyes for free. But you, you didn't pick up nothin'? No knowledge of ingredients from that friend o' yourn?"

"It's very hard to keep track of everything one knows, especially when you're the newly appointed reeve of a feuding town... Is that an imp then? Trapped in your head?"

"Not a bloody imp," Vicente snapped, glaring now. "Think I'd trap an imp in my skull? Imps take on the likeness of one's appearance. Play some tricks, cuss out yer father and get you a whoopin'. Pranks. No, nothin' like ol' Scratch. Can't do alchemy no more. At least not much. Would risk letting the thing out. It would kill me if it escaped. Kill a lot of other people too on its way out. Some say demon blood would make it smoother, but I manage enough with my own drinks and draughts."

219

Edmond held up his hands in mock surrender. "I wouldn't know—like I said, I'm no alchemist, just an appointed reeve.

"Strange appointment though," said Vicente. "Interesting you took the job. You were the wealthy son of a rich noble on the coast. And yet, for some reason you decided to travel two hundred miles south into the middle of nowhere. Taking a position where the mortality rate is higher than that of even *your* coastal friends."

Edmond stiffened. "What do you know of my friends?"

Vicente was now eyeing the knife, tossing and catching it again, chortling delightedly as it flashed in the moonlight. "Oh," he said, "nothing much. Just rumors is all. I hear a cart of them end up dead though." His gaze flipped up, piercing Edmond in the dark, and pinning him to the shadows. "Especially the female sort." He glanced at Edmond's fingers. "I used to hear you had a collection of rings. What became of those?"

Edmond did not like the direction this conversation was going. He glared at Vicente, then tried to amend the expression into a look of surprise and uncertainty. "I don't know what you're talking about," he said. "It's true, I have lost some friends, but who hasn't during these hard times. What with the pox, pirate raids on the coast, and accidents."

"Oh, aye, accidents of course." Vicente nodded, wagging his head up and down in theatrical agreement.

"Like I said, is there something I can do for you?"

Vicente flashed a smile, revealing rum-stained teeth. "No," he said simply. "Vicente doesn't require favors. It's what Vicente can do for *you*. What Vicente can do for Augustin. Always what can *Vicente* do!"

"Sounds like maybe your boss doesn't treat you well. Maybe you should seek different employment."

"You offering me a job then?"

Edmond shrugged. "Are you dependable? I pay my men well. You can ask them."

"What a funny little thought. Delightful, delightful, delightful. But, alas, I'm stuck to stay with the Order of the Lily. Through thick or thin; been through too much blood and seen too much death to not stand with the boys." His expression softened somewhat. "And Catali."

"If that's the case, do you have more boring questions, or can we get on with it? The man might be fighting for me, but he's your friend. Unless you want Augustin to be trounced by six men wielding swords, perhaps you should stop nattering and help me with the rest of this armor."

Vicente chuckled again, and shifted his weight in a sort of dance from foot to foot. "Aye, aye we could do that." Though, his eyes narrowed. "I have to suspect that perhaps there's more in it, to you, than just some title. I would never say it of a man, but you seem up to something Reeve Navara."

"Anything I'm up to, you're a part of now, as are your *friends*. And your Catali." Vicente stiffened. "Best be careful about who you say those sorts of things too, aye?"

Vicente gave a slight shake of his head, and rubbed his shoulders. "Gives me the chills that, almost like you weren't the same person—someone lurking behind that face of yours, someone wanting to come out, but can't."

"That's the rum talking," Edmond muttered.

Vicente took another long swig, then raised his hands in mock surrender, and turned back to the armor. He said nothing further and continued whistling as he sawed at the leather and poked at the metal. Edmond, frowning at Vicente's back, eyed the man's skull. For the faintest moment, he felt the surging desire to stab the blade home, burying it in the old knight's back. This man was a threat. A threat to Edmond's plans. A threat to Edmond's wife... He *needed* her back. This was all taking too long.

River's Gift... All rivers meet again... Edmond swallowed back his burning temper and closed his eyes, shaking off the mood. He shook his head and kicked the knife away into the shadows, watching it clatter beneath a shelf. He wasn't a murderer. Killing Navara—a serial killer was one thing, and even that had twisted his stomach leading up to it. But, to kill a knight while his back was turned? No. Edmond refused to traverse that path. That's not who his wife would want to return to... *But first she has to return...* Edmond clenched his teeth as if gritting against a chill.

Whatever this man suspected, or thought of him, Edmond didn't care. By the sound of things he knew a thing or two more about Matimeo than Edmond was comfortable with. But, soon enough, he would change his face again. He just needed to last longer. The tournament would be over within the week. By then, Edmond would have what he wanted. And he would leave this cursed town, and this cursed face far, far behind him.

With that thought echoing in his mind, he picked out a small vial from his right pocket and approached the next suit of armor. With Vicente still whistling, twittering in the background, Edmond went to work, dabbing corrosive potion on the weakest parts of the armor. The second potion bulged in his pocket as he worked—he would have to stop by the kitchens on the way out. If this didn't save Augustin, nothing would. The rest was up to the swordsman.

CHAPTER 21

STARING ACROSS THE TOURNEY field, Augustin waited for the other team to arrive. The crowd buzzed with an agitated energy at the delay, and as he gazed up to check the sun, Augustin saw the bent figure of Baron Genevese in his box, his long beard whipping back and forth as he frothed and shouted at the younger men around him. Whatever caused the delay, it seemed to enrage the Bull.

"M'lord reeve?" The hesitant voice, light with youth, came from a line of five men on Augustin's left. Each wore a shoddy assemblage of mismatched plate armor so dingy that it seemed to swallow the sunlight. Each held a round shield, and all but two held blunted arming swords, while the others held warhammers with steel heads the size of a closed fist.

"Yes, Migo?" Augustin replied after struggling for a moment to remember the man's name.

Migo pointed to the empty space on the opposite end of the field. "How long are we meant to wait? The trumpet sounded three times and I'm sure at least half the hour has gone by. Aren't they disqualified?"

"No."

"But then how long are we meant to wait? Surely there's a limit."

If there was, the reeve had not seen fit to tell him, and Augustin hoped one of the other members of the team would jump in to answer the youth's question. Augustin tried to say as little as possible. He doubted any of these men had met the reeve before, but he didn't want to leave anything to chance. He fiddled with the blunted longsword in his hand, giving it a few practice swings.

"Patience," he said when it became clear no one else would answer for him. He stepped away from Migo as if the matter were settled.

They had been waiting, but in reality, Augustin would have been surprised if more than ten minutes had passed since the third trumpet. He couldn't blame the man for his anxiety. The young man had been jittery and had paced the line ever since the first trumpet's blast. If he had to guess, Augustin would have bet money that it was his first time at tournament, and he was probably nervous to be paired with even a minor noble like the reeve.

Looking back over his shoulder, Augustin held up a questioning hand to Cristobal. The big man shook his head from the edge of the field, then bent to say something to Catali. She nodded and Cristobal turned and ran into the cluster of tents and pavilions at the field's edge. Tristan and Vicente exchanged a few words that Augustin could not hear but assumed must have been some joke from the way Vicente grinned and Tristan looked down, flushed with embarrassment.

Maybe they would get lucky. A part of him balked at the idea of being put through by the other team's disqualification, but his leg still ached, and if he got lucky enough to have another day of rest for it, he would take it.

A flurry of commotion drew his attention to the herald's stand on the edge of the field. The same pale skinned man from the day before threw the drooping tail of his silk head wrap over his shoulder as he rushed out from the tournament committee and took the platform.

"Good people of Titan's Folly," he shouted, bringing a hush over the crowd. "Sad news comes to us this day." A murmur of concern rolled through the audience, and the herald waited a moment for the swell to pass. "The sponsored warriors of the Genevese have fallen ill. Unable to rise from their beds, this noble band of six is reduced to three." The herald lifted three fingers, showing them around the crowd like a magician beginning a trick.

Augustin heard Migo and the other men of his line chuckle and turn to each other with softly voiced comments of relief. Augustin himself let out a slow breath. He couldn't help, but be relieved as well. With half the men sick, they would have to call the bout. Delay the match, or disqualify the hindered team.

"However," the herald's strong voice continued. "The gods smile down on us, for as three have fallen ill, three have swiftly volunteered to take up their places. Let your voices be heard for their selfless intercession."

The herald waved to the empty end of the field, and the crowd cheered with wild enthusiasm as six men stepped into view. Augustin could hardly believe his eyes. Three of the men were so broad across the shoulder that they could have seated an ox collar. Their armor, like his own team's, was unmarked, but unlike his teams, it looked polished and well-made. They held no shields, but instead one carried a two handed halberd on a wooden haft that stood six feet tall, another leaned a large, blunted mace on his shoulder, while the third held a two-handed greatsword. Behind them, three more men, each nearly as large as Cristobal and bearing enormous drooping battleaxes, stalked forward. Augustin's breath caught as he saw they each wore a black tabard with the Genevese serpent.

From her box, the baroness Alverdo, swept to her feet. "What is this nonsense, Niko! No combatant may name a second. And to blatantly use three of your own men?" she cried across the rumbling crowd.

The Bull gripped the edge of his own box, his mouth hanging open in a scarecrow smile. "My dear baroness, I assure you I had nothing to do with this. My noble knights saw the need and volunteered of their own accord. Is this not so?"

"It is, my lord baron." The three Genevese knights replied in unison.

Holding his hands up in a gesture of resignation, the Bull's grin split even further. "Who am I to deny such noble action? Would you deny your own warriors the chance to prove their valor? Would you deny the people this combat?" His voice rose louder than Augustin would have guessed possible for the old man, and as he mentioned 'the people' the crowd raised their fists in an uproar.

Within moments the commotion took shape and out of the rolling cheers came a rhythmic chant of 'Let them fight! Let them fight!' The baroness' expression soured, and her eyes narrowed, but Augustin guessed even she knew better than to fly in the face of an excited mob. Smoothing her expression, the baroness smiled down on the crowd like a grandmother doting on her grandchildren with some sweet-treat.

"Very well then, Niko. I grant my permission for your knights to take up the honor of the sick men who could not fight. I am confident in the valor of our reeve." She turned a smile as soft as broken glass towards Augustin, and he could feel the edge behind it. He nodded to the baroness and raised his blunted longsword, hoping there wasn't some secret message in her words intended for the reeve. The crowd roared in response to his gesture, and he watched as the other team lined up across the field.

Turning to the helter-skelter grouping of his own team, he called out with the clear clip of command. "Form a line." The men stared for a moment, then Migo stepped in beside him. As he did, the others begrudgingly fell into formation. It wasn't much, but it would have to do. Tightening his grip on the longsword, Augustin waited for the herald's call.

"Sponsored of the Genevese, are you ready?"

Each man across the field raised their weapon in response.

"Sponsored of the Alverdo, are you ready?"

Augustin raised his longsword again. A burst of laughter went up from the crowd and Augustin glanced to his left.

"Migo," he growled.

The younger man's helmeted head twitched towards him.

"Raise your hammer," Augustin said.

"Oh, right." Migo lifted his hammer over his shield. Another fit of laughter went up from the crowd before the herald raised his hands for silence.

A breathless moment passed, and the herald shouted, "Lay on!"

A cry went up from the Genevese line as they rushed forward. Dust churned under their feet, and the sun sparked off their weapons in a flitting dance. To Augustin's left, the men of his line let out a cry, and he swiftly cut his longsword out in their direction. The flat of the blade fell across the nearest men and they turned to face him, the furthest man taking a few halting steps before realizing no one had charged forward with him.

"Do not charge until I say," Augustin barked, pulling back his longsword. The men stared at each other then stepped back into position, casting uneasy glances to their reeve.

"If the Genevese want to wear themselves out dashing across the whole damned field, let them. We charge when we're ready." Augustin hoped the excitement of the match would distract them from his voice. If they had any hope of winning this, they would have to fight smart, and he couldn't afford to stay quiet any longer. "As we charge, keep pace with each other. You have shields. They don't. Stay close and use each other's shields for protection. Strike only when you have an opening. They'll try to batter your shields away. Don't let them."

He had more that he wanted to say, but no more time to say it. The Genevese line had crossed more than half the distance to them and would be on them in a moment. It was time.

"Make ready... Charge!" Augustin shouted. He dashed forward, keeping his longsword back and ready for his opening strike. The others followed him, keeping their shaky line together.

As they crashed together, the clamor of the crowd disappeared under the crunching of steel as the arms and armor of the two lines scraped together. A rapid-fire chunking erupted from the line of shields as the blunted weapons rebounded off of their metal rims.

From his place at the right extreme of his line, Augustin's longsword swept in to meet the armored warrior wielding the greatsword. The greatsword's heft gave it the advantage on reach, and its heavier blade would hit like a hammer if it could make contact, but Augustin's own longsword had one advantage. Speed. As the greatsword moved to intercept his slash, Augustin levered his blade, arcing it over the greatsword's guard and crashing into the bigger man's helmet. Staggered, the greatsword lifted his blade to fend off any other attacks and stepped backward—out of line.

With his ally out of position, the Genevese with the large mace now stood with his side completely exposed. Too sluggish to respond, Augustin leapt forward and landed three succinct blows across the mace's legs and ribs. To his surprise, the mace wielder's cuisse fell from his thigh, clanging to the ground and leaving the quilted padding beneath exposed. Migo's warhammer fell into the gap, with a crack like a snapping branch, and the mace tumbled back from the onslaught, falling into the man beside him with a scream that cut through the cacophony. It had worked. The Genevese line

230

fell into disarray, and Augustin urged Migo to turn his attack down the line. Their last blow had broken the mace's thigh bone, and Augustin had seen enough battles to know the man would either pass out from his pain or be too bound up in it to do anything but scream. He also knew the man would likely never walk again, but he pushed this thought aside. Unless he wanted the same, he had to stay focused.

As Migo pressed the attack against the four remaining men in the Genevese line, Augustin turned his attention back to the greatsword. The warrior had recovered, and taken the opportunity to shift around Augustin's side. They faced each other perpendicular to the two striving lines, and in that moment Augustin rushed the man. If they were akimbo to the main fight, he would rather turn it into a duel than risk tangling up his allies. Five to four, he hoped his men could hold the line for at least the moment.

The greatsword let out a series of broad sweeping cuts, and Augustin ducked and slid around them as best he could. A heavy downward slash came for his head and forced him to parry. He felt the flat of his longsword driven down against his pauldron before the greatsword's blade scraped clear of him. Augustin tried to angle his attacks around the heavy steel, but the greatsword had found his rhythm and now the large two-hander moved at speed. Augustin desperately interposed his longsword, narrowly deflecting blow after blow, but each strike slammed his blunted blade against his armor and sent shockwaves through him as if he were an anvil and the greatsword was a blacksmith's hammer.

Come on, give me an opening. Augustin gritted his teeth, but the warrior's attacks were relentless. *I can't just stand here,* he thought. *He's going to batter me to pieces unless I counter-attack.* At that moment, as though one of the gods had heard his words, the greatsword abruptly stopped. The man stepped back, and for a moment his helmed head stared down at the greatsword in his hands as if he didn't know what it was.

Augustin did not wait to analyze the moment. He leapt forward, craning his longsword in a cascade of arcs across the greatsword's body. Now the greatsword fought on the defensive. A few of Augustin's blows managed to break through and the blunted steel rang on the knight's arms and thighs. One of the man's pauldrons sloughed off his shoulder, and Augustin focused his attacks on the exposed padding beneath, forcing his opponent to shield himself with his weapon. As Augustin rained blows down on the greatsword's guard, the sound of the clashing blades felt wrong in his ears. Some discordant tone rang from the song of steel that he knew so well. The greatsword raised his blade again to block Augustin's attack, and all-at-once, the blade's hilt fell loose from its crossguard. Pommel, blade, and crossguard fell to the dirt at once, leaving the Genevese warrior holding the wooden handle of his sword and nothing else. Augustin's longsword swept through the open air where the greatsword had been and rang his helmet like a bell. The man staggered and fell to the ground, clutching his head. As Augustin rushed over him, he held up his hands, gesturing quickly as he shouted, "I yield! I yield!"

Augustin watched him as the man left his broken sword on the field and retreated to the edge of the arena. He looked down at the discarded pieces, confusion tugging the edge of his mind, but with the gravity of a soldier, he turned away to rejoin his line.

As he rushed back, his stomach fell. Three of his men huddled behind their battered shields in a tight circle. The other two lay unconscious on the ground. Around the shield circle, the Genevese knights coordinated a thrashing assault with their axes, and even with blunted edges, Augustin saw the rims of his men's shields bent and splintered under the furious attack. Beyond this, the halberd arced his polearm over the shields, dropping the heavy steel across the men's shoulders and helmets. Since the axemen had tried to encircle his men, one of them had their back to him. With no war-cry to draw attention, Augustin rushed toward the Genevese axeman. He stepped within three paces of the man when the halberd whirled to intercept him.

Augustin drew up short as the steel-bladed polearm dropped between him and the axeman. The man knew his craft as he drew back the metal head and lashed out at Augustin with a vicious spear-like thrust. If the weapon had not been blunted for the tournament, Augustin would have had a spike as long as his forearm thrust into his chestplate. As it was, a blunted nub knocked the wind out of him and knocked him onto his back. Starbursts rose in his eyes as he coughed and gasped. He saw a vague flicker of darkness cross the sunlight overhead and rolled to the side as the steel head of the halberd slammed into the ground where he had been. He continued to roll, twisting his hip to put himself up on one knee, his longsword angled into a hanging guard. Once again, his instincts spared him as the halberd collided with his guard and drove him back to the ground. The halberdier pressed him with another series of thrusts, and from his back, Augustin desperately parried the heavy polearm. One blow slammed into his shoulder, another into his side. He could feel the welts and bruising beginning to blossom as his aching muscles fought to maintain his grip on his longsword.

"Why won't you just die!" the halberdier grunted as he drew up his polearm for a downward thrust. A shadow appeared behind him, and with the ringing of metal, the halberdier dropped the heavy weapon and fell to the ground senseless.

Blinking up into the light, Augustin saw Migo with his warhammer, his body turned from the swing, standing where the halberdier had been.

"Get up, m'lord reeve. We have to—" The young man didn't finish his statement. From behind him, two battleaxes rang concurrent blows against the back of his helm and the base of his spine. He let out one stifled sound, like someone talking in their sleep, then fell to the ground.

Rushing to his feet, Augustin saw at once what had happened. When Migo had fled the line to help him, the Genevese axemen had swiftly overwhelmed the remaining two men. They likewise lay unconscious now. Once they were taken care of, the axemen had no difficulty in coming up behind Migo.

Augustin's hot breath echoed inside his helmet. His sweat had soaked the linen coif around his neck, and stung the corners of his eyes. In front of him, the three Genevese knights casually stepped into a semi-circle. They turned their heavy battleaxes with seeming indifference. Three to one. Augustin swallowed and fought down the small voice in him that told him he had no chance. True or not, that thought did him no good. Not now. He didn't have the luxury of losing. He had to win, the only trick would be figuring out how.

He tensed, looking across the encroaching line of axemen. They were spreading out to encircle him, just as they had done to his teammates. If they did, he knew he was finished. His eyes flicked inside his visor. A plan beginning to form. He gave the axemen a few more moments, letting them spread.

Almost, he thought. His legs tensed. He would only have one chance. If he failed, they would swarm him, and he couldn't allow that. The axeman in front of him tilted his head, as if looking to the other two that had spread around him.

Now! Augustin twisted on his heel, dashing for the axeman to his left, swinging his longsword in a one handed swipe that gave him extra reach. The axeman seemed surprised by the sudden attack, and threw his weapon up to catch the slash. Augustin had not truly expected to hit the man, even if he did, it wouldn't have been a dangerous blow, but just as he hoped, the axeman's instinct to protect himself drew up his weapon, and it gave Augustin just enough time to break free of the circle.

Now, on the outside, Augustin launched an attack of his own, throwing himself against the axeman like a wild dog. He wasted no energy on defending himself. He had the faster weapon. As soon as he went on the defensive, they would surround him again, and this time there would be no breaking out.

The other two axemen quickly dashed in to support their ally, but Augustin focused his attacks solely on the one he had already engaged; only throwing a sporadic slice towards the other two to keep them on their guard. Glancing blows from the axes danced off his plate as he maneuvered to keep all three of the axemen in front of him, always in front of him. Herding them like sheep, he sliced for their legs and shoulders when they wandered, but returned to the center. His arms burned. Sweat poured from his body, but he fought on.

A beautiful shock of ringing metal sprang from the lead axeman's helmet. Augustin's cut had caught him dead center, and as he fell Augustin saw a dramatic trough of bent mental collapsed across the crown of the helmet. The man fell silently to the ground, and Augustin paid him no further mind, driving his attacks on to the next axeman.

His vision flashed red as Augustin felt the shock of a blow to his own helmet. He lost his sense of the ground as the glancing blow sent his senses reeling, and with only his training to guide his arms, he executed a swift counter stroke. He felt the shock of impact rocket through his arms and up into his shoulder, then swung for the other axeman. His longsword fell through empty air, and a moment of panic gripped him. Deaf from his heaving lungs, his arms trembling with strain, Augustin stepped back, throwing up a desperate guard while his vision cleared.

At his feet lay the second axeman. The third stood three paces back, his axe held in one loose hand. With his second, he motioned his surrender.

"I yield, dammit! I yield!"

The man's shouts broke through, and Augustin managed to let out a shaky nod, lowering his sword. The roar of the crowd around the tourney field reverberated off the plateau wall and echoed in his helm. Augustin wanted nothing more than to remove the stifling metal. Instead, he looked up to the sky. He stayed that way for what felt like a long time, afraid if he moved he would collapse.

He had done it. He had survived.

As his breathing steadied, the cries of the crowd began to twist. A low booing began to roll from the Genevese side. Augustin looked around. Feeling like he had missed something important. It had been a good bout. Great even. Why were they booing?

He looked up to the Genevese box. The Bull was nowhere to be seen. When he lowered his eyes, Augustin saw the small Genevese, Ciso, on the field. His sister glared at Augustin while Ciso plucked up the fallen cuisse. He held it delicately, inspecting it like some exotic animal. He pointed and whispered to his sister, who leaned down to hear. Tiny's sister and brother were an odd coupling. Ciso Genevese was the oldest of the Baron's children, but stood no more than four feet in height. Magdela, on the other hand, stood taller than most men and was a knight herself. She had proven deadly with the enormous 150-lb pull bow on her back. Among a series of Alverdo tournament victories, five years ago Magdela had claimed one for her own family. She was also inseparable from her oldest brother, Ciso.

Magdela Genevese's face drew into a dark storm of anger as she took the cuisse. She held it up for the crowd to see, and in her bellowing voice, she shouted. "What is this farce? Cut straps? Crumbling swords?" She threw the piece of armor against the ground amid the pieces of the broken greatsword. "Is this a tournament or a fairground play?" Her call invoked outrage from both sides of the field as those on the Alverdo side called for her silence, while those on the Genevese echoed her words.

"I don't know what you're at, m'lord reeve," she spat the words, "but our tournament isn't a game." The crowd shook the tourney ground around him with their outcry. Magdela opened her mouth to say more, but her words were swallowed in the swell of the crowd.

What could he do? What could he say? If he stood now to proclaim he had no idea why the armor or the sword had fallen apart, surely someone would know he wasn't the real reeve. How could he defend himself without giving away even more?

The wooden fence encircling the tourney field shook and swayed as the violent energy in the crowd pressed forward. If no one did anything, they would have a riot on their hands. Augustin turned and looked to the baroness. Her glowering eyes did not meet him, and when Augustin followed her gaze, he saw that the baron's box was empty. Ciso and Magdela were down here, but where was Tiny or the Bull?

Augustin turned and strode towards the field's edge. He did not look back, but kept his eyes locked on his companions. Catali, Vicente, and Tristan were looking around him anxiously, but Augustin kept his gait smooth and confident. He hoped he aired the manner of a man refusing to dignify such outrageous accusations. He thought momentarily about the gigantic bow on Magdela's back. She wouldn't shoot him in the back. Would she? It was difficult to tell in this damned town. All around him the chaos and the noise grew and grew.

As he stepped off of the field and between the tents and pavilions, Tristan leaned close, pressing his back as he said into his helmet, "Get in the tent, now. We have a problem."

A pistol shot blasted from the edge of the field, and the crowd grew silent.

He wanted to turn and look, but Catali and Tristan urged him forward, pushing him into the tent. Reeve Matimeo sat there, his foot tapping nervously. He avoided Augustin's eyes, instead looking to Tristan.

"Get him out of his armor. Fast," the reeve said.

As the flap fell behind him and his companions rushed to comply with the reeve's command, Augustin managed to catch a glimpse out onto the field. The Bull had joined his children on the dusty grounds along with several more of his guard. Between them all knelt a bruised and bloodied figure.

"No," Augustin gasped. On his knees, slumped Cristobal. Augustin tried to move for the tent flap, but Tristan grabbed his shoulders to hold him back.

"Nothing you can do. It's on the reeve, now," he said as he yanked off Augustin's gauntlets, tossing them to Matimeo. A moment passed where Augustin felt all his blood and sweat turn to ice across his body, then he snatched at the breastplate's buckles as he rushed to doff the dented armor.

CHAPTER 22

EDMOND COULD FEEL THE nervous energy radiating off of Augustin. The duelist paced beside him like a caged tiger, glaring black murder at the doorman to the inn.

"Let us in to see your mistress or I swear to Mercusi the surgeons will require new words to describe the way you are killed!" Augustin cried, his face red.

The doorman spluttered on the threshold, but stayed his ground, refusing the odd group admittance into the inn, standing resolute in the moonlight glinting from the darkening sky.

Edmond shot a sidelong glance at the once-captain, struggling to keep his expression neutral. He'd never seen the man this agitated before.

"Was bloody and beaten," Augustin muttered, tapping his fingers across his rapier's grip in time with his pacing. "Blue fire and black fish, if I had the whole Order back together, we would have sliced through the bastards like a scythe through a field!"

The tomb raider shifted uncomfortably at the exchange, doing his best to keep his body angled, so the man wouldn't see down his shirt and spot the tell-tale black vial. Mirastious had told him to keep it out of sight, but Edmond refused to let it part from him. Still, it was a close thing, especially when Augustin grabbed him by the shoulders and shook him. "You're the reeve—do something you conniving bastard! This is *your* fault!"

"That's why we're here. Getting yourselves killed back in the tournament grounds wasn't an option," Edmond said, trying to keep his voice calm.

Vicente, for his part, looked as if he had wasps in his stained pants, dancing about from foot to foot and muttering dark obscenities beneath his breath while his fingers curled around his dagger, then his pistol grips, back and forth, back and forth. The doorman to the inn kept quiet, glancing wide-eyed between the three of them though, clearly conveying a sincere desire to be anywhere but there at the moment.

"Ten of the baron's men," Augustin spat. "Dragging him away. You should have let me at them! I would have sliced them to ribbons."

Edmond shot his eyes to the heavens, trying not to sigh in impatience. "Yes," he said, "I remember you wanting to do that. Especially since you punched me when I stopped you. But do you also remember the part were the baron threatened to shoot Cristobal if we neared?"

The doorman to the inn swallowed now, swaying as if he were seasick.

"It was because of the cheating!" Augustin said, shaking his head. "I *didn't* though. Their armor just fell on its own. I had nothing to do with it—I swear!"

Behind Augustin, Vicente and Edmond shared a look. "I believe you," Edmond said, and this time it was Vicente's turn to roll his eyes. "But I don't think this had anything to do with the armor. The baron said Cristobal was spotted *robbing* an old mineshaft where they kept the remains of the titan's armaments. Two giant rotating canons and four ornithopters. Stolen! They said Cristobal was behind it!"

"Gave 'em what for, though, didn' we!" Vicente crowed, still dancing agitatedly around in tiny circles. "A slash, a bash, the ol' fuckery! Got one good right in sack, ey."

"We landed a stroke or two, aye, but I wish we didn't have to flee," Augustin said, some of the color draining from his face, his hand trembling where it rested against the hilt of his rapier. His voice pleading, he eyed Edmond. "So? Why have you brought us here, *exactly*? How is this detour going to help Cristobal?"

Edmond scratched the back of his head, adopting a quizzical expression. Inwardly, his thoughts were rampant. Just before Cristobal had been captured, Kurga and his boys had shown up to the arena grounds. Across the tents, the short bravo had caught Edmond's eye. The diminutive bravo leader had looked miserable beneath his floppy hat—as he had ever since he'd agreed to don it. But the bravos respected the contract. They were being paid for their new ensembles, and, if Edmond could count on anything, it was the bravos' loyalty to gold.

Kurga, despite looking uncomfortable and itching at his scalp every couple of seconds, had managed to snap his fingers two times, quietly, hand against his thigh. A sign of affirmation.

Edmond had inflected an eyebrow. And both of Kurga's albino sons had also nodded.

Good. Edmond had thought. *The plan worked.* It had taken him a while to learn the location of the titan's remaining guns—the ornithopters had been sheer luck. He hadn't, however, counted on Cristobal being blamed for the theft. Kurga's boys were tall—perhaps someone had seen them near the mineshaft.

But to mistake them for Cristobal?

No. The baron was using this as an excuse to settle a petty score.

"Well?" Augustin was saying, glaring at Edmond. "What now? Do something. If they lynch my friend, I'll kill you myself."

"No need for lynching nor killings," said Edmond quickly, shaking his head. "Look, the baron won't do anything immediately. Not while the tournament is in full swing. If they execute a man on mere suspicion it will be considered a breach of peace. The Genevese and Alverdos skirt, bend and sometimes flat-out subvert the peace treaty, but they *won't* break it. No one wants war."

"What does that *mean*?" Augustin snapped.

"It means... they'll likely hold a trial. Some sort of hearing. They'll have evidence, witnesses—only *then* will they kill Cristobal. Probably by hanging, but maybe a firing squad. Hard to tell with these mining folks."

"Oh, only *after* a trial will they murder my friend," said Augustin stiffly.

"Mayhaps you ain't properly motivated, ey?" A pistol suddenly appeared in Vicente's hand and pressed against Edmond's forehead. "Reeve Navara, whatever twisted past you might have—no concern to Vicente at this moment. Do reevey things to rescue the giant, or I'll drill your skull for gold."

Edmond kept his expression as calm as possible with a pistol to his skull. He inhaled momentarily, but then winced against a sour smell wafting over from Vicente. He was nearly certain the man had been wearing the same clothing for seven days now. Again, Edmond noticed the doorman turning a shade of green, his face pale. Edmond kept his eyes fixed on Vicente's—the old knight's yellow band swirling and twisting as it scanned the doorman and Edmond.

"Don't do anything rash," Edmond said through tight lips. "Obviously, I'll help your friend. That's why we're *here*. I need you in this tournament, don't I? Can't let you be distracted..."

"Or kill you," said the old knight.

Edmond swallowed. "Or that." He tried to lean back, but Vicente's arm followed, keeping the cold barrel pressed into his skin.

"*How* will you help him?" Augustin demanded.

"The baron has him, you say? Well—then he'll likely blame the baroness."

244

"So?"

"She's our sponsor! And, last time I was there, she seemed to take a liking to me."

"Find a good number of ladies likin' you, eh? Do you prick 'em then stick 'em, or the other way 'round?"

"Vicente!" Augustin snapped. "Not now."

Again, Edmond was reminded that the old knight seemed to know a thing or two about Matimeo Navara's eldritch past, but for now, Edmond's main concern was the circular indent in his forehead. He swallowed. "We have time... That's what I was getting at. They won't execute your friend until—well, at *least* this evening. The baroness is staying here," Edmond jerked his head at the inn. "If anyone knows what to do, she will!"

Edmond had wanted to visit Fort Dentemosi to check on the titan's guns and ornithopters, but he hadn't been able to extricate himself from the Order of the Lily. Now though, at this latest pronouncement, the doorman stopped quavering like a leaf in a gale, and stood his ground, back pressed against rough wood.

"No one may enter," said the guard in the clipped tone. "Not while the baroness is dining in her rooms. On strict orders we is!"

Edmond quickly stepped forward, interjecting himself between Vicente and the guard. "Understandable," said Edmond with a nod. "By any chance do you know where Fero is? Last time I spoke with *him* at the gates."

The guard frowned in confusion, giving a slight shake of his head. "Falo? What's that?"

"*Fero*. The baroness' child."

The guard wrinkled his nose, shaking his head impatiently. "There's no one by that name here. Most of the baroness' bastar—er, children stay in their rooms, except for Dante. But there is no Fero."

Now, Edmond's brow was scrunched together, and he found himself gnawing on the corner of his lip. He felt no small part of annoyance at the guard, either. Edmond knew what it was to grow up under the whispered label of 'bastard': a title designed to diminish and ostracize. There were some who said it merely as a description, with no malice intent, but the slight curve of the guard's lip hinting at a sneer, suggested he had meant it to dig. Edmond thought of how Dante had reacted to the guards' teasing at the baroness' mansion, and he knew, from his own childhood pain, but the pain hadn't lasted for ever. He had found a soothing balm... *River's Gift* she had called him. He could still smell the ocean breeze on the summer day, the cooling grains of sand pressing between their toes. She had insisted on walking barefoot, as he often had. A stray, shattered shell had nearly cut her foot. Instead, though, she had cut her palm and then his, pressing bleeding fingers together, intertwining in an unyielding grip. "*There*," she had said. "*Now you have blood relatives too.*"

She had always known what to say.

Edmond snapped out of his reverie, a frown on his face, at someone insistently tugging at his sleeve. Augustin cleared his throat emphatically, and

Edmond could hear Vicente shifting in agitation behind him. "Are you new then?" Edmond asked the guard.

The man shook his head, the arrangement of his slitted eyes and pursed lips transitioning seamlessly from impatience to outright annoyance. "Been serving at the baroness' pleasure for nearly ten years now."

"Then you're lying to me. I met Fero back at the mansion. Dante introduced him as his brother."

The man scowled though. "Careful who you call a liar," he said. "If anyone is leading you one way or another, it's the fire-mouthed bastard." Again, he said the word with intent to sting, and Edmond found his fists balling up at his sides. "There is no one by that name that lives here. All five of the baroness' children are accounted for, and none of them are called Fero."

Despite Edmond's mounting resentment, there was something about the man's anger that had the ring of authenticity to it. Edmond glanced uneasily at Vicente and Augustin, but then frowned again and returned his attention back to the doorman. "Five?" he said. "The baroness has ten children."

The doorman smirked, but then seemed to realize Edmond wasn't joking and his eyes widened in a look of surprise. "Are you off your kettle? Been huffing the tar—is that it? *Ten* children? Blue fire and briny bits—where you hearing such nonsense?"

"I don't—what are you," Edmond stammered at first, catching his breath, then blurted out, "The baroness has ten children! Everyone knows that."

The man shook his head again. "Five children. Always been that way. Dante is her oldest."

"Dante is... He's *fourteen* years old," Edmond exclaimed. "He's not the oldest. He's one of the younger ones!"

"The bastard alchemists are young'ns, that's how the baroness likes it. Easier to train—to mold. Dante is the oldest. There is no one named Fero. And there are only *five* of them! Fair enough?" The guard's cheeks were tinged red at this point, and he looked on the verge of throwing fists. "Perhaps you'd better spend more time getting to know the town you're in rather than harassing doormen doing their jobs."

Edmond fidgeted uneasily. None of this made sense. Why was the doorman lying about how many children the baroness had? Mirastious and Edmond had researched extensively, piecing together all sorts of reports that the baroness had filed with previous reeves. She had ten children. It might not have been common knowledge in the town, and it would make sense for her to keep it from the likes of the baron, or Tiny, or any of the Genevese, but a doorman who'd been in her employ for ten years? He would know. There was no doubt she'd adopted ten children. That—at the very least—was what the records had shown...

Now that Edmond thought about it though, he'd never actually *asked* the baroness, nor Dante how many siblings he had... But... Edmond could have sworn Dante had told him he wasn't the eldest child. The last adoption had been sixteen years ago, and the child's age had been listed as ten, at the time. Edmond couldn't recall the name he'd read on the form... But he knew he'd read it... His own name had once been on a form like that, framed above his mother's bed as a prized possession.

Edmond swallowed back the surge of emotion, focusing on the task at hand. Certainly, there were strange things about the baroness' children, or at least, the two Edmond had met. They had the same red hair and freckles as the baroness had. It was also unusual they lived in a mansion filled with all sorts of imbued crystals and alchemical defenses. It was equally strange that a hellcatcher in the form of Uncle Rodergo lived on the premises, keeping eye on things and watching his sister. There was something more going on here, something Edmond wasn't privy to. The guard clearly wasn't telling the truth—but the kicker seemed that he didn't *know* he wasn't telling the truth.

"If you've really been with the baroness for ten years, how come you don't know how many children she has?" Edmond said, his eyes narrowed.

"Matimeo!" said Augustin his voice harsh. "We don't have time for this. We need to hurry. Cristobal's life is on the line!"

"I know," said Edmond through gritted teeth. "But..." he waved a hand towards the doorman.

"Oh come now," Vicente snapped. "This is how they teach you to reeve where you're from? You're as useless as Tristan at an orgy." The old knight stepped forward, growled once and then slapped the doorman upside the head, sending him reeling to the side of a railing. The man shouted in alarm, nearly tumbling over the rail, and lashing out with his hands to catch himself and right his balance. Before he could retaliate, a knife appeared in Vicente's hand and pressed into the nape of the man's neck. "Now you can let us in," said Vicente. "Or I'm gonna slice you open and play with your spine."

The doorman's voice quavered as he said, "I don't know who you think you're meddling with, but the baroness will—"

He received another slap from Vicente.

"Stop doing that!" the man howled, his voice carrying into the night air.

"Then step aside, you pompous-toad-licking-ass! And don't make trouble. We're on unofficial reeve's business, or some such saying," said Vicente, with a disinterested wave of his hand.

"Oh—lookie! Hey, perv," a voice called out from the second floor window in a friendly tone. "What are you cocksuckers doing round theseaways?"

Edmond knew what he would see before his eyes whipped up. Dante sat in the window, legs dangling over the sill and arms pressed against the shutters.

The doorman glanced up, and then cursed. "What did I tell you about sitting like that! You'll fall and break your neck."

"Not that you'd care, though, huh Morga?" said Dante with a wink. "But a broken neck is bad for ambition, right?" Dante stuck his tongue out at the guard. "Haven't broken me neck yet, you magnificently syphilitic prick, and I've snuck up three times since we've been here."

The doorman growled, shooting a sidelong glance of fury in Vicente's direction, who nodded almost sympathetically. "Itches something fierce, doesn't it?" said the old knight.

"I don't have syphilis!" snapped the doorman. "Stop telling people that!"

The boy in the window gave a bemused shrug as if he didn't know what the guard was referring to. He redirected his gaze to Edmond. "Well, brought some more pervs with you? Looking to have an explosive, slippery orgy ey? Gonna braid each other's' hair after? I see one of your friends likes it rough, all grip'n steel and like."

Vicente glanced up at Dante, frowning slightly. "What are you saying about old Vicente, you wretched-piece-o-fire-headed-flotsam?"

Dante's eyes widened, and he smiled in surprised delight. In a chipper tone, he replied. "Nothing much *worth* saying, about you old-prick-suck-ling-snake-headed-ship-whiffing-ass-nuzzling-bodice-ripper."

Vicente shook his fist. "Double goes for you, you damned-knuckle-drag-ging-piss-guzzling-gargoyle!"

"I'd be impressed if you knew how to double anything. You stupid, rum-soaked, cunt-munching-glinty-eyed-lay-about!"

Edmond, Augustin and the doorman's gaze bounced between Dante and Vicente. For a moment, the gravity of their endeavor slipped their memory as they witnessed the exchange. It was much like a repellent rallying howl of two long-lost wolves of kin. But after a while, Augustin interjected himself, and asked, "Who is this foul-mouthed child?"

Edmond waved a hand. "Dante. Don't worry about him."

"Don't worry about me?" Dante frowned as if he didn't like the sound of that. He started making a sucking noise, sloshing something around in his mouth.

"If you spit on us," said Edmond with a glare, "I'm going to climb up there and pull you down myself, making sure you land on your skull. Though, perhaps your head is so full of air, you'll float."

Dante considered this for a moment, but then spat anyway. The gob of spit landed just shy of the men, and he seemed to deflate with disappointment.

"You here to see mother, perv?" Dante said before Edmond could make good on his threat.

"That's about it," said Edmond, keeping his calm. "Is she inside?"

"She's having dinner. Doesn't like to be disturbed when she's eating. She's in her room with Uncle Rodergo."

"Dante!" snapped the guard.

"What? You have a knife to your throat. You stupid ponce."

"Child!" Augustin snapped. "Mind who you speak to in that way!"

"I," Dante said slowly, like addressing a very slow child, "Was speaking to *him*." He pointed at the doorman. "I called Morga—him again—" still speaking insultingly slowly, "A *stupid* ponce. Stupid means dum-dum in the head thing," he tapped his skull with a finger. "Ponce means his wife's a whore."

The look of sheer annoyance on Augustin's face only served to boost Edmond's secret liking of the boy.

Dante waved airily at Augustin, a cheerful look still etched across his face. "You don't mind making death threats, but you have a problem with how I speak? Strange notions from the perv's friend."

Edmond glanced from Vicente's knife to Augustin's frown, and gave a sort of half nod. "He does make a good point."

Dante was now practically leaning out of the window, peering down at the men below him with a look of glee.

"Dante," said Morga, in a careful voice. "Please," the word sounded like it pained him. "Tell the others there are hoodlums out here threatening one of your mother's men."

Dante considered this for a moment, then sagged, as if exhausted. "Truly," he said, "I wish I could. But the others are all the way downstairs—ugh. The walk alone... I can't imagine. No, no, it's much better I don't tax myself so."

The man spluttered, and Vicente shook him to quiet him. "Why not?" the doorman said, a note of panic to his voice. "They're in the basement—just go!"

Dante began picking at his fingernails, and gave a sort of half shrug with one of his shoulders. "Busy," he said. "If I move, I could fall. Might break me neck. No, no, best I stay here."

The guard devolved into a series of dark expletives beneath his breath, including words like *bastard* and *son-of-a-bitch* but then his eyebrows ratcheted up, and in the tone of someone who knew they had the upper hand, he declared, "If you don't get someone now, I'm going to tell your mother that you sneak out at nights. I'm gonna tell her where you go to!"

At this, Dante stiffened. He glanced nervously in Edmond's direction, but Edmond gave the slightest shake of his head. And mouthed, "he's bluffing." He wasn't sure *why* he cared for the boy. By all reasoning, Dante was annoying pain in the ass, but there was something about the bastard alchemist that Edmond couldn't help but like.

Dante didn't look particularly reassured, but he recomposed himself and glared at the guard. "Oh, and where's that?"

"I-I know you're up to no good," the guard finished lamely.

"Pshaw. That's not news, that's history," said Dante with a scornful laugh. He returned to picking at his nails, and managed to tear one off, flicking it. The thing arched through the air, carried further on the breeze, and as if guided by the god of luck himself, it ricocheted off the doorman's nose.

This only set the man into another string of expletives.

"Enough of this," Augustin snapped. "We're going inside. If swords and guns await us, may the gods pity those standing in our way."

Vicente tapped his knife against the doorman's throat and pushed him roughly towards the door. "You first," he said cheerily.

The man reluctantly pulled a key set from beneath his tunic and set to the door, after a couple of false starts, the door lock clicked and it swung open, revealing a strangely gloomy, dark interior to the inn.

The baroness, Edmond knew from asking around, had rented the entire place out for the week long tournament. However, he hadn't been expecting this. There were almost no lights, save a few red glows from imbued crystals in the wall. There were no guards either.

"Where are the others?" Edmond said.

The doorman muttered a bit, but finally, with a grim look, he said. "They go downstairs to the basement when she's dining."

"Why?"

"Them's orders. I don't know, I just obey. Boy too; he wouldn't be in his room if it wasn't locked. Dante likes to assault and belittle the guards when he's allowed reign of the house. The shit stain doesn't like to sit still."

"Assault the guards? He's half your size. What does he do exactly?" said Edmond.

"Does it matter?" asked Augustin, but the doorman, Morga, answered anyway, glaring from beneath a sun-freckled forehead.

"Likes puttin' things in our drinks, sometimes. Makes us have to piss while on duty. Once, I caught him filling my pillowcase with badger shit. Another time, he dyed the fur of Captain Amos' hound—made the creature bright pink. All because it nipped the boy a couple'a times. He deserved the nipping. It's a good hound."

"That doesn't sound like assaulting guards," said Edmond. "They're harmless pranks."

255

The doorman's eyes narrowed. "Harmless? Tell that to half the town who think I have syphilis. Nearly impossible to bring a lass home nowadays."

Vicente patted the man comfortingly with the flat of his knife.

"So where's she?" said Edmond, his voice carrying in the gloom as they inched, as a group, into the room. The red glow illuminated the darkness like blood peeking from behind a scorch wound, and a quiet creak preceded the whistling sound of wind slipping through the now open door.

Edmond glanced around, licking his lips nervously. There was something off about this whole thing. He wished he'd brewed a couple of potions before coming, but the urgent nature in which he'd been found had made that an impossibility.

But the doorman stopped moving. He shook his head once. "I'll not betray my honor!" he declared into the darkness, trembling slightly. "I'll tell you nothing. You can't make me—there's nothing you can say to—"

"If you don't tell us, I'll cut you," said Vicente, matter-of-factly. Edmond believed him.

So, apparently, did the guard. "Upstairs," he said with a squeak, pointing hastily towards a turning staircase at the back of the room. "Largest door, largest room, the far end. It'll be locked though. The hellcatcher won't be happy that you broke in. Secured funeral, crossing one of those."

"Not scared of a hellcatcher," grumbled Vicente.

The man muttered softly, shaking his head with a dark scowl. "Well maybe you should be. Or maybe you're as stupid as you look." He winced as Vicente swept the knife out with a lightning fast twist of his wrist.

At first Edmond thought the swipe had missed, then a hair thin trickle of blood rose from the doorman's neck. The man quailed as Vicente lowered his chin and said in a low voice, "I can go as deep as I need." After that the doorman made no more comments.

"Well," Edmond said uncertainly, "We're here. If you want to rescue your big friend, she's the only ally we have. I'm just a reeve. Newly appointed one at that. No one's going to listen to me. But her, she has clout."

Augustin glanced at Edmond, nodded, and then said. "Just so you know, if my friend dies, or you try something funny, I'll tell her exactly who's been fighting in that tournament."

Edmond winced, glancing quickly at the doorman, but he seemed too distracted by Vicente's knife to pay much mind to anything else.

Edmond said quickly, "I want this to work out for both of us. A mutually beneficial relationship."

"We'll see about that. You might not know what it is to have blood on your hands," Augustin said, coldly. There was a way to his words though that hinted at lower and deeper meanings. "But, if you do, you'd better not be hoping to add me or my friends to your list."

Not only Vicente, but Augustin as well seemed to know something about Matimeo's past. Everything seemed to be balanced precariously. The robbery of the titan's guns and the ornithopters had gone without a hitch;

this capture of the giant was only a mild distraction. Edmond cared for the bravos that worked for him, and would have done his best efforts to keep Kurga and his boys, or any of his employees safe. But Cristobal was no friend, nor employee.

The tournament was going well too. But at every opportunity, the more progress they made, the larger the chance it all came tumbling down. This complication with the Dumasian only further proved to Edmond they needed to hurry. Everything was counting on this plan to succeed, but with so many moving pieces, and possibilities of error, Edmond wasn't sure what the result would be.

For now, he needed to help Augustin reclaim Cristobal. If only to assuage his temper. Edmond nodded once, and then marched to the bottom of the stairs, hands clenched at his sides. He heard the others quickly following him. Without a glance back, Edmond started up the steps, eyes narrowed on the dark hallway that led deeper to the second floor. It was like the slit eye of a demon, spilling with inky blood, and threatening to reveal distasteful things beneath. Edmond stepped through the hallway, and found himself facing a long corridor flanked by doorways. One doorway, set at the far end, facing him, seemed to have a strange red light glowing beneath the door. Even up here, the torches had been snuffed, and no lights were emanating except for the red glow.

Edmond hesitated outside the door. Something was brewing here—more than what he'd bargained for. He recalled the strange glove on the baroness' hand. The unusual change in the doorman's claim of the baroness only having five children instead of ten. No one in Titan's Folly had told Edmond that she had ten children, but he and Mira had researched with the census-keepers, and tracked down the number of names the baroness claimed to house in her home. Ten names. Ten children, adopted, spanning back nearly sixteen years. Wasn't that when Dante had told him the baroness' accident had happened? Or, not an accident, but an attack by the Genevese that had injured her, taking away her ability to have children.

Edmond fidgeted nervously, pressing one shoulder against the left side of the hall, for no other reason than it felt good to have something solid against his back. The hairs on the nape of his neck prickled as he scooted by; he knew Augustin and Vicente were likely watching his every move. He heard the guard grunt and struggle, being prodded and pushed forward. Edmond reached the door, grabbed the handle, but then thought better of it. The prickle from his spine had reached his fingertips now, and they seemed to be buzzing with a strange apprehensive energy. Hesitantly, his throat dry, and his mouth suddenly filled with a strange cottony taste, Edmond gently tapped against the door.

As they paused, the sound of their creaking footsteps fading against the floorboards, waiting for a response, Edmond could have sworn he heard crying in the background. He frowned again, and tapped a bit louder this time. There emitted a sound like rattling chains, and then a snarl. Edmond felt a cold shiver shoot through his body and he glanced over his shoulder at Augustin.

The swordsman gripped the hilt of his rapier, and stared at the door with a wide-eyed look of uncertainty.

Edmond tapped, for third time, this time much louder, clenching his fist and using the bottom side to pound against the door.

Suddenly, the clinking chains and crying sounds of anguish faded, almost as if they'd been snuffed out like an extinguished torch. There was a little grumbling, and the thrum of quietly exchanged words. Then, the tap of feet against wood. A rattle, followed by the sound of a bolt being drawn, and the door cracked open barely an inch. Through the gap, Edmond spotted the dark, glaring eye of Rodergo Alverdo. "What?" the hellcatcher demanded, his voice laced with fury. "You know the rules," he spat. "No disturbing us when—"

He froze, glancing uncertainly from Edmond to Augustin to Vicente and the knife pressed against his doorman's neck. "What is this," he said, no less fury in his tone despite the transition.

Edmond decided not to comment on the kidnapped doorman. "We're here to speak with the baroness," said Edmond. "There's trouble, and we need her help."

"You can't just come barging in here," snapped the hellcatcher, his teeth gritted. The silver swooping tattoos across his face glinted in the faint red glow emanating from the room. His fingertips clasping the edge of the door also were traced with silver tattoos.

"My apologies for the disturbance," Augustin said, tight-lipped. "We don't mean to intrude on your supper. But, my friend has been falsely imprisoned by the baron. We need help setting him free."

"We're not going to pretend like we didn't hear that are we?" said Vicente frowning at the hellcatcher, but addressing the others. "The clinking of the chains, the snarling, the crying? I'm not the only one that heard that, right?"

The hellcatcher fidgeted slightly, and the door closed a fraction of an inch. "Oh," he said hesitantly, "that was just silverware against plates. I can be a bit of a loud diner, you know how it is."

Vicente scowled, shaking his head rigorously. "I don't know how it is. That's an utter load of tripe."

But Augustin held up a hand pressing it against Vicente's chest, in a placating gesture.

"Perhaps now's not the time," said Edmond glancing significantly at Vicente.

The old knight shot daggers at the eye in the doorway, but fell silent.

"Why is there a knife against my doorman's throat?" said the hellcatcher, a ripple of anger riding the words.

"Just a matter of misunderstanding," said Vicente with a would-be appeasing smile. He lowered his dagger, allowing the doorman to quickly step away from him with a relieved sigh and burst into a series of apologies and explanations which were waved away by the very tips of Rodergo's fingers.

"Leave, and don't come back, or else," the man growled in a nearly draconian tone, the single eye visible through the crack flashing with malice. Then, the door slammed shut. A split second passed where an ominous silence hung over the group, but before anyone could comment, the door cracked open again, and Rodergo glared at the doorman. "You personally had better see them out, or it'll be your tongue I take with my silver pincers—Melayna hasn't taken a tongue in a while, and she's grown restless."

Then the door slammed a second time. There was the rattling of a chain, the drawing of a bolt. A couple of moments passed and the sounds of crying and clinking could be heard once more fading through the doorway and emanating from inside the room.

CHAPTER 23

THE DOORMAN ROUNDED ON them, and, in a would-be commanding tone, he said, "We're leaving, you stupid chuckleheads. *Now*. Don't give me—"

Halfway through the gesture he quailed, however, when Vicente's blade shot back up, pointing towards his throat. "Try again," Vicente said lazily.

"I mean to say," the guard cleared his throat. "The baroness and her brother are indisposed. We can come back some other time, if you wouldn't mind."

"Better," said Vicente.

Augustin was shaking his head though. "We don't have time to wait. Reeve, what's the plan now?"

Edmond sighed. "Just give me a moment." He turned to the door adjacent to the baroness' room and tried the handle. It wouldn't open. Edmond moved to the door across from it and tried the handle, it too wouldn't open.

It took him three more attempts, but finally, halfway down the hall, in one of the middle doorways, he found a handle that would turn, and pushed it open, allowing himself into a clean, neat room. There was a small bed and dresser, old, varnished wood and shag carpeting. There was also a window.

Edmond fidgeted slightly. He felt naked without the alchemy satchel he normally carried, but it had been decided between Mira and him that an alchemist satchel on a reeve unknown to perform alchemy would only arouse suspicions. Kurga and his boys were still hanging on to it, but that didn't leave Edmond feeling any less exposed.

Vicente, Augustin, and the doorman spewing a stream of protests, moved to follow Edmond into the room, but found the tomb raider holding up a hand, flat at chest height.

"Give me a moment," he said with an attempt at a reassuring smile. Then, before anyone could reply, he slammed the door shut and bolted it.

He heard muttered voices in the hall, accompanied by a couple of offers from Vicente to stab the "bloody bastard", and Edmond was pretty sure he wasn't referring to the doorman. Still, he drowned the voices out, and hurried over to the empty dresser, desperately scanning the surface of the furniture and his own memories for some sort of recipe. He knew what he needed next, but the necessary moonlight liquid and sea turtle shavings were rare to find at best. And he didn't have time to visit one of the local apothecaries. He would have to improvise, the sort of improvisation that would leave Mirastious furious with him, but it was the only option.

Edmond glanced frantically around; there was no moonlight, at least not of the liquid variety, but there was moonlight streaming through the open window. He would just have to use that, and keep the concoction exposed longer for the diluted form. As far as sea turtle shavings, he would have to skip that ingredient entirely. He *did* know of a lesser version of the potion he was angling for that skipped the turtle and used the contents of a beaver's stomach instead. Now, as far as Edmond knew, Beavers spent a lot of time gnawing on wood, and the pulpy mixture found in their intestines often contained a good number of splinters. In a room full of wood, the splinters he had would have to do, accompanied by a good dose of his own spit, and he winced at the thought, whatever amount of upchuck he could manage to regurgitate in the short time span he had. That only left the final ingredient, which, as it was, would actually be the easiest to procure. He needed something from the body of someone who would kill him if given the chance. Thankfully, three such sources were sternly standing outside the door.

Edmond hastily grabbed a handkerchief from his pocket and hurried to the door, he cracked it open again and pushed the handkerchief through. "Here," he said. "Sneeze into that."

"What? No," said Augustin. "What does that have to—"

"Questions just waste time," Edmond said, nervously. "Just do it. I need the...er...the stickiness. For adhesion to a wall. Just trust me for a moment; I'm not going anywhere two floors up."

"Who should sneeze into it?" Augustin said, after another series of grumbling.

"Doesn't matter, any of you. Sneeze." He hesitated, then slightly pulled the handkerchief back. "Have you killed someone before?" he said to Augustin.

Augustin nodded solemnly as did Vicente vigorously and even the door-man reluctantly. "Perfect," said Edmond and he jammed the handkerchief into Augustin's hands. "Sneeze into that. You don't like me very much do you?"

"I don't see what that has to—"

"—perfect. Just sneeze into it."

"I don't have to sneeze."

"Well blow your nose dammit, you're the one wasting time now."

"I still don't see what this has to—"

"You don't have to see, just do it."

Vicente, growing bored with this exchange, grabbed the handkerchief, snuffled a few times, and blew into the center of the handkerchief.

Edmond winced in disgust. "Perfect," he said halfheartedly.

Vicente held up a hand though, indicating he wasn't finished yet. He blew a couple more times, pressing one nostril closed to clear out one nasal passage, then pressing another to clear at the other. He also, for good measure, spat into the handkerchief. Then, delicately, folding it at all four corners, he handed the handkerchief back to Edmond. "Thank you," Edmond said sarcastically.

"My pleasure," said Vicente.

Rolling his eyes, Edmond grabbed this handkerchief and tried not to press in the center or think about what would have to come next; he returned to the room, slammed the door and hurried over to the desk. He opened the handkerchief, determinedly not staring at what lay inside, and, his stomach turning slightly which would only help with his next step, he peeled splinters off the bottom of the dresser. It took him a couple of tries, and he had to pull one of the knives from his pockets to do it, but at last he had the contents laying in the handkerchief. Then, with a slight sigh of resignation, he jammed his fingers down his throat, practically tickling the back of his gullet. He heaved and gagged, and a couple minutes later, the eggs and partridge that had been cooked for him the previous morning met the handkerchief.

Now, completely disgusted and wincing in pain. Edmond hovered his hand over the contents. Focusing, and reaching out despite his disgust towards the part of him that could summon alchemy, Edmond concentrated on what he needed next. It took him a moment, but then, he managed to feel warmth spreading from his fingers. Blue vapor descended like falling mist from his palm into the waiting ingredients. Alchemy was no respecter of disgust, and soon, the offensive contents of the handkerchief began to turn to a clear liquid. Alchemy had once been the pursuit of transmuting gold from lead, and the magic had an ability to entirely alter the properties of whatever it touched. Edmond focused on the spell; he knew that if it failed, it would only summon an imp. He had dealt with imps before; they were more tricksters than malicious. Though, they had the annoying habit of taking on similar appearances to their causer—sometimes older, posing as the summoner's parents, or younger, passing for their children. Always with the intent to perform mischief. But, he didn't have the time or the inclination to chase around a humanoid demon trying to get it to return from whence it came.

Thankfully, after another few moments of focusing, Edmond managed to complete his alchemy. It wasn't pretty, but a glinting pile of clear bluish ice fragments now lay on top of the handkerchief, basking in the moonlight from the window.

Edmond sighed softly, then reached out and grabbed the ice chips, feeling them frigid against his fingertips, and popped them into his mouth, swallowing.

It tasted, as he knew it would, exactly like ice. All signs of the previous contents had been changed, claimed as an offering by another plane and replaced with something far less offensive.

Edmond swallowed the ice chips, inhaling deeply through his nose and pocketing his handkerchief once more, then, thinking better of it, he pulled the handkerchief out and threw it behind the dresser. None of the remnants of Vicente's contribution remained, but he would never be able to get the image out of his head.

Still, slightly gagging, Edmond approached the window and pushed it open. Over his shoulder, lest the others try anything rash, he called, "Just a few more minutes. Trust me!"

It occurred to him that if he had to ask someone to trust him, it likely was a failed venture to begin with.

Then, as he had done many times before in his tomb raiding, Edmond flung himself out the window and pressed his hands immediately against the wall.

His body jolted, but his hands stuck like glue to the side of the building. It took him a moment, stretching his shoulders, rolling his muscles, but then Edmond, like a spider, or a crab, began sidestepping, using his hands' suction against the wall to pull him towards the next window. Like this, crawling against the face of the building, with his back to the streets, beneath the winking moon in a dark sky, Edmond passed one window, another, and then rounded the side of the inn. There was no risk of falling; the Draft of Adhesion would see to that, and unless he willed it, his hands would act as a welded bond against the rock wall. He didn't have far to go, however, and he managed to reach a large window facing south in the back of the inn. Across from the window was a taller building with dark walls and no windows of its own. Vaguely, Edmond wondered if this was intentional. Did the baroness desire secrecy so much?

Edmond hesitantly, and carefully, scaled up to the window. He was grateful Augustin and the others couldn't see him now, as he didn't need anyone else to suspect his ability with alchemy. Already, Vicente knew he had used potions when he'd raided the Genevese tournament barracks, but he managed to pass them off as the potions of a friend. But if they'd seen him doing the brewing himself, that would ruin the illusion for sure. He was so close; with the theft of the titan's guns earlier that day, and the successful escape of the bravos who had brought the cannons to Fort Dentamosi, Edmond was worried that more meddling and more distractions like this would undermine everything they'd worked for. Still, there was a chance it would all come to fruition. Besides, he needed Augustin to win the tournament. That was the linchpin. In order to secure Augustin's continued aid, though, Edmond would have to help rescue his galoot of a friend.

And it wasn't like Edmond didn't like the giant Dumasian in a distant sort of casual admiration. The idea of someone dying when he could help had long since been numbed in him, consumed by his own pain. Spikes of mourning that rallied people to action had no hold on Edmond—he lived from an agonizing pit of grief. He woke with it every day. More grief was a redundancy, like trying to spit in the ocean to raise the tide. Many people died, and many times he didn't help. But, he wouldn't have been human if he didn't care at least a little about the thought of a man like Cristobal; a devout person, someone who worshiped a god that Edmond's wife would never have served, but at least he shared her fervency of faith. Edmond would not wish to see the death of such a man.

Then again, he could always just close his eyes.

That's what the man who'd killed his wife had said. "*No worries lass—close your eyes and it will all be over soon.*" Edmond hadn't been there to hear it, but someone who had been there told him, right before Edmond cut his throat and pushed him into the sea. Edmond shivered at the memory, goose pimples crawling like spider legs up his arms and neck. A pure jolt of hatred coursed through him, and a revulsion, stronger than what his recent alchemy had evoked, arose like bile in his chest.

Shaking his head, and forcing himself to focus on his current venture, Edmond scaled the face of the inn until he was just below the window facing the blank wall of the building opposite the street. Hesitantly, heart in his throat, Edmond inched his face up, wondering vaguely why he still couldn't hear the sounds of clinking and crying. Another thought, just before his eyes crested the sill: *Do I want to see what's inside? Should I look?* A shiver and a shudder crept across his body that had nothing to do with the ice chips he'd swallowed. He'd already come this far. With a swallow and a groan, Edmond pulled himself like a spider an inch more, peering through the window into the room.

Through the smudged glass hazy with his reflection from the moonlight, Edmond managed, after a couple of moments, to readjust his gaze and make out the contents of the room.

He nearly fell, and a small scream of horror stoppered his throat like a cork on sordid whiskey. He stifled the yell, his muscles tensing, every bone in his body seemingly going rigid. Edmond tried to choke out a word, to speak as if to remind himself he was still there, but he couldn't find the strength to utter anything, and he couldn't tear his gaze away from the contents of the room.

A dark, looming shape, in form, reminiscent of some of the larger shrubs in the baroness' courtyard on top of the Stern. This, he knew, not from sight, because he had never seen one in the flesh before, but from stories. However, what stooped over the bloodied carcass in the middle of the room was no shrubbery. A large, looming shape, with ridges of sapphire, emerald, and diamond tracing through dark scales and tufts of fur and leathery membrane, crouched over a pile of broken, splintered bones, blood seeping from its mouth. This demon was smaller than any greater demon Edmond had ever heard of... Was it some form of marid? Gods' eyes, it wasn't an *archfiend* was it? Its face angled away from Edmond, and he could only see one curled ear, and a jutting jaw covered in blood dribbling out of the corner of its mouth, but that was enough. The fear coursing through Edmond was unlike any he'd experienced before. This was clearly a greater demon—but it seemed small, malnourished even. Edmond had

271

never heard of one that could fit comfortably inside a normal room before. Still, one of the most powerful demons of alchemy sat in the center of the room, feasting on—on what?

I know what, said a small voice in Edmond's head. Those bones were in the distinct pattern of a human rib cage. A bloodied skull lay discarded beneath a banister bed a few paces away. But, as Edmond stared, he realized the skull was misshapen, with bony protrusions in strange places, as if making room for multiple, additional eyes. A demon then? A demon feasting on a lesser djinn, perhaps?

Rodergo was in the corner of the room, murmuring softly, and talking quietly as one might do to calm a beloved pet. He was making soothing noises and gestures in the direction of the feasting demon. Edmond squeaked, stuck to the face of the window as if he'd been soldered. "Dear gods," he murmured softly to himself. A greater demon loose in the middle of Titan's folly. And a hellcatcher who had loosed it. But where was the baroness? Where was...

Then, Edmond noticed something curious. On the creature's left hand, it wore a thick, leather glove, with dark stitched seams. On the demon's other hand, it wasn't a demon's hand at all, but rather a female woman's hand, smooth pale and tan, resting gracefully against a scaly, tufted leg.

The human hand clutched at a couple of arm bones, and then pulled delicately on a bloodied piece of flesh. Daintily, the pale, woman's hand lifted the meat to the monstrous muzzle, and pressed the delicacy into the mouth.

Edmond tried to look away, but found he couldn't. The whole spectacle was so nauseating and fascinating at the same time, he'd forgotten to
scream.

Just then, Uncle Rodergo ceased his cooing noises and glanced towards the
window with a sharp look. Edmond immediately ducked out of sight, burrowing his head beneath the window sill. He heard scraping from inside;
the sound of a chair moving, followed by a couple of muttered comments,
and then the sound of distant thumping footsteps to the window. Cursing
to himself, Edmond began to quickly sidle along the wall, desperately
attempting to return around the edge of the building. He'd seen something
that had nothing to do with him—something that Rodergo and his sister
had been hiding for decades most likely. Exactly *what* he'd seen, he wasn't
sure. He'd never heard of a tame demon before, but by the way Rodergo
had managed to stay alive for more than a split second within grasping
reach of the greater demon, Edmond knew some strange sort of fuckery
was afoot.

He knew he shouldn't have investigated. But, he hadn't been counting on
the sheer idiocy of what the hellcatcher and his sister seemed to be up to.
And, all this talk about the baroness' adopted children, and whether there
were ten or five, or if something fishy abounded, seemed to be swaying more
and more in one direction. Edmond couldn't climb around the corner of
the building fast enough, even scraping his cheek and arm in his effort to
put as much distance between himself and what he'd seen as possible.

He was the reeve, but even reeves had limits. A runt-sized marid—for it
couldn't have been greater than that at its size—was still a marid in the heart

of Godshaven. Edmond wasn't sure what had become of the baroness, and he wasn't sure what the gloved hand and dainty pale fingers had indicated.

For now, whatever foolishness abounded, it seemed to be under some semblance of control. Though with demons, there was no such thing—not really. Edmond would have to send for hellcatchers himself in a week's time. But... For now...

He half glanced back along the carved stone wall, his skin buzzing.

For now... perhaps he could wait to report what he'd seen. Just until the tournament ended; just until he put things in order...

Still, beating his hasty retreat, he traversed across two closed windows and made a beeline towards a third open one and into the room where he'd escaped the others. Before he passed the second window completely though, there was a shuddering sound, and an arm snaked out, grabbing Edmond around the ankle and yanking sharply.

Chapter 24

Edmond practically wet himself; the sensation of sheer terror was accompanied only by his shrill scream. "Blue fire and black fish!" he screamed at the top of his lungs. Edmond kicked wildly out, trying to dislodge the grip of whatever had grabbed his ankle; he screamed again, and, only after the third shrill shout, did a voice behind him start giggling in jittering fits.

Edmond spun, glancing sharply back, angling himself on the wall so that one arm was above his head and the other was at his side groping for a dagger. He froze however, when he spotted Dante leaning out the second window, hand extended, and a giddy expression on the boy's freckled face.

"You should have seen yourself!" he cried, laughing uproariously. "Like a dainty lass accosted in a tombyard you were! Like as not that's the scent o' shite on the breeze! Aha!" he cackled again, giggling so hard that his shoulders shook.

Edmond's eyes narrowed; through a hooded gaze he glared at the boy, teeth clenched. "That's not funny," he said, shaking his leg and dislodging the child's grasp on his ankle. Dante slipped a little bit, nearly tumbling out the window, and this caused him to stop giggling at least for a moment. But then, dangling by one hand gripping the inside of the window frame, the rest of his body leaning out angled upward so that he had the best possible view of Edmond, Dante began laughing again, and clapping uproariously. The boy was giggling so hard now that he lost his grip on the shutter, and he yelped once before tumbling out of the window.

Edmond's hands shot forward, grabbing the boy by the shirt. The Draft of Adhesion worked as it was meant to, his hand welding to whatever it touched. Even though Edmond wasn't closing his fist, the boy's shirt was stuck to his palm as if stitched there. Dante fell only a short ways, but then jolted to a sudden stop, dangling from Edmond's arm.

And while the potion did cause his hands to stick to whatever they touched, it did not improve his strength. Edmond's arm groaned, popping from the effort of hanging the fourteen-year-old child aloft.

Dante began kicking and thrashing and waving his hands. "Let me go! Let me go!" he cried.

"Stop struggling," Edmond snapped. He hated this part. No one ever listened when he told them to do something. And inevitably it got them killed. Like the pearl divers back in the crypt, or the bravos who, upon the end of the contract, had tried to take his ship.

To his surprise, however, the moment Edmond said it, Dante stopped wiggling. He went rigid, and glanced over his shoulder, glaring at Edmond. "You made me do that," he said.

"I made you laugh so hard you fell out a window?"

Dante crossed his arms, still dangling from Edmond's hand, apparently determining that he wasn't going to plummet to his death after all. "Well, you did part of it at least."

"Nice to hear you taking responsibility for your own choices."

"Response-a-what? Never heard'a it."

Edmond was still struggling to make sense of what he'd seen back in the baroness' room.

He shivered a couple of times, his skin crawling and buzzing. With a good amount of effort, and muttering, inter-spliced by an impressive treasure load of cursing, Edmond managed to lift Dante up back to the window and instruct the boy to pull himself through. Edmond willed his hand to stop sticking to the boys shirt, and watched as Dante scrambled back to safety.

Glaring sharply at the child, Edmond said, "Stay in your room. Lock the door if you can. There's something dangerous in the inn."

But Dante didn't look concerned. He gave a halfhearted wave in Edmond's direction. "Nothing dangerous," he said. "Not with Uncle Rodergo and mother around."

Edmond shook his head quickly. "You don't understand. They're up to something. I saw, I'm not sure what I saw. But it was—"

Dante shook his head. "Not supposed to bother mother when she's feeding."

"What, like in ever?"

"She only eats once every couple years anyway. Though recently, it's been getting quicker."

"Excuse me?"

"Quicker means things is movin' faster—"

"I know what quicker means you shit-flinging monkey. The other part!"

"Mother only eats once every couple of years? That part?"

"Your mother doesn't eat more than once a year?"

Dante frowned slightly, glancing at Edmond's lips, then his own lips, his eyes going crosseyed to peer down his cheeks. "Am I—Am I using these right? I thought I spoke plainly. Honestly, none of them are particularly *large* words. Which one are you struggling with, maybe I can act it out."

"I should have let you fall out the window. Tell me about this. Most people eat more frequently—you know that right?"

Dante shrugged one shoulder. "It is what it is; always been that way. Something to do with her alchemy from before I suppose."

"And what happened to your older brother. Fero, the one who met us at the gates."

Dante scrunched up his face, his nose wrinkling, his brow creasing. "What bullshit are you on about? You fucking daft? There ain't no one by the name of Fero."

Edmond stared at the child to see if he was having a go, but Dante looked serious. The glowing red veins beneath his skin pulsed even brighter as Dante met Edmond's gaze, illuminating his pale flesh in the dark room.

"You are sure?" he said. "Dante this isn't funny; what happened to Fero?"

"There ain't no one by the name of Fero. What are you smoking old man?"

"You're joking."

"Usually."

"No, I mean now. You're joking now."

"Not joking. I've only got four brothers and sisters. None of them are named Fero."

Almost in the distance, Edmond could hear the sound of crying and clinking chains.

A new shudder crept up his spine. Suddenly, as if listening down a well, or through layers of walls, Edmond heard a crack, followed by a greater grunt. And then, the crying and clinking of chains stopped abruptly. "There's only five of you?" Edmond said.

"Five?" said Dante frowning. "Five? What five?"

"Five brothers and sisters. Five bastard alchemists?"

279

"Where the fuck did you hear *five?* No. There are only four of us. Me and my three siblings." A strange sort of stunned look had fallen across Dante's face. The red crystals in the room behind him seemed to pulse brighter, if only for a second. His eyes flickered and his pupils widened momentarily, and he shook his head as if trying to dust cobwebs from his face. "Four," he murmured quietly. "No, no never five. There was never *five* brothers no, no, *four*. Three including me. That's four. I only have three siblings." Dante looked dazed and confused for a moment longer as the red crystals dangling from the walls glowed, but the light dimmed again, and he stared at Edmond with a bemused expression.

His pupils widened again, and all sounds from the distant room where the baroness and her hellcatcher brother were hiding had faded completely.

Whatever had come over Dante, and whatever had happened in that room beyond them was connected—Edmond was certain of it. He shook his head in confusion. "I don't understand," he said. "What are you hiding for your mother?"

But Dante didn't wear an expression of guile—if anything, he looked as confused as Edmond. "I don't know what you're fucking talking about," he said, his tone surprisingly gentle. He was watching Edmond now with a look of concern. "Are you feelin' alright? There's never been anyone by the name of Fero. And I only have three siblings."

"You just said *four*, a minute ago."

"No, I didn't." Now Dante sounded as frustrated as Edmond felt. There was too much alchemy, too many moving pieces, and Edmond wasn't thinking straight. He wished he'd brought Mira—she never got scared.

"I need to speak to your mother, now. You really should stay out of the way, she's not right Dante. I don't know where she is, but there's something wrong with the baroness."

"Oi, don't speak about my mother that way you puffin."

Edmond held up his hands in mock surrender, and then quickly had to slam one back to the wall so he didn't fall.

"Why are you here?" Dante snapped. "Miss my scintillating good looks, ey? You perv."

Edmond thought to question Dante further, to dig deeper, but for the moment, he discarded the notion. They were running out of time for the real reason they'd come. "A friend of ours was captured by the baron. A tall fella, name of Cristobal. He's a good man and it'd be a shame to see him killed. Lynched actually—lynched by hanging." Edmond raised his eyebrows, allowing the inflection and the obvious tone to speak for him.

Dante shifted uncomfortably, subconsciously his hand fluttered to his neck, as if to stroke his fragile throat. He swallowed. "Not a right way to do one in." He said. "But mother won't be able to help you. Usually takes her a few hours to recover after a meal."

"And she only eats once, every couple of years."

"That's what I said—now about this friend of yours; you say the baron has him?"

"That's right, why do you ask?"

"Because," said Dante. "What the hells. I might be able to help after all."

"How are you going to help?"

"No need to sound so doubtful. I can help. I know where they're staying."

"Who?"

"The baron, and his children."

"Would they take Cristobal there?"

Dante was shaking his head already though. "You're pretty much a dimwit for a reeve aren't you? No, that's not where they'd would take him. They would take'em some place safe, guarded, maybe somewhere dark, and unknown. Maybe one of their mines, or one of their hidden burrow holes were they're drilling on our family's land like a blacksmith in a brothel with—"

Edmond interjected before the boy could finish the metaphor. "So then what are you suggesting?"

"Well," Dante scratched his head. "They take one a yours, so the only thing you need is a bargaining chip. In exchange."

"And what might that be?"

"I told you, the baron and his kids stay at the same place whenever shite hits the ceiling. I know where that is. It's a riphouse on the other side of town."

"I'm still not understand—"

"Double dimwit, for fuck's sake, what's wrong with you? Try to read my fucking lips."

It struck Edmond in that moment, how there was an irascibility to Dante that was more reminiscent of someone very, very old, rather than a child... He wasn't sure why the thought came to him, nor why his eyes flicked to the glowing red crystals dangling on the wall. Dante's veins were also glowing red again, pulsing beneath his skin. Edmond brushed the thought away, hiding his annoyance at Dante's ceaseless nattering.

"What you are going to do," said Dante, "is take one of the baron's over-grown teet-suckers. His children. Exchange one for another. I'd recommend Ciso, he's the most fragile of the lot. Smarter than Tiny, but not particularly dangerous on his lonesome. Though if he's near Magdela, stay clear. She'd split ye in two. Though, perhaps it's nothing an alchemist can't handle," Dante said.

"I'm not an alchemist," Edmond replied almost reflexively.

Dante raised a skeptical eyebrow, and glanced at Edmond's hand which was still adhered to the wall.

"Whatever," said the boy, rolling his eyes, the glow of his reddish veins pulsing beneath his skin. "Whatever you do, don't mess with Magdela, she's deadly with that bow of hers, and is one of the only knights to win on the Genevese side of things. Five years ago, she destroyed the competition. Not worth messing with her, she fights dirty; never plays fair. Goes for the double danglers every time."

Dante smiled in approval.

"Okay, so that's your plan, you'll show me where they're staying, and we kidnap one of theirs?"

"Pshaw. I don't want to get within a thousand feet of Magdela and her longbow. I'll *tell* you, if you ask nicely."

"It's not much of a plan."

"Well you're not much of a man."

"You better watch that tongue of yours or it's going to get you in trouble."

Dante flashed a grin, then stuck out his tongue, peering down his cheeks again at the reddish tip. "S'haw ti twak wish mosshot." He said, his tongue sticking out.

"It may not be much of a plan, but it's the only one we have."

"Ithjo shaw shee. Ib sho—"

"Stop watching your fucking tongue!"

Dante returned his tongue to his mouth and flashed a toothy grin. And, though he had wanted to remain the mature one of the two, Edmond couldn't resist reaching out and flicking the boy on the nose.

"Hey!" said Dante.

"Hey yourself. You're showing me where they're staying. No arguments. Do it, or I'll throw you out the window."

"You wouldn't actually—"

Edmond's hand darted forward, grabbed the boy and yanked him from the window until he was dangling upside down.

After a series of squawks and indignant kicking, Dante grunted. "Fine! I'll show you. Don't drop me you shit-sniffing loveless bastard."

Edmond gave Dante a little bit of a shake, for no other reason than his own enjoyment, and then, he scaled down the front of the building, bouncing Dante off the side of the stone wall every couple of feet. Edmond wasn't about to stay and ask for the baroness' help, not after what he'd seen. He wasn't even sure what that was, but by the lack of screams emitting from the room, or shouts from the hellcatcher it seemed as if perhaps it was under control for the moment. Besides, the person Edmond would contact in manners of released and escaped demons was already in that room.

He filed the information away in his mind, and decided to leave it until later.

He reached the ground, loosing his grip on Dante's leg a couple of feet up so the boy thudded into the alley floor on a pile of garbage.

Slumped upside down, against the wall, his head in a pile of refuse, his legs still against the stonework over his head, Dante peered up at Edmond. "How," he said, "may I be of service to you? Perv."

Edmond shook his head slowly. "Your plan is ludicrous, but I'll give you credit for audacity. Fine—show me where the baron and his children are. You're right, we need a bargaining chip."

Dante flashed a thumbs up, upside down, then kicked off the wall, rolling into a backwards sort of somersault and leveraging himself back to his feet. He skipped a couple of steps ahead of Edmond, then turned around and flung a bag full of rotten vegetables, plastering the tomb raider in the face.

"Aha!" Dante guffawed. He didn't try to run away though, and, if anything, he was watching Edmond's expression eagerly, as if searching for some sort of approval there.

He only found a frown, though, as Edmond wiped kitchen waste from his shoulders and the side of his cheek. As Dante skipped along ahead, though leading them to the mouth of the alley, Edmond sighed wearily, and said, "It's not a terrible plan, boy. You're clever for your age. Though, you're still a shit-flinging monkey."

Dante's face lit up in delight at the praise, and he became even more energized, setting a rapid pace that Edmond—even in all his active years of looting and climbing and crawling into tight spaces—found difficult to keep up with, weaving through the gloomy streets of the old mining town.

CHAPTER 25

EDMOND GLANCED OUT OF the corner of his eye, down an alley, then glanced over his other shoulder to see if they were being followed. So far they had been left relatively untouched as they moved quickly through the nighttime streets.

Augustin and Vicente wouldn't have wanted to be left behind, but Edmond hadn't given them a choice, seeing as he hadn't told them where he was going. He'd left word with one of the servants that Augustin and Vicente should stay put, and to tell them that he was going to handle it. Right now, he didn't need the distraction of the knights. From what Dante had described, violence wouldn't solve anything here. The Genevese were more than a match for just the three of them.

"You're an alchemist aren't you?" said Dante as he led Edmond through the labyrinth of streets from the Alverdo side of Titan's Folly to the Genevese. "No," he quickly interrupted, "don't pretend you're not. Normal people can't just climb on walls. Tell me, you are, aren't you?"

"I am, not that it is any of your business."

"Keep your dick out of a knot, I'm not trying to make anything of it, and I'm not gonna spill no secrets or nothing. Just interesting is all. My mother likes alchemy."

Edmond glanced at Dante. "You mean like those caps in your teeth?"

Dante wrinkled his nose though, and gave a slight frown. "What caps?"

Edmond waved vaguely in the direction of Dante's exposed veins in his arms glowing slightly orange. "That's not normal," he said. "You're specialist; an amateur alchemist focused on only one part of the craft."

"I'm not."

"Yes, you are."

"No, I'm fucking not."

Edmond frowned. "A potion then? You drink it before you leave the house."

Dante hesitated. "Mother has us drink potions sometimes. Says it's supposed to remember things proper. Other than that, though, she doesn't permit us to use alchemy."

"Wait, hang on. You spewed fire. Your veins—even now, they're glowing. They call you the bastard alchemists!"

"I—I know. I mean, I, I," Dante looked confused and flustered all at once. It was the same expression that had crossed his face when Edmond had asked about his ten brothers and sisters. *There's only five of us*, that's what he'd said at the time. Then, he'd nearly instantly, changed his tone and with equal conviction said there were only *four*.

"Forget it," Edmond said, shaking his head. "Perhaps I don't even want to know. Not now. How far are we?"

"Not—not far," said Dante, a troubled expression on his face. He reached up and scratched thoughtfully at the side of his head, but then just shook his head and took off again, leading Edmond further into the Genevese part of town.

***

"This is one of their riphouses," Dante said eyeing the dark, ash-streaked building with a look of severe distrust. Twisting metal rails curled beneath tar-stained windows, curling around a second and third floor like the hoops on a lady's dress. "The whole place could go up like kindling if you're not careful; there are all sorts of strange contraptions and alchemical solvents inside. None of them are as sophisticated as anything my mother used to brew, and there have been rumors that the alchemists working for the Genevese are self-taught." Dante shuddered at the thought. "Just," he glanced at Edmond shooting a sidelong glance. "Be careful," he said.

Edmond smirked. "If I didn't know any better, I would think you were worried about me."

"What? Don't be gross. I just don't want to have to explain to your drunk friend with the knife what happened to you."

Edmond gave an understanding nod. "Normally, I'd like to take some time to plan, to determine our best entry and exit points. Alas, the knights don't think their friend has much time left. If we want to make sure they don't do anything rash, I'll have to be quick."

"So what can I do?" said Dante.

"You?"

"I didn't come all this godsforsaken way to play with my ass—you lump. What can I do to help?"

"I seem to recall that you *offered* to come."

"Wha—what? Offered? You dropped me on my head you puss-sucking galoot of magnificent proportions. Go boil your tits! On second fucking thought, never mind. I can see my services aren't appreciated by your cream puff self. I said I'd show you the way, and I've shown it. It's fucking there." Dante pointed towards the dusty, dark building up against the side of the mountain.

"No—no, wait, one moment," said Edmond. "I might actually need some help. A distraction. You're a natural nuisance; think you can put your annoying qualities to something constructive?"

"What? You mean like blow something up."

"No—no, don't do that," Edmond said quickly. "You said that whole place could go up like kindling—so no fire. I'm going to be inside. Try something... fake sick, or scream, or something else. No explosions, got it?"

"You *don't* want me to blow anything up?"

"Dante. Read my lips. Don't, blow, anything, up."

Dante clicked his fingers twice against the side of his leg in the universal sign of agreement. "I'll make the best distraction you've ever seen."

"No fire. Tell me you won't explode anything."

Dante rolled his eyes, but then made the sign of Pardi across his heart and said, "I swear on the health o' me cock and the sight in my eyes, I'll not blow nuffin' up. Fair?"

Edmond nodded appreciatively. "You have to wait though," He said. "At least five minutes. Do you have a way to tell when that will be?"

Dante hesitated, then said, "I can count in me head."

"You can count?"

"Old perv coming full force with the funny. I can count, and I can also leave. How about that?"

"No, no. Don't leave. Go ahead and count. If I'm not out in five minutes, then you'll need to start your distraction. Make it big, and make it loud. And don't, don't kill anyone. And *no explosions.*"

"I wasn't gonna kill anyone," Dante said sullenly.

291

"Dante. I'm serious. No killing."

The boy nodded demurely, but Edmond caught him muttering, "Spoil-sport," beneath his breath.

"Well this old perv doesn't have to be fun," said Edmond. "I just have to be quick, and convincing." He licked his lips, steeling himself for what lay ahead, then, hurrying forward, he approached the riphouse. He hadn't had time to brew anything particularly substantial over the last few hours. Normally, alchemy didn't work unless given time to form and bond. The shorter time one let a potion sit, the higher chance something would go awry. He'd risked it before, like with the draft of adhesion for the windows, but that didn't mean it would always pay off. The last thing now that he needed was to summon a demon in the middle of this place.

The thing would likely kill him. So, carefully, creeping around the side alley and moving through an upper floor window, Edmond made his way into the rafters of the riphouse.

CHAPTER 26

IN THE DISTANCE, EDMOND heard an earth shattering explosion, and he immediately cursed Dante in his mind with every expletive he could imagine. The men and women gathered around the makeshift tables below him, in sight of where he rested in the shadow of the rafters, leapt from their seats with yelps of surprise and surged towards the first floor's windows, rounding in the direction the explosion had come from. The second floor wasn't a proper floor, but more of a walkway that rounded the room with metal railings and wooden platforms. Edmond was above, stuck to the beams supporting the third, and final floor—a storage space of some sort. He peered down at the Genevese below.

A few of the more adventuresome sorts abandoned caution and pressed their faces up against a window, peering out into the street beyond. One of the men yelped, shaking his head and pointing through the open window; at the top of his lungs, he shouted. "The gold," he screamed. "Melting! The gold is melting."

A few of the men in black tabards began hurrying out of the riphouse, barging through the front door, shouting warnings at the top of their lungs; others hung back, staring uneasily out into the street, their faces aglow with a flickering orange light.

Edmond was still sitting on one of the rafters, hidden in shadows and watching those below, one hand pressed firmly to the wooden beam. If he fell, he'd stay stuck to the wood, but it would alert everyone in the room that he was there. This, he surmised was just as quickly a death sentence.

Magdela Genevese sat straight backed in a chair, staring at a pewter goblet in her hands and ignoring the commotion. Upon the tall, flaxen-haired woman's back there was a magnificent composite bow—a new design coming out of The Crook, said to hit with twice the impact and puncture plate mail. Edmond wasn't sure if he believed the rumors, but the strangely curved bow was the thickest he'd ever seen, and if she could fire that thing, it would skewer him to the ceiling as if he were a moth in a collector's book.

Ciso, for his part, had pushed out of a seat so low to the ground they must have ordered it special from a carpenter. The diminutive man quickened over to the window, moving as fast as his small legs could carry him. He hopped up onto a stool, peering out into the night. Then, clicking his tongue, Ciso said, "He's not wrong. Someone set fire to the trailings cart."

Edmond wasn't sure what a trailings cart was, but he sure knew what melted gold was. Dante was obviously sending some sort of message, and, despite Edmond's insistence on anything but an explosion that could spread fire to the riphouse, Dante had, perhaps predictably, taken things his own route.

Eventually, the remaining soldiers assembled under Ciso's instructions. Anytime someone hesitated to obey, Magdela glanced up from her drink, fixing the man with a furious glare, and he'd double time whatever Ciso had instructed. Finally, once Ciso had organized a group of soldiers into two columns with various instructions—Edmond was too distracted to listen to such mundane exchanges, though he did hear the word "water" and "pail" bandied about—Magdela finally rose from her seat, pushing nimbly away from the table and hurrying out the front door with her older brother scurrying at her side, his legs moving at twice the speed of hers.

A few of the men stayed behind, as well as Tiny, who Edmond hadn't initially spotted lurking in a dark corner, brooding over three different bottles. He was a hard man to miss, built like scaffolding—his limbs didn't quite match to his body, giving him a stretched look, like taffy drawn into the shape of a man. Tiny was too drunk to do much, and Edmond cursed as he stared at the man. He'd been counting on Tiny leaving with the others. Out in the chaos beyond, Edmond had hoped to find an opportunity. Now though, with Tiny lingering behind, sheltered by four walls, and defended by four remaining men watching their master drink, Edmond would have to improvise. His initial plan, of spiking Tiny's drink while he was out of the room, or accosting him in an alley wouldn't work now. Somehow, he had to get the enormous scarecrow-sized man out of the room, without anyone else stopping him.

The only way he could think to do it was willingly.

So, licking his lips nervously, and clearing his throat, Edmond dropped from the ceiling joist, dangled beneath a platform, eased himself to his full length like stretching cat, and then released, landing with a dull thump next to a large metal vat with an empty grate.

A couple of the guards in black outfits swiveled towards him, eyes widening in surprise. Edmond though, was striding confidently forward, approaching Tiny's shadowy table.

"Stop!" shouted one of the guards.

Edmond ignored the man. A difficult feat on account of the sword raised towards his throat. Still, he knew he had precious few words to pull this off, and he didn't want to waste them on some lackey.

"Tiny," said Edmond, his voice sure and confident, despite his swallowing past the edge of the blade.

The large man looked blearily up from a black-stained glass bottle, shaped like a square with a spigot. "Who is it that speaks my name without knowledge?" said the man in a would-be significant voice that came across as petulant from behind a rosy nose and flushed cheeks set against a skeletal face.

Edmond didn't comment, and instead said, "I'm here from your father. There's going to be a hanging—he needs you there to officiate."

Tiny stared, and the four men around him, who had initially moved to intercept Edmond, stiffened, glancing back and forth in confusion. Their black uniforms with frayed ends and dirt stains, as well as some darker stains did little to assuage Edmond's fears. But for the moment, they didn't move to intercept him, glancing in Tiny's direction as if waiting for instructions.

"Well," said Edmond. "What are you waiting for?" he said brusquely. "Didn't you hear? Someone stole the titan's guns and the ornithopters from one of your family mines!"

Tiny pushed the enormous bottle out of his line of sight, and gave a small growl.

"Magdela told me," he said, "but equally so, the divines revealed it during my private solace."

"Well, like I said, you're needed there."

"Father doesn't need me for an execution. He's completed a proper number on his own; who are you?"

"It's the new reeve," said one of the men in a black tabard. "He's one of them who done in Gregor the miner."

Edmond winced at this; he hadn't anticipated his past actions coming back to haunt him. But quickly, he shook his head. "I did have an unfortunate run-in. And my men did protect me from his choices. But I don't want any trouble."

Tiny pushed slowly to his feet, bringing himself a full foot taller than Edmond.

"I know you," said Tiny Genevese, his eyes narrowed shrewdly. "You're the knight with the ruined armor. The cheater. The one who's been breaking the rules. We don't like cheaters. Magdela!" He cried, facing the door. "Come hither!" To Edmond, he said, "Maybe it's due for your soul to meet a real knight."

This clearly wasn't going as Edmond had hoped. "Come now," he said fervently. "Your father wants you!"

"No, he doesn't." Tiny glared at Edmond. "He personally told all three of us to come here, and to stay out of it. The large thief is going to be executed within the hour. They're stringing him up from the Prow. Gonna make an example out of him for cheats and thieves, not unlike you."

Edmond licked his lips nervously, and shook his head. "And why would he send you three away?"

Tiny gave a sort of half shrug and tapped the holy symbol on his chest of a golden skull above a crossed pick and shovel—the sign of Corundos, the god of mining. "It isn't mine to know all things; omniscience lies only in the hands of the holy and the devout. And I myself am just a humble leader of those who are in the truth. You are not in the truth. Neither is the baroness. My father notes that if we kill one of her men, she will retaliate. And he wants us to—"

One of the men behind Tiny cleared his throat. And the Genevese son quickly changed the subject, "It doesn't matter why we're here. Just know that your accomplice in iniquity will die within the hour. And so will you." As he said this part, he lashed out, his enormously tall frame shooting towards Edmond like a whip.

Edmond shouted and stumbled back, tripping over his own feet in his attempt to get away, but he wasn't fast enough to avoid the gangly Genevese devotee. The man grabbed hold of Edmond, gripping his arm and yanking him one way then another as if trying to shake him. It was then that Edmond realized he'd latched his hand around Tiny's wrist. The alchemy was still in effect, and whatever he touched, he wouldn't let go unless willing to. Currently, he was sealed tight against Tiny's forearm. The scarecrow of a man frowned, cussing and cursing, and kicking out with one leg. The foot struck Edmond in the stomach, causing him to gasp for air, but at the same time Edmond instinctively lashed out with his other hand to block the blow, and now he had one hand gripping Tiny's forearm, and another latched onto the man's ankle.

For a moment, they stood like that, Edmond's joints and sockets groaning in protest from the effort of holding the enormous man aloft by his arm and ankle. Tiny hopped around, looking quite the fool in front of his men as he stumbled and then fell over. As he toppled, Edmond quickly willed his hands to release, and backed quickly away. Then, thinking better of it, lest everything be wasted in the last couple of hours, he surged forward towards where Tiny sprawled. A dagger procured in Edmond's hand, and one of the guards lurched, slapping it with a gauntleted fist, but again, Edmond's Draft of Adhesion held true, and he managed to keep his grip on the knife. He surged forward like the tide, moving like one of the Signerde—a side-effect of having grown up among the seafaring race. He ripped at the front Tiny's shirt, pulling aside his holy symbol of Corundos, revealing a bare throat. "No one do anything," Edmond cried out, knife extended against the Genevese man's exposed throat. The guards around him hesitated, their black ensembles dull in the shadows of the room. In the distance, Edmond could still hear the shouts and blasts of explosions. Whatever Dante had done, he'd done so with style, but Edmond was running out of time. He didn't want to be here when Magdela returned.

"Don't stay back!" Tiny snapped at his guards from where he lay on the ground. "Do something you infernal things!"

"Don't listen to him," Edmond cried, also directing his comments to the guards who were shifting tentatively on their feet. "I'll kill him—slit his throat. What will The Bull say then? His youngest son—killed under your watch. You know his temper. Stringing up will be the least of your worries!"

"Think of *my* temper," Tiny roared, still frozen stiff, eyes on the knife at his throat, veins pulsing in his neck, reaching out to meet the sharp blade.

"I'm taking him with me!" Edmond insisted. He reached out with his free hand and tried to drag Tiny's enormous frame, but it was a futile effort. The man had gone limp like a child throwing a fit at bath time.

"No, he's not!" Tiny cried, trying to shuffle on his hands and knees away from the knife, but unable to due to the table at his back.

"Shut up," Edmond said. "Or I'll cut you open."

"If you cut me open, *they'll* cut you to pieces, you blasphemer. And then they'll come for your friends too. That pretty little woman that walks around with you; they'll visit her next and purify her with fire. Is it a good thing to pour out wrath on your enemies, and even the divines know the need for justice."

"That would be justice?" Edmond shook his head. "I'd like to see you try to accost Mira. She'd pick you apart, discovering ever hidden fear, insecurity. She'd lay them out for you to study, and witness you shrivel like a plant in the hot sun."

"Nameless Death comes for all."

"Not all," Edmond snapped, his hand moving reflexively to the vial dangling from his neck. "Not forever. But for now, you should be more worried about *your* life. And what I'm going to do to you, unless you come with me now!"

Tiny glared up at Edmond through hateful eyes; he stuck out his lower lip like a petulant child, and said, "No. I won't. Do your worst."

Edmond's knife hovered over the man's throat. Of course, he knew he was bluffing. And somehow, this overgrown gangly holier-than-thou man also knew it. There was a wicked gleam in this man's eye: the look of a zealot; the look of a man resting in the absolute certainty of his belief. And, as he glared at Edmond, Edmond knew that whatever Tiny would see in Edmond's eyes wouldn't speak of kinship. Whatever Edmond was, he did not delight in the suffering of others. It didn't absolve him of his own faults, but he'd chosen to kill Matimeo Navara as a sort of justice...

He shook his head; he was thinking in Tiny's terms, and he couldn't risk that now.

"Fine then," Edmond said. Then, he threw the dagger at the nearest guard, aiming towards his face, in the same motion, he spun on his heel and sprinted away.

A sword clattered at his feet as a guard threw his own weapon towards him; Tiny shouted furiously. "Magdela! Sister! Brigands, thieves, assassins!"

Edmond didn't look back. He could hear the sound of hurrying footsteps thumping after him, but he wasn't worried. Half those men were clad in armor, weighing them down. And by the looks of them, they weren't used to chases through the labyrinthine city. Edmond though had always known cities were his friends. They hid thieves and obscured the passage of grave robbers. He'd spent a good part of his life running from people, and so, still not looking back, he hastened out of the riphouse at a dead dash.

It didn't take him long, as he raced onward, to spot the blaze, an enormous inferno churning out from the mouth of a mine shaft, sweeping rivulets of smoke towards the darkened sky which only darkened further from the streams of soot. Around the mouth of the cavern, there were scattered pieces like a wheel well in one spot, and a large chunk of wood in another, spokes over on one side, and the meaty slabs of what looked like it had once been a horse now charred beyond recognition. Edmond felt a small surge of sympathy for the creature, but ignored it, continuing to race in the opposite direction from the men and the large woman and the small man who were fanning at the flames and passing buckets from a nearby pump. As Edmond raced away from his pursuers, he felt his hand tighten around what he clutched. It had been impossible to let go once he touched it, and he hadn't. He glanced down at the holy symbol—Tiny's crest clutched in his hand, the gaping sockets of the skull seemed to glint with a strange green light—then Edmond spotted two emeralds twinkling, embedded in the gold. There was a time, Edmond would have been enthralled to have scored such a treasure in his looting. But times had changed.

With a grim look, and a determined huff as he put on an extra burst of speed, Edmond rounded one building, then another, bolting down a side alley and skipping through a private garden to hop a wall on the other side. As he ran there was something almost cathartic about the moment. This was as things were meant to be: Edmond fleeing, danger chasing him, just out of reach. He'd played this tune before and danced this dance many a time, like a shy girl playing coy with a lustful suitor. Death often grasped for him, and Edmond narrowly avoided it at every turn. His wife had once told him she prayed for him: the Betrayed Mother would protect him, watch over him. But look where that had gotten her...

Edmond cussed and hopped another fence. He hoped Dante had taken advice to return home the moment he had caused the distraction. Thankfully, he hadn't seen the boy or heard him anywhere in the vicinity, so he hoped that at least Dante had escaped. For now though, Cristobal would be executed within the hour. Edmond had to hurry to the Prow, where Tiny had said they were going to kill the man they thought responsible for the theft of the titan's guns and ornithopters. Edmond, of course, knew that it wasn't Cristobal's fault at all. Then again, Edmond knew a lot of things that he wasn't willing to share.

It took him nearly half an hour, and two hitched carriage rides, to reach the hanging site, indicated by the crowds gathered beneath the shadow of the Prow. From the bowsprit dangled a long trail of rope. The rope was wrapped around an enormous neck which belong to an enormous man. As he approached, he saw Cristobal standing precipitously atop a wooden pedestal.

Below him, Baron Genevese, the Bull, shouted and waved his hands, much like he had at the tournament when Augustin had bested his men. This time though, as he spluttered, sending spittle flying into the crowds around him, he was indicating Cristobal. Four different knights were standing next to the baron, all wearing the black tabard's indicating they were of the Genevese clan.

"Caught red handed!" said the baron, shaking his jowls and raising a fist to the sky.

Cristobal glared at the back of the man, but beneath his breath he seemed to be muttering something, and his hands which were tied in front of him were rigid but the fingers continued to move in different symbols of prayer.

Edmond shoved his way through the crowd, actually pushing people one-way than the other, muttering, "Official business. Reeve business. Out of my way."

As he moved through the crowd, he spotted a bearded man he recognized as one of the miners who had accosted Dante. The miner glanced over at Edmond, then his eyes went wide and a hand quickly shot to his hip where he kept a pistol. Edmond gave the man a wide berth and made a beeline in the other direction, around the circle. He knew the man was following him, but didn't care. What happened next required boldness, and he was meat in a den of lions.

But even lions feared something.

"In Titan's Folly, we don't accept rampant theft and villainy!" The baron was shouting. "When guests come and rob us of our hard labor—*your* labor. He's an *outsider*." The baron winced at the word as if it gave him pain to utter it. "And this," he waved his hand towards Cristobal, "Outsider tried to steal from us, and he got away with it, or at least he thought he did. Currently, his accomplices are at large, but we will find them soon enough. Where they've stashed the loot, he refused to say."

Edmond spotted scrapes and bruises and cuts all up and down Cristobal's arms and face. He guessed by the way he was wincing with every shift of his shoulder blades that if the man were to remove his shirt, those torture marks would continue across his whole body.

"Hello!" Edmond called, waving a hand. He glanced towards the miner moving towards him and then stepped outside of the circle, putting a foot onto the steps that led to the gallows. "Excuse me," he called.

The baron had been in the middle of a particularly colorful tirade, but at the interruption he scowled, and attempted to speak again, but Edmond stepped up the gallows once more, reaching the platform, and the baron now rounded on him, jowls quivering and eyebrows furrowed.

Two of the Genevese knights immediately moved towards Edmond, their hands reaching towards their swords. But Edmond made a tutting sound, holding up a finger like a teacher admonishing a pupil.

"Wait a second, you don't want to do anything rash," he said. "Look here." He opened his hand, allowing the metal chain to loop around his fingers, and the talisman to drop from his palm, and bounce in line with his elbow, dangling against his arm and swaying slightly back and forth.

Judging by his sharp glance towards Edmond, and a deep inhalation, the baron immediately recognized the talisman.

"What is the meaning of this?" snapped the baron.

"So boring," said Edmond, rolling his eyes. He needed to keep the man flustered, and angry. Angry men were dangerous. But angry men were also stupid. They rarely thought through things. And for this bluff to work

Edmond couldn't let the baron think much. He would just have to hope the man didn't kill him outright.

"What is the meaning of this," Edmond said mimicking the baron's vernacular. "Why can't people ever come up with more interesting expressions? You could've just said *what*? Or perhaps you could say, *how may I help you*? That, at least, is polite." Edmond made a series of sharp tsks, gauging how far he should take it by the red shade of the baron's face. Once the man had reached a particularly vibrant hue, Edmond cleared his throat, and said, "You recognize the holy symbol of your youngest son Timeteo—Tiny they call him, yes? Well, we have him. In the same way you have one of ours. I am the reeve; unless you haven't familiarized yourself with the goings-on of your town yet."

"I know who you are," the baron said, his voice rasping, his eyes narrowed.

Edmond had heard a good few stories about the baron in his preparations for the feud of Titan's Folly. He was a man known for fits of rage. It was always during a black tar infused haze, or alcohol imbued state. The man was extremely doting and kind to his children, almost over protectively so. That, Edmond assumed was why all three of his children had been sent far away from the hangings. If he expected a retaliation from the baroness, the baron likely wanted to keep his children out of the line of fire. Some people would have picked on a child like Ciso, but the baron had given him status and positions of authority. Some families like those in Titan's Folly would not have allowed a daughter to become a knight. It was an old way of thinking, but still one subscribed to by many in the deeper parts of Godshaven. And yet the baron had allowed his daughter to become a knight. Tiny was an insufferable ass, that was all. And yet the baron seemed to care about that child too. He was clearly a doting father, and it would be what Edmond used against him.

Likely, over a lifetime of feuding, losing relatives left right and center to bloodied attacks from the Alverdo, Baron Genevese had grown scared of losing his own children. A more compassionate man would never use such knowledge against a father, but Edmond's compassion had left him nearly seven years ago, and for now he didn't care so much about compassion as he did about making sure Cristobal wasn't murdered.

"This man had nothing to do with the thefts. A tall, intimidating looking fellow may have been seen in the area, but our evidence shows it that it was Tiny Genevese. We currently have him in custody. Awaiting trial." Edmond declared this as loudly as he could towards the assembled folk, ignoring the baron's protests and spluttering outcries of rage and indignation.

"Oh yes," said Edmond. "We found him in the riphouse where you were trying to stow your children. Your daughter put up a big fight, but she's mostly unharmed. If you hurry now, you might be able to heal her injuries. Of course, the youngest one, Tiny, we had to take him into custody. We're keeping him currently at gunpoint in the reeve's dungeons."

The baron was shouting now, trying to override Edmond's speech, but failing as Edmond continued, also screaming at the top of his lungs. "And so, this is a stay of execution. You will remand the giant into my custody. As the reeve, I'll determine who is actually at fault. We'll hear the evidences, and present each other with the facts. All eyewitnesses must come and give a public testimony, as I'm sure everyone knows that's the code of the law."

"Give me back my son!" The baron shouted, eyes fixed horrified on the talisman in Edmond's still upraised hand. "Give Timeteo back! Where is he! Give him now!" The baron had rushed across the stage and was coming straight at Edmond, shouldering past two knights, an axe now in his hands as he tried to reach Edmond.

Edmond found it quite easy to dance out of the way of the corpulent man, continuing to dangle the emblem in front of the baron's eyes.

"I came myself," Edmond cried, "because I wanted to show you that respect. But if you try to kill me or kill this man, there are orders to execute Tiny. It's as straightforward as that! Think carefully!"

"You'd kill an innocent child for vengeance!" the baron roared.

"Tiny is no child," Edmond retorted. "Like you said, Titan's Folly has different rules," he continued, still speaking loud enough for everyone to hear. "You wouldn't condemn your own child to death would you? What sort of message would that send to your people? Could you not even protect your child, then how could you be expected to protect them?"

With each word, some of the wind seem to be blasting out of the baron's sails. The knights around him were looking at Edmond with hate. One particularly scowly fellow in a muttering voice said, "What if he's lying, sir?"

Edmond licked his lips, but didn't reply, as the baron did it for him.

"Don't be an idiot, Tiny doesn't go anywhere without that symbol, he wouldn't have given that up without being captured."

"But what if they just stole—"

"Shut up!" the baron screamed. "Shut up!" He turned and slammed a beefy hand to the side of the man's metal helmet with a loud clapping sound, and the knight went stumbling off the stage, crashing in a clattering heap on the ground.

One of the other knights raced over, trying to help his friend back to the stage, but the other two kept their hands on the hilts of their swords, waiting for instructions.

"Don't hurt my boy," the baron kept saying. "Don't hurt my baby." His voice picked up in volume. "Don't you dare. I won't kill you; I'll cut you into pieces over a period of years. You'll never, never recover. I'll take your eyes, your balls; I'll feed pieces to you one bit at a time. I'll have the hounds feast on your intestines, while you watch!"

Edmond wrinkled his nose in distaste. "It all sounds quite lovely, but I'm afraid I have to pass. I won't kill your son, but you can't kill an innocent man. Cristobal has nothing to do with it."

"He was seen!" The baron cried.

Edmond's eyes narrowed, peering at the baron, and glimpsed a swallow, a puff of the cheeks, a tilt of uncertainty in his eyes. It was as Edmond thought: the baron was making it up. The Bull didn't know who stole the titan's guns, and he was using this as an opportunity to lynch an enemy—someone assosciated with the Alverdos, as he saw it.

"Whoever saw him," Edmond said coldly, his gaze locked with the baron's, "Should step forward. Who was it?"

The baron spluttered, but quickly recovered, shaking his head. "I won't tell you; you might just kidnap them as well."

"Enough of this," Edmond snapped. "You either release our friend, now, or we kill your son. Simple."

"What are you? You're no reeve. That's not how things are done around these parts!"

"Well, the way things are done seems to end with my friend strung up with a broken neck, so I'm willing to change the process a smidge."

"You don't know what you're messing with!"

Edmond rolled his eyes. "Again, again with the generic applications; just let him go. Now!"

They had reached the crux of the matter and a point of decision. Edmond had stopped talking. Even the baron quieted. The crowds though were in full whisper frenzy, muttering and crying out and taking sides. The miner shouted from the crowd. "He's the one who killed Gregor!"

The baron's eyes narrowed, his cheeks puffed and flushed, as he seemed to be trying to make a decision.

Edmond, tantalizingly extended the holy symbol towards the baron, praying—in his mind, to no one in particular—his bluff worked. At last, the baron cursed Edmond in such a manner that Dante would have blushed, and then waved at the gallows. "Cut him down," he said in a fuming voice. "Cut him down now."

310

A minute later, Cristobal joined Edmond, rubbing at his wrists and his neck, but keeping any comments or thoughts to himself. Wisely so, because they weren't out of the woods yet.

"So, give me my son."

"I told you," said Edmond. "He's in the dungeons."

"I'm not going to just let you go free until you give me my son!" The baron roared, swinging his axe from side to side.

Edmond nodded thoughtfully for a moment. Then, ignoring the baron for second he turned. "My large Dumasian friend, how are you feeling?"

Cristobal glanced out of the corner of his eye at Edmond, but shrugged, then winced at the gesture. "Bruised, battered; the bastards pricked me up a bit, but I can move."

"Can you run?"

"I," Cristobal frowned in mild confusion, "suppose I could do."

"Perfect." Edmond launched the pendant at the baron's face. It wasn't a unique strategy; in fact he had just employed it only minutes before with Tiny. But Edmond didn't care about originality. For the moment, they just needed to get away. Obviously, Edmond didn't have Tiny to trade, and Cristobal's life was still in danger. Not to mention Edmond's—which mattered far more to him than any Dumasian knight.

"Make a hole!" He cried, and then he pushed Cristobal off the stage, shoving back towards the crowd and sprinting in the wake the large man made among the people.

There was the predictable roar of the crowd, and shout of Genevese knights. Cristobal, for his part, reacted surprisingly astutely to the interaction. He lowered his shoulder and began barreling through the crowd like a bull. The Bull himself shouted in rage and screamed. "Catch them! They're going to kill Timeteo! Catch them!"

A far calmer, though no less fervent voice behind them rattled off a series of orders. "You two after them. You there, go search the riphouse—make sure Tiny isn't there."

Edmond surmised that this was the scowly-faced guard. It was the smart choice, and the choice that the baron should've made before releasing Cristobal, but that was why Edmond wanted him riled up. Smart choices were hard to make when one was fearful for the death of their child.

By now, the crowd parted, lest they also be bowled over by the enormous knight and his smaller companion. Sprinting away, Cristobal and Edmond raced from the shadow of the Prow, putting as much distance between themselves and the clanking knights as they could. Again, Edmond was relieved to hear the sound of metal as the knights tried to give pursuit. Running in armor was an impossible task.

Before they'd gone too far though, there was a pistol blast, and Edmond felt a sudden sharp pain against his palm, which had been extended behind him, swinging back as he ran.

He yanked his hand forward and glanced down, stunned to see a bullet resting in the middle of his palm. It hadn't burrowed in, but had stopped the moment it touched his skin. He supposed that piercing his flesh was a bit like letting go. He hadn't known the potion could prevent bullet penetration before. That was something worth noting. Cackling to himself and sprinting along, the Dumasian and Edmond made good their getaway, weaving through the streets and racing into the labyrinth of the town beyond and back towards the Alverdo section of Titan's Folly where Augustin and Vicente were still waiting at the inn.

Chapter 27

"These knights are going to get me killed," Edmond muttered, staring into his empty glass and leaning back in his chair once more. It was only the mid-point of the tournament, but thankfully a day of feasting. There would be no fighting. Only drinking and eating. A day of rest. Again, Mira sat across from him, her lips pursed, her back straight as she eyed a set of regional sketches similar to the ones she'd been examining before.

"I told you not to fool with them," she said primly. "It's a powder keg of interaction."

Edmond sighed, leaning back in his chair, relaxing as best he could. "At least Augustin agreed to continue the tournament."

"Mhmm," said Mira distractedly, pointing at something on a map before her. "He was grateful you rescued his friend..."

"Vicente looked ready to shoot me. He doesn't trust me at all."

"Do you blame him?"

Before Edmond could reply, there was a sharp knock on the door. Edmond didn't even have time to reply, before Kurga and his boys stumbled into the office. Edmond frowned, preparing to scold the interruption, but then stiffened.

Calub, or was it Dorgo—Edmond could never tell—was limping, leaning against his brother. Kurga had a long scratch down the side of his face beneath his floppy hat and a scowl twisting his lips.

"Assassins," Kurga snapped.

"Excuse me?" said Edmond.

"Fort attacked," said Kurga, still scowling and glancing worriedly over at his limping son.

"Attacked? By who? Genevese, Alverdo?" Edmond sat up in his chair, shooting a worried look at Mira.

"No," Kurga said simply. "Not. Assassins. The sniff of death and dying. Murderers—killed ours."

"They killed your comrades? I'm—I'm sorry. The titan's guns though? The ornithopters, are they safe?"

Kurga nodded curtly, one of his small hands playing feverishly with the trigger mechanism of a pistol. "To a fish, dirt is death."

"I don't—don't under--"

"Buried guns. They no find, uh?"

Calub muttered something in Chellek, which Dorgo repeated louder so their father could hear.

Kurga waved a hand and then inclined his silver ear to the air. For a moment, the room hung in silence, watching the diminutive bravo listen to the breeze. Inclined like this, he seemed to calm somewhat, but said, after a moment. "Assassin fish. Cold, dark fish."

"Excuse me?"

Kurga's gaze bore a hole into Edmond. "Muergo," he said simply.

The word meant nothing to him, but the intensity of Kurga's stare sent a chill down his spine. "And where are these assassins now?" asked Edmond

Kurga jerked a thumb over his shoulder. "Still in fort. They camp for now."

"Camped in our fort, is it?" Edmond glared into his cup, shaking his head.

"Edmond," Mira said, calling back his attention.

He met her dark, dispassionate eyes. She glanced down at the map, then raised a delicate hand and tapped a heavy leatherbound book that lay across the desk. She tapped with the singular emphasis of a ticking clock, and the tap of her nail on the binding sounded like the distant clip of an approaching horse.

"We need that fort," she said in a tone that brooked no argument.

Edmond considered the situation, nodding in agreement. She was right of course, but how—He snapped his fingers as the idea came together in his mind.

"I'll send in the knights—they owe me for rescuing their big friend."

Mira folded her arms with a skeptical smirk, "Are you certain? You're relying on them an awful lot for a man who claims he wishes to be rid of them."

"That's because you've only heard the first part of the plan. You three... I need something else from you."

Kurga and his boys stepped in close, leaning in to listen to Edmond's instructions.

Chapter 28

As Augustin rode into the Choking Pass, the shade of the narrow canyon walls sent a chill across his parched skin that drew a consoling mutter from his lips. Around him, he heard similar sighs of relief as the Order hurried their mounts to follow him. They had grown more acclimated to the dry heat of Titan's Folly these last few days, but the wasteland of the Folding Valley still demanded its tribute in sweat. It had been a close thing with Cristobal, and Augustin was relieved to have the large Dumasian at his side again. He was indebted to the reeve—as much as he hated to admit it.

"Stay sharp," Augustin called over his shoulder. "We won't be long to the ruins of Fort Dentimosi."

His companions readily complied. They had done plenty of bandit hunting in the last year together, and they knew how easily the ambushers could become the ambushed. If the reeve was right and these brigands had dug in at the fort's ruin, then they were going to have a nasty time drawing them out.

They rode for another hour, following the stone bridges and paths that zig-zagged over the sharp teeth and sudden drops of the pass. The vine choked stones were uneven and cracked, but the smoothed grooves from two centuries of wagon wheels provided at least some semblance of order to the road. The sun fell low in the western sky at their back, casting distorted shadows into the growth ahead of them, and out of those twisted shadows lurched the crumbled ruin of the imperial fort.

Augustin lifted a fist and the Order drew up their horses behind him. As quietly as possible, they dismounted and tied their horses by the side of the path. Fort Dentimosi had been built where the floor of the pass fell off into a chasm. The leafy vines of the canyon wall dripped down its dark stone walls into an impenetrable blackness, while a stone bridge, only a single wagon wide, gently arced over to meet the empty mouth of the fort's former gatehouse. For a long moment the companions stared up at that looming entryway. Apart from climbing the smooth stone and vines, the only way to cross the chasm was over the bridgeway, exposed to the dark arrow loops and crumbled parapets of the fort. No fire light flickered within. No sounds other than the buzzing insects that crept between the filthy stone and undergrowth. No sign of patrolling guards.

At his side, Catali whispered, "Where are the bandits?"

Vicente shifted, "Maybe, they all gone away?"

It was certainly possible, but the reeve had seemed confident the bandits had set up their base in the old fort, and the position made sense. It was defensible, dry enough, and travelers had to pass through if they wished to enter or leave the valley. And yet, no movement betrayed the presence of even a single person. Augustin turned to Cristobal. The big man squinted through his bruised eye, but he shook his head.

"Alright," Augustin said at last. "The light is behind us. If anyone is there, the glare from the sun should blind them. We'll move up, but keep your weapons ready."

Wordlessly, Tristan pulled the leather sheathe from his spear head. Vicente slowly cocked a pistol, and Catali drew her curved surgeon's knife. Together they moved up the bridgeway with Cristobal at the rear.

It wasn't until they reached the gateway of the ruined fort, that the smell reached them.

From the inner wall of the ruined fort, with the trailing light of the setting sun landing on them in golden stripes, hung five bodies. Dark flies crawled over their exposed skin and up the ropes cinched around their necks. Everyone except Catali, covered their noses against the scent. She stepped forward instead, tilting her head as she stared up. Augustin followed her in, eyeing the shadows around them anxiously as he stepped beside her. The men's faces were obscured by shoulder length hair that hung in intricate braids, and bits of glass and bright stone caught the orange light of the setting sun.

"Bravos," Augustin said.

Catali lifted a thin finger to gesture to the hanged men. "Dead at least a day I'd guess." she said in a low voice. "I'm not seeing any other obvious wounds. Look like they were hanged to death."

"You are correct."

Augustin spun to face the new voice, lifting his rapier. He saw no one, but after a moment he recognized the melodic Trabson accent, rising and falling as if every word were a question.

"No point in torturing bravos. They never talk until their contract is complete."

Out from the shadow a pale face rose. Milky eyes under black hair that hung like seaweed across a nearly bald scalp.

"Muergo," Augustin said.

As he stepped out from the ruin's shadowy corner, Muergo's dark cape and leather clothing began to take form around him, just as six more men, wrapped head to foot in wraps of black linen, slunk forward to join him.

Augustin's fingers squeezed the hilt of his rapier, eliciting a groan from the leather wrapped grip. "What are you doing here?" he demanded.

"I imagine I'm here for the same reason you are, dear lad," Muergo said in the muted tones of a clerk, tiredly reciting the contents of his ledger.

"I very much doubt that," Tristan said, stepping forward to join Augustin. "Don't talk around the matter. What are you doing here? Why did you murder these men?"

321

"It's not murder to carry out the law, noble Tristan," Muergo replied. "These were bravos. Mercenaries and pirates, hired by a criminal to aid in his escape. I've found a few of them here and there over the last few months. Finding these, and particularly finding you, Augustin, confirms my suspicions. I'm close."

Muergo stepped closer, holding out his empty palms as his men in black drew up beside him. Augustin stared at them, then to the men on the wall. Something didn't feel right here. Why would Muergo be hunting bandits at the edge of nowhere?

Augustin lowered his rapier, but only fractionally. "We came here because we were told there were bandits in the pass, killing people."

"The only people killed in this pass are the vermin hanging from the wall," Muergo said. His flat grey eyes narrowed. "We let a couple of the bravos snoop around the other day, let them find the other bodies, let them know we were here hoping to draw him out. But he didn't come. You did."

"Who? I have no idea what you're talking about." Augustin felt himself getting angry. Muergo's self-indulgent way of talking scraped at his nerves, and frayed the small amount of patience he had for the man.

"The tomb raider," Muergo said.

Shock shook Augustin. His eyes widened as he felt the tip of his rapier scrape the ground at his feet. The tomb raider, the Viper, the man who had cost him everything. He was here. Somehow, Muergo had tracked the man across the sea. He had followed his meager trail, and it had led him here of all places.

"You didn't know? Interesting," Muergo muttered. The comment roused Augustin from his stupor.

"Where is he? How do you know he's here?" Augustin took two steps forward. The sunset light through the gate made him blink. "Tell me, Muergo."

Muergo's entourage followed him as he stepped within arm's reach of Augustin. The air seemed to somehow chill with the man's presence, but Augustin did not recoil. He needed to know.

"Still haven't given up, Augustin? I'm glad. It would have been so unlike you to surrender." Muergo ran an appraising eye over Augustin that made his skin crawl, then shook his head. "No," he said. "No, I don't think that I have any reason to tell you, Augustin. Perhaps you will find the man anyway. Consider it a boon that you chanced upon me and now know he is near, but we are not allies."

Augustin's heart sank, then the chill in his blood began to churn and boil. He opened his mouth to speak then, when Muergo suddenly grabbed one of his black-clad assistants and yanked him, pulling the man off his feet as Muergo took cover behind him. A sound like distant cannon fire roared from the pass as the black-wrapped man's chest exploded in a spray of bright red gore. Dropping the dead man, Muergo dove back into the shadows of the ruined fort, while Augustin turned and drove his companions back into their own corner.

With the open gate between them, Augustin and Muergo stared at each other from the shadows.

323

"What was that?" Catali called out from her place crouched against the stone wall.

"A sniper," Augustin said quickly. "From back up the pass, where we came from. Did anyone see a flash or smoke?"

The group shook their heads. On the other side of the fort, Muergo raised his voice. "That shot was meant for me. Were you sent alone, Mora?"

Augustin beetled his dark eyebrows. His breath came in quick gasps as he steeled his nerves, the rough stone scraping against his back where he sheltered. He glanced over, relieved to see the other knights and Catali similarly sheltered. The reeve had made no mention of sending anyone else. "Yes," Augustin said, quickly, keeping his voice low and head in the shadow of the stone. "We were sent alone. Perhaps it's the other bravos you didn't murder?"

"Perhaps," Muergo replied—no sign of worry or fear in his tone. He seemed to be commenting on the weather. "But either way, you were the better target. You were the better target and yet they shot for me. Why is that, I wonder?"

"I don't know what you're getting at, Muergo. But we have more pressing matters. There is a narrow bridge between us and that sniper. We can't hide in this fort forever. So what do you suggest?"

Muergo turned to his men. He seemed to talk in a hushed conference with them. Then he turned back to face Augustin. "There is only one sniper. He can't shoot all of us, and he must reload after each shot. We will flood the bridge. Rush across all at once. When he fires, we will see the flash and we can swarm his position."

Augustin frowned. "It's not much of a plan. If we do that, someone's getting shot, probably more than one of us."

From his side, Cristobal spoke up. "I don't know if we have a choice. I can take the lead. Cover for the rest of you."

Augustin looked at the big man's missing ear and criss-crossed scars across his arms and neck. It was true that Cristobal had been shot more than any man he'd ever met, but this wasn't a simple musket ball or pistol. A sniper's rifle was made to fire over vast distances with large shot. His eyes strayed to the man who had been struck. He had fallen on his face, and Augustin saw the wound on his back, a ruin of blasted flesh and bone as large as his open palm. It was not the sort of wound even Cristobal could shrug off.

"No, Cristobal," Augustin said at last. "There has to be another way."

This time Vicente spoke up, "Gus, I know you're trying to protect us. Stop it. The longer we sit here, the more time the drownin'-sonno-va-bitch-shite-shooter has to change his position. We need to charge him, now!"

Augustin gave Vicente a hard look, meeting his one yellow eye, but he did not back down. Augustin turned to look across the sunset lit gap to Muergo.

Muergo stared back, his eyes flat as those of a dead fish sitting in a marketer's stall. "Your man is right," he said. "The longer we wait, the worse this will be. Take up Cristobal on his offer. He's good at catching musket balls if I remember correctly. And, if it makes the matter sweeter to you, I'll make you a deal. If you go out ahead and follow through with the plan, I'll tell you what I know about the tomb raider. We can 'work-together' if it pleases you. It'll be just like old times."

Vicente threw up his arms in theatrical shock and said, "Muergo. Not helping."

Augustin glared at Muergo. Sniper or not, in that moment he wanted nothing more than to wring his neck. It was only after Vicente and Cristobal's hands landed on his shoulders that he felt calm enough to answer. As much as he hated it, he couldn't think of a better plan, and time was running out.

"Fine," Augustin shouted. "But, Cristobal, everyone, you're behind me. I'm leading the charge." He held up a hand to stave off the big man's protests. "No, that's my last word on the matter. If anyone sees smoke or a flash, call it out. This only works if we can swarm the sniper's position. Get ready. And, Muergo, if you betray us on this they will never find your body."

"Was that a threat, Mora?" Muergo gave a low tone-deaf laugh that sounded like a pack of barking dogs.

Augustin swallowed a retort and stepped to the edge of the gateway. His companions gathered behind him, with Cristobal shadowing him like a heavy cloak. Tristan's melodic voice intoned a rhythmic prayer.

"Pardi, watch over us. Shield us and guide us. Give us eyes to see our adversary, and the strength to fight them. For your glory, Sun Lord."

On the other side, Muergo's men silently swept around him like a shield wall, as he crouched behind them. A twinge of disgust pulled at Augustin's stomach, but he let the sensation go. The sniper would demand all his attention for now. As Tristan continued to speak, Augustin waited. He did not know the right words, but he wasn't about to rush his devout friend.

A cricket chirped from the shadows nearby. A breeze moaned over the top of the pass. With a nod, Tristan finished his prayer.

"Alright," Augustin muttered, taking a deep breath. "Forward!" As Augustin gave the call, he dashed around the stone entryway, the Order hurtling onto the stone bridgeway behind him. He shielded his eyes with his forearm as best he could. The glare of the setting sun cut at his eyes, and for a moment he slowed, afraid he might accidentally lose his footing and tumble from the bridge. He passed the midway point of the bridge before he heard the first shot. He couldn't see a flash for the sun's glare, but as he squinted and adjusted his arm, he heard Tristan's voice behind him.

"There! Smoke!" he called out.

"I don't see it," Augustin replied. "Take the lead."

Augustin didn't know how he could see anything through the glare, but as Tristan ran forward, the point of his spear flashing in the western sun, he moved with a fluid surety that quickly left them hurrying to catch up.

Another shot rang out, echoing through the pass. Augustin thought he could hear the whistling of the bullet as it whipped through the air this time. He tried not to think about how close the shots must be coming.

Two more shots rang out as Tristan led them through the tangled brush at the edge of the pass. They must have been running for at least a minute. Augustin didn't dare look back. He knew the fort must have grown small behind him, but over the ringing of the shots and the pounding of the blood in his ears, he did not know who had been shot.

And then the shots stopped.

Augustin followed Tristan as they wound further and further up the pass. Following the congested rock and tangled vines off of the road stone. They ran for what felt like another full minute in silence. When Tristan stopped, Augustin nearly ran into his back. They both took heavy breaths as their lungs fought to recover from the uphill sprint. At their feet, branches and leaves lay bent and broken. A light depression in the foliage marking where a man had lay.

With a tromping of heavy feet Cristobal stepped beside Augustin. At his heels came Vicente. Augustin looked up from inspecting the ground.

"Where is he?" he asked.

Tristan looked around, scanning the brush and the road through the pass below them. Shaking his head, he said, "This was the last place I saw the flash of his gun. You can still smell the smoke."

Augustin could. The scorched scent of gunpowder hung in the air like the ghost of violence. With a bitter twist of his head, Augustin looked to his companions. "He's escaped then. We couldn't get to him in time, and we'll never find him in this tangle unless he fires again."

The tangled green of the pass around him seemed menacing to Augustin's eyes. They had come close, but now they had no way to know who the sniper had been.

Looking around him, Augustin felt a rush of fear rise in his chest. "Where is Catali?" he asked. The Order looked to each other, and Vicente looked back the way they had come.

"She was right behind me," Vicente said as he turned and started back down the slope towards the road. The rest of the group fell in behind him. There was nothing more to be gained by looking at the bare ground where the sniper had been.

"Catali!" Vicente called, "Where are you, you marble-headed-man-butcher?"

The call hung in the oppressive canyon for a moment before an answer rose up from the road below.

"I'm down here, you lousy-vermin-toothed-drunk."

A wave of relief ran over Augustin. None of them had been shot. As he cleared the brush and stepped out into clearer air, he saw Catali standing beside Muergo. At his feet lay another of his black wrapped men. He looked back towards the ruined fort and Augustin could see three more bodies, all wrapped in black.

As Muergo stepped to Augustin's side, he said, "You say you came here alone, yet our sniper seemed to intentionally avoid you. Shooting past all of you to get at me. Who did you say sent you here?"

"I didn't say," Augustin replied. "But that wasn't part of our deal. The sniper is gone, for now. So, what do you know about the tomb raider?"

CHAPTER 29

MUERGO'S LOOSE BLACK CAPE hung from his shoulders, limp and damp, a look not unlike a used dishrag. His thin hood suited the hateful sun, filtering the light and keeping his pale skin free of its blistering touch without trapping the heat to an unbearable degree. Augustin and his pompous band of vagrants had not spoken to him the entire ride back to Titan's Folly, and that suited him just fine. He preferred not to waste his breath in banal platitudes. Inevitably in his travels, some ignorant merchant or clay-brained caravaneer would try to make small talk with him, talking about the road, the abundance of rain or lack thereof. He would stare back at them, letting their fetid breath hang hot in the air. That stifling stink rose like the gas of a corpse bloated with rot, sure proof of the decay in the speaker's mouth and mind. It disgusted him. In those moments he could almost see the face of the speaker blacken and slough, the corruption of grave moss and nightsoil stuffing them upright like a scarecrow. No, after he had told Augustin what little he had gathered from his months of tracking the tomb raider, the Order of the Honorable Lily had been content to let him slink behind, ignored as thoroughly as any street corner beggar.

The city of Titan's Folly swayed drunkenly under the red and green of alchemical lanterns. Paper decorations strung across the streets from brick roofs, and the scents of peppery desert herbs mingled with sun-baked shit and the human heat of laughter and festive conversation. The tournament field lay bare, and in the back of his mind, Muergo remembered what he had known about the Titan's Folly tournament. Five days. Four for fighting. One for feasting. The final two days of combat must begin the next day he realized with no particular emotion to the thought. What he found more interesting was the collective look the Order gave the field as they rode past. In the pressing crowds, the Order's horses moved no quicker than those walking beneath them. Muergo dismounted, letting his own stolen mount wander away towards a cart of sugary baked apples.

Who sent you to the old fort? Muergo wondered as he let the Order believe they had lost him. Drifting back, following them by a hunter's instinct, he alternated between frantic bursts of speed and rigid stillness. He watched from alleyways and rooftops. He became swift wind and silent shadow, watchful moss and patient stone. And, as the hours of the night drew on, he saw the Order stabling their horses within the courtyard of the reeve's mansion.

With grasping fingers and flexible limbs, Muergo mounted nearby buildings. Part gargoyle, part spider, he blanketed his moist flesh in cool shade and watched the streets beneath him empty, his milky eyes fixed on the reeve's mansion with unblinking restraint.

Sent by the reeve? He considered the possibility. Augustin Mora did not have a heart for subterfuge. If he had been sent to clear the Choking Pass, then he would confirm the task completed with whoever held his leash at the earliest possible moment.

The tomb raider employed a number of bravos. Muergo did not know precisely how many, but it had to be quite a few the way that he spread them out. They were spinning some web; that much he was certain of. He had seen them these last months, dissonant and incomprehensible as an orchestra bringing itself into tune, but moving with purpose. Men like this tomb raider did not faff about. There would be a purpose to all of it. Once his disparate plans were brought to harmony, what song would they play?

And if the tomb raider left those bravos in the pass for some purpose, he would use whatever tools he had to recover that purpose. Even ignorant tools, like Augustin Mora and his order.

And if Mora should prove inadequate to the task— he thought of the roaring sniper fire as it had torn through his crewmen. The bravos had attacked no travelers. Bravos were always as good as their word. Muergo and his crew had taken no lives on that road, but for the bravos. The reeve would have no reason to clear the pass unless he were invested in the presence of those bravos; that is, unless he was the tomb raider.

Muergo's thin hands caressed the cool leather grips of the daggers hanging from his hips, lightly tracing them like a harpist drawing out a shimmering glissando. A spark of electric eagerness thrilled his body, and his flat, fish eyes dilated, momentarily catching the cloudless starlight above. He drew one of the daggers free, letting the polished steel tip scrape his inner thigh as he pulled it up. He held it point down like a fang in front of his face.

That was it. The reeve was the tomb raider in disguise. It was the only option that made sense. No, that wasn't entirely true. Perhaps the tomb raider held the reeve's ear? Muergo knew the man was an alchemist, and a face-changer at that. If he had ingratiated himself to the reeve and persuaded him to act on his behalf. The animation behind his eyes evaporated, and Muergo looked down on the quiet compound of the reeve with the grey petulance of an old dog called to heel. Dockmen and filthy fish-lickers were one thing. If they went missing or turned up one piece at a time in the alleyways of the Gilded Isles, no one would miss them—no one of any consequence anyway. If he were wrong, or even if he were right, killing a reeve would not be easily accepted. No, here even he must be sure.

And so, Muergo crouched on the rooftops at the heart of Titan's Folly, feeling the night air pull the warmth from his bones with an undead indifference, watching the doors and gates of the reeve's mansion.

***

Ana looked down at the basket in her arms. The chilly air drew spectral trails of fragrant steam through the cloth she had tucked over the bread. Pulling the warm armload in towards her chest, the smells of baked in rosemary and hard cheeses swam in the air around her. It had taken longer than she thought to get the loaves done, but she was used to late nights.

Since her conversation with Augustin in the reeve's courtyard, the uneasy feeling that the Order might show up at her door in the middle of night needing her help made her ear turn at every small sound and robbed her of more sleep than she cared to admit. Still, she wanted to help, and the thought of Augustin showing up at her door in the midnight hours wasn't all unpleasant. She imagined the neatly cropped black of his beard, salted with the early uneven traces of grey, the strong slope of his shoulders and tightly muscled forearms as he held the mansion's gate between them. She smiled again as she indulged in the thought of those arms wrapping around her, pulling her to his chest and feeling the light scrape of his beard against her ear as he pressed his lips down to her face. A warm flush spread beneath her shawl, and Ana chewed her lip to suppress a small laugh.

When she looked up, she had reached the gate of the reeve's courtyard. No one stood within, and she frowned. It seemed obvious to her now. The nights were cold, why would Augustin, or any of them, just stand out in the cold in the middle of the night? Ana hoisted the basket onto one hip, and reached for the gate, rattling the cold iron lock as she attempted to push it in. With an exasperated sigh, she stepped back.

Well, what did you expect? That the reeve just leaves his home unlocked all night? Blooming Ververiona, I know we've had a bit of a dry spell, but come on. Get it together. Ana shook her head and frowned down at the basket in her arms.

"He probably doesn't even like rosemary," she muttered.

"Are you locked out?"

Ana jumped at the unexpected voice, close behind her. Turning around, at first she saw no one, then she saw what seemed to be a ghostly head floating in the midnight air, but as the figure stepped closer she saw that the pale man simply wrapped himself in a black cape and hood. Putting up a reflexive smile, Ana's eyes flitted up and down the street. She saw no one else, and tightened her grip on the basket, bringing it between her and the pale man. Blue fire and black fish, but his eyes were foggy as sand scratched glass.

Ana shrugged. "Ah, I'm just waiting for my friend to come out and let me in. He should be here any moment," she lied, hoping the man would simply leave.

Instead, he stopped barely three steps from her, staring into her eyes. Ana stared back, unease growing in her chest. The muscles of her cheeks twitched as she struggled to maintain her smile. She wanted to look away from the man's gaze, but she knew better than that. As one tense moment slipped into another, she maintained eye contact, pouring her anxious focus into the delicate muscles of her face and hoping that her expression looked confident and unafraid.

"It is terrible of your friend to leave you in the cold like this," the caped man said. "Are you sure they are coming? I had heard a group of mercenaries have taken up residence with the reeve. Such men can be—demanding."

Ana gave a mild chuckle, and stole a quick glance over her shoulder into the courtyard. Was it her imagination or had the man stepped closer? He still held the same stoic posture as before, but his caped shoulders seemed to loom more than they had a moment ago.

"You're right. They can be a handful. My friend is actually one of them. Great with a sword. Quick as lightning. I-I'm bringing him some fresh bread."

She had hoped that would do it. The chill in the air mingled with the anxious unease that radiated off of the dark man, and she didn't want him to hear the tremble in her voice.

"Oh," the man said, "I know the man. Augustin Mora. He's an old friend of mine. He works for the reeve now?"

His eyes and mouth seemed to be drawn on marionette strings, as he woodenly mouthed the pleasantries.

Ana nodded, confusion and unease tumbling in her like rocks thrown into a rushing stream. The man stepped towards her. Retreating, Ana felt the freeze ebbing from the iron gate as she nudged the bars.

"I think," said the man, "that you and I have much to discuss."

It would be another twenty minutes before the bread went cold. An hour would pass before the rats dragged the loaves from the fallen basket, and three more would pass after that before the first of the toasted brown larks would descend on the morning air to peck at the remaining crust.

Chapter 30

"A JOUST BY THE look of it," Tristan said thoughtfully.

"That's fine," Augustin replied. "It's a formality. Tradition more than a genuine test. I doubt any of the remaining fighters have ever used a lance in ernest."

From the shade of a marketer's stand, they stared down into the valley floor. The rest of their companions had stayed back at the reeve's mansion, and long lapses of silence fell between them after each comment. The tournament field had been swept and the bright streaks of fresh planks showed where the encircling fence had been reinforced. Distant men carried long poles onto the field, and Augustin saw the glint of gold over the flowing robes of the tournament committee as they directed the installation of the barrier running up the center of the long field.

Augustin was the next to break the silence. "Tradition is important. Can you imagine a tourney without a joust?"

"Times have changed," Tristan replied, a note of sadness in his voice. "Gone are the days of grim faced knights riding barded steeds into battle. They are fading. Fading into the realm of myth as surely as the Ghost Warriors of Salamaron or the valor of King Ebaer the Stoneheart. Can't you feel it? I can. In my bones. Pardi above us, the last time I saw a line of knights charging into battle they hadn't carried lances, but rifles. No glittering steel into the flank of an enemy line. No archfiend breathing blue fire and poisonous black smoke. Just men and horses racing into the mud spray of flying iron and the fire of eight-pounders."

"I remember," Augustin said. "I was there."

A silence fell between them, muting the haggling merchants and the commotion of the market street. It was a silence of shared memory, and unspoken acknowledgement. It was the silence of survivors.

The pair shook their heads as the committee men below wrangled with their workers, and Augustin turned his head to look up at the wrecks of the ancient titan overhead. The sea had long ago surrendered to the power of alchemy and black powder, further back than many people realized. Control of the sea meant control of the isles, and so the sea had been the proving ground of great powers. Who knew how many of the world's greatest weapons lay rusting in the ocean's heart? Maybe the Signerde. Augustin had heard once that the Signerde and their Betrayed Mother believed that the world had once been entirely underwater, and one day it would be again. Straining his eyes, Augustin looked at the barren floor of the Folding Valley and the distant grey ring of the Monta Gabri that wrapped the land. He tried to imagine all of it underwater, but after a

339

moment, the bright sun began to hurt his eyes, and he looked back to the tournament field.

Though no combat had been held the day before, he still felt the bruises and aches of the last few days settled against his bones. He was careful to keep himself walking, stretching his legs to bring nourishing blood to the wounds. It was an easy enough task as the thought of Muergo lurking somewhere in the city put an anxious energy in his bones that made him want to pace. He had told Augustin what he knew about the tomb raider's whereabouts, but it had been infuriatingly little. He could be anywhere in the Folding Valley, and Muergo had hounded him by the bravos in his employ. None of them had seen a single bravo since they entered the valley, and with their traditional braids bound in silks and jewels, they should have stuck out like a pearl-boned Signerde in the parched land. But, Muergo had relayed what he knew, his voice impassively tolling out the information like a clock announcing the passing seconds. It bothered Augustin that he did not know where Muergo had slunk off to. The man had a tendency to appear and disappear like a ghost, but everywhere he went blood would flow behind him.

"I shouldn't have let him go," Augustin said.

"Muergo? What else could you have done?" Tristan replied.

"I could have killed him. Thrown him in the chasm. Left his corpse in the valley to feed the vultures," Augustin muttered bitterly. The thought galled him, with the unique jabs that only hindsight could deliver.

"But you didn't," Tristan pointed out.

Augustin flashed him a narrow eyed glare, but Tristan's honest smile soured the expression, and he turned to look back over the tourney field.

"You know why you didn't?" Tristan asked. The expression would have sounded condescending from the lips of anyone else, but from Tristan it held a genuine tenderness that was hard to discount.

"Why," Augustin replied flatly.

"Because you're an honorable man. You know that murdering a murderer is not justice. Muergo's time will come, but you're a good man," Tristan leaned on his spear as he spoke, his voice melodic and reassuring. "The gods would not ask you to pollute yourself with murder."

Augustin let out a long breath as he considered this. He didn't know if he believed any of it, but Tristan seemed to believe it, and that was a small comfort. But then again, Tristan didn't know the whole story.

"I made a promise," Augustin said at length. When Tristan showed no sign of interrupting him, he continued. "Months ago, before we found you again, and I was still Lord Captain, back when I started chasing the tomb raider, I found an accomplice of his—no, a friend—a Signerde. Muergo had tortured him. Murdered him, slowly and painfully," Augustin hesitated as the memory of the Kindly Roost in Carabas and the Signerde's opal bones, peeled from his flesh like smooth stones from a clay pit, flashed in his mind's eye. He took a moment to rebury the image, exhaling the disgust rising in his throat. "The Signerde called the tomb raider *deniz dostu*, sea-friend. He made me promise that I would not allow Muergo to kill the tomb raider. Even as he lay dying, wracked with pain, his last thoughts were of protecting this man, this viper who has cost me everything." Augustin turned his head, looking back to Tristan. "Muergo is a mad-dog," he continued. "And a part of me hopes he catches him. Despite my promise to a dying man, in spite of everything I hate about Muergo, a voice in me whispers that I should let it happen. That I should let Muergo catch him. That's why I didn't kill Muergo in the pass." With a self-deprecating twist of his wrist, he spitefully muttered, "Still think I'm an honorable man?"

The look of pity from Tristan's eyes stung, and Augustin blinked as he felt the dry air tug at his eyes, trying to coax tears from him.

"Augustin, I've known you too long," Tristan said at last. "Yes. You want to do the easy thing. We all do. Your mind is telling you that it would be so easy to let the tomb raider die, but your heart knows better. I know what caliber of man you are. You prove it every day. I know when it comes down to it, you will do the right thing, and yes, you will do it because you are a good and honorable man."

Augustin felt the muscles in his back and neck beginning to strain, and he closed his eyes as he tried to release the tension mounting in his body. As he did, he cast Tristan a look that carried a silent conversation between them.

We'll see, he said.

Yes, we will, Tristan replied.

Fuck you.

I love you too, my friend.

As the muscles in his neck began to unwind, and his back popped with the uncoiling tension, Augustin put Muergo and the tomb raider from his

342

mind. His knee twinged, and he picked up his leg, stretching the joint. The last two days of the tournament lay in front of him still, and the last thing he needed was a distraction or a stiff joint betraying him. Whatever Reeve Matimeo had planned or plotted, they would need to be ready for it.

Tristan sighed. "You should let me look at your leg."

The note of concern in his voice drew a look from Augustin, and he saw the fair face of his friend turned down with concern.

"I know. I know," Tristan continued, holding up a hand almost apologetically. "We have Catali now, and she's a godsend, but Pardi, preserve us, sometimes I get the impression she's just looking for an excuse to use that bone-saw of hers."

Augustin laughed. "You're afraid she's getting bored bandaging sprains and stitching up cuts? That she's going to take off my leg just to get some variety?"

"No, not exactly, but I get the impression she wouldn't lose any sleep over it." Tristan smirked, scratching at his scalp and setting the golden locks of his hair tumbling. A pair of passing market girls slowed down to give him an appreciative look. He waved to them with genial kindness before they turned and skipped away, giggling to each other.

Augustin shook his head at the display and said, "One day you're going to regret spending your youth on brotherly love. Gods, you make me feel like a lecherous old man the way you act with the ladies. I don't think Pardi would mind if you flirted back a little."

"I've had sex, Augustin," Tristan said flatly.

"Could have fooled me. What? Didn't care for it?"

Tristan shrugged. "More or less."

The moment felt odd, and Augustin looked away to the field once more. His friend had turned down his eyes, and he did not wish to make him uncomfortable. Not knowing what to make of the exchange, Augustin chewed the inside of his cheek for a moment.

"I'm sorry," he said at length. "I feel like I've overstepped somehow."

Beside him Tristan stirred, shifting to lean on his spear as he hastily put a hand on Augustin's shoulder.

"No, I'm sorry. Let's change the subject," he said with an amicable chuckle. "So this evening will be the joust. That leaves tomorrow with the last day of the tournament. Has Matimeo told you what you'll be facing?"

"No," Augustin replied. The reeve had been tight-lipped and distracted when they returned from the Choking Pass, and Augustin had been forced to ask around the town to find out what the last day would hold. "But, I know that the final day will be another round of duels. There will be eight of us, and I have a feeling I know who I'll be facing off against. The first round should be simple enough. There's really only one fighter left who I'm worried about."

"The Gamorian?" Tristan asked.

Augustin sighed and gave him a knowing look.

"Well, then," said Tristan with a hopeful chuckle, "We'd better make sure that leg of yours is in good shape."

344

As he suspected, Augustin swept the joust, shattering at least two lances on even his worst match. He managed to unhorse most of his opponents, to the crowd's delight, and even the baroness seemed to enjoy the spectacle, raising a golden goblet in smiling salute when he bowed to her from the saddle. The only serious opponent he faced had been the Gamorian, and in their first pass he only barely managed to keep his saddle by throwing his shield and grabbing the horn. He had been nearly sideways as he pulled himself back upright, and from within his dark helm, the Gamorian had given him a nod of respect. In the end their match was decided by points, with Augustin's truer strikes edging him ahead. The exchange reminded him of his tournament heyday, and Augustin would have loved nothing more than to open his helm and talk with the Gamorian. Instead, he sighed within his visor as he rode Bellenio from the field like a spoiled child. No word of congratulations for his worthy opponent. He knew he couldn't risk exposing the charade, but the lack of decorum still galled him, and as he rejoined his companions, he hoped he would have some chance to congratulate the warrior when he was free of this farce.

"That was well done," Cristobal said, with an encouraging chuckle as he helped Augustin remove the heavy breastplate. Inside the reeve's tent, the Order sat alone, the reeve had not deigned to join them that evening, though none of them could say where he had gone. Augustin, though, had the impression of a gathering storm—Matimeo Navara at the center of it, waiting to unleash... unleash *something*.

"Only one more day of this damned tournament," Augustin muttered in response, shaking out the sweat streaked tail of black hair from beneath his helmet. He looked around to his companions. "Did you find anything?" he asked.

Tristan shook his head. "I found a few locked doors, but the deputy ran me out before I could get anywhere."

Vicente huffed, "Yeah, that paunchy-sonnovabitch is under orders. He run me out of the stable the other night, an' I wasn't even spyin'. Just digging around for a spare bit of the whiskey we put by, but no, he starts barking ol' Vicente's ear off about 'curfew' and 'respectful guests'. Never found that whiskey by-the-way, so if—"

Augustin locked his hawk eyes on Vicente and cleared his throat.

Taking the hint, Vicente trailed off, shaking his head like a man trying to clear water out of his ears, muttering, "Fine, fine, we'll solve the murder and circle back to Vicente's missing whiskey.

"I managed to get into his office, just like you asked," Vicente said, the strength returning to his voice. "Nothin' odd to my eyes, just a map of the valley, a stack of letters, and a dusty tome on Imperial law. Those as were opened, I read, but they were nothing interesting. If I had to guess by the stack, I'd say the man finds being a reeve as boring as I do. Unanswered reports, and surveys of the valley, a few maps, but nothing marked on 'em. Nothing pointing back to Wickwood or those bodies we found in the Navara garden. Nothing to or from his family at all, leastwise as far as I could see."

Augustin nodded. He had hoped for more. Perhaps not a signed confession, but some evidence of disagreement between Matimeo and his step-brother.

"You found nothing odd, in his desk drawers? You checked them," Augustin asked.

Vicente swept his arms up, falling back in mock astonishment. "Pardi, Tempa, and Nameless Death, why didn't I think of that? The desk! Of course!" Vicente scoffed and swatted the air with a derisive shake of his black hair. "Yeah, I checked the desk with the rest of it. Nothing there. Except... there was a couple of coins... And—oh, dear, they must have fallen into my pocket."

Vicente made a show of astonishment and scooped out a couple of thick gold coins. These, however, weren't d'oro.

"Old coins," said Augustin, slowly. "Just like Lady Navara warned us about—Matimeo's ransom money was paid in king's gold."

"He's a conniving son-of-a-bitch," said Vicente. "Don't mean he's a murderer, though. Took his father's gold on a ploy, aye, but that's the sum of it from where I'm sitting."

Augustin replied, keeping his voice low and indifferent. "You didn't see any of the rings Lady Navara mentioned?"

"Oh, yes. Those I definitely saw, I just decided not to mention it. Pesh-Ah!"

Vicente slumped back into one of the low stools at the tent's edge. Despite his careless attitude, Augustin knew the lack of evidence was eating away at Vicente as well. He simply showed it in his own way.

A quiet moment hung in the air, then Catali said, "I managed to get a better look through the pantry and buttery. Just like you thought, they were cellared where it would be cooler, but it was strange. While I was down there searching, I saw someone."

Cristobal raised an eyebrow, "One of the reeve's manservants?"

After they had seen the trio in the reeve's tent, on the first day of the tournament, they had reappeared in and around the reeve's mansion. The tall albinos and their diminutive companion with the belt full of pistols—more even than Vicente—sometimes they led Matimeo away. Sometimes they spoke in hushed conference, going silent if any of the Order happened upon them with the reeve. Cristobal had taken to calling them the reeve's manservants, but truthfully they still didn't know who the men were, and the reeve had been exceptionally evasive on the topic. Catali shook her head, and absently whispered, 'no', but left the group in silent suspense.

Augustin dropped his gauntlets and moved on to unbuckling his cuisse and greaves. Asking Catali to search for a cellar pantry had been a long-shot, but in the hard ground of the plateau, and with the tight confines of the city around them, it made a certain sense. If the reeve was their murderer, maybe he had continued killing here. If he did, he would still need to dispose of the bodies. Augustin met Catali's eyes. She seemed distracted and hesitant, chewing her lip while her eyes seemed to search back into her memory.

"Catali?" he prompted.

"Sorry," she replied, shaking her head. "It was just strange. I was moving a few of the barrels and kegs around the buttery floor, just trying to make certain I didn't miss any patches he may have dug up, when this woman came into the room with me."

"A woman?" Augustin tried to think if he had seen any women around the reeve's mansion. "Ana? The innkeeper from the Pipe and Lady?"

"No, I didn't recognize her. She had dark hair, straight like yours, but it hung down past her waist. Her skin was pale too, not splotchy like the Alverdo, almost like a river stone or porcelain. When she came in, I made some excuse that I was looking for something. She asked what I was looking for. I panicked, so I just shouted out the first thing I saw. 'Salt! I'm looking for the salt.' She didn't look around, she just gave me this kind-of eager smile. She asked if I knew the prayer for 'returning what once was lost'. I haven't heard that expression since my nan died." Her voice had the far away quality of remembrance, and what she said next, she said in the sure rhythm of childhood, the familiar cadence of the old songs that you never really forget.

"Keeper of what disappears

Return the lost to find me here.

Mistress of elusiveness,

Black-root and dust, Mirastious."

Catali let out a slow breath. Somewhere in the back of his mind, Augustin felt a memory stir, like a familiar scent on the wind. He tried to hold onto it, but the thought fell to smoke through his fingers, leaving him with the vague impression of salt and shadow.

"I didn't have black-root, but there was plenty of dust," Catali continued. "The woman knelt and traced her finger in the dirt. I've never seen a wandering star so perfectly symmetrical in my whole life."

"Wandering star?" Vicente asked, "Was she doing some kind of alchemy?"

"No," Catali said, "It's not alchemy, it's kind of a sigil or like a written prayer. It's one of Mirastious's secret symbols. Not secret like it's forbidden or anything, they're just really hard to draw correctly."

Tristan had a peculiar look in his eyes. He opened his mouth to speak twice before the question finally came to his lips. "Why do you think she was there?" he asked, cautiously.

Catali shrugged her shoulders, her eyes relaxing, resigning to her confusion. "I can't say," she answered. "But that wasn't the oddest part. After she drew the wandering star and we said the prayer together, she seemed to get this— look— on her face. She put my hand to the star, muttering about how *hers didn't work*. I didn't know what she meant, but I knew that look. It's the look people get when I give them senza. Pain melting back into relief. Then, she looked around the cellar like she was just seeing it for the first time. Like she'd just woken up. For a moment it was like she forgot I was there, and when she looked back at me, she just said, 'What you are looking for isn't here.' No doubt in her voice. And, I know she wasn't talking about the damn salt."

They sat in silence for a moment. Augustin set aside the final piece of the ornate armor, waiting for her to continue.

When she didn't, Augustin asked, "That's it? She didn't say anything else?"

Catali shook her head abruptly, making a small noise before she hurriedly said, "No, nothing else. Just that."

Something in Catali's voice sounded odd. Distracted, embarrassed even. Augustin opened his mouth, but closed it again as Tristan shot him a warning look.

"What did you do?" Tristan asked her softly.

Catali ran her hand over her shaved head with a soft scrape, and let out a sarcastic laugh, "I got the hell out of there." When she lifted her eyes, she looked at Augustin directly. "I don't know what's going on in that mansion, but that woman scared the shit out of me. I felt like she could see straight through me. Almost like she could hear my thoughts as clear as if I were speaking them aloud. Murderer or not. Something is about to happen, and she and the reeve are part of it."

Without anything more to say, the Order gathered up their horses for the ride back to the mansion. As usual, the sun would be set before they reached the gate, though the true cold of the night would still take another hour before it settled on the plateau.

One more day, Augustin thought to himself. One more day and the tournament would be over. Without the threat of discovery over their heads and without the reeve running them between the tourney field, the mansion, and the pass would it be easier or harder to investigate the man? The question turned fitfully in Augustin's mind, like a dog circling the ground for a place to sleep, until they saw the iron bars of the courtyard gate.

Vicente pulled up his horse with a hiss between his teeth, and Augustin peered ahead. The reeve stood in front of the open gateway. He was on one knee, his hand stretched into the shadow under his hunched form. As the Order drew up their horses, he stood, looking up at them with eyes withdrawn in cheerless reflection. His hand extended, and Tristan gasped.

"Pardi, be merciful. Is that—?" His voice faltered and Tristan couldn't finish.

Phantom hands gripped Augustin's lungs as a chill spike arrested his heartbeat for one desolate moment. Reeve Matimeo held a severed hand dangling between his pinched fingers. A pale gold ring on the bloodless knuckle, holding a swaying gold bracelet by small chains.

Ana.

Augustin would not remember leaping down from his horse or drawing his rapier, nor did he quite remember shouting, "I'll gut you—you murderer!" but as Clasco's truncheon slammed into the back of his head, and he fell to the ground, he saw the reeve clutching at his arm, pulling his palm away from the slashed fabric to reveal a bright red stain on his palm. A burst of pain exploded behind his eyes, and everything went black.

CHAPTER 31

WHEN AUGUSTIN STARTED AWAKE, his bleary eyes could not determine if it were day or night. As they focused, he realized the warm glow at his side came from a candle. His skin's chill told him night still hung over the city. He groaned as he rubbed the scum from his eyes, and touched the back of his head, feeling the hot swelling where a bruise rose. His vision cleared, and Augustin recognized the room as he sat propped up in his bed within the reeve's mansion.

At his side Cristobal hunched on a low stool, glowering at Clasco. Clasco leaned on the wall beside the room's open door, his truncheon tucked under one elbow. The reeve's deputy looked even worse than Augustin felt. Purple lumps rose across his cheeks and forehead, and one eye had swollen almost completely shut.

Clasco snorted and tilted to shout out through the open door. "He'sh awake," he said around his swollen lips and jaw.

Moments later, Tristan entered, followed by Catali and the reeve. Reeve Matimeo gave Augustin an appraising look, and the two locked eyes for a moment. There was no anger in the gaze, just a cool assessment.

"You're awake. That's good. How do you feel?" Matimeo asked.

Turning to look to his companions, Augustin did not reply.

From beside the reeve, Tristan nodded. "It's ok, Augustin," he said in a reassuring voice. "We are here, but we need you to talk to us. Do you remember what happened before Clasco knocked you out?"

Augustin closed his eyes as the throbbing in his head made him dizzy for a moment. His heart hammered as the scene came back to him. "The reeve," he said, "He had Ana's hand. Just holding it, cut off. Did you kill her?" The last words held an iron edge, as Augustin looked to the reeve.

Matimeo shook his head. "I don't even know who that is. I told your companions I had just returned. I almost walked right by the bleedin' thing. I spied it just as you came riding up. Ana. You knew her then?"

Augustin nodded. The implications of the hand made his blood race, and he pushed back the blankets, swinging one leg out. He almost rose, but a rush of dizziness stopped him where he sat, and he felt Cristobal's heavy hand gingerly take his shoulder to steady him.

"You shouldn't try to stand," Catali said. "You took a knock to the head. Take it slow. We're here."

Matimeo pushed an irritated sigh through his nostrils. "Who's Ana? Why is her severed hand at my gate?"

354

"Innkeeper," Augustin managed. "At the Pipe and Lady. We saved her when the Genevese and Alverdo shot up her bar."

The reeve snapped his fingers, nodding to himself. "That's it," he said, pointing to no one in particular. More subtle looks of recognition passed between the other members of the Order, and a concerned tension seemed to fill the room like a pungent incense.

"So," the reeve continued, "Again, why is her hand on my doorstep? Best guesses?"

"Why don't you tell us?" At the door, Vicente stood holding the bloodless hand, turning it with a curious expression.

"What? I told you, I don't even know her," Matimeo said, as he shot a menacing look around the room. "I find a severed hand on my doorstep. Someone that *you* know, not me. I pick the bloody thing up, and all of a sudden *you* come charging at me like you're going to run me through. If my deputy hadn't been there, who knows what would have happened!" he shuddered slightly. "So why don't we stop pretending like this has anything to do with *me*, and tell me what *you* know? It's a warning, that much is clear. So who did *you* piss-off in my town?"

With each *you*, Matimeo jabbed a finger towards Augustin. The appealing face he had seen before was gone. In its place, the reeve wore a mask of furious accusation.

From his seat on the bed, Augustin took a long breath. He couldn't exactly tell the reeve that they were investigating him for killing and dismembering people, but that was exactly it. He had recognized Ana's hand and just acted. There had been no thought, just the instinct that he was seeing a killer at work. Now, in the stifling space of the bedroom, he saw the holes in his thinking, but then, if it hadn't been the reeve, who left the hand?

"It has to be the families," Vicente said. "Poor girl."

Augustin looked up with a sudden twist that made his head spin.

Vicente's yellow eye flicked from the severed hand over to meet his anxious gaze. With a somber frown, he nodded.

"Shit," Catali said.

That was it then, Augustin thought. He had been right. She tried to help, she'd been killed for it. The anger he had felt before stilled with the cold certainty of Vicente's confirmation. He would know. The demon in his eye made sure of it.

As Vicente set the hand down on a vacant dresser top, he crossed his arms. "So, Genevese or Alverdo?"

The reeve shook his head. "It doesn't matter," he said. "Not after tomorrow anyway." Looking around to each of them, Matimeo put a hand over his heart. "I don't doubt you're right. This is exactly the sort of petty and vicious message the families would send. You see why I need your help. This damned feud has eaten so many people. Stay with me. Just one more day."

Augustin felt sick. Some of it was probably the head wound, but as the reeve made his speech, Augustin wondered if he had said similar things to his neighbors in Wickwood when their wives and daughters went missing. He had no way of knowing. Not yet.

"Alright," Augustin said. "One more day."

"That's all I ask," replied Matimeo.

***

Roberto deCorvago rose early. In the narrow cotton walls of his tent, he underwent his morning stretches with strict attention, minding his body for any signs of stiffness or pain. In his mind, the body of a warrior was just one more piece of equipment, inseparable from the sword and shield he carried, and just like he knew a sword must be oiled and sharpened to keep its strength he knew that if he was careless with the day to day maintenance of his arms or legs, they would betray him.

He let out a long deep breath as he rolled back out of his stretch, letting his warmed muscles relax even further. It was the last day of the tournament. His last chance to prove himself. He thought back on the previous bouts. Some of the boys he had squared off against had been laughably easy to overwhelm. He had expected with an open tournament like this that there would be a spectrum of skill, some better, some worse, but passable for the most part. Instead, it was a circus. A bumbling cavalcade of clowns with only a small handful of true warriors among them. Even the muscular ones wielding their two handed axes were little better than the sort of thugs you'd expect to find watching the door at one of the Kindly Roosts back home. On the first day he'd even seen a group of five boys who had gone in together on a suit of armor. One would strap it on for his duel, then after getting his head hammered in, his friends stripped him down and suited up the next one. A circus. A godsdamned circus. There were no warriors. They were boys, the lot of them.

Well, that wasn't entirely true, Roberto thought as he fetched his longsword from the corner of his tent. He was here. And early on he'd seen a Dumasian with a heavy black mustache who seemed to know what he was doing. Unfortunately for him, his teammates didn't. He was eliminated during the lesser melee on the second day. What a mess that had been. Roberto tested the edge of his blade with his thumbnail, then fetched out his whetstone to sharpen it regardless.

That was when he had noticed the reeve. When he'd seen the ornate armor, with its pinkish shine and gold trimmings, he had shaken his head in disappointment. Any real warrior knew the style was trash. You want your armor smooth. Soft curves to deflect strikes. Trimmings and ornaments like that could catch a weapon, and then your opponent is dragging you around like a dog on a leash. That's the best case. At worst, the blow would ricochet and hit something vital, like your neck. When he saw the Genevese side march out with three sworn swords, he almost left. No point wasting his time on what would clearly be a massacre. But, somehow, the reeve pulled it off. The Genevese made a lot of noise about cheating and broken armor and the like, but Roberto knew skill when he saw it. The reeve, in his shitty pink armor, that was his real challenge.

He pushed the whetstone across his longsword with a grin on his face, listening to the metal's song. It would be an exciting match today. He had no doubt about it. Behind him, Roberto deCorvago heard the flap of his tent open, and he twisted to look.

"Pardon me, but you are Roberto deCorvago?" a hunched man in a dark cloak asked. The early morning sun coming into the tent from over the man's shoulder made him difficult to make out.

"Yeah?" Roberto replied. "Can I help you?"

"You are the one who will fight the Reeve Navara today, correct?" The man's voice had a hollow sort of tone, like a man talking in his sleep, but Roberto thought he picked out the sloping rhythm of Trabson in the accent.

"That's right. We have the first round when the fourth bell rings. After I win that, I'll be facing the reeve," Roberto said, putting his whetstone back to the longsword in his lap. He had a routine, a rhythm to his morning, and this was an important morning. He hoped the stranger would take the hint and leave.

"You seem confident," the stranger said. "With another match between, what if the reeve should lose?"

Roberto gave a derisive snort. "Not likely," he said over his shoulder. "I've seen him fight. I know who he's facing off against before me. He'll win."

"And when you fight him. Your blades will be keen, yes? No blunted blades for the final duels?"

"Yes," Roberto said, unease growing within him. "Why do you ask? You betting on the fight or something?"

The stranger did not reply, and Roberto passed his whetstone over the blade three more times, feeling the skin on the back of his neck prickling.

359

He suddenly felt very uncomfortable with the stranger standing behind him. He lowered his sword and shuffled around, turning to face the tent's entrance.

The stranger was gone.

"Creepy sonnovabitch," Roberto muttered, lifting the longsword to inspect its edge. "Wonder what he's after?"

No clear answer came to Roberto deCorvago, and within the hour, he had pushed the stranger's appearance from his mind, losing himself in the rote rhythm of his hands as he polished his sword, and cleaned his armor. Every detail mattered, and he was determined that if he lost today, it would not be due to his own carelessness.

CHAPTER 32

THE FINAL DAY OF the tournament progressed much as Augustin had imagined it would. Though his head ached, he declined Catali's offer of senza. He did not want his reflexes to be dulled when he faced off against the Gamorian. He could not afford to trifle with Roberto deCorvago in his present condition. He knew he should have taken the reeve's offer of breakfast. He would need his strength for the matches, but grief throttled his guts and he found no will to eat.

The mid-day sun dipped, and for the first time since the tournament's beginning, Reeve Matimeo rode with them to their tent. As they approached the ramp to the base of the city's plateau and the flat, salt-washed floor of the valley opened up before them, he seemed to watch the western sky, and if Augustin had not known better, he would have thought Matimeo scanned the horizon for signs of rain. When Augustin asked the reeve what he was looking for, Matimeo gave him a twisted grin and said enigmatically, "A change in the wind." The reply did nothing to ease the souring in his stomach, but he did not press the reeve further. That well had been sealed. Whatever the reeve planned, it was a secret to all of them.

As much as he tried, Augustin could not keep the image of Ana's severed hand from his mind. Following Vicente's eye, they had recovered her body the night before from the dusty basement of an abandoned house. Whoever had killed her left her there, her limbs heaped and bent like the pages of a dropped book. No effort made to hide the crime, whoever had done it did not seem to care about being found out. Augustin remembered the brazen audacity of 'Tiny' Genevese as the gaunt giant instigated the fight in the Pipe and Lady. The families didn't care if they were found out. Who would hold them accountable?

We will, Augustin said in answer to his own thoughts. He glanced again to the reeve, and the inscrutable grin that ticked beneath his searching eyes. He hoped that he could trust the reeve's intentions. The families needed to be brought down, that much was clear to Augustin, but how it was done mattered as well. Would they end the feud and save the city, or were they about to spark a bloody coup? Perhaps both.

As they reached the tent, the reeve knocked aside the flap with an enthusiastic slap, and led the way in. About to follow, Augustin felt a hand on his shoulder. It was Tristan. His eyes were heavy, and a weak smile tripped across his chin. When he spoke his words had the soft reassuring quality of linen bandages.

"I just wanted to say, no matter what the reeve has planned, no matter what happens today, we don't belong to him," Tristan said. "Before anything else, we are the Order of the Honorable Lily. We are your friends." He gave

Augustin's shoulder a reassuring squeeze as he said this last. "You're a good man, and we stand with you."

From over his shoulder, Augustin saw Cristobal folding his massive arms, nodding in agreement. Vicente also met his eyes, and gave a firm grunt, while Catali gave a grave nod of her own.

Cristobal added in his rumbling voice, "We don't play politics. We help people."

In that moment, Augustin felt his breath come a little easier, as if he had unshouldered a heavy pack. He looked to each of his companions. He saw the commitment in their faces.

"We have been swept along in the current of Titan's Folly since we arrived," Augustin said. "That ends today. No matter what the reeve plans. We protect the people. We protect them, by Mercusi, Pardi, and all the rest."

Tristan's smile broadened, drawing strength as Augustin spoke.

"We protect them," Augustin repeated, "No matter what it costs us."

Augustin put his hand on Cristobal's massive shoulder. One by one the rest of the Order around him put their hands to each other's shoulders until they connected in a living chain, feeling the strength of their wills feeding into each other. The strength to continue. The strength to try.

The tent flap stirred and Reeve Matimeo's hand came down on Augustin's shoulder.

"What are we doing? Pep talk before the big fight?" Matimeo asked. "Fine. Whatever. It's cute, but inside the tent. You bunch of weirdos are drawing looks."

The first duel drew excited cheers from the crowd as Augustin squared off against a Northern mercenary. The man wore a blackened breastplate and a dark steel helmet in the shape of a roaring panther. It was an intimidating looking piece, and Augustin had to admit the man had a clever strategy. Getting quality blackened steel from an alchemist made a superior piece that would neither rust nor go brittle, but it was an expensive process. Much easier to simply soot the armor with the scraped-out leavings of lamps and campfires.

After a few passes with their longswords, Augustin drove his opponent to the ground and the man yielded. The crowd seemed disappointed by the bout's swift ending, and the tournament committee gave Augustin a line of withering stares as he retreated to the tent. Well, no matter, he thought. It was the last day. He wasn't about to chance a loss to give a good show.

Doffing his armor, Augustin drank from the water barrel by their tent and returned to watch the Gamorian's match. The man fought spectacularly, though apparently he had a greater flair for showmanship. He let several openings in his opponent's guard pass, luring him back and forth across the field with goading attacks. It appeared as if he were trying to give each section of the crowd a close up look at the fight. *Look closely, you might not see fighting like this again!* Though showier than Augustin liked, the Gamorian's skill was clear. He had measured the extent of his opponent's skill and, despite the appearance of danger, his opponent may as well have been wielding a wooden training sword.

As Roberto deCorvago's final blow sent his opponent sprawling across the dusty field, Vicente turned to Augustin and said with a voice more than half question, "You're gonna beat him huh?"

"Yes, Vicente. That's the idea," he replied with mild irritation.

Vicente whistled then turned to face the rest of the Order. "Hey, beautiful, you got-eh- any prayers for winnin' fights? I'm feeling religious all-offa-sudden-for-no-particular-reason."

Tristan smirked. "I do, but wouldn't that be cheating?" he replied.

Vicente let out a harsh barking laugh. "Listen to him," he said, poking a finger into Augustin's shoulder as he thumbed back towards Tristan. "Prayin' is not cheatin'. Cheatin' is stuff like- erm- sneaking into the opponent's barracks and sabotaging their weapons and armor, maybe putting a little somethin' in their food,"

"Wait, what?" Augustin said, jerking his head to look back to Vicente.

"Just for-as-an example," Vicente said dismissively. "That would be cheatin'. Prayin' is not cheatin'."

Tristan gave a small tilt of his head, sending his golden hair over his ears. "It is when they listen," he replied. "Besides, I have faith in Augustin."

Roberto deCorvago held his longsword to the sky in a gesture of triumph and the crowd answered him with riotous cheers. Turning to face Augustin's side of the field, he lifted his visor and his deep green Gamorian eyes scanned the wooden barrier. With one hand he leveled the longsword's point at Augustin.

Feeling the challenge in the gesture, Augustin started. Then, looking over his shoulder, he saw Reeve Matimeo give a single cocksure wave to the warrior and disappear into his tent. Augustin let out a sigh of relief. For a moment he had been sure that the Gamorian had figured out his secret.

One more duel, then the charade is over, he thought. *For better or worse, one more.*

Within the hour, Augustin donned the reeve's armor and stepped onto the field. The westward sun hung heavy and accusing in the sky. From her box, the spider grey form of Baroness Alverdo smiled and drank deeply from a ruby stained goblet. The Bull hunched over the heavy black of his family banner, while his children lurked behind him, grey statues in the shade of their box. Tiny Genevese held his golden amulet in front of his throat and Augustin could see his gaunt jaw flapping with some prayer too faint to be heard outside the family's box, while his sister leaned on her great bow and eyed him with thinly veiled irritation. The herald stepped out from the cluttered committee stands and took his place.

"Peace and Honor!" he called out with upraised hands.

The crowd echoed his cry enthusiastically, and the herald's lips tugged up a smug grin.

"This is the final duel of our honorable tournament. Today the efforts of our brave and noble combatants come to fruition. All will be decided in this final contest of arms, and the victor shall receive their prize. They will be brought into the retinue of their sponsor, with all honors and prestige. They will be named Lord of the Pass, and given the keep of Dentimosi for their own. A Lord beholden to their liege, with all the rights and privileges thereof."

Augustin stretched his neck as best he could beneath his helm. He wished the herald would simply announce them and let him get into the fight. Each mention of honor and prestige felt like an indictment and soured the energy of the crowd around him. Looking across the field, he saw Roberto deCorvago. It may simply be that the Gamorian had his visor down, but something in his posture seemed to echo Augustin's own impatience. He did not have the same restless energy that Augustin had seen before his previous bouts. No pacing. No sweeping his sword. No attention to the crowd whatsoever. The animated warrior had a grave seriousness about him that made Augustin wonder if he had been holding back his true skill for this final duel. The thought was not a comforting one.

"Reeve of Titan's Folly, Matimeo Navara!"

The herald's introduction, roused Augustin from his own thoughts, and he swept his longsword up to his face in a clean salute to the other warrior. A hearty cheer went up from the crowd in answer, but with a turn of his palms the herald silenced them.

"And sponsored by the Genevese, Roberto deCorvago!"

The crowd roared again, and this time the herald patiently waited for the wave of their enthusiasm to crest before he gestured for their silence. The whole while Roberto made no move to return the salute. He held his longsword's grip in one hand and the blade in the other as he let it hang in front of him. Like a statue in a Lord's garden, he stood utterly still while the crowd's cheering died.

The herald raised his hand and shouted, "Are you prepared?"

Augustin raised his sword, and across the field Roberto mirrored the gesture.

"Then, *lay on!*"

Roberto surged forward. A shark cutting through the sea could not have performed a more terrifying charge, and the aura of predatory hunger that rolled off of him nearly checked Augustin's own charge.

His own discipline kept him from freezing, and Augustin rushed out to meet his opponent. Their longswords changed position several times before they met, like the opening moves in a game of chess before either side has a chance to claim a single piece, they felt out how the other would respond with each adjustment to their steel.

In the first exchange of blows, Augustin nearly lost his sword. Gone were the plunging thrusts and strong slashes that he had seen in Roberto's earlier fights. Instead, his attacks were met with cunning back edged cuts and intricate twists that threatened to tangle their guards. Roberto pressed closer and closer, disdaining the longsword's natural reach he pressed until they stood so close that Augustin could have reached out and touched his opponent.

Trying to reclaim some space, Augustin shoved forward with his hilt. As Augustin's hands went forward, Roberto stepped into his extended hands, hooking the guard of his longsword around Augustin's blade. They stood locked together by grinding steel as the sharp blades scraped harmlessly across each other's breast plates.

368

With one hand, Roberto reached to his waist and came back with a thin stiletto dagger. The narrow point thrust for the gap of Augustin's visor, and without thinking Augustin ducked his head and rammed it forward. As the dagger scraped a bright line across the top of his helm, Augustin's visor crashed into Roberto's. Their eyes met, but he did not see deep green Gamorian eyes. These eyes were the pale grey white of milk that had begun to turn.

"Mora."

Close enough to feel the fetid heat of the words, Augustin saw Muergo's pale eyes squint in a look of cautious confusion. At once the dagger withdrew, and Augustin let him go as Muergo stepped back from the grapple.

"Of course," Muergo said, turning left and right to scan the crowd. "That is what she meant. The reeve would not risk fighting this battle himself."

"What are you doing here?" Augustin demanded, raising a gauntleted hand in confusion.

"Hush, lad," Muergo replied. "I thought she was protecting the reeve's secret, but no. It was your secret. Interesting," he muttered to himself.

Around them the crowd rippled with muttered confusion. A few loud shouts of "Get on with it!" and "Take his head off!" rolled across the field as agitation at the duel's abrupt interruption began to mount. Muergo paid no attention to the goading voices, instead locking eyes with Augustin.

In that gaze, Muergo's words took form and realization settled into Augustin's chest.

"It was you!" he shouted. "You killed Ana, not the families!"

Muergo nodded absently. Ignoring his dropped longsword, he sheathed the stiletto at his waist and stepped past Augustin. His voice low, he spoke over his shoulder as he walked slowly for the field's edge, "And for it, I know all I need. The reeve is likely watching us. If I don't catch him quickly, it could be months before I—"

Augustin swung his longsword in a brutal, two-handed chop. Like a lumberjack felling a tree, the blow drew strength through his entire body, concentrating into a resounding clang as the steel blade crashed into the back of Muergo's helm. Unconscious before he could even lift his hands, Muergo's body sprawled out in the dust as his helmet bounced off the ground with the impact.

All around him, the crowd erupted into a cacophony of disparate, animalistic sounds. High chittering laughter peaked over a thunderstorm of grumbling voices. A few clapping hands and shouted insults punctuated the dangerous sound, and as Augustin let the longsword slip from his fingers he saw the wide-eyed committee members tripping over themselves as they rushed to meet him in the field. Practically dragging the herald with them, the squat committee man with the golden monocle reached into his voluminous robes and withdrew the silver broach he had so ceremoniously displayed at the tournament's opening, holding it high in the air as he gesticulated to the herald.

"Well fought my lord reeve," the herald called out in a voice that was loud if not particularly confident. His hands upraised, the herald kept his ear tilted to the committeeman as he spoke to the crowd.

"For your valor we commend you, and declare you, Matimeo Navara, as master of the keep at Dentimosi, and Lord of the Pass."

The committeeman pursed his lips in a frustrated glare as he took Augustin's hand and slapped the broach into his grip. He did not trust himself to speak, and Augustin simply stared down at the mark of office. It was over.

From the edge of the field a boisterous voice called out, "Thank you!"

Augustin spun to face the voice, his face blanching within his helm.

Matimeo Navara swung over the fence at the field's edge, waving to the crowd as he jogged to join the small gathering at the field's center. Some in the crowd gasped, and a fresh round of urgent whispering roiled through the press of people. The herald and committeemen stared with eyes agog as their heads swiveled between Augustin in his copper-pink armor and the rapidly approaching reeve.

"Thank you!" Matimeo repeated, flashing a charming smile around as he made two flourishing bows towards the baron and baroness in their boxes. Once finished, he turned to Augustin and took him by the hand, shaking it firmly as his grin met his eyes with a mischievous twinkle. When he withdrew his handshake, he took with it the silver broach of office and quickly lifted it aloft, holding it in the sun.

"What is the meaning of this?" The Bull roared from his box. His dark Dumasian features flushed a fiery orange as spittle frothed from his mouth with the accusation.

Matimeo withdrew from the group, standing alone on the field, he spoke to the crowd around him. His arms moved with theatrical grace and he spoke like the hero of a play as his strong voice reverberated off the plateau's walls with hypnotic effect.

"I am the Reeve Matimeo Navara. I am Lord of the Pass and master of the keep at Dentimosi. Baron Genevese, Baroness Alverdo, your feuding has been a blight on these lands. You have innocent blood on your hands. By my right, as the master of a keep and protector of the people, I call for the surrender of your titles and lands. I give you one chance and one chance only. Surrender now peacefully, or it will be war between us."

Augustin gaped at the reeve, lifting his visor to be sure he had heard correctly, but there was no mistake. He had just watched a mouse declare war on the lions.

CHAPTER 33

IT TOOK A MOMENT for the laughter to fully subside. As it did, though, Edmond stood confidently in the center of the bloodstained arena, clutching the silver broach and raising it high. Sunlight glinted off the broach. Edmond winced slightly in the light—was the sun brighter than usual?

He glanced quickly over his shoulder in the direction of the mountain pass to the east. *Come on*, he thought to himself. The glinting from the broach should have been visible through Kurga's scope. That was the sign.

"Come *on!*" he repeated, realizing only a moment later than he'd uttered it aloud.

"You declare *war?*" said Baron Genevese, glaring in fury at Edmond across the arena. The man looked like—if the railing could support his girth—that he wanted to vault onto the sand and come charging towards Edmond. Clearly, he hadn't moved past their previous interaction. Threatening to murder someone's pretend-kidnapped son had that effect on people. The Bull's hands seemed to be flexing in his black gloves as if anticipating the feeling of Edmond's throat in his grip. "You're the charlatan who pretended to kidnap my son! You're a *cheater*!" The baron roared.

"Even so," Edmond nodded slightly in agreement, "I ask for your surrender."

The baron roared, shoving one of his guards to the side and grabbing another one's pistol. He fumbled with the weapon for a second, and Edmond didn't move. He was nearly sixty paces away—the wheel-lock mechanism wouldn't be accurate at this distance, plus the baron had been drinking just moments before. Not to mention, Edmond had once again imbibed the Draft of Adhesion, which, as he'd discovered only by accident, allowed his hands to block bullets.

He kept one arm upraised, another held out towards the baron in a gesture as if to say *Stop!*

The baron cursed and fired, but the pistol shot went wide and Edmond lowered his hand. Again he glanced towards the mountains. He thought, for a second, that he could see movement, but perhaps it was a trick of the light.

The sun *really* seemed brighter than usual.

The handsome companion of Augustin's with the spear and that stupid grin, was basking in the glow, head tilted back, a smile whitening the lower half of his face.

Edmond rolled his eyes, but returned his attention to those he had just declared war on.

"You can't declare war!" The baroness was saying. She too looked angry with Edmond, but also quizzical. "Firstly, you don't have an army. Secondly, only title holders are *allowed* to declare war. They must own *land*."

Edmond smirked and jiggled the broach. "This is mine. I won it fair and square by cheating something fierce. It's why I entered the competition in the first place. So I could do this." He wiggled the silver pendant a second time. "You are now my prisoners of war!" he called out, scanning the green tabards and tunics of Baroness Alverdo's knights and soldiers, and the black uniforms of the Genevese.

"He's a puppet for the baroness!" a voice called out, full of feigned solemnity and malice. "The divines look upon us with scorn to allow such company to burden our midst. The baroness has used him as a catspaw! First to assault me, then to insult my father! And he *stole* my holy symbol!" Tiny was practically screeching at this point, frothing at the mouth and waving his large arms expressively. He too pulled a pistol, this one from his own belt.

Edmond raised his hand again, preparing for impact, but as Tiny prepared to fire, Edmond's eyes narrowed. Did the scarecrow-sized man think the *Baroness* had ordered him to declare war?

"Hang on!" Edmond called. "Just to be clear, everyone, *I'm* the one who is—"

But before he could finish, Tiny screamed, and instead of firing at Edmond, he spun around, sighting down the pistol barrel and pointing it across the stands. It was as if time seemed to stand still momentarily. There was a blast of gunpowder, a gasp from the crowd, and then a painful yelp.

A second later, Baroness Alverdo crumpled over, bleeding from a wound to her face.

It had been an impossible shot.

A shot worthy of Kurga.

Perhaps the divines did smile on Tiny after all, if only for a moment longer.

Uncle Rodergo loosed a feral, freakish scream that sent Edmond's hair standing on end. The Alverdos reacted in fury, taking aim and firing as well.

The first salvo of shots peppered Tiny, sending the large man toppling—dead before he hit the ground by the looks of it. The baron screamed in agony, his shouts mirroring those of the hellcatcher.

Rodergo was stooped over his sister's fallen form, screaming, and pulling things from his pocket. A vial appeared in his hand, he ripped off a cap and began pouring something dark and congealed into his sister's mouth.

But her body was still.

Except her gloved hand.

The gloved hand was twitching. The moment the baroness had fallen, the hand had become erratic, like a caged bird desperately trying to be set free, finding—for the first time—its cage's door unlocked.

Rordergo began shouting incoherently and took a few hasty steps back, but before he got far, the baroness' gloved hand lashed out, ensnaring him around the ankle. More spectators began to shout.   In the distance a rolling crack like cannonfire erupted. An explosion. And one by one hands in the crowd pointed to the West. The tomb raider squinted to follow the crowd's gesture, and beneath the rising smoke and dust he saw the sparkle of water trickling down the grey wall of the Monta Gabri. A scream brought Edmond's attention back to tournament grounds.

Edmond stared up into the Alverdo box in growing horror. Frantically, he tried to piece everything together. Why did no one remember all the children Baroness Alverdo had adopted? Why had he only seen two of those children? Fero. Dante. The others had always seemed to be cooped in their rooms. But now, as Uncle Rodergo scrambled back, his tattooed face morphing from grief and fury, to stark terror, Edmond realized what had happened.

"What is wrong with you!" snapped Augustin at his side. He tried to grab the broach back, but Edmond kept it out of his grasp like a child playing keep away.

Still though, as he retreated, holding the silver broach close to his chest, he stared up into the baroness' box.

Augustin followed his gaze, a note of genuine worry rising in his voice now. "What did you do?"

"I didn't—I hadn't—I-I didn't know," stammered Edmond, his words coming weakly. His mind reeled as the pieces clicked together. He had doomed everyone. Titan's Folly wouldn't survive. Even if he started running now, he couldn't make it far enough. They were all going to die.

"Archfiend," Edmond said, his voice so weak that it felt like it would collapse in on his throat.

"What was that? Augustin demanded.

"It's an archfiend," said Edmond, his breath coming in a shattered gasp. His skin prickled with terror and strange numbness had come across the tips of his fingers while the words tumbled out of him in a half-coherent jumble, "That's why she stopped practicing alchemy twelve years ago. A godsdamned archfiend broke through, but she contained it, trapping it in her soul. Or a piece of her soul. The gloved hand—but I bet you anything that she didn't have a human hand!"

"Slow down. What are you saying?" Augustin demanded. At his side, Tristan shot a worried look between his friend and Edmond.

Tristan examined Augustin and Edmond's expressions, and then he began to slowly mutter a series of prayers to the sun god Pardi. To Edmond's ears they sounded nothing like the rigid rhymes and chants that Mirastious had been fond of. Tristan spoke so conversationally, that at first Edmond's distracted mind assumed he'd been speaking to Augustin. But, no. In the midst of it all: As a hellcatcher screamed above them, the crowd rushing in mad circles, and the mountains at the valley's edge began to spill in great gouts of water, he smiled.

Edmond didn't wait to listen, but he couldn't turn tail and run either. There was nowhere to run. No amount of alchemy—nothing would contain an archfiend once it broke free, and as the flooding waters rushing from the erupting face of the Monta Gabri attested, soon they would all be trapped on the plateau with one.

The baroness' corpse shook and shuddered now. Beside it, Rodergo clutched the stained black vial uselessly. Back in the inn, Edmond hadn't realized what he'd seen through the window. He'd known it was a demon, but it hadn't been an archfiend, at least not fully. It had been a sort of hybrid between human and demon. They had been containing it. *"She eats a meal, once every year."* That's what Dante had said.

And that was what had been happening to her *children*.

Scenes from the last several weeks flashed through Edmond's stunned mind. Rodergo's knights bringing the shuddering crate to the baroness. A live capture. A demon they could nurture and raise, fattening them like a calf for the slaughter. The black vial. Demon blood could keep it at bay. Satiated for a time, but not forever. The listed names, the pretend adoptions—they were to throw people off the trail. To justify the number of rooms, the noises—the continued alchemy in the baroness' home... There were no children; only imps, djinn and marid—meals. Sacrifices to help contain the monster. But an archfiend? For an archfiend that wouldn't be enough. Edmond thought of the imbued crystals back at the inn, glowing red.

This was why the baroness didn't venture from her home, why she had reserved an entire inn when she needed to venture out for the tournament. Demon blood and imbued crystals and demons masquerading as children, only to be eaten.

Behind him, Edmond could hear the rushing sound of water tumbling down the mountainside, the clacking of boulders ripping from their purchase. He heard cracking and snapping as trees were torn from their beds and roots were lifted up.

He heard Vicente and Augustin turn sharply. But Edmond ignored them.

They were now muttering and pointing and shouting, and more of the crowd had spotted whatever was over Edmond's shoulders. But he didn't turn. He knew what was coming. He'd planned it all, he'd intended it all. And all of his intentions and planning had led to this moment, and everyone was about to be killed because of him.

The baroness' body was now covered in black scales and tufts of fur. Fangs the size of scythes were now sprouting from an enormous head that seem to be multiplying in size with each passing second. A hand lashed out an enormously impossible long arm, snaring the hellcatcher, and ripping a leg off.

Before Rodergo even had time to cry out in agony, another sliding hand sprouting from the baroness' once chest, eviscerated the man, ripped him in two and allowing his halves split as if he were a human log. Blood and entrails spilled onto the ground, while the archfiend's wretched, corpulent, shambling form got to its feet. From the gloved hand, there was pulsing radiating darkness that with each vibrant glow seem to continue to transform the rest of what had once been the baroness' body. The archfiend was escaping. Edmond remembered his conversation with Vicente back in the armory of the Genevese knights.

"Can't do alchemy no more," he had said. *"At least not much. Would risk letting the thing out. It would kill me if it escaped. Kill a lot of other people too on its way out. Some say demon blood would make it smoother, but I manage enough with my own drinks and droughts."*

The baroness had managed to contain the fiend. All up until now. Tiny had murdered her, his bullet like a key in a lock.

Edmond risked a glance over, to see more black-clad men on the ground, bleeding out, dead, and more men in green livery pierced with bullet wounds or swords also scattered among the stands—the latest contribution of a century old feud.

"Godsdammit," said Edmond.

***

Augustin stared at the back of the reeve's head. "Navara!" he kept shouting. "Reeve Navara!"

But it might as well not have been his name; the man didn't reply; he didn't seem to be able to as if caught in some sort of trance. Next to them, Augustin could hear Tristan muttering a series of prayers, crossing himself in holy gestures and lifting his eyes to the sky. As he did though, looking up to the sun, and somehow not blinking, the man still had the wherewithal to take a couple of steps forward, placing himself protectively between Augustin and the chaos ensuing in the arena stands.

Augustin was still breathing heavily from the bout, bruises from the last week straining his body. The appearance of Muergo had been enough to stun him, but this declaration by the reeve, this declaration of war had been something else. He still wasn't sure what it meant. Clearly the man was joking. Had he really declared war on behalf of the baroness? Well she now lay dead in the dust and—

"Godsdammit!"

Augustin look sharply over at Cristobal who had cried out, pointing.

Vicente had a pistol leveled at the back of the reeve's head, seemingly waiting for permission to fire, but at Cristobal's exclamation, even Vicente turned, and all of the knights were staring at a strange, black, scaly, furred creature rising from the dust and blood where the baroness had fallen. Augustin could no longer see the baroness. Nor could he see the silver clad man with the many weapons who had been tending her. Now, this thing continued to grow, and grow. Soon, it was nearly half the height of the Prow. At this rate it would be the size of the titan itself within a couple of minutes. It was lashing out at the stands now, stomping with feet the size of carts and groping with tentacles protruding from a chest covered with crystals amid flesh and scales. It was hard to count the number of tentacles because they kept squishing back into the abdomen and protruding out another part like wisps of splattered ink. The ends of these tendrils were covered in wretchedly jagged talons, and enormous teeth sprouted from the creature's face. Though it was hard to call it a face. There were too many teeth and too many eyes. It almost seemed like each eye had a tooth protruding from its pupil.

The creature was the most horrific thing Augustin had ever laid his eyes on. But by the way the reeve was behaving, not only was its appearance terrifying, but what it could do would also be equally devastating. The reeve kept muttering again and again. "We're dead. I've doomed us all. We're all dead."

There was no real emotion to the reeve's tone; it was more like he was commenting on the weather.

Now silence had fallen on the stands between the baroness' men and the Genevese. Ten or so men and women lay dead, draped across the seats where they'd struggled to get each other. Others were limping away or dragging each other bleeding and injured, but their gazes, for the moment no longer fixed with hatred on one another, and rather levied with terror at the demon rising from the dust.

"Give me two damns for alchemy," said Augustin.

"And a third for my troubles," Vicente murmured, completing the age-old expression.

"What do we do," said Cristobal, his voice low. His pistol was out too and pointing towards the monster. Tristan and Augustin also fumbled for weapons, but Augustin took a moment to remember that he hadn't been allowed a pistol in the arena. Thankfully, Tristan had a spare and handed it to him. Now all four men were pointing the weapons towards the demon. Well, all three of them. Vicente still had his pistol aimed at the back of the reeve's head. Augustin wasn't sure whether or not the man was wiser than the rest of them in determining the true threat.

Behind them, Augustin had seen an explosion in the mountains, and water was now spilling like an ocean cresting, pouring into the valley and sloshing up around it like a basin.

This man who had just declared war though seemed the sort who knew a thing or two about mysteries.

"Reeve Navara!" Augustin shouted again, but again he received no answer.

A few pistol shots resounded, and the demon jerked and shuddered slightly. But it seemed no more injured than if a couple of small gnats had nipped at its heels. Still, Augustin did notice, each time a pistol shot struck it, the demon seemed to shrink ever so slightly, or at the very least, it stopped growing.

"Do you see when you wound it—" Cristobal began to say, and Augustin nodded quickly.

"What! What is it," Tristan said. His eyes were still towards the sun, astoundingly, not blinding him.

"Perhaps if you weren't so fixed upon what's above you might see for yourself," Vicente said out of the corner of his mouth.

"I'm sorry," said Tristan. He didn't, however, look down,

"Every time we strike the beast, it seems to shrink a little," said Cristobal. His voice grim. "Here, friend, give me your spear." He reached out and before Tristan could protest, Cristobal snatched the weapon from him.

Cristobal glanced over at Augustin. "Just like in Borgo Tortugha," he said with a leer.

"Not like then," said Augustin, still standing tense, pistol extended. "We barely made it out alive. Just like in Sile... Wait, no we barely made it out there either."

"Just like in Dumas," Cristobal said with a good-natured nod, testing the spear, and putting on an air of feigned levity.

Augustin knew better though. His friend wasn't the sort to project fear, but Cristobal, despite his steady hands and firm gaze, had a slight inflection—a minor quiver to his voice that spoke volumes to someone who had known the Dumasian for more than a decade.

The demon had turned, at this point, sniffing the air. It made short work of most of the people in the stands. Scores of bodies lay scattered everywhere, broken and bloodied pools forming on the ground and in the sand near the stands, missing limbs and pieces were scattered every which way. Every so often, the demon's arms darted towards its toothy eyes and there'd be a sipping sound as if it were tasting something, though Augustin saw no tongue.

The demon then turned fully, fixing the knights and the reeve with a ravenous look. Reeve Navara squeaked in fright, and turned, trying to run.

Vicente growled, but didn't shoot.

The reeve scampered back, crying, "Not good! Not good!" He said. "You can't kill that thing. Don't be stupid. Back off."

"Not even with a blessed weapon?" said Cristobal, hefting the spear.

Augustin looked sharply at his friend and shook his head. "No, don't. We harass and harry it and beat a retreat. Maybe we make it out of town." He glanced back at the reeve. "When will it stop growing?" he demanded.

"Never," said Matimeo Navara. "Never, it always grows. Each time it takes a life it'll grow. If you hurt it, it'll stop for a bit. But there's nothing you can do. I'm-I'm sorry, I didn't know."

There was a childish, almost boyish look to the pleading expression on the reeve's face. But a second later, the reeve's fists curled, and a steely glint crept into his eye. "It's not my fault," he snapped. "The baroness should not have been dabbling in those things. She should never have tried to keep it alive. She should've died—by trying to live herself she kept feeding, allowing it to live and grow. The hellcatchers should've been sent. Only they have the power to do anything. One holy weapon, it won't be enough."

"We'll have to see," said Cristobal with a grunt. He looked over and flashed a small smile at Augustin, clapped him on the shoulder and winked, and then turned and began sprinting towards the demon, roaring at the top of his lungs, spear ahead of him, pointing towards the demon's thigh, which he could just about barely reach at his full height with the spear extended.

"Dammit!" said Augustin. "Dammit, fuck, dammit." He began to sprint after Cristobal, but Vicente caught him by the shoulder, trying to drag him back.

"You're in no state!" he cried. Gripping Augustin's shoulder with one hand and wheeling around with his other, Vicente let off a shot, and Tristan soon followed. The bullets whipped through the air with brief whistles and caught the demon, though it was hard to determine where amidst the fleshy, scaly black skin.

For a moment, the demon seemed to almost shrink a little, like a shadow infringed by daylight.

But then, the demon roared and surged forward swiping at Cristobal.

The giant Dumasian swung his borrowed spear once, twice, catching a tentacle, then an arm, and stabbing the demon in the foot.

With each attack, the beast roared in fear and horror. The holy weapon, the spear of a blessed man was doing its work. Over the chaos. Over the roar of the oncoming flood. Above the insane gibbering screeches of the demon, and the thunderous clap of muskets and pistols. Tristan prayed *loud*.

"Pardi—my light and my friend, blessings on all—your light shines and guides the wicked and the good alike. You smile upon the children of mothers, and you bless and tend to the lowest of the low. You grow even the most fledgling of crops, and you kiss the brow of anyone who meets your acquaintance. I pray to you now, that you come, and guide us out of this dark place. Where there is sun, the night cannot exist. Where there is sunlight, the darkness cannot prevail."

Augustin hesitated slightly; it was almost as if Tristan's skin was now glowing. This, he certainly hadn't seen before. Golden sparks seem to be dancing across Tristan's arms and face. But Augustin couldn't see any more than that, and he didn't have time to watch. Cristobal was in danger.

He yanked himself free from Vicente and tried to surge forward again, but this time the reeve caught him. He hadn't been gentle either, tackling Augustin, bringing him slamming to the ground.

"I can't let you die on my account!" He screamed in Augustin's ear, clutching him around the chest, and wrapping his arms tightly across Augustin's sword arm. "We can't make it out of here, but, perhaps, maybe, Kurga and his boys will hurry. Maybe they'll be able to find us before we drown. I don't know. But we can't stay on the platform. The thing will grow to the size of a mountain within the hour!"

Augustin wasn't listening though, he was kicking and biting and scratching and clubbing with his spent pistol. His hand scrambled frantically for the sword, but the reeve seemed to know what he was doing and pinned his body against his leg. "No," he kept crying. "Don't!"

Tristan's prayers were now pouring even more fervently, there was a heat coming from over Augustin's shoulder where he lay on the ground—coming from Tristan's direction. Augustin couldn't see though, his face buried in the sand.

Desperately screaming, he tried to look up, and he saw Cristobal battling the thing, holding it off, for the moment, at the very least, and protecting his friends and everyone else in the arena as they made good their getaway.

"Get out of here!" Cristobal shouted. "Run! Flee!"

But as Cristobal jabbed at the thing, swatting it with the spear and stabbing, drawing black blood in gouts from the thing's sides, Augustin knew it still would not be enough. The demon staggered beneath a ferocious jab, skewered through a tentacle, but then tottered forward into a pile of corpses. Then, the blood almost seemed to leach into its foot like a plant sucking up water or roots taking in nutrients. As it stepped in blood, the being started to grow again, and at renewed rate. It was struck once more by the holy weapon, and then grew again. Back and forth, back and forth. And while Cristobal was striking a good number of times, he was making no progress in injuring the thing. The Demon continued to strike back at Cristobal.

He was fast—far faster than the enormous demon. But the archfiend only had to hit once to make its mark.

For Cristobal, it took more than one strike.

A scything blow caught Cristobal across the back, sending him reeling to the ground; another blow nearly severed his head, but he ducked.

Vicente was cursing now and charging at the beast himself, with no one out to interrupt his pursuit.

He had been the one to hold Augustin back at first, trying to preserve his leader, but Vicente seem to have no such regard for his own life with Cristobal's at stake.

Catali's voice could be heard screeching from where she had been in the tents with the wounded. Vicente flinched at Catali's voice, stalling slightly in his dead long sprint. He shook a fist at the demon, screeching, "You-thrice-fucked-evil-slime-bastards-phlegm-blood-sucking-piece-of-hells!"

But Vicente had only half sprinted across the arena before Cristobal caught another blow—this time across the face. His good ear, and one of his eyes seem to rip from his flesh. Cristobal emitted an enormous groan, and reached up, stabbing the spear, burrowing it deep, almost halfway into the flank of this massive thing. He lost his grip, and another slicing claw flashed down. Cristobal slumped over, on his knees now, shaking at the shoulders almost as if he were crying.

Augustin stared, the weight of the reeve pressing down on him like an impossible burden. Tears were now pouring from Augustin's face as he screamed helplessly in rage and fury. He clubbed the reeve again and again with the pistol grip, catching him in the ribs and in the arm, but the reeve wouldn't let him up.

"You can't die," he said. "No you can't die! You have to come with me—get up, all of the rest you. What about the rest of your men? See them. This one gave his life for them. Don't waste a sacrifice."

The reeve lifted his pressure slightly, but Augustin didn't care what had been said; he spat and scrambled up slipping on sand and sending grains scattering every which way as he began sprinting towards his friend's side. There was nothing he could do. His sword would be useless against the thing; it wasn't even a holy weapon. He wasn't as strong as Cristobal either. By now the enormous monster had grown another few feet despite the attacks, now seemingly feeding off of Cristobal's blood. There were two more slashes, and Augustin dropped, as if he'd been shot, collapsing face first into the dust with a wretched bone-deep wail of anguish. Tears were now streaming hot down his face, and he could hear the knights around him admit mournful wailing screams. Vicente fired off two more shots from pistols in his bandolier, but there was little impact. As for Cristobal, there was nothing left of Augustin's best friend except for blood and torn flesh.

He was gone.

The reeve's words were echoing in Augustin's mind. *Save the others. Don't let a sacrifice be in vain.* Augustin was a professional. Augustin had lost men before. It came with the trade. He would never, ever, not even with Cristobal, become the sort of man to allow his own emotions to take precedence over saving others. Never. Furiously he wiped his face, coming to his senses, in as commanding a voice as he could, he shouted. "Flee! This way. Through the tents, out the back!"

But, though Vicente and Catali moved to obey, bolting with tear-stained looks of sheer horror, Tristan stood where he was.

He was no longer praying. Augustin had turned, leveling his gaze on the gentle-hearted man, and he couldn't help but notice the expression of peace hovering on Tristan's face.

The glowing sparks across his skin began to lift up, swirling like lightning bugs, and then they coalesced, forming a cloud, and then the cloud formed a glowing, golden form, almost like a haze in the breeze, or a golden ghost.

A very large, golden ghost.

A thousand voices suddenly echoing in the air, like giggling, burbling laughter. The tittering of birds, but in human voices—or human-like voices. The chortling sounds of mirth were carried on a warm breeze swirling through the arena, the sun above shining brighter than ever...

Then the ghost gusted towards the demon.

Tristan laughed.

The glowing apparition of the golden ghost seemed to extend like tendrils of fog creeping across a forest floor, weaving through roots... There hadn't been trees before, but they were now here, rapidly growing wherever the ghost hovered. Everything the gold mist touched seemed to glisten and sparkle, and Augustin stared in wonder and amazement. The tears on his cheeks still trailed, but as the golden mist passed him, the trailing vapors of the ghost seemed to dry the wet on his face. The agony in Augustin's chest couldn't be offset, not even by something as marvelous and wonderful as this, and yet still he couldn't look away. It couldn't be real. He stared in awe as the golden ghost sped on the breeze towards the giant demon.

The enormous archfiend stood in the pool of blood, soaking it through its feet and growing even larger, but the moment it spotted the glowing sun being, it seemed to recoil on itself. As the glowing form of what Augustin could only assume was a god, what he could only believe was Pardi himself, sped towards the demon, the creature loosed a screeching howl of agony. Blisters started to form across it's skin. A golden tinge crept along its body, creeping towards the being's wrist and then its fingers where the glove had once resided. Scales and clumps of fur began to fall, along with flesh, fleeing like shadows on the breeze, carried away by gusts of gold.

As the golden form passed, trees continued to sprout from the ground, laden with fruit in full bloom, flowers out of season also appeared, immediately exuding a redolent aroma. Sparrows birthed in the branches of the trees began to sing, the hatching of eggs evident in the crackling gaps between the demon's howling. The golden ghost made no sounds, but everywhere it went blood seemed to evaporate; the hazy mist fell over the arena, and the demon kept trying to crawl back, recoiling. But by retracing it steps, it was no longer stepping in blood, which meant it was no longer replenishing. And now, it was shrinking at an alarming speed. Tristan's ghost continued to speed towards it; two large arms extended as if in an embrace, ensnaring the demon in a hug. Where the arms and the ghost touched, more flesh was seared and more agonizing cries rent the sky.

Tristan had tears streaming down his face now; tears of joy, and he had a smile across his face as if he had seen the birthplace of the divines.

"In all my days," Tristan was saying, his voice barely a quaver. "Pardi above, how you've blessed me and honor me!" Tristan dropped to his knees now, unable to rip his gaze away from the ghostly apparition.

Soon, the demon had faded to nothing but shadow, and the golden apparition turned and began floating back towards the stunned men. It settled, hovering over Tristan. There was a close clacking sound, and a spear fell from the creature's body, as if suspended by the mist and released just now.

It was the spear Cristobal had used, and it was now glowing gold.

A glistening vaporous hand reached out, touching Tristan on the side of his face; where it touched, one of Tristan's eyes began to glow with a resplendent light, his hair turned white immediately. Tristan though just smiled still on his knees, staring up, enraptured.

And then, there was a swirling wind and the ghost faded.

"I don't—what was—how did..." Vicente was shaking his head, trying to make sense of things but his words wouldn't come, slurring more than usual. "I-I," then, as if realizing something important, he spun sharply towards Augustin. He glanced once again towards were Cristobal had fallen, but now the whole area was covered in grassy hills and fruit laden trees and fields of flowers.

"Augustin," said Vicente, rasping. "I'm so sorry."

But Augustin just shook his head, keeping his lips firm. "We need to make sure everyone is okay. Go check on Catali. I'll tend to Tristan once he snaps out of it. The reeve has some explaining to do."

Augustin turned, looking sharply at the man who had instigated this all.

CHAPTER 34

EDMOND STARED IN RELIEF, scarcely daring to believe his luck. The gods had blessed his endeavor, it was the only way to think of it. The Betrayed Mother, reaching beyond the grave had come to his aid. Or, had sent someone else. The sun god wasn't known for being an ally of the Betrayed Mother. But there was no other explanation. When everything had gone horrifically wrong, and everything was at stake, after a year of planning and effort, and it all came down to this, the divine had helped him.

Edmond grinned, beaming. Lives had been lost, but that was unavoidable in war. None of his men had died. Though, he had grown fond of the giant Dumasian, in a way. He frowned slightly, his smile diminishing. He glanced towards Augustin who was shooting him a fearsome look, but then looked away.

He didn't accept the blame. He had no interest in pointing fingers or accusation. He had known what he was up to, when he'd started this. And he had known people would die. It had never been his fault that the demon was trapped inside the baroness. It certainly had not been his fault that Tiny had executed her in the arena. And it doubly hadn't been his fault that the hellcatcher had shirked his duty and kept an archfiend alive and trapped in his sister's body. And now, all of them had paid with their lives, and it had cost some good men too. At least one good man.

Edmond heaved a slight sigh, shaking his head in regret. But there was no time for regret. Not now. Now, things were back on track. Now—

Just then, an angry voice shouted across the arena. Most of the spectators had fled, leaving the moment the demon had appeared and started attacking the stands.

Now though, a few seemed to have crept back in, and in the lead, stood the baron. The Bull and his enormous daughter with that huge bow of hers were marching towards Edmond and the knights. At their back nearly thirty men, all of them garbed in black tabards. All of them with equally furious expressions on their faces and dangerous weapons glinting in their hands.

Edmond winced, but didn't hesitate. He took a few hurried steps to one side, standing where he'd stood when he initially declared war. This was the portion of the arena closest to the precipice. And, he knew, it would strike the most impressive spectacle.

Kurga and his boys had plenty of time now. Now, Edmond was in control at last. The baron just didn't know it yet.

"Declare war will you?" The baron shouted. "Killed my son!" he screamed, his face red, tear-filled eyes glaring hatefully in Edmond's direction. "I'm going to gut you," he said. "I'm going to rip you to pieces one at a time and fry your bollocks. I'm going to, I'm gonna..."

The baron faltered though, words fleeing him as all thirty of his followers circled around him approaching Edmond. A second later, they too were glancing over Edmond's shoulder, staring in horror. Their weapons dropping to their sides.

Edmond smirked. He too glanced back.

"Ah, there we are at last," he said with a slight smile.

The water pouring from the mountain pass had now formed a lake, flooding the entire area below the plateau. Everyone had heard rumors of how the titan had gotten to Titan's Folly. Some said it came a piece at a time. Some said that it had been put here by the gods as a joke. Others said that a river had once run through this place and dried up.

Mirastious, though, had a deeper memory than most. She had known of Titan's Folly, and she had equally known that a river had been dammed off. An underground river prevented from pouring into the valley to open up mine shafts.

But now, the dam was broken. It had been blasted to pieces by Kurga and his boys and the other bravos not long before. That had been the sound of the explosions. Mira had known exactly where to find the dam, and she had known exactly where to apply the alchemical charges to make sure that the work was done well. According to her, one of the architects all those centuries ago had been a devotee of hers.

The frigate though was Edmond's own contribution. His Imperial Majesty's Ship *Intrepid* coasted along on the water with nearly a hundred bravos dangling over the edge with swords and flintlock pistols in their hands. The frigate cut through the water in a straight line directly towards the edge of the platform where Edmond stood. It had cost him a good sum of gold to hire the extra bravos, but the ransom gold from Reeve Navara's father had paid for that well enough. The two enormous titan's guns which Cristobal had nearly hung for were protruding from the edge of the ship, through makeshift gun ports gouged in the hull. The gigantic, rotating canons would have been threat enough—Edmond had lost the ship's canons nearly a year ago. But the threat was only doubled by the ornithopters flying above, swooping one way then the other and churning and chugging towards the shore. The alchemical flying contraptions were enough to put the fear of gods into any town or village. Four of them, over a ship with two titan guns, and one hundred bravos was enough in any battle.

Edmond had declared war after all.

He'd hoped to catch the baron and the baroness and their most trusted men and women in the middle of the tournament in a way they never would've expected—caught by a frigate in the middle of Godshaven. But now, all that remained was the baron and his thirty men.

Edmond turned back towards the baron. "Consider your daughter," he said slowly. "Consider your children. All of you die if you don't lay down your weapons right now. See that ship, see those bravos, they get paid whether you're alive or not. But I have to imagine they enjoy some violence every now and then. So please, if it was up to me, you'd put your weapons *down.*"

Before the words had even left Edmond's mouth, there was a resounding blast as one of the barrels of the titan's guns rotated back into place, spewing shot towards the now half-submerged tournament grounds. A hole as large as a castle gate erupted in the side of the plateau as the Alverdo and Genevese boxes erupted in a shower of wood and stone shrapnel.

Barely a moment after that, there was a clatter of metal striking ground as thirty men dropped their swords and turned tail to flee. It took the baron a second longer, then he cursed at Edmond as he turned and ran as well.

A couple of ornithopthers sped overhead. Their pilots weren't the best. But the baron didn't need to know that. In fact, one of the men he had encountered before. A man by the name of crewmaster Agreo had changed his tune about bumping shoulders with bravos when he'd been offered an exorbitant fee for his training. Edmond could glimpse the frog-faced man, lounging on the deck, leaning over a railing with a swivel gun between his hands grinning in delight at the thought of more violence.

The man was accustomed to imperial traditions, and had known how to fly the ornithopters. Apparently he had served on a titan in his youth. By the looks of things he had trained the bravos well enough. How they'd managed to entice Agreo to join the crew was a long story in and of itself... Though it had a thing or two to do with the ransom and Edmond's current face.

CHAPTER 35

FROM THE TOP OF the southern wreck, Edmond stared out over the glittering water that surrounded his newly minted island. His ship lay anchored where the tournament field had been only hours before, and her sails hung limp in the wind starved air. The occasional blast of a musket or pistol sounded from the streets below, sporadic and weak. The last faint coughs of a dying regime. At his back, Mira stood next to Kurga with a distracted smile lounging at her lips. At the edge of the wall sat Dante, kicking his legs over the waters with the vertigo inducing nonchalance only a child can manage.

Watching the boy, he could see clearly now what should have been so obvious all along. The red hair, the freckles, even the attitude. Imps adopt the forms of their alchemists. Sometimes older, sometimes younger, sometimes a different gender, but the familial resemblance would be there. The boy had even tried to tell him, in his own way. Dante had said that no alchemy was involved in his fire. Edmond simply hadn't believed him. Was it the baroness' alchemy? Had Dante really not known what he was?

Fero had disappeared because he had been eaten. That was what Edmond had witnessed through the inn's window. The baroness' alchemy, woven into the Alverdo family household: every time her demon needed to feed, she could alter the memories of the household and its guards... *"Mother has us drink potions sometimes. Says it's supposed to remember things proper. Other than that, though, she doesn't permit us to use alchemy."* That's what Dante had said. The potions *altered* the consumer's memory. Dante hadn't remembered how many "siblings" he had midway through the eating of Fero—the red crystal in the wall glowing bright behind him.

"What are you staring at, perv?" Dante asked, raising an eyebrow.

"Nothing," Edmond said, with a small shake of his head. "Hop down now, and go stand by Mira for a bit. The Bull should be here soon."

Edmond didn't want to spend another minute in the same room as the raging Genevese patriarch, but according to Mira, the surrender had to be official. "To stop future headaches," she said, "And unwanted questions about legitimacy."

And so, Edmond had ordered the baron brought to him. The old man had shown an uncommon resilience in the face of his coup, almost as if it were a play. Waiting at the edge of the ruined titan's prow, Edmond had expected the Genevese patriarch to bluster and bellow the whole way as Edmond's bravos brought him up to the overlook. He had prepared himself to smile in the face of furious shouting and to cow the baron with threats and displays of power. He had not prepared himself for this. But... something in the man almost seemed broken now. The loss of his son had done something to the Baron—and it almost aroused pity in Edmond to see it.

The Bull plucked a golden ring from his finger, and the sunlight flashed briefly across the pale ruby set in its band as he turned it in his palm. He pulled another and another, until his fingers were bare, then one by one he tossed them over the wreck's edge. His wrist flopped with the easy motion, like a child feeding the fish from the edge of a pier, and they dropped silently to the new waters below them. And for the first time since he had arrived in the city, Edmond saw the patriarch as an old man. Standing under the weight of his years, tired and worn.

"I presume you've brought me up here for some reason?" the Bull said in his gruff voice. "Other than to admire your handiwork."

Edmond gripped the railing of the deck as he replied. "The Alverdo are broken. My men are enforcing the peace, and rooting out the few groups still hellbent on continuing this damned feud. It's over already, but it will go easier on everyone if you surrender."

The old man turned from his overlook. He looked into Edmonds eye as if trying to determine whether he was joking.

Edmond gave a soft sigh, "You might say we had something of a bad start. Regardless of how it may seem, I have a keen interest in handling this transition as smoothly as possible. So I'm giving you a chance to *lay down* your power, before I have to take it from you. So, I'm asking you for a second time. Surrender."

The Bull chuckled, a bitter laugh that fell in on itself with a low shake of his head.

"My surrender," he repeated. "Already twisting my arm, it's time for me to say 'uncle' or you'll break it, eh?" He had tossed the last of the rings from his hands, and Baron Genevese patted his rough palms together, wiping them as though he had handled something unpleasant.

Behind them, Mira spoke up. "It would be best for everyone. This wasn't even his first plan. Trust me, you would have liked the others even less."

"Really?" the old man replied. "I'm still trying to puzzle out how you accomplished this much. Did you pray to Corundos to open his mountain or for Nepir to raise her seas?"

Mira gave a derisive snort. "Please. Corundos wouldn't stir himself from that damned throne of his if the whole world were on fire. And Nepir, in all her wisdom, would still be debating the merits of the plan."

The Bull turned and gave her a strange look. Again, Edmond was struck by how deflated the old Genevese patriarch seemed, then, he realized, the rosy red had left the baron's cheeks and nose. This, perhaps, was the first time Edmond had interacted with the Baron sober. Staring at Mira, the Bull wore the sort of look one might have when they can't quite remember someone's name, but feel like they ought to know them from somewhere. He seemed on the point of asking some question when Edmond interrupted his thoughts.

"No, no gods needed for this one," Edmond said. Mira gave him a pointed look, and he turned his wrist in a subtle gesture to let him talk. "There was an old sea gate, a locke system for letting ships in and out. It was forgotten long before the Empire ever came and after a while the valley just dried up.

So we thought, this might be the perfect time to see if the old sea gate still worked."

Edmond folded his arms. Despite the Bull's indifferent eyes and cold stare into the sunset waters, Edmond could see he was listening. His ear twitched and his fingers curled as Edmond described the sea gate's discovery.

"Turns out it didn't work, and we still had to blow the damned thing open, but near enough to the mark. Mira is right, though," he continued after a brief pause. "We went out of our way to do this as bloodlessly as possible. Surrender, and we keep it that way. Best for everyone."

"Best for everyone," he muttered, dragging the words across his teeth.

A few long moments passed while the comment hung in the air, but Edmond could already tell which way the die was falling. There would be nothing for it. He would have to let the Bull speak.

"What about what is best for my family? Hmm? What about what is right?" Turning his dark eyes on Edmond, the Bull gave him a baleful glare. "The Alverdo did my family a grave injury many years ago, and half a hundred more since then. Blood has been spilled. So much, you would drown before you reached its edge. Peace." He scoffed at the word. "I have seen what comes of peace, and I have lost so much in the name of peace."

As he looked out into the setting sunlight, the sparkling water cast a dappling reflection across the old man's face. His eyes narrowed and squinted, but Edmond could see a familiar sadness in them that told him the Bull did not see the water or the sunset. Not now. And so he waited.

"Thirty years ago. My daughter Bianca was married to an Alverdo. Branco was the whoreson's name. They were to be our peace. Their children would bury our sins and smooth over the hard brows of our warring houses. She died," the baron said. He released the words in a sigh that was half a groan, like a house settling in a winter's chill, and Edmond could hear the weight of the memory. Something in the way the baron spoke told him he had not said these things aloud in many years, perhaps never before.

"They found her. She had been cut. Slashed so many times she looked like a portion of roast beef. No children. No love. No one there to hold her in her final moments. I opened my heart to peace once and it cost me my daughter. So I ask you," the Bull turned to face Edmond. The folds of his eyes overflowed with the first weak forerunners of tears, and they caught the twilight, drinking its warmth greedily. "I ask you, why should I stop? Why should I surrender? Why should I cheapen the memory of my daughter, and of all my kin who have died at Alverdo hands, to appease some vague ideal of peace?" His voice came hard, but clear with conviction. He waved a sweeping hand over the wreck and the watery basin of the Folding Valley as he stared Edmond in the eyes and said, "If it were you, if someone took the most precious thing in all the world from you, would you let it go? Would *you* surrender?"

Something glinted on the Baron's chest. Tiny's holy symbol—the golden skull of Corundos. It rested high on the Baron's chest.

Edmond felt the chill glass of the potion vial pressed against his own chest. As he stood staring into the eyes of the grieving baron, he could see the echo of his own sorrow. Inarticulate and formless, like the impression of a wave rising from the swelling sea, he remembered her. In a feeling, without words or pictures, he remembered Ailsa dancing on the beach in the glow of their campfire, the sublime slip of her body as she swam in the ocean beside him, the cool feeling of her pearlescent ridges of twining bone softly scraping his skin as their bodies wrapped around each other. Edmond felt the accusation of the baron's question, and he knew what his answer would be. Someone had taken what was most precious to him in all the world. Would he surrender? No. He would fight until he pulled her back from beyond the gates of death. Even if he had to cheat, lie, and steal from every lord between him and the Emperor's throne. Even if he had to pry her out of Nameless Death's frosty hands himself. He felt all of this in the span of a heartbeat. Then he raised another man's eyebrow, turning up the lips of another man's face in a gallows grin, and he lied.

"I would," he said. "I would surrender. If it saved my family." Edmond let his words hang for a moment. He could see the baron taking in the measure of his reply, but before the old man could speak, he pressed on. "Any simpleton can get into a feud. You are the baron of the South Fold, at least for the moment. The Emperor holds you to a higher standard. Your position demands that you avoid such extravagances as personal vendettas, and if they do arise, you are expected to put them down swiftly. The mere fact that you and the baroness kept this feud going as long as it has is proof alone that neither of you are fit to rule."

"And who are you to judge!" the Bull snapped. His face began to flush. This was the reaction Edmond had expected. This he was ready for.

"I am the reeve of Titan's Folly and the Lord of the Pass, or had you forgotten?" Edmond touched the silver broach at his lapel with a sharkish smile.

"And I am the baron of the South Fold. Depths below, with the bitch finally dead, I should be baron of the whole of the Folding Valley! You've no right to bring war on this realm! I'll see to it that the Commodore has you hanged from the tallest mast of his titan, you mongrel. "

"Wrong," Edmond replied sharply. "I have every right. You gave it to me."

"What? I did nothing of the sort!" the baron said with a flustered huff.

"Yes, you did. You made me Lord of the Pass through winning your little tournament."

"Invalid! You cheated!" the baron spluttered.

"A technicality," Edmond replied with a casual wave of his hand, "and one I think is likely to stand given our current position. You see, when I was proclaimed the winner and awarded the keep of Dentimosi, I was made a protector of the realm. 'Any lord who does possess a goodly strong keep is honor bound to protect the peace and prosperity of our good-realm'," Edmond said with an imperious lilt.

Mira sighed from her place beside Kurga. "It's 'Any lord who doth possess in his household the means of a goodly and strong-kept keep—"

"That's what I said," Edmond replied.

"That is most definitely not what you said."

"I was near enough."

"The book was very exacting on the wording, and we have to be precise with these matters," Mira said with growing impatience.

"And if I had the book I would read it out of the book, but he gets the point." Shooting her a last exasperated stare, Edmond turned his attention back to the baron. "The point is," he said, "You gave me a castle, a little out of shape, but a castle. That means I am honor bound by the Emperor's code to protect the peace and prosperity of the land. And I have a feeling that since your feud is over, and believe me, it *is* over, we're going to see a bit more peace and a whole lot of prosperity over here. All well and keeping with the spirit of the Emperor's Law."

The Bull's eyes darted to Mira, the same haunting look on his face. "The Commodore will never let this stand. I'm a baron. True nobility, not some pissant reeve with delusions of grandeur. He'll never let this sort of nonsense stand. You think you're clever opening the sea gate and sailing in on your little frigate? We'll see how clever you feel when Commodore Radichelle sweeps in on the prow of his titan." The baron drew up his lips in a defiant snarl. "You will hang."

"Actually, the Commodore has been very understanding of the situation." Edmond reached to his breast pocket and withdrew a folded letter. The setting sun illuminated the paper, showing the dark ink through its folds as the heavy wax seal drooped one corner over Edmond's knuckles. "I expected he would need some convincing, but blue-fire and black-fish, you all must have pissed him off something fierce. He practically leapt at the idea. At least, that's the tone I got from this."

Edmond flapped the letter in front of the baron, but he made no move to grab it. Instead he closed his eyes.

"What will become of my family?" the Bull asked.

"That depends on you," Edmond said, tucking away the letter. He let the flippancy drop from his voice. "Surrender to me formally. You can't stay a baron, that much is certain, but," Edmond tilted his head with the hint of a reassuring smile. "I don't see any reason to kick you out of your house. I don't need your mines or your businesses. With the baroness dead, I think I can arrange for whatever is left of the Alverdo to leave Titan's Folly for good. Obviously some of her family and supporters will stay. I can't exile half the bleeding city, but if you surrender, and swear there will be no reprisal or revenge, well," Here Edmond paused until the baron opened his eyes, waiting until their gazes met, "I think we could have a rather profitable partnership, don't you?"

***

The evening air hung with an eerie silence around Augustin. The sporadic pop of musket fire faded into the background, as did the moans of pain from the wounded men and women who lay on tables and blankets all about the room. Outside, a child cried out for his parents, and Augustin heard the shaking sobs that poured from small lungs drift away to join the rest of the muted tragedy. He sank into it, like a stone house built on soft ground, he felt himself being swallowed in the thick, viscus murk. Deeper and deeper, the battle's aftermath, gods, could he even call it a battle? The massacre? The riot? The calamity? Nothing felt right. It was a churning sort of chaos that he thought he had left behind. It was precisely the sort of mindless, hateful violence that he never wanted to see again. And there, in the shade of the Pipe and Lady's front room, he saw the cost of it.

On the floor in front of him, lay Cristobal's body.

He was too big to lie on one of the round tables. He barely fit through doors or into beds anyway, and none of his friends had the strength to bear up his prodigious weight for long. A blanket had been pulled from one of the inn's rooms and draped over the giant. It covered his head and ran down to his knees, but the scuffed leather of his boots protruded, pointing grotesquely to the ceiling at a splayed angle, as though he might any moment kick his heels and drag off the boots for bed.

Tristan had cried the entire time as they carried Cristobal back to the inn. They thought to take him to the reeve's mansion, but after what they had seen, Augustin wanted to be as far from the man as possible. There would be no telling what he might do next. Demons. Cannon fire. The hum of ornithopters overhead. And the sea. The rushing sea spilling out over the valley floor, swallowing the tournament grounds and overrunning the lowest portions of the market had sent them all into a primal mindset. All of their training had come back in those moments, and a small part of Augustin made a note to commend his companions for the admirable way they had leapt to the town's defense. They had done their best. They had acted selflessly. Cristobal had acted selflessly. Augustin put a hand over the blanket, feeling his friend's cold body beneath.

No words would come. He was not ready to let him go.

Augustin stood, and strode out of the inn. Catali and Tristan both attended to the wounded villagers that choked the building, directing a few pale faced assistants as they set broken bones and sewed up slashed skin. As he passed, Catali shot Tristan a worried look that Augustin pretended not to see. He had no words for them either.

Vicente was nowhere to be seen. He had come with them to the inn, but Augustin could not remember if Catali had sent him on some errand or if something else drew him away. It did not matter. Vicente could take care of himself.

Outside, Augustin stared out the main street. Through the clear avenue, he could see the shimmering layer of sea water that had flooded the valley. It unsettled him to see so much water with no sound of waves or gulls. After the initial rush, the tide had fallen still, like a muddy puddle after a deluge. The distant shape of a ship drifted into his view, but it was difficult to make out. He could tell it was a frigate, but beyond that— he realized he was squinting and blinked to relax his eyes.

"We're too full already! Set him down there and we'll get him."

Augustin turned to see two men pulling a small handcart with the crumpled body of a man inside. As one of Catali and Tristan's exasperated assistants stepped back into the inn, the men set down the cart. The figure within trembled as he fished out a small handful of d'oro, handing the coin off to the men. His hand shook so bad, he dropped a few of the coins and one of the men knelt and scooped them up with a muttered curse. At that, the figure in the handcart flapped his wrist and dismissed them, and the men departed without another word.

From the little of the man he could see, Augustin could tell that he wore a dark gambeson and he heard the scrape of metal ring mail against the cart's metal sides. Drawn by the uneasy feeling in his stomach, Augustin stepped closer. Within the handcart, his face bruised and split, lay Muergo.

Augustin felt a sudden upwelling of disgust, and reflexively clutched for the dagger at his side.

"M-Mora?" Muergo's flat, grey voice came out weakly, like chipped flecks of slate that might snap at the slightest impact.

Augustin did not reply, but released his grip on his dagger. The sight of the broken man made him think of Cristobal's body, laid out under a blanket, and he could not bring himself to draw the blade.

"Mora," Muergo repeated, this time his split face gave a lopsided grin. "You have to help me,"

Augustin's lip twitched in anger, his sorrow vanished, swallowed up in a flash of fury, and now he drew his dagger. He held the steel to Muergo's quivering throat. "Help you?" Augustin growled. "Why should I do that? You have given me nothing. You have taken everything. You tried to murder me in the tournament, and you killed Ana. I should bury my dagger in your chest and be done with you."

Muergo's smile lingered, completely unperturbed by Augustin's outburst. He swallowed, clearing his throat to speak, and as he did he shifted his head as if he were trying to use Augustin's dagger to shave the pale grey stubble from his neck.

"A misunderstanding, and a miscalculation. Even I can have bad days. As you can see, I have miscalculated gravely this time." Muergo's rolling Trabson accent animated the words as he puppeteered the expression of regret with none of its implied emotion.

412

"The only miscalculation I see is where I did not gut you like the fish-eyed monster that you are." Augustin could feel the heat rising in his neck as he spoke. "Whenever I think to trust you, people die. Whenever I think listening to you may help me, people die."

Now Augustin shook as well. He felt his blood pounding in his ears as his grip shook the knife in his hand, drawing a bright bead of blood from Muergo's pale throat. His words came in halting breaths as his heart drew up his grief like a well of black oil.

"Cristobal would still be alive. Ana would still be alive. And I would have captured that damned Viper. That godsdamned tomb raider!"

Muergo chuckled, his pale eye wobbling in the waning twilight. Augustin froze. An icy feeling seized his heart. He could not place it at first, but then he knew what it was. He had never heard Muergo laugh. Not really. Not with any kind of delight. As the chuckle rattled in Muergo's crumpled body, his eyes flitted towards the open avenue. Augustin stood and followed the gaze. The frigate had drawn closer now, as it turned, the drooping sun caught its bright masts and pale wooden hull.

"Mora, lad," Muergo gasped between his painful chortles. "You need to keep your eyes open. You look, but you don't see."

Augustin squinted now, and he caught the lettering on the ship's hull. *HIMS Intrepid.*

Beneath the additional guns and modifications, the outline of his former ship suddenly leapt out like the familiar face of an old friend behind the creases and wrinkles of intervening years. What was it doing here? Now? The reeve had—

Augustin felt the ground go out from under him. His body went numb as a chill slowed the blood in his veins, and when he spoke the words came as a whisper. "Reeve Matimeo is the Viper."

Muergo drew a harsh, rattling breath. "Do you still know how to use that sword?"

EPILOGUE

THE SOUTH OF GODSHAVEN had not seen a storm of its like in forty years. As rain fell in a deluge, thunder boomed like the close roar of cannonfire. For three days and nights, the storm clouds blocked out the sun, and the only light that came to those places the storm touched was the fire of the lightning that heralded each clap of thunder.

The roads of Wickwood and Shalhaven became impassable as heavy drops battered the muddy ground into a pulpy mush that swallowed up the dirt and gravel of the roads and vomited back the wriggling pink flesh of earthworms and darkling beetles. Howling winds tore the leaves and bark from ancient trees, and pulled them over while their desperate roots tried to hold them to the soaked earth. Shutters were ripped from iron hinges as ditches and gutters overflowed with forgotten refuse. As the rain drove down across the swollen earth, rivers overflowed and where no water would normally run, small creeks and tugging streams drew rivulets through the ground, pulling away the dirt and muck bit by bit.

And a quarter mile from the road, in a copse of dark-needled fir trees, the spider-thin fingers of the streams drew along the body of Matimeo Navara.

Black and bloated with rot, Matimeo floated on currents no deeper than a finger. His handsome hair, stringy and snarled with twigs and stones, caught on grasping roots and pulled free as the waters, murky with his corruption, carried him under those black and storming skies. He drifted through ditches and canals, and over muddy slopes barely an inch deep. The waters carried him South, until they could carry him no further. Dragging his flesh-scraped corpse over sandy earth that drank the rainfall, until the water beneath him disappeared.

The corpse of Matimeo Navara lay there a long time; until the rain blew away and the sun dried what remained of him into a leathery sheathe to wrap his bones. But South of Matimeo's body, the ocean tide rolled in its hypnotic murmur, calling out to his bones.

South. South. South.

And the bones of Matimeo Navara drew up their skeletal hands beside their hollow face, pushed themselves to their feet, and walked.

The End

Except just like last time, it's not the end at all. Scroll down or turn the page to see the next title in this series.

READY FOR THE NEXT ADVENTURE?

THE STOLEN KING

THE CRIME LORDS OF Carabas don't take kindly to strangers meddling in their affairs. Interfering with the gangs and the guilds of Gamor is the surest way to float south. Edmond is being hunted by the fish-eyed assassin . The killer has been picking off his bravos one bloody death at a time, prompting Edmond to decide the time has come to leave Titan's Folly. Mirastious has the perfect destination in mind: the Godforge-a powerful, magical artifact capable of creating the gods themselves. With the recent kidnapping of Isobella Morecraft--arch hellcatcher--the location of the Godforge is now compromised.But Edmond and Mira aren't the only ones seeking the threshold to the realm of the gods; Sofia Diladrion, and her Roosters are hunting it as well. Augustin and the remaining knights also set out, hired by an old acquaintance-none other than Tristan's sister, and Augustin's old love: Serenia. Hellcatchers, gangsters, tomb raiders and alchemists all collide while hunted by cannibals, Signerde pirates and Nameless Death himself. Will Edmond and Augustin survive the threshold of power, or will the Godforge and its denizens claim their souls as tribute.

JK DANIELS & B.A.
STEVE HIGGS

THE RAIDER & THE RAPIER 3:
THE STOLEN
KING

WANT TO KNOW MORE?

Greenfield press is the brainchild of bestselling author Steve Higgs. He specializes in writing fast paced adventurous mystery and urban fantasy with a humorous lilt. Having made his money publishing his own work, Steve went looking for a few 'special' authors whose work he believed in.

Printed in Great Britain
by Amazon

86162604R00244